What readers are saying about previous books by

DIANNA CRAWFORD:

"Your stories have been the refreshing oasis that I so often need but can never quite find."—Kathryn Soulier, Louisiana

"I could not put your books down! I have highly recommended them and passed them around to my friends."—Mary Lou Hess, Illinois

"So real, exciting, and funny. We have problems every day, and it's so much fun to see how God will help us. Your story shows this in a big and wonderful way."—Sherrie Sumner, Texas

"I used to laugh at my mom whenever I'd see her crying over something that happened in the book she was reading, but now I understand why she does. Now it's her turn to laugh at me, because I have been crying over your books."—Quimbly Walker, Texas

"I loved your book so much that I read it over and over. I thank you for writing such wonderful books that have to do with God, romance, and our nation's history."—Kim Hanson, Maine

"I can't begin to tell you how much I enjoyed your book. Please keep up the great work."—Jo An McNiel, Texas

"My seventeen-year-old daughter and I just finished 'devouring' your Freedom's Holy Light series. We both enjoyed them tremendously. Could hardly put them down."—Doy Groenenberg, Washington

"Definitely the best books I've ever read."—Jasmine Madson, Minnesota

"Your books have turned many a boring night into a wonderful evening and a trip back in time."—Stephanie Bastion, Illinois

"You don't just tell a story, you make it live. I look forward to each evening when, once again, I laugh with true enjoyment and get to know the oh-so-interesting family of characters you have created."
—Deborah Jones, Maryland

HEART
QUEST®

HeartQuest brings you romantic fiction
with a foundation of biblical truth.
Adventure, mystery, intrigue, and suspense
mingle in these heartwarming stories of
men and women of faith striving to build
a love that will last a lifetime.

May HeartQuest books sweep you
into the arms of God, who longs for you
and pursues you always.

Freedom's Hope

Dianna Crawford

Tyndale House Publishers, Inc., Wheaton, Illinois

Library of Congress Cataloging-in-Publication Data

Crawford, Dianna.
  Freedom's hope / Dianna Crawford.
    p. cm. — (HeartQuest)
  ISBN 0-8423-1917-4
    1. United States—History—Colonial period, ca. 1600-1775—Fiction. I. Title. II. Series.
PS3553.R27884 F73 2000
813'.54—dc21   00-028648

Printed in the United States of America

06   05   04   03   02   01   00
9   8   7   6   5   4   3   2   1

I dedicate this book to my almost always,
very nearly perfectly patient husband.

Acknowledgments

I would like to acknowledge several people for the invaluable assistance they graciously rendered during the writing of this book: Frances Young and Robert McGennis, who work with the McClung Collection at the Knox County Public Library System in Tennessee, and the Enoch Pratt Free Library, Maryland Department, Baltimore, Maryland. Also Rachel Druten, Mary Firman, Sally Laity, and Sue Rich, my critique partners, along with Denise Bean, my proofreader.

1

Tennessee Country
November 1786

Lurkin' and lurin'.

At that thought, Noah Reardon grinned.

Every time he caught his younger brother staring intently at
something along the riverbank, he smiled in remembrance of the
accusation that had been made against the lad . . . an accusation
that had persuaded Noah of the prudence of bringing Andrew
along on this trip. It would seem young Drew—as he preferred to
be called—had been paying entirely too much attention to one of
their neighbor's daughters. That accounted for the lurking part.
The luring off into the woods, though, Drew had not quite
managed. Thank goodness.

It was hard enough to start a new settlement without the lanky
seventeen-year-old creating another scandal. One was enough at
the moment.

At the rear tiller, Noah steered the cumbersome log raft round
a bend between a new stretch of banks. He searched both, but still
there was no sign of a landing on either side. What was supposed

1

to have been a simple wagon trip from Reardon Valley to the Watauga settlements had turned into a drawn-out float down the Tennessee River.

Impatiently, he watched the last remnants of autumn scatter orange and gold across the water as the flatboat moved slowly with the current. Here they were, a good hundred miles from where they'd left their wagon and team of Clydesdales to go after something that should have been readily available at any settlers' store. Salt. All because Storekeeper Keaton's party had been run off when they'd gone to the remote salt lick to boil down a supply last month.

Hunkering deeper into his heavy wool frock coat, Noah gazed skyward with added disgust. It was near noon on the fifth day of this bone-chilling, unscheduled trip with Andrew and the frontiersman Ethan Yarnell, and the sun still shone only weakly through a haze . . . not even enough warmth to burn off the mist hovering over the murky water. The trees and vines along the shores were stripped half naked in this dreary change of seasons before the snows came and blanketed everything in beauty again.

This time of year was too busy to be away from home so long—hog-killing time, as his father had called it—the time for salting down a winter's supply of meat and for pickling vegetables. But instead of merely going to purchase supplies and file deeds for his new neighbors, his small party was on a mission to secure a supply of the vital mineral.

And Noah knew trouble awaited them at the salt lick—maybe even deadly trouble.

He glanced just ahead of him on the flatboat to the cauldrons they would use for boiling down brine—if they got the chance. He then looked just beyond to the five ponies Storekeeper Keaton had supplied . . . upon which, God willing, they and the salt would make the return trip north.

Fortunately, Ethan Yarnell had volunteered to come along. The buckskinned hunter, who'd dropped in and out of his life on rare occasions since their days of fighting in the Revolution, had been at Keaton's store when Noah arrived. At the moment, Yarnell appeared all the more woodsy as he warded off the cold in a buffalo robe fashioned into a crude-looking coat.

Drew looked just as miserable with a gray knit scarf wrapped between his low-hanging hat and his heavy wool coat. Drew was almost as tall as Noah's six-foot-three, but it would still be some time before he filled out his Nordic frame.

Yarnell stood near the front, opposite the lad, his pole poised to push away from any sandbars or half-submerged logs the craft might encounter. Like Noah, the long hunter seemed more intent on searching the overgrown banks than the current. Instead of thinking of this trip as an adventure as Drew did, Yarnell fully knew the dangers.

Besides the armed resistance they probably would face when they arrived at the salt lick, every hour they floated ever deeper into Muskogee country. The Muskogee Indians had been very hostile since the war with the British.

Yarnell glanced back at Noah with piercing dark eyes. Noah nodded and smiled slightly in a silent gesture that conveyed that all was well . . . for the moment.

Ethan Yarnell was always a good man to have around in a crisis, and his years of wandering the frontier had paid off this time. After hearing the name and description of the fellow who had run off Keaton's salt-boiling party, Yarnell was almost certain the man who called himself Pizar Jones was in actuality Pizar Whitman, a thieving scoundrel who had been chased out of Shawnee country for watering down his trade rum once too often. And now, claiming to hold a deed to the salt lick, Whitman was asking an exorbitant price for what should have been free to anyone who took the effort to boil it down himself. He wanted fifty cents for a twenty-pound bag of salt.

Folks didn't have that kind of cash money to toss away.

But then, any man who would take advantage of the Indians by selling liquor to them in the first place surely lacked moral character. Noah knew for a fact that South Carolina, Georgia, and Spain each claimed this southern territory, not to mention the claims of the various Creek tribes. Until the matter was settled, neither franchises nor deeds were supposed to be issued.

Therefore the Indian trader's "deed" was almost certainly a forgery. Noah, being the only person within a week's ride of Henry's Station who'd actually studied law, had been commissioned to judge the authenticity of the deed . . . one way or another.

He glanced at his Pennsylvania rifle lashed to the top of the nearest crate. In the three years since he and his two brothers had settled their valley between the Watauga settlements and Nashville, they had maintained good relations with all men, red and white. Aye, three years of peace were now threatened by this one greedy trader.

Another bend was coming up. Maybe this time, there'd be some sign that they were nearing the lick. Noah leaned to one side to get a better view.

The only difference, though, was a shift in the icy wind. How he wished he were snug in his warm tight house right now, sitting close to the fire with his collection of books . . . even without the woman he thought he'd be married to by now.

As usual, Lorna Graham popped into his thoughts. Beautiful Lorna. But he would have none of that. Turning his attention to the shoreline, he scanned as far as the next curve. Nothing again. No sign of life, not even a bird perched on a tree branch.

Growing impatient, he tied down the tiller stick and made his way across the lashed logs to Yarnell. "You'd think we would've come upon that trader's place before now," he said close to the man's ear. "Keaton said it shouldn't take more than five days."

Yarnell raised a hand in a manner that Noah understood from their army years to mean they were to maintain silence.

A second later, he knew why. The smell of woodsmoke wafted stronger than the other forest scents. Woodsmoke and something more. A briny smell. The ocean? No, the salt lick. Most likely just around the next curve.

Noah dashed back and shoved the tiller to one side.

The sluggish raft began edging toward the bank. They would need to scout out the situation before exposing their presence.

His kid brother glanced back at him, a youthful excitement shining in his eyes. The towheaded lad was always too eager for his own good.

Noah beached the unwieldy craft just below a marshy canebrake, and Drew hopped ashore with the tie-off rope and wound it around a sturdy sycamore.

As the lad struggled with blue fingers to make a knot, Noah came up behind him. "Drew," he said in a low voice, "stay here with the raft while Yarnell and I check out what's ahead."

"I wanna come. The stuff'll be all right."

"You don't know that," Yarnell muttered, coming up beside Noah, his bone-lean hands now gripping a long rifle. "Redsticks could'a been trackin' us all mornin'."

"We ain't seen a soul in the last four days," Drew argued.

Noah ignored him. "If you see anyone on water or land, don't you try to take them on by yourself. Then, and only then, do you come after us. We'll be cutting into the woods that way," he added, pointing toward the unusual smell.

"You do as he says, boy." Yarnell gruffed out, just as adamant. "And don't show yourself. The Muskogee sided with them bleedin' redcoats durin' the war. Can't trust 'em."

Leaving a disappointed Drew behind, Yarnell strode off on almost soundless moccasined feet, while Noah attempted to be equally quiet in his tall boots. An occasional twig snapped as they traversed the molding tangle of woods, cutting across an area surrounded by a half-moon bend in the river. Few pines grew this close to the water, mostly the hardwoods that were nearly bare, but Noah was pretty sure they provided sufficient cover.

Following their noses, they hadn't trekked more than a quarter of a mile when they saw two log cabins, smoke spewing from the chimney of the closer one, and just beyond, stood an animal shed. The crude buildings were situated on a treeless rock table that gently tilted until it sheered off abruptly. The salt lick most likely lay below. Near the bluff, three campfires made bright splashes of color on a day that was mostly drab grays and blacks. Great iron cauldrons sat over the flames, and steam billowed up from them to evaporate before reaching the hovering clouds.

Someone tended the fires. But at this distance Noah couldn't tell much about the person's size, particularly since a bulky bearskin draped most of the body. Only the person's head stuck out of a hole in the heavy pelt, and that was covered with a dark floppy hat. Noah did, however, easily recognize a musket that lay nearby on the ghostly white stone surface.

They'd been told the salt trader had a grown daughter and a son of about fourteen living with him. "Woodsy as they come," Keaton had said. The lad had seemed more Indian than white, and the girl he'd called "real standoffish."

Loudmouthed Donald Mackey, who'd made the unsuccessful trip with Keaton, had added his own farthing's worth. In a sneering taunt, he'd said the female might be more to Noah's liking, since the lovely Lorna had apparently not been.

Little did Mackey—or anyone else at Henry's Station—know that the choice had not been Noah's to make. He'd been jilted. Lorna had taken a good hard look at life on the frontier and had run off down the Cumberland River to the Mississippi and New Orleans.

With his best friend.

Yarnell nudged Noah out of his dismal thoughts and pointed toward the water.

Beached not a stone's throw from the cabin lay a trio of rafts and three birch canoes. Rafts, which could only be navigated downstream, were expected to be abandoned here . . . as his own would be. But the sleek, lightweight canoes were a different matter. They could be paddled both ways. The trader surely wouldn't own that many. He must have visitors. And those particular canoes had Indian markings.

Yarnell dropped onto his haunches behind a densely limbed shrub.

Without speaking, they both knew they'd have to watch the place until they could get a head count. All the while, Noah prayed that the Indians would leave soon and head downstream—away from Drew and their outfit.

But suppose they didn't.

Noah knelt on one knee beside his bearded comrade. "I'm going back," he whispered, "to help Drew unload the raft and get our supplies out of sight."

Without taking his eyes off the cabin with the smoking chimney, the hunter nodded his agreement.

But as Noah rose to leave, Yarnell caught hold of his maroon coat sleeve and pointed with his rifle toward the log houses. Quickly, silently, Noah squatted again beside his friend, suddenly wishing their cover was more than a thick bush.

A man emerged from the cabin. He was bundled in a European-made blanket of red and gray, but a spray of feathers decorated his hair. An Indian. Musket in hand, he toted a large deerskin bundle over one shoulder. And, thank Providence, he gave no sign that he suspected Noah and Yarnell were spying on him.

Another stepped outside, a two-gallon keg crooked in his arm. Probably rum. This Indian wore the more traditional fur and fringed leathers of his own people. A third Indian emerged, along

7

with a bearded man who had to be white, since Indians kept their beards plucked clean. Probably Pizar Whitman.

The white man, bundled in a heavy blanket, stopped a few feet away from the cabin, but the Indians continued on without him, down to their canoes.

As Noah watched them place their supplies in two of the swift crafts, tension built within him. Those same men who came to peacefully barter for European goods could just as easily slaughter a lone traveler for his possessions, then return to their village bragging about their brave deed.

Anxious for Drew's safety, Noah renewed praying that the braves would head downriver. If they didn't, he'd have to cut across the woods and fast. But even knowing he would beat them, how could he and Drew get the horses unloaded and the raft concealed before the Indians spotted them? They'd have to fight for their supplies if not for their lives. As eager as young Drew was to prove his manhood, was he really ready for that?

Two of the Indians pushed one of the canoes out into the shallows, then hopped in, while the other shoved off in the smaller one.

Noah exchanged tense glances with Yarnell. Which way would they go?

The first bow turned south and glided away, followed by the second. Downstream. Thank God!

A relieved sigh whooshed from Noah. Settling on his heels, he waited to see if anyone else would come outside. One of the trader's family was still unaccounted for.

The bearded man, who seemed rather short and thin-legged beneath his blanket, watched the Indians only long enough to see them rounding a bend, then returned inside. That left only the one out in the open, tending the fires.

Several minutes ticked by with no change except for when the person draped in bear fur picked up a ladle and scooped the salty residue from the bottom of a boiled-down cauldron and dumped it into a cloth sack. The worker then poured more briny water into the empty pot.

Noah shifted his weight as he watched steam roil up when cold water hit scorching-hot iron. Otherwise, all seemed tranquil.

After what seemed like an hour, he leaned closer to Yarnell. "We can't take them by surprise if we don't know where the third person is. You stay here and keep watch. I'll go back and get a couple horses loaded with goods—but no kettles. Mayhap this bunch will think we're just passing through and not try to get the drop on us."

Yarnell, never much for words, again nodded his approval.

Noah kept low until he was well into the woods, then headed back toward Drew. In the silence broken only by the steady murmur of the river, he was reminded again of how thankful he was for the woodsman's quietude. Not once since Noah and Yarnell had been fortuitously reunited at Henry's Station had the hunter brought up the subject of Lorna—a subject Donald Mackey had delighted in bandying about. Noah knew his wartime friend couldn't help but be curious about the missing bride, the fickle lass who'd been brought all the way from North Carolina only to disappear with Jigs Terrell the very day before they reached the valley. Thank goodness, no one at Henry's Station knew the actual details. Not yet, anyway.

Ethan Yarnell, a true gentleman despite his lack of genteel manners, talked only about where he'd been since the war, the new country he'd explored to the west. Noah chuckled, knowing Yarnell had talked far more than he probably wanted to because Drew had been relentless in his questions. Like most untried young men, his kid brother lusted for excitement, whether it was chasing after a pretty skirt or trekking off into the unknown.

Once Noah reached Drew and their outfit, it took a good half hour of unloading, packing supplies on one horse, and saddling two others before he could return to where Yarnell waited. Noah left the animals tethered about fifty yards short of the hunter. Then, bending low, he made his way back to his friend. "Seen anything of the third one?" he asked in a whisper, though he knew the steady roar of water would muffle his words.

Yarnell grimly shook his head.

"Thought we could cross the creek up there before it runs past the lick." Noah pointed east of the cauldrons and the chalky gray bluffs leading down to where the salt lick surely lay. "Then circle back like we're riding in from the southeast."

Yarnell rose and deftly followed Noah back to the animals.

Yessir, Yarnell was sure a restful man—especially after Noah had just dealt with Drew. Noah had practically had to club his brother to get him to stop yammering about coming along and to stay put until they came back for him. But Noah couldn't bring himself to put the lad at risk.

After circling the salt lick in a wide arc, the two men recrossed the creek just above where the fires burned—they didn't want to get in the cross fire of the two Whitman positions they knew about. Still, they didn't sneak up. They made enough noise not to seem suspicious.

However, before they'd ascended the bank, the one at the fires had a bead on them.

Without stopping, Yarnell raised a hand in a sign of peace.

As they rode nearer, Noah couldn't decide whether the one aiming the musket was the son or the daughter—since the drooping hat covered much of the person's face. On closer examination, he noted that the jawline appeared too delicate for a lad's. But the charcoal-blackened hands gripping the weapon were sure and steady, and a powder horn hung from the belt that cinched in the bearskin robe. Below the coarse black fur were deerskin leggings and muskrat-lined moccasins.

"How do, Jay Jay," Yarnell drawled as they stopped before the trio of fires.

At his words, the kid pushed back the felt hat . . . catching Noah completely by surprise.

Firelight danced bright in eyes that reminded him of an opal he'd once seen at a jeweler's in Philadelphia. Despite the smudged face and her being called Jay Jay, this had to be the girl—make that *young woman*. This unkempt but enchanting creature could hardly be considered a mere girl.

A small frown marred her ash-smeared brow as she stepped closer to the frontiersman's horse and stared up at him. The fire no longer reflected in her eyes, yet the remaining hint of color was equally remarkable. They were a rare capricious shade of aqua that Noah had seen only in the depths of river ice. Her eyes now widened with recognition, and she lowered her weapon. "Mr. Yarnell. It's been eons. 'Tis an unparalleled pleasure to see you again."

Eons? Unparalleled pleasure?

But Yarnell didn't look the least surprised by her use of scholarly words. He grinned. "Aye, it has, Jaybird. A coon's age. Ye've grow'd up. This here's my friend Noah Reardon. We fought in the Revolution together."

Even framed by two dark, straggly braids, those fathomless eyes weren't diminished in the least as she turned them on Noah.

He did his best to stop gaping and compose his features. "How do you do, Miss . . ." After mentally discarding both *Jay Jay* and *Jaybird* as inappropriate, he thought to add, "Whitman."

"I'm afraid 'tis Jones, these days," she said.

"That's what I hear." For once, Yarnell carried the conversation instead of Noah, who couldn't quite believe what he'd just seen or heard. "Noah's thinkin' of startin' a settlement hereabouts. We traipsed out this way to look the country over. Hear tell of any recent troubles with the Muskogee?"

"No. But Americans aren't inclined to inhabit this area. Princi-

pally since no one's in accord as to where Spain's domain ceases
and the various states' claims commence."

Noah wished Yarnell hadn't deceived her. Those fairy-hued
eyes might very well see past the lie.

She looked at Noah again, studied him. "But I do understand,"
she finally said, "why a community of people would accompany
this man. He appears to be a leader of stalwart heart and height,
with a pleasurable girth to him. And his face is princely handsome." She added that last observation with no discernible affecta-
tion whatsoever, as if she were discussing the latest litter of pups.
"And there's a charity and clemency in his eyes. His wife and children undoubtedly flourish in his felicitous favor."

Noah knew all those educated words couldn't be coming from
the mouth of this woodsy lass. He must be dreaming. He had to be.
Why else would the painful subject of his marital status be
mentioned so unexpectedly?

"Speakin' of family," Yarnell said, "is your pappy and them
brothers of yourn layin' up by the fire whilst you're out here
workin' all alone in the cold?" He nodded in the direction of the
two cabins farther up the bank.

"'Tisn't overly frigid, long as I keep these fires stoked."

"Then your menfolk's all inside?"

"My father is. But my brothers—" she glanced away, and much
of the inner radiance fled her eyes—"they've all gone hither and
yon. Even Little Bob, he ran off with a tribe of Muskogees just
after the leaves turned to the flames of fall."

Now the woman was spilling into poetic phrasings? If Noah was
the superstitious sort, he'd be inclined to think she was some
bizarre forest creature like in the tales of yore. Except for that
smudged face.

Someone tugged on his sleeve. Yarnell.

"Are you going deaf?" his friend asked. "I said, let's go on in and
say howdy to Jay Jay's pappy."

12

Realizing he'd been standing there like a fool staring at the young woman, Noah quickly tipped his tricorn to bid her adieu.

The lass casually returned the gesture, doffing her own hat and nodding. In spite of all the fancy words she'd just spouted, she was blithely unaware that it was men who did that in parting, not women.

"Noah, let's go," Yarnell repeated brusquely as he turned toward the cabin with smoke spewing from its chimney.

Feeling like a giddy fool, Noah caught up, purposefully matching his steps to his friend's.

About halfway between the woman and the cabin, Yarnell sidled a bit closer. "This ain't no time to get all addlepated over that gal. Her pappy's the one you need to set your mind on. He was one of them hoity-toity English officers what come over here back in the fifties. Resigned his commission, hopin' to make his fortune tradin' the redsticks outta their furs. But he's spent too many years pickled in rum to ever get rich, and he's turned too woodsy to ever go back to what he was. Plus, he's sneaky mean. So you stop moonin' over that gal an' keep your guard up. Stay sharp."

2

A settlement of American families! Moving into the area! A thrill
spiraled through Jessica as she watched the gentleman and the long
hunter walk up the barren rise to her father's cabin. Since the
nearby Muskogee village had moved on last month in search of
fresh soil, taking Little Bob with them, there weren't even any
Indians within ten miles. But if the people coming with Mr.
Reardon were anything like him, mayhap her yearning to leave this
forsaken place wouldn't be quite so desperate. Every day since her
younger brother had left, it had grown stronger. No reason for
staying remained—except, of course, her sense of duty. If she
didn't linger till spring, Father would probably freeze to death
during one of his drunken stupors.

   Shaking off that unpleasant image, she concentrated again on the
departing gentleman. He had a tidy look about him, similar to the
storekeeper from Henry's Station who'd come for salt a few weeks
ago. But this man was younger and taller and altogether more
pleasing to the eye. She especially liked that his face was as clean of

whiskers as an Indian's. And no buckskins or coarse linen hunting shirt for him. This one dressed as proper as anyone she'd seen in the woodcut pictures featured in the newspapers and broadsides that occasionally reached the wilderness. Aye, just like the pictures, except he wore tall boots instead of buckle shoes and stockings. But that only made him seem more manly.

Yes, everything about Mr. Reardon was a pleasure. From the three-cornered hat stylishly set over his light-colored hair to the store-bought black ribbon that tied it back. The spotless berry-colored coat was made of any number of pieces and fit over his shoulders like a second skin.

And this beautiful man had smiled at her. Tipped his tricorn, too. Just like her brothers said gentlemen did. A gentleman from across the mountain this one surely was. Maybe even all the long way from Baltimore.

She continued to watch the two men as they neared the hide-hinged door of her father's cabin. Suddenly her moment of happiness evaporated. Once a proper gentleman like Mr. Reardon spent a few moments with her father, he'd most assuredly take his leave . . . just as everyone she'd ever cared about had done. As long as her father kept his finger crooked in the ring of a rum jug and as long as he refused to take up the banner of justice and honesty, no one would stay. Her days would continue to spill endlessly away, one after another, going the way of her father's drunken promises. Unless she hardened her heart to his needs and took off as her brothers had done.

And she would. She'd trek over the mountains and travel to the ocean and the splendors of Baltimore—her mother's city. Most important, she'd find out why her older brother Spencer had gone there, never to return for her and Little Bob as he'd promised. At the first hint of spring.

Jessica's hand came up to rest on the bearskin cloaking her. Even through its bulk, she could feel the large ruby stone set in the cross

she wore around her neck. It had lain hidden next to her skin for
more than four years now, since the day she'd turned fourteen and
Spencer had left—as her oldest brother, George, had done years
before him. Her father knew nothing about the cross. It was the
proof she would take with her that she was the daughter of the
long-deceased Jessica Jane Hargrave of Baltimore.

Next spring . . . and in the meantime, she might have the
company of Mr. Reardon's settlers—if, after meeting her father,
he ever came here again.

She glanced again at the men closing in on her father's foul
hovel.

Noah watched the door and the wooden shutter for any movement
as he and Yarnell strode up the knoll, leaving the young woman
behind. When he saw none, he stepped closer to Yarnell. He
wanted to address the subject of Yarnell's lying out of her hearing—he hadn't wanted to reprimand his friend in front of someone
else. Nonetheless, being untruthful never set well with him.
They'd come here to expose Whitman's dishonor, not add their
own to it.

But just as he was about to speak, Yarnell called out, "Halloo the
house."

Gripping his rifle tighter, Noah surveyed their surroundings
once more, then glanced back at the girl. She seemed totally at ease,
busy again with her chore. Returning his attention to the cabin, he
saw no one come to the door or open a shutter to peek out. Either
the trader hadn't heard them—or he was waiting with his rifle at
the ready.

A deeply tramped bog fanned out from the cabin's entrance for
several feet. The thought of stepping through it irritated Noah.
The mess could easily have been prevented by making a path with
a layer of straw or even a few fir branches. He glanced around but

saw nothing handy on the bare rise, just a broken bench and some crockery pieces scattered about.

And still there was no response from inside.

Yarnell called the greeting again as they reached the door.

Noah noticed that it sagged, leaving a space at the top where freezing air surely whistled into the interior. To fashion some new leather hinges would take no more than a half-hour's worth of labor. This was undoubtedly the dwelling of a very lazy man. And, hopefully, one who was more careless about keeping guard than Yarnell feared.

"Anyone to home?" Yarnell asked, scraping in the heavy door across the packed dirt floor.

From the darkness within, Noah heard an unintelligible grumble of a reply as he followed his friend past the portal. Assaulted by the sour smell of sweat and rum worse than any waterfront tavern, he staggered back a step. The acrid mix of wood and tobacco smoke only added to the stench.

Steeling his senses, Noah strode into the room, which was lit only by the fireplace and one candle on a table cluttered with what looked like a week's worth of rotting food. As his eyes adjusted to the dimness, he saw that the walls and floor were crowded with barrels, bundled pelts, crates, and sacks that gave some semblance of a trading post. The closeness made the air seem even thicker with the odor.

Then he spotted Whitman near the fire. With a rum jug hooked in one finger, the man pushed himself out of a crude stick-framed chair. When the buffalo robe Whitman was wearing fell away from his shoulders, Noah saw that the man was much thinner and smaller than he'd expected. His face was dried up and withered beneath a wiry brush of a beard.

"Who is it that graces my humble establishment?" the trader asked in a decidedly English accent. "From whence doth thou venture?" His squinting, red-rimmed eyes followed Noah and Yarnell as they moved around the table to reach him.

"It's me, Ethan Yarnell, from up Kentucky way."

"So it is." Holding unsteadily on to the back of his rickety chair with his free hand, the man regarded the armed Yarnell suspiciously, then shifted his attention to Noah and the rifle in his hand. "What brings you down into Muskogee territory? 'Tis a considerable distance. Are the Shawnee on the rampage again?"

"Nothin' more'n usual," Yarnell replied in his lazy drawl. "A body's just got to watch he don't get hisself catched out by his lonesome."

Whitman nodded in agreement, but his gray eyes remained as cold and hard as the iron plate on Noah's weapon. Comparing the father's eyes to those of the daughter, Noah was suddenly, unaccountably, glad that this smelly sot's eyes were nothing like hers.

"I hired on with Mr. Reardon here," Yarnell continued, "to scout out some land along the Tennessee. His company is thinkin' on startin' a settlement just to the south."

The man's used-up features became even more drawn as he cocked his grizzled head at Yarnell's continuation of the falsehood. "This far south?"

Noah was further disturbed by the hunter's lying. This was no way to approach the matter. "Yarnell, maybe I'd better handle this."

"Handle what?" Whitman asked, shifting suspiciously to Noah. Yarnell quickly changed the subject. "I hear tell you're goin' by the name of Jones now 'stead of Whitman."

"Where did you glean that tidbit? I don't recall posting any banns about it." The trader eyed his rifle leaning against a crate beside the chair while setting his jug on the table, freeing his hands.

Yarnell seemed not to notice as he grinned. "No, I don't 'spect you'd be announcin' the change. Back in Spartanburg we was told

19

a Pizar Jones had hisself a tradin' post out here on the Tennessee. Figured it had to be you. You're the onliest Pizar I ever heared of. And, well, you did disappear real suddenlike from up on the Ohio."

Whitman harrumphed. "Since, as Mr. Whitman, I'm the royal subject of the British Crown, I thought it prudent to make a few changes, considering the outcome of the rebellion."

Yarnell, in a disarming move, leaned his own long rifle against the table and warmed his hands at the blazing fire. "In your place, I would'a did the same. Ever' man deserves a new start . . . a new start to go along with our new freedom."

"Speaking of something new," a more relaxed Whitman said, retrieving his jug, "just when did the territory this far south open up for settlement? Did that rabble you call a Congress get together and decide which inept colony has jurisdiction?" The soiled and smelly man eased back down into his seat. "The Muskogee shall be most displeased to learn they're to be invaded by a mob of hare-brained colonists."

Grunting, Yarnell nodded his agreement. "Whether we like it or not, we can't keep all of overmountain to ourselves much longer." He sighed and took a step closer. "Enough of wishin' for what can't be. We come by here to boil us down some salt and maybe do a little tradin'. We should be camped hereabouts for several days."

After all the man's lying, Noah was surprised Yarnell had come right out and told Whitman their true intent. Keeping an eye on Whitman's rifle leaning against a crate not more than four feet from the trader's grasp, he clutched his own a bit tighter and waited for Whitman's response.

The trader leaned forward in his seat. But instead of reaching for his weapon, he looked interested, his watery eyes sparking with greed. "No need to trouble yourselves. I have an abundance of salt already bagged to sell. As you undoubtedly observed, I keep my girl occupied with that chore."

Noah moved closer to Whitman and spoke for the first time. "Have you got two hundred pounds?"

"Aye, but why would you require such an excessive amount?" The trader's suspicions were aroused again.

Yarnell beat Noah to the answer. "A couple men in Reardon's company brought hogs."

The man certainly was quick to talk when it came to lying. Noah had to set this matter straight. "Trader Whitman, that's not exactly—"

"Pork!" Whitman's shout overrode his words. "I haven't had roast pork since the last time I was in Spartanburg." He licked his upper lip—a disgusting sight, considering the nasty beard around his mouth. "Two hundred pounds of salt, you say." He scratched his head.

Noah's own scalp started to itch just thinking about the possibility of lice. For an educated man, Whitman certainly had sunk to a low state.

"That'll cost you ten dollars American or Spanish."

"Ten dollars!" The price was as outrageous as Storekeeper Keaton had said it would be. Noah and his brothers were selling land in Reardon Valley for fifty cents an acre, and this man wanted the same for ten pounds of salt! Noah moved back a bit. "Your price is much too steep for us. We'll just have to take the time and boil down our own."

"That won't be possible." Whitman struggled to his feet, but not before Yarnell deftly sidestepped between him and his rifle. Whitman nervously shifted his gaze between the two men, then stiffened his shoulders the best he could, considering his drunken state. He doggedly went on. "I own the rights to this salt lick. And I'll not allow any poaching."

In one smooth motion, Yarnell reached across and caught up Whitman's rifle, then swung back and retrieved his own.

Whitman's reddened eyes flared. "What's the meaning of this, Yarnell? I thought we were friends."

"We are. Just tryin' to keep it that way."

"You say you have a right to the lick," Noah questioned. "What exactly is your claim?"

The frail man again attempted to gather himself. "I've been issued a deed. Legal title."

The miscreant was caught in his own lie. Noah stifled a smile. "How is that possible? As you yourself just said, deeds aren't being granted this far south due to a border dispute."

"But Yarnell just said you have a township to settle."

"I lied," Yarnell bluntly admitted. "Just like you."

"My good sir," Whitman puffed out his bony chest. "How dare you come into my home and call me a liar. My deed is a special grant. I have the document to prove it."

"If we're mistaken, Mr. Whitman, we'll gladly apologize," Noah said, though he wished he hadn't been put in a position that needed amending. "If you don't mind, I'd like to see your deed."

Yarnell edged one of the rifles up, aiming it at Whitman. "Slowly, Pizar. Keep your hands where I can see 'em all the time. Don't want you comin' up with a pistol you got hid. Us bein' friends and all, I'd hate to have to put a ball in ya."

Whitman narrowed his gaze on Yarnell. "I don't need trickery, unless you've abandoned all sense of honor and fair play." He plucked the wax-encrusted candleholder from the table and walked at a slight tilt to the nearest corner. The flame cast a dim circle of light onto a rumpled bed.

Yarnell followed, watching closely as the smaller man stooped before a black chest at the foot of the bed.

While Whitman rummaged through a pile of what looked like rags, Noah decided to check on the young woman outside. With a pa like hers, she probably knew she had to stay close by in case he got himself into trouble. Noah cracked open the sagging door.

Icy air blasted his face. A blessed relief. Breathing in the forest freshness, he didn't even mind the strong briny smell coming off the lick. Glancing out at the trader's daughter, he saw that she seemed concerned only with keeping her bearskin covering from falling into the flames as she pulled a kettle to the side and began scraping salt from it. But then why should she be suspicious? She trusted Yarnell and had no idea the two of them had deceived her about their purpose for being there. Noah was going to have to make that right somehow. He doubted she'd think he had such a "stalwart heart" then.

"Here it is," Whitman said from behind him.

Noah turned back to see the Indian trader and Yarnell returning to the table.

Setting down the candle, Whitman cleared a spot by using his already soiled deerskin sleeve to push aside a cup and two trenchers of spoiled food. He dragged the fringe across one of the wooden plates as he spread out the paper in the light. "I'll be expecting a proper apology now," he huffed.

Despite being soaked in rum, the man played his part to the hilt. If Noah didn't already have very real suspicions, he'd believe the man was telling the truth.

Noah stepped forward and leaned over the document. It did appear as authentic as Storekeeper Keaton had said. It had actually been printed by a press. It had an official-looking heading, and next to the signatures was a wax stamp that replicated North Carolina's insignia.

Would he and Yarnell have to eat crow over this?

Then he saw the error. It was *South,* not North, Carolina that was disputing with Georgia over this region. The deed would have been issued by one of them. Noah folded up the document and handed it back to Whitman.

Standing behind Whitman, Yarnell's brows dipped in a questioning frown.

"I thank you," Noah said to the scrawny trader, "for allowing me to view it. It is a truly remarkable forgery."

Whitman's mouth popped open. "How dare you!"

"I dare because, I'm sorry to say, whatever you paid for this was wasted. North Carolina would never grant a deed on land this far south. Yarnell, we'll be boiling down our own salt."

"Over my dead body!" Whitman roared, then lunged at Noah.

Even with a rifle in each hand, Yarnell's attempt to stop the rancid fellow failed.

Whitman piled into Noah, clawing at him with dirty nails.

Noah caught the weaker man's wrists and thrust him away to arm's length. Whitman continued to struggle, the stench of his breath blasting Noah's face.

Noah grasped tighter. "Calm down, Trader Whitman. Or we'll have to tie you up."

What little strength the man had seemed to go out of him. He sagged against the table and looked around at Yarnell. "I thought we were friends of long standing. Or you never would've caught me unaware."

"Sit down." Noah pulled him toward the rickety chair. "Relax. We wish you no harm. We're here merely to take what we have as much right to as you do."

Whitman dropped into his seat, but his hate-filled eyes didn't leave Yarnell. "You duped my daughter, too, didn't you? Otherwise she never would've let you in here without shooting off a warning. I'll not soon forget what you've done."

Reminded of the young woman outside, Noah started toward the door, not relishing the thought of explaining their actions *or* of recanting Yarnell's lies.

"We best get the old coot tied up first," the hunter said. "He's a slippery one, and he's certain to have weapons stashed all over the place, seein' as how he trades 'em to the redsticks for pelts. He'll have a store of lead and gunpowder, too."

"Cheating me out of what's rightfully mine won't suffice?" Whitman railed. "Now you plan to add theft? Oh, how the mighty have fallen." He glanced toward the door, then, filling his lungs, opened his mouth.

Yarnell clapped a hand over it. "A gag wouldn't be a bad idea either." Yarnell dragged the trader with him to the open chest and lifted out several rags, then sat him down and started tying the man's wrists to the chair frame.

Noah was exceedingly glad Yarnell had taken on the task of securing the smelly man—until the frontiersman looked up and said, "Reardon, I can handle this alone. You go on out and disarm that little gal. And be careful. She can shoot straight as you or me."

3

Both hands encumbered, one with a bucket and the other gripping her rifle, Jessica carefully made her way down the steep bank of the stream that fed into the river and into the great oozing bowl of brine. Even now, after almost a year of this work, she hated descending into the sink. Jutting bones of long-dead animals were always a reminder that one slip of a step and she could end up like them. Several times since her family had moved here, an animal had become hopelessly bogged. The bellows of the last one—a terrified elk—still echoed in her brain, as they had echoed off the hills until she shot the suffering animal.

Of all the places her father had brought her to over the years, this was by far the worst. Plus the work was grueling. Small wonder Little Bob had run off with the Indians. But then, unlike her, he'd always been welcome among them.

Reaching the bottom of the path, she leaned the rifle against the crumbling cliff and stepped across the stone surrounding the gray white sump to a spot where she'd dug today's hole out of the pale mush. It had again filled with salt water. She stooped and slowly submerged her container, careful not to disturb the sides of the already slumping cavity.

Little Bob.

Her thoughts returned to her younger brother as she gazed down the creek toward the wide Tennessee—a river with so much force it vibrated the chalky stone beneath her moccasins—and so long, it could've carried him all the way to the Mississippi. Would he ever come back? At only thirteen, he was too young to be on his own. Her oldest brother, George, had been that age when he, too, had escaped, and they'd never heard from him again. But then, he'd run off with their Susquehannock slave girl. A bad time, that had been . . . one she didn't like to think about.

Jessica dug into the hard surface with her toes and grasped the bucket handle with both hands. Straining, she labored to lift the heavy receptacle straight up the center of her unstable well. Before Little Bob left, they'd done this together. Now, dredging up a much needed reserve of strength, she hauled the liquid up to the ledge and wondered which missed him more—her yearning heart or her aching back.

But her baby brother going off with the Muskogee was no surprise. Most of his life had been spent near one Indian village or another, and since their mother had died giving birth to him, he'd had Indian nursemaids until he was five and Jessica was old enough to take over. Small wonder he'd always moved among them with so much ease and acceptance. Particularly since he didn't have her almost colorless eyes.

Jessica's puffing breaths turned into a chuckle. If the Shawnee up along the Ohio had shunned her for being a witch when she was a mere child, they should see her now . . . down here in this eerie place of death and desolation, stirring up stinking brews in great black cauldrons.

Well, at least the odd pigmentation of her eyes had kept her family safe when the Indians went on the warpath. Even those times when they'd caught Father cheating. Their fear that she'd call down some curse upon them was far greater than their anger at him or even their desire to steal his rum and guns.

And it wasn't as if the Indians were cowards. As a rule, they had a penchant for taking whatever they wanted by force. The tribes had been warring against each other as long as anyone could remember. Spring raids on other tribes were as predictable as the rhododendron blooming on the hills. Now isolated settlers were prone to be targeted as well. Sometimes even trading posts. But never theirs.

Shoving the heavy fur robe to the side, Jessica rose to her feet, wondering about the new settlers who were coming. She wished Mr. Reardon had described his company. How many white women would he bring? Except for the few she'd seen the Shawnee sorely abuse during the war, she could scarcely remember what one looked like—not even herself. Her mother's mirror had shattered several years ago.

But then she might not be a proper example of a female. She couldn't help noticing that whenever a long hunter or a trader saw her for the first time, he always stared, slack-jawed, for a second or two before collecting his manners. Most, anyway. Some had been brash enough to mention her peculiar eyes.

But from what George and Spencer had said, her mother's eyes had been the same light shade, and no one had thought *her* odd. Jessica's older brothers had said the women at Fort Pitt had been very friendly to Mother and were sad when she died. Spencer had always said white women were kind and they cooked an abundance of the most delectable things to eat.

A pleasurable warmth coursed through Jessica as she shifted the weighty bucket to one hand. For certain, she'd go visiting these women just as soon as they arrived.

She felt a presence behind her. She swung around. Not three feet away stood Mr. Reardon, holding two firearms.

She shot a glance past him. Her musket was no longer where she'd left it. It was in his hand!

Her chest tightened with fear. She'd been dreadfully wrong about him. He wasn't a gentleman. He'd come down here out of sight of the cabin, alone, like some mountain cat, and disarmed her. The look in his eyes was that of a hunter. And she was his prey.

She grasped the bucket tighter. So he was the sort of man who would try to have his way with her. Leave her with the shame of an illegitimate child. Father always threatened to kill her if she ever let that happen.

But she was trapped. The tall man stood between her and the path up out of the sink. Behind her, the quagmire was at least an acre across before it oozed off a sheer twenty-foot drop to the boulder-strewn creek below.

Trapped with nowhere to go. She had no choice but to talk her way out . . . put him at ease, then push him into the sump. "I see you've taken a fancy to my rifle," she said in a falsely calm voice. "It's unequivocally accurate. I can shoot the eye out of a gobbler at a hundred paces." It didn't hurt to let him know she was someone to be reckoned with.

He stayed where he was, just watching her.

What was he thinking? Was he planning to make a lunge for her?

Finally he spoke. "Are you sure? I couldn't even *see* a turkey's eye at a hundred paces."

"Let us climb up out of here, and I shall give true evidence of my proficiency."

"You first." He stepped back, flattening himself against the cliff to make room for her to pass—a leeway of less than two feet. But would he actually let her by? Or was this just a ruse to more easily catch hold of her?

Well, it wouldn't be all that simple, since his hands were filled with weapons at the moment. Gripping the bucket with both hands—the better to swing it into him if he tried to grab her—she sidestepped along the narrow stone ledge. Keeping her gaze locked on his, watching for any sign of a sudden move on his part, she was forced to crane her neck upward as she came abreast of him. Up this close, she saw he was even taller than she'd first reckoned, and his shoulders were much broader. His frock coat expanded impressively with each of his steady breaths. Easily, he made two of her. She grasped the bucket all the tighter, hoping desperately he didn't sense her fear.

As she reached the base of the path, she was still within his reach. With trepidation, she turned her back to him, knowing she was now even more vulnerable to capture. Powered by her panic, she raced to the top of the bluff on swift, sure feet, reaching it far ahead of the long-legged Mr. Reardon.

Though her fear told her to run, she waited at the head of the path, knowing that a well-placed slam of the bucket just before he reached the flat would send him tumbling back down and into the quagmire.

But he was smiling almost apologetically when he climbed up to where their faces were level. And his gray eyes were not hard and steely like her father's but more like the soft silvery feathering of the mockingbird. Had she been wrong about him?

Her hesitation cost her the chance to vanquish him. He stepped onto the shale surface and moved clear of the edge.

She backed out of reach.

"Here," he said, holding out her musket.

A ploy to bring her close again? Or a genuine offering?

Cautiously, she stepped forward just far enough to stretch for it. And he actually let her firearm go.

"Thank you." Relief flooded through her—the man truly had come to assist her. Then the realization sprang forth. How very close she'd come to knocking him down the cliff and into the deadly muck.

"Let me pour the bucket into the kettles for you," the gentleman offered as he took the carrier. "That looks mighty heavy for such a slip of a lass."

Such thoughtfulness, she mused as she watched him walk to the trio of fires, then remembered she'd promised to demonstrate her shooting ability. Starting for her cabin, she called, "I'd better fetch more of my paper cartridges if we're going to—"

"Wait!" He swung around as if her halting were of vital importance. Then, in a sudden change of expression, he shrugged and smiled ruefully. "How much water do you want me to put in each kettle?"

"Oh, just divide it betwixt them. And if you don't mind, toss on some extra wood. I don't want the fires to go out whilst we pursue some edible game. I reckon I should advise you, I don't shoot anything just for sport. If it can't be put in the cook pot, I won't kill it."

His doubtful smile turned into an infectious grin that showed off a perfect row of gleaming white teeth and pleasing creases on either side of his mouth. "That's good to know."

She grinned and started for her cabin, which, thankfully, sat a good fifty yards upwind of her foul-smelling father's. Whether seriously or not, she knew Mr. Reardon had entertained a few doubts of his own about her intentions.

Noah was relieved to see the lass walk up the rise to the second cabin and away from her pa's. At the same time he could kick himself for not capturing her when he first came up behind her at the salt sink as Yarnell had sent him to do. It would have been so easy to have scooped her up then and there. But when he saw how her delicate hands strained as she pulled up the brimming bucket, he became so overwhelmed with compassion for her that he couldn't bring himself to do it.

But he knew he'd have to act before she walked into her pa's hovel and found him bound and gagged.

Carrying the large bucket of murky water, he stopped before the closest of the large-footed kettles set on a ring of stones over fiery coals. As he poured liquid into the dry iron pot, the beading water danced and sizzled. Steam billowed up, burning his face and hands, then quickly diminished as he hastily added more water. Cheeks stinging, he knew he'd have to be more careful in the days to come, during his own labors. This would be hot, hard work. Drew, who would always rather go hunting than do any mundane chore, was not going to be happy when Noah asked him to help.

When he'd replenished the water and wood from a nearby pile, Noah started for the cabin Miss Whitman had entered. He couldn't afford to have her head over to her pa's before he did something about her.

But what? He didn't want to subdue her by force. At least not until after he'd told her the truth—the whole truth. Perhaps if he explained their position in an amicable way, she might not react with too much violence. She *did* say she shot only edible game. The thought no longer amused him. He prayed she would understand his position. But could she, being raised by that odious sinner of a father?

Yarnell must have been right when he accused Noah of being addlepated over her. Was he a complete fool when it came to women? Like he'd been with Lorna?

No. There was no comparison. This was an open, intelligent woman who deserved honesty and compassion. Besides, he sensed a goodness in her—unlike her pa. And, who knew, beneath all that char, tangles, and bear hide, there might even be a presentable young woman.

Just before he reached her door, she came out with the straps of her powder horn and ball pouch slung over the coarse black fur. "Shall we go now and find something succulent for our evening repast?" she asked, strolling cheerfully and unsuspectingly to meet him.

Suddenly a shadow clouded her gay expression.

Had she noticed something at the other cabin? Noah shot a glance over his shoulder but saw nothing.

"You and Mr. Yarnell *are* staying for supper, aren't you?"

Now he really felt guilty. Her change of expression had merely been caused by the thought that they might leave before she had more chance to visit with them. "Aye, we'd count supping with you a true pleasure."

"Wonderful!" A burst of light danced in the depths of her amazing eyes. "Follow me!" Holding her floppy hat down, she took off at a run, heading east.

Noah remembered Drew back at the raft. "Miss Whitman," he called. "Wait a moment."

Stopping, she turned back questioningly.

"Would you mind if we went through the woods to the north?"

She glanced in that direction, then to the east, as suspicion once again stiffened her countenance. "We'll be blocked by the river if we venture that way."

Taking three long strides, Noah's long legs ate up the distance between them. "I know. But that's where I left my kid brother to guard the rest of our supplies until we knew it was safe."

Keeping close watch on the direction she kept her musket barrel pointed, he explained, "Drew is the baby of our family. I promised to keep him unharmed."

She relaxed somewhat. "I understand. I've been worrying about my own little brother since he left me." Turning, she headed north. "So I reckon we better go fetch your Drew. Did you beach your raft in that cove on the upper side of the bend?"

"Aye." He followed after her, feeling even less worthy of her good opinion. The fact that she'd said her brother had left *her*, not *them*, only made it worse. Miss Whitman felt abandoned. He'd heard it in her voice.

She headed toward the November-dead woods. Noah knew he could wait no longer to tell her the rest. He stepped up beside her and placed a hand on her fur-covered shoulder. "Miss Whitman, could we pause a moment? I'm afraid I have something else to confess."

As she gazed up at him, her eyes looked even larger than usual. "Yes?"

"We really came here to boil down some salt. But your pa said we couldn't because he held title to the land—a title which we have since found to be false. You see, I am rather learned about such matters since I've been reading for the law."

She studied him a moment. "Then you should know all about the principles of truth, justice, and propriety, and the great men who wrote about them."

"I reckon." He was feeling more uncomfortable with each word that passed from her lips. "And, as I said, I found your pa's deed to be a forgery."

"That doesn't surprise me," she replied matter-of-factly, a far cry from the outrage he'd expected. "Hard drink has long since destroyed all virtue in my father and in his business practices."

Noah took a fortifying breath. She had yet to hear the worst. "Miss Whitman, I regret to tell you that your pa tried to shoot us when we informed him that he had no right to stop us from boiling down our own salt. We were forced to disarm him."

"Oh la." She instantly stepped back, out of reach, her own weapon firmly in hand.

"I promise you we have no intention of abusing him in the least. When we leave, he'll be as unharmed as before we arrived."

She glanced behind her through the brush and trees that

impeded the view of the cabins. "Father won't let you prevail over him for long. He's a sly old fox. We'd better return before he shoots Mr. Yarnell."

Noah put a staying hand on her slender arm. "Yarnell's safe. I'm sorry, but we had to tie up your pa."

"Oh, my." Her gaze darted back and forth. Undoubtedly, she was caught in a dilemma. Which would claim victory? Her honesty or her loyalty?

Finally she aimed her attention, not her rifle, on him. "Well, I reckon we'd better go fetch your brother and hunt us up something for supper. The rest I suppose we can sort out later."

4

Jessica led the way to the upper side of the river bend, but all she could think of was her father, bound hand and foot. Glancing back at Mr. Reardon, who followed a few steps behind, she wondered if he had any idea of the danger he and Ethan Yarnell had placed themselves in, not to mention his younger brother.

Father never forgot and never pardoned. She couldn't even imagine what manner of vengeance he was planning at this very moment. And if they deprived him of his jug, he would accept nothing less than their deaths by torture. Father knew those who would do the deed for no more than the cost of a rifle.

Perhaps Noah Reardon didn't understand the enormity of their folly, but surely Mr. Yarnell did. Any long hunter who managed to keep his scalp this many years overmountain couldn't be that much of a fool. He should have known better.

One thing for certain—Mr. Yarnell never would have left her armed. No doubt the grim-faced hunter had sent his partner down to the salt sump to take her prisoner as she'd suspected. But Noah

Reardon was too much of a gentleman and a scholar to commit such an ignoble act. The man was as truehearted as he was handsome. A man as worthy as Thomas Paine or General Washington himself, or—

The snap of a twig close behind served to remind her that no matter what she hoped he was like, the man walking behind her was still a stranger. If she knew what was good for her, she'd better stop placing so much trust in someone she'd just met.

No, she was right about him. Any man who read for the law must love justice and honor as much as she did. Hadn't he already confessed the lie he'd told her without the least prompting?

Her father, on the other hand, had no problem at all being deceitful. Lies issued from his mouth as easily as water poured from a gourd.

Yes, Mr. Reardon was a man to be admired, like those patriots who'd fought in the war for valiant principles . . . a real Baltimore man.

Jessica turned back to him. "Sir, perchance did you fight alongside General Washington in the great battles for freedom and justice?"

Noah Reardon paused. His gentle gray eyes, as friendly as ever, smiled along with his lips. "Why, yes I did, Miss Whitman. My older brother and I spent almost eight years in his army. From Boston to North Carolina and back again."

"My father was a military man once too. He came to Maryland from England. That's where he met and wed my mother, may she rest in peace. I was born after he was transferred to Fort Pitt on the frontier." She started to say more but stopped, remembering how her older brothers always called her Jaybird because she talked too much.

Mr. Reardon came alongside and began walking again—beside her this time. "You were born and raised on the frontier? Tell me, have you ever been to any of the Eastern towns?"

"To my utmost regret, no, I have not. Father resigned his commission soon after I was born and became an Indian trader. When my mother died, he took us with him down the Ohio to the Indian towns. But I've read every newspaper and broadside that's found its way to us. As you have, I've studied the new proclamations and rulings, embraced all the patriotic essays."

Admiration for her shone in his eyes. "You never cease to amaze me. Perhaps we can discuss our mutual interests this evening over supper."

More confident now, she ventured the question she'd been yearning to ask. "Perchance, do you hail from Baltimore?"

"No, I was born on a farm just south of Salisbury in North Carolina. But I've been to Baltimore . . . as lovely a city as any on the seacoast." Then he raised his gaze from her and looked beyond. "It shouldn't be much farther to the raft."

He'd been to her mother's city! She had so many more questions to ask. But there would be plenty of time. Several days, anyway—*if* they could come to some agreement about Father.

Off to her right, she heard the distinct gobble of a wild turkey. "Tonight's supper," she whispered, allowing a bit of happiness to swell within her. "We can chase it down after we fetch your brother."

The raft was exactly where Jessica thought it would be. Through a break in the trees she saw it bobbing gently in a protected inlet, totally unloaded, yet only a couple of crates and several large cauldrons were stashed behind the river brush. But then, Mr. Reardon and Mr. Yarnell had come to the lick with loaded horses, she remembered.

Jessica surveyed the woods but didn't see the younger brother. A rustling in the fallen leaves drew her gaze to three horses tied to tree branches a stone's throw from the bank. Then she saw the lad, standing on a boulder at the water's edge. Tall, like Mr. Reardon, he also wore a fitted coat, his the darkest of blues. He didn't wear the stylish three-cornered hat, though. His was more like hers, the brim low all around, shading his profile as he entertained himself, skipping stones across the water.

Beside her, Noah whistled in imitation of a wood thrush.

The younger, thinner brother swung around. Grinning, he tossed the remaining stones aside. "It's about time," he called as he leapt from the rock and trotted toward them.

Suddenly he stopped short and gaped at Jessica, his mouth wide enough to catch a mouse.

"Drew. Andrew," Mr. Reardon scolded. "Where's your musket?"

"Leanin' against yon tree," the lad absently murmured as he continued to stare at Jessica as if she were some strange creature that just crawled out of a bog.

"If we were Indians, you'd be dead," Noah retorted.

The younger version of the good-looking one finally stopped gawking and turned to his brother. "For Pete's sake, Noah, it's cold as January. Redsticks ain't gonna be skulkin' around on a day like this."

"You mean like the three who just paddled away in their canoes?" Mr. Reardon expelled a frustrated breath, then turned to Jessica. "May I present my rather foolhardy brother, Andrew."

"It takes a fool to know one." The younger one sounded as irritated as his older sibling. Then, with a sudden sweep of the hat from his head, he bowed low. "How do you do, miss. The name's Andrew Vickersund Reardon of the Carolina Reardons, but my *friends* call me Drew."

With the hat removed, the sandy-haired lad looked about seventeen, the age her own brother Spencer had been when he ran off to Baltimore. Jessica couldn't help but warm to him, despite his rude ogling. In an effort to make him feel welcome, she did her best to return his greeting, right down to the deep bow. "How do you do. My name is Jessica Jane Hargrave Whitman Jones of . . . of the

Baltimore Hargraves." Replacing her hat, she added, "But everyone calls me Jay Jay or Jaybird because I have a tendency to talk too
much."

"Is that so?" Drew Reardon said with a spark of merriment in
his voice. He reached out and took her hand in his much larger one.
"It's a real pleasure to meet you, Jessica Jane. A *real pleasure*."

"Drew," Noah said, his voice even more assertive than before,
"you and *Miss Whitman* will have opportunities aplenty to resume
this conversation later. We'll be here for several days. Right now,
we need to reload the horses and supplies and float the raft down to
the salt lick." He was obviously still irritated with the lad.

Continuing to hold her hand, Drew's jaw muscles knotted as he
glanced at his brother. Then in a mercurial change, he returned his
attention to her and smiled lightly. "Miss Jessica, may I be permitted to help you board?"

He was even more of a gentleman than his older brother, she
thought as unexpected heat rushed to her cheeks.

Before she could gather her wits to answer, the elder Mr.
Reardon intervened. "She has game to shoot for supper."

"Huntin'?" Drew responded with enthusiasm, dropping
Jessica's hand. "You're goin' huntin'? I'll get my musket and come
with you."

Jessica glanced up at Mr. Reardon questioningly.

Brow furrowed, he glared at the lad. "I need your help with the
raft, Drew." His curtness brooked no argument.

She knew Mr. Reardon could easily navigate this gentle stretch
of river without assistance. Did he lord it over his brother as a rule,
or was Mr. Reardon trying to protect her from a brother whose
motives might be less than worthy? At that idea, a wondrous swelling took place in her bosom.

But then another thought came to mind. Perhaps he was trying
to protect his brother from her . . . perhaps he was afraid she might
take the lad hostage to trade for her father's release. He had yet to

tell Drew about the situation at the cabin. Too many questions needed answers that she feared would not be forthcoming as long as she was present.

"I bid you adieu," she abruptly said. "The sooner we each achieve our goals, the sooner we may exchange our latest bits of news from the East and perhaps have that stimulating debate of the prevailing philosophies." Turning from them, she made a hasty retreat, wanting to remove herself from their view as soon as possible.

She couldn't have been more than twenty yards away when she heard a burst of laughter. Glancing back, she saw that it came from Drew.

"Hush," the older brother said and yanked the giggling lad toward the horses.

A stone's throw farther, Jessica dropped down behind a tangle of berry vines and stealthily started working her way back toward them. She had to know more.

Drew's laughter sputtered to a stop. Almost, anyway, as he said, "'A stimulatin' debate of the prevailin' philosophies'? Comin' out of that dirty face?"

He was making sport of her! Angry, mortified, she wanted to run away, but she crawled closer.

"That's enough," Mr. Reardon said, untying the first horse. "I know she takes a bit of getting used to, but from now on I expect you to behave like a respectable adult."

Jessica, who had managed to get within easy hearing distance, slithered beneath the drooping branches of a river willow, where she had a good view of Drew as his face reddened and his fists clenched.

"You expect me to act like an adult when you treat me like a half-grown colt?" The lad sounded furious. "Ever since we left the valley, you've been bullying me around. You wouldn't even give me a few pence so I could stay at Henry's Station whilst you came down here. No, you wouldn't have it no other way than to drag me

along on this cold, miserable trip. You ask me, I think you're takin'
it out on me for what Lorna Graham done to you!"

"That's my business, and at the moment, so are you. You are to
treat Miss Whitman with the utmost respect."

"For Pete's sake, Noah, her pa's nothin' but a thievin' pirate.
'Sides, someone that peculiar should be grateful for any crumbs we
drop her way. I mean, just take a gander at her clothes, if that's
what you want to call 'em. And where in this wilderness did she
come up with all that fancy talk?" A grin snaked across his face
from ear to ear, and he shook his head.

Every word he'd said slapped Jessica in the face harder than the
back of her father's hand.

Mr. Reardon walked two horses to his brother and handed him
their leads. "Are you finished jawing now? Good. Because I'll not
tell you this again. That young lady's face is smudged with char-
coal because she tends three fires all day long—just like you're
going to be doing. She may have lived in the wilderness her whole
life, but she's still a valuable human being. Just because she's been
deprived of a proper upbringing doesn't mean she deserves any less
respect. You do the least thing to shame her, and if I have to, I'll
keep you tied up just like we have her pa."

Drew froze. "You got her pa tied up?"

Reardon settled back on his heels. "He gave us no choice. Now
get those horses loaded on. And I mean it, Drew; all we came here
to do is boil down some salt. No more, no less."

Jessica had heard all she could bear. More. As the nervous
animals created a racket, whinnying and dancing about as the men
pulled them toward the raft, she backed out from under the willow
and began moving from tree to tree. Once she was a safe distance
away, she broke into a run—one she couldn't bring herself to stop
until she was too winded to go another step.

Gasping for air, she propped her rifle against a fallen pine and
slumped down on it, feeling a chill that came not from without but

from within. She no longer had to guess about what people thought of her. Now she knew exactly . . . especially gentlemen who came from the East.

She was laughable, dirty, and the daughter of a thief. And dressed so peculiar that the younger one laughed out loud. Could that be why her brother Spencer had never come back to fetch her as he'd promised? He said he'd go to Baltimore, find their grandparents, then return for her and Little Bob. But that had been more than four years ago.

Jessica ran fingers down her nose and over her lips. La, how she wished she had a looking glass so she could see what the Reardons saw. Then she noticed how rough and calloused her palms were from the gritty salt and from lifting iron pots every day. Like her face, they were smeared with soot. She hadn't noticed how unclean they were when Drew had taken her hand into his.

Cringing at the thought, she rubbed her hands on the coarse black fur. Tears pooled in her eyes. She rarely cried, and to make matters worse, she was certain the tears would make streaks through the ash that smeared her cheeks.

Realizing she was wallowing in self-pity, Jessica leapt to her feet and swiped the wetness away with the almost-clean back of her hand. "To weep is a fruitless expenditure of energy. Fruitless," she repeated several times. "Useless waste."

Wrapping her fur tighter about her, she picked up her musket and headed toward where she'd heard the gobbler several minutes ago. No matter what Drew Reardon said, supper had to be hunted up for their guests.

But soon her steps slowed again. How could she ever sit at the table with her guests when she knew what they really thought of her? And what about her relatives in Baltimore—would they be as condemning? Her hand flew to the bejeweled cross as it always did when she thought of her mother's people. Would she never be able to go to them?

Of course she would.

The dirt was easy enough to wash away; it simply took some water and a little lye soap. And she did have those coins squirreled away. Enough to buy some proper clothes when she reached Henry's Station up in the Watauga settlements and enough to see her overmountain. Aye, and that storekeeper, Mr. Keaton, had seemed kind. He'd help her find the right clothes . . . or some fabric to make herself a new day gown . . . a day gown like in the drawing she had. Maybe she could make it out of that pretty calico Father used to sell to the Indians. Yes, she could do that.

But the "peculiar" part Drew mentioned . . . that was another matter. She had learned to read from her brothers, just as her mother had taught them. She'd thought that was the first step to being the same as the folks over the mountain. All the years she'd spent poring over the newspapers and broadsides until she could quote every word—the articles, the fascinating essays and letters she'd memorized—had been for naught. Drew had laughed at her. There must be so much more to learn before she could present herself in Baltimore.

Jessica stopped. Didn't Mr. Reardon say they had come here to boil down salt for his settlement? That would take them several days at the very least. Mayhap longer. And he was a kind gentleman—he'd proved that by defending her against his brother. He'd teach her what she needed to know—show her how to be acceptable. She'd wasted too much time waiting for Spencer to come back for her. Too much time.

Her heart picked up its pace. Yes, she might even be out of here before the first snow.

But her moment of elation quickly evaporated. She couldn't leave Father, not with winter coming on.

Maybe not—but she would be ready when the thaw came. "Aye." She stood up and lifted her chin. "With the help of Noah Reardon, I'll do just fine overmountain."

5

"Steer the tiller for shore," Noah shouted from the front of the raft. Turning to Drew at the rear, he pointed to where the three abandoned rafts were beached.

Drew, holding a square of muslin over his nose, nodded, then leaned his shoulder into the thick rudder guide, not willing to forgo the kerchief to use both hands.

The lad had yet to learn how much worse than the salt lick the interior of Pizar Whitman's cabin smelled. Noah chuckled and looked up at the limestone rise.

Yarnell stood just outside the door—probably stepped out for a breath of the less-offensive odor of brine. Seeing them, he headed toward the beach.

Noah tossed Yarnell a line, and he secured the raft to an abandoned one as Noah and Drew led the animals off to dry ground.

Drew still looked foolish, keeping his nose covered while working awkwardly with only one hand.

"Might as well get used to it, boy," Yarnell said in a gravelly voice. "We'll be stayin' a spell."

Reluctantly, the lad stuffed the piece of cloth into his coat pocket. "This must be what hell smells like."

Yarnell grinned, exposing a gap in his front teeth. "Me and your brother has smelled a lot worse. Ain't we? *Recently.*"

"Aye," Noah agreed, trying to conceal his own amusement. "I remember it like it was only today."

The leather-clad hunter turned to Noah. "I was startin' to fret about you. You went to disarm the lass and never come back." He glanced around. "Where is she?"

"Sorry about that. We came to an understanding about her pa. She's out now, hunting up our supper."

"She still has her *gun?* You didn't take her musket?" Yarnell sounded incredulous.

"I think it's all right. I told her everything, and she doesn't want anyone shot anymore than we do. And she seemed bent on cooking us a nice supper."

Yarnell raised his brows dubiously and glanced around with piercing eyes. Shrugging helplessly, he hopped aboard and hoisted a wood box up to his shoulder. "I hope it's just our supper she's a-huntin'."

Starting toward the animal shed with the horses, Noah waited for Yarnell to catch up. "I trust her. Let's just wait and see how this evening goes."

"Tell you one thing," Yarnell said, shifting the weight of the box he carried, "I ain't stayin' in yon stinkin' hole with Pizar all night."

Drew, tagging along, asked in disbelief, "It's worse in there than out here?"

The two men looked at each other and grinned.

"I reckon the other cabin is crammed with stores," Yarnell drawled. "But I'll manage to carve a space out for myself."

"I'm afraid you'll have to ask Miss Whitman about that," Noah said. "I think that's where she sleeps."

Yarnell groaned his disappointment. "Well, I reckon we'll have to clean up ol' Pizar's slop hole then, or sleep outside. And," he said, peering skyward, "it looks like rain."

Noah handed off his horses to Drew. "Why don't you two tend the livestock and finish unloading. I'll start some more fires and get our kettles going. The sooner we boil down our salt, the sooner we can get out of this place."

By the time the light began to fade from the heavily overcast day, Noah had Storekeeper Keaton's five large cauldrons going alongside Miss Whitman's. A single line of fires had been extended from hers so he could tend them all more easily. Caring for her pots was the least he could do, considering she was hunting for their supper.

At least that was what he hoped she was doing. Perhaps he'd played the fool again by letting her go off alone. He'd heard only a few shots, and those could have been a ploy to trick him before she went after some Indians to free her pa.

Every few seconds now, Noah glanced into the dark woods surrounding this eerie place. This may not be the hell Drew thought it was, but it very well might be the site of their deaths.

A sudden bang caught Noah by surprise. He swung around.

Only Drew. The lad hurried out of the cabin with an armload of clothes. Grim faced, Drew headed for a washtub that sat on its own fire not far from Whitman's door. He dumped the ragged wear into the heated water, where it joined every other washable item Drew and Yarnell had unearthed in the cabin . . . and that was after they had used the tub to scrub down Pizar Whitman himself. And cut off his unredeemable hair and beard.

At the far side of the cabin, Noah spotted something move.

Drew, unaware, started back to the door, blocking Noah's view.

Noah's rifle was propped against a stack of wood several yards away. He dove for it. Sprawled on his belly, he brought it up and aimed . . . then recognized Miss Whitman's bear fur. But before he lowered the gun barrel, he scanned the woods behind her for any other movements. Had she brought Indians with her?

Seeing none, he finally rose to his feet.

Drew started toward the young woman, an eager expression on his face.

Then Noah saw why. From one of the lass's hands dangled a wild turkey and what looked like two grouse—the chickens of the forest. And propped across one shoulder, along with her rifle, lay a pointed stick with a big fat perch impaled on it. She had enough meat for several days.

"Thank you, Lord," he mouthed as he returned his own rifle to lean against the woodpile. He'd been right about her.

And she'd been right about her prowess as a huntress.

Miss Whitman spotted Noah. Stumbling over a broken jug, she glanced down at the debris they'd dragged out of the cabin and frowned. Did she think there'd been a brawl . . . that they'd harmed her pa?

Drew murmured something to her, and the young woman glanced back at the cabin, her weapon clutched tightly in her hands.

Again Noah wished he'd kept hold of his own weapon.

Finally, she nodded and walked on, coming in his direction. But when she reached him, she didn't quite look him in the eye.

What did that mean? Why had she turned suddenly shy? "I see you had good success," he said, hoping to ease her mind.

"Aye," she replied softly, addressing his left ear. "There's always an abundance of game in the proximity of a salt lick." She glanced past his arm. "I see you've maintained my fires too."

"I thought it only fitting since you stopped working on our account."

She moved her gaze to him, with those lightest of aqua eyes. "'Tis a kindness I hadn't anticipated. I thank you." Then just as quickly, her attention returned to his ear. "Your brother said you've cleaned Father's cabin and bathed him, and you even gave him a haircut."

"Aye. That we did. I do hope that doesn't upset you."

Still without looking directly at him, her lips lifted in a quick smile. "No. I suppose I should've tied him up myself ages ago and done the same. He's gotten worse than an old squirrel storing nuts for winter. The more he crams into his trading post, the better he likes it. He flies into a rage if I even mention touching a thing. That's one of the reasons I reside in the storehouse." She glanced down at the fowl dangling from her hand. "If you don't mind, I thought we'd have the grouse and fish this evening, stewed with some squash and onions the Indians brought today."

"That sounds delicious. We ate mostly dried meat and hard bread on the trip down."

She glanced up for an instant, her dark lashes fluttering like butterfly wings. "As soon as I get the stew to simmering, I thought I'd pluck the turkey and dig a pit to slow-roast it overnight with the coals from today's fires."

"Don't you give that a second thought. I'll take care of the gobbler."

"*You will?*" Her mile-wide gaze met his full on as he took the large brindle-striped bird from her. Nonplused, she stammered, "Br-breakfast. We'll—uh—have it for breakfast."

"Makes my mouth water just thinking about it," he said, trying to put her at ease.

Abruptly she glanced back at her pa's cabin and caught her lower lip between her teeth. "Oh la, I do hope you're plying my father with his doses of rum. If you don't, he'll commence with the sick shakes and turn fearsome mean."

Everything that came so unexpectedly from this young woman's mouth ripped at Noah's heart. He wondered if she even knew how ill treated she was. At a loss for the proper response, he searched for something appropriate to say. "The apostle Paul wrote that we are not to become slaves to drink," he finally murmured.

She seemed less timid now as she held him in a steady gaze. "Aye, Father is that for certain—a slave to drink. Everything he barters or buys goes to support that one master." She shifted the weight of her heavy musket. "Well, I'd better take my leave and commence with supper preparations. I'll bring your victuals over to you."

"You don't eat with your pa?"

"No. Me and Little Bob always partook in the other cabin."

"But we've cleaned your pa's cabin up. I thought you'd join us for supper and some stimulating conversation."

Her fairylike features brightened, then quickly dimmed. "I perpend that Father would not be gladdened to see me since I have not attempted his rescue."

Noah placed a hand on her fur-draped shoulder. "I will speak to him, explain the folly of any effort on your part to try. Surely he would not want any harm to befall you."

In an abrupt move, she stepped out of his grasp. "I don't reckon he'll concern himself overmuch with that. If I don't try, he'll brand me a traitor, like he did the patriots during the war . . . and all three of my brothers when they left."

"I'll speak to him. And in the next day or two when he calms down, we'll turn him loose."

Her mouth parted in amazement. "If you do, you'll be dead before the sun rises again."

He smiled reassuringly. "No, we would make certain no weapons were within his reach."

52

"Don't be a ninny. He wouldn't kill you himself," she countered as if she were speaking to a brainless child. "What's done is done, so it's best to keep things as they are till you're ready to leave." With that said, she strode away.

There was a strength in the lass Noah hadn't expected and a clear, direct mind. And she'd left no doubt about one thing—if Pizar Whitman was freed, he'd set the Muskogee on them for sure.

The next morning Noah walked outside to the pinkening dawn. The day promised to be clear and sunny. Only the faintest of mists hovered over the river. But it was still bitterly cold, and for one brief moment he let himself think about what the morn would have held had he stepped outside his own place: the air fresh with the scent of pine and freshly mown hay, the gentle slope dotted with only a few magnificent old trees that glistened in the morning frost, and beyond them, their own gently flowing river. The remembrance gave him purpose as he asked his heavenly Father to see them safely and swiftly home again.

Keeping the collar of his heavy wool coat turned up, he quickly dug up the turkey pot and retrieved some live coals surrounding it to get fires blazing under the salt kettles again . . . as much for the warmth they would provide as for their eventual purpose. While completing the chore, Noah glanced now and again up the rise to Miss Whitman's cabin. He'd spent a miserable night in her father's cabin, listening to him snore. But what had bothered him even more was that not once did Whitman ask about his daughter's welfare. It was obvious the trader thought she would burst in at any moment to save him. He'd watched the door like a sly old fox . . . until Yarnell dropped the wooden bar into the slots to secure it for the night.

Noah poured brine into the kettles, fed and watered the horses, including the Whitmans' three, then returned to tend the fires. And still no one else had stirred.

Finally, from the farthest cabin, the young woman stepped out into the cold, wearing her bearskin cloak and carrying her floppy hat. Spotting him, she waved and walked down the barren rock in his direction.

As she neared, he noticed a marked difference in her appearance. She'd scrubbed her face. Her cheekbones seemed more pronounced, her chin more delicate. Quite a pleasing face she had, and her eyes . . . their netherworldly absence of color still startled him.

Her hair was divided into two ponytails that were tied with thongs and spilled over the coarse fur in shining strands as rich and deep a brown as mink fur. She must have spent half the night washing and brushing it smooth. Her neck, now more exposed, seemed almost too slender. She was no more than a wisp. The thought that her pa might abuse her after they were gone was unthinkable. But the possibility was very real. The miscreant thought of no one but himself and his jug.

"Greetings to you, kind sir," she said, putting her hat on and tipping it in the same way that she'd mimicked his greeting the day before. "The aroma of roast turkey floated up the rise and teased me awake. I see you've already uncovered it."

"Aye." Noah looked to where the iron pot held the succulent meat. "I used some of the live coals to start this morn's fires."

She scanned the long row of steaming cauldrons, then the still low slant of the sun. "You are men of great industry. But I don't see your companions. Where are they?"

"Still abed, I believe."

"I see." From beneath her black hat's wide brim, she looked at him with admiration. "Then the diligent pursuits on my behalf have been all yours."

Feeling a bit unworthy of such laudation, he plucked a drumstick from the pot and offered it to her. "I'm certain you do as much—*more*—every day."

As she accepted his offering, her half-hidden eyes sparked with pleasure. "Thank you most kindly."

She took the food in a hand that he noted had also been scrubbed, the nails clipped and cleaned. It pleased him yet made him uncomfortable that she'd felt obliged to go to all that effort. He hoped Drew hadn't made her uncomfortable the day before. He busied himself by tearing off a piece of thigh meat, then joined her at the nearest fire.

Bowing his head, he prayed. "Father in heaven, thank you for Miss Whitman's gracious hospitality and the bounty you have provided. We pray this in the precious name of your Son. Amen."

Raising his gaze from the flames, he saw that she stared at him as if he'd lost his wits. Why? He'd merely thanked God for the food.

Quickly she looked away, then she turned back as if she had something very serious to discuss. "Please, tell me about Baltimore across the mountain. Someone once said the cities there have more cabins and lodges than the biggest Shawnee town. And in Philadelphia, where the Congress meets, traders have stores lined up in precise rows—one selling nothing but hats, another baskets, or firearms, or fancy jewels."

"Aye, that's true. Silks and spices, tea and coffee—all manner of wondrous things are brought on ships from around the world and can be purchased in the stores. Belgian lace, crystal from Germany."

"Crystal?" She cocked her head curiously, then pressed her lips together. "When a person goes to Baltimore, how many of those accoutrements does she have to own to be accepted? How much money would it take? Or beaver pelts?"

At a loss for words, Noah stared at her. She was as ignorant of life over the mountain as he would be if he were suddenly deposited in India or China. "Being accepted is more than just acquiring possessions. It's thinking the same way about things as the other folks around you do."

"But I do. Despite what my father says about the patriots, I agree with everything I ever read about their zeal for liberty and about having sound principles and the utmost decency."

How he loved her bright, open inquisitiveness—so refreshing in comparison to his own "polite" society, which frowned on women betraying any intelligence that might equal a man's. "That's commendable, Miss Whitman. But I'm afraid there's so much more to learn than merely their political beliefs. It's knowing their social graces, their customs."

"I understand what you mean. When we first came into Muskogee country, my younger brother, Bob, had problems. He would return from the Muskogee village all befuddled. Not only did they speak another language than the Shawnee or the Chickasaw, but they had different chants and dances." A smile spread across her full lips. "What bothered him most, though, was that the Muskogee played a different game of stickball. He came home covered with bruises at least a dozen times before he caught on."

"I take it you didn't go to the village with him."

"No. Father has always forbidden me to mingle with the natives, even when they come here. They believe my eyes are bewitched—and Father likes to keep it that way. They think if they look into my eyes, I'll steal their sight. Yet they fear harming me, lest I call down some curse on them. So I mostly keep to myself when they come to trade." With a nonchalant lift of her shoulder, she took a bite off her drumstick as if she'd shared a simple, ordinary tale. "So tell me," she continued between bites, "what manner of customs do the Baltimore people have?"

"Customs?" Still digesting what she'd just said, it took a moment for Noah to recall any. "Oh, I reckon one would be that men are expected to help women down from wagons and carriages and to open doors for them."

"Men doing things for women," she said slowly; then she

brightened. "I favor that. Like yesterday when you tended my salt pots."

"Aye," Noah said automatically. Her enlivened expression had returned his thoughts to what she'd said about the Indians. He could easily see why they might be fooled by eyes that were as mercurial as quicksilver.

But the young woman had real questions that needed clear answers. Noah's dilemma was in how to gently explain that she would most definitely *not* fit in if she went to Baltimore. "Miss Whitman, to be accepted in what is called 'polite society,' one must know the right thing to say in each circumstance. That's something that is learned over time. And just as important is knowing when *not* to speak."

She nodded earnestly. "Like knowing when even the tiniest whisper will send Father into a rage." She stepped closer. "Mr. Reardon, I'll pay whatever you want in salt and pelts for you to teach me all those things. Please, teach me how to be a Baltimore lady before you go."

"*Before we go?*" The incredulous words came from Drew.

Noah spun around and saw that his brother had walked up, unnoticed.

"Now that sounds like a barrel-load of fun." The lad's expression shifted to a mischievous grin.

6

"You're going to have fun today, all right," Mr. Reardon quipped
to his younger brother, "making salt."

Drew's mischievous expression faded. "I'd rather do the huntin'."

"Wouldn't we all?" the older one agreed, arching a sun-bleached
brow.

These two seemed to have a running battle, Jessica noted.
Perhaps that was the natural way of families. She did remember
that her two oldest brothers had argued quite a bit before George
ran off with the slave girl. But after that, the only one Spencer ever
argued with was Father, and then usually over her and Little Bob.
Until Spencer left, he'd always stood between them and Father's
mean spells. It was still hard to believe he had never come back
for her and Bob as he'd promised. Yet she refused to accept the
possibility that he hadn't survived the trip out of the wilds.

Drew swung away from his older brother to her. The thin line of
his lips relaxed as he addressed her. "Miss Jessica, last night your
pa said he wanted to see you soon as he wakes up."

59

Father. Dread spiked through her. He would make her pay dearly for not stopping these men. Jessica took in a breath. "He doesn't usually rise before noon. I'll go up to him then."

Noah Reardon stepped closer. "If you would prefer not to be put in the middle between us and your pa, you don't have to be. I could forbid you entrance to his cabin. I can tell him that I thought it best if you two don't talk to each other whilst we're here."

"*Are* you forbidding me?" She didn't like the sound of that.

"If that's what you want. Otherwise, you're free to see him anytime you wish."

"Then I suppose it would be rather nice to have a few days' freedom. Unless, of course, he becomes overly agitated."

The older Reardon nodded and turned to his brother. "Now, Drew, I suggest you grab yourself some roast turkey and start helping with the salt. The sooner we finish here, the sooner we'll be heading back to Henry's Station."

At the mention of leaving, Drew became all smiles again. He glanced toward the fires. "Where's the coffee?"

"Why don't you break yourself off a piece of meat? Then go fetch our pot and the fixings," Mr. Reardon suggested in an offhanded manner, no longer at odds with his brother.

Jessica picked up a bucket of briny water and went to add some to each of the cauldrons. She wanted a moment to mull over all Noah Reardon had said to her. Most particularly, she enjoyed knowing he was determined to protect her from her father, whether she needed it or not. This man truly was as beautiful in thought and deed as he was in appearance. A veritable prince of the realm.

Her heart warmed strangely at the thought, and a smile spread unbidden. To disguise it, she wedged her drumstick between her teeth on the very valid pretext that she needed both hands to pour water into the first cauldron.

Then a sobering question resurfaced. She removed the turkey leg. "I, too, will do whatever I can to aid you in obtaining your quota, Mr. Reardon, because I'm certain your wife and children are eagerly awaiting your return," she probed.

Pulling some thigh meat from the bird, Drew sputtered, "Noah? He don't have a wife or kids. He couldn't even keep hold of his betrothed."

"Coffee, Andrew," his brother reminded in a low stern voice and pointed toward Father's cabin. "Get the coffee fixings."

"Let me get mine," Jessica offered, her own spirits soaring. "I'd be most happy to make it." As unbelievable as it was, Noah Reardon did not have a woman. Gathering her bear fur tightly around her, she took off at a run. Then she stopped and turned back. "How would you like it, Mr. Reardon? Weak, strong, or medium?"

Near noon on the same clear, cold day, Jessica was scraping salt into her sack from a fiery pot held by Drew, when she realized she'd reached her daily quota. She already had a ten-pound sack full of the grainy substance. With the three of them working together, her chore had been completed in record time.

But she reminded herself, the two brothers had good reason to hurry—no one would want to stay in this smelly place if he didn't have to. No matter how much she wished they would.

She caught a flash of movement up by the cabin.

Mr. Yarnell. He'd stepped outside as he had on numerous occasions this morning. He'd elected to split his time between guarding her father and keeping watch for the Muskogee, rather than joining in the tedious labor of boiling down salt. But that was typical of a long hunter. They always saved their strength for moments when it was most needed—like making certain they kept their scalps during the extended months they stayed in Indian country hunting and exploring.

"Miss Jessica, this pot is gettin' heavy," Drew grated out. Dripping with perspiration, he was bent spraddle-legged over a fire while straining to keep the large cauldron tilted.

"I do apologize." Securing her bear fur more snugly, she spooned the last of the salt into her bag. She was finished, yet she'd not asked nearly all the questions of Noah Reardon she wanted to.

As Jessica tied off her sack with a strip of deerskin, Drew returned the pot to its upright position and picked up the bucket. "I'm goin' down to fetch more brine," he said and took off at a fast trot. He certainly was in a hurry to conclude their business here.

But Jessica didn't want them to go. She'd learned precious little of what she needed to know before going to Baltimore. Every answer Mr. Reardon had given her only prompted more questions. Gathering her sack under her arm, she walked over to where he gathered wood from the rapidly depleting pile.

With a load in his capable arms, Mr. Reardon turned toward her. "Don't worry about the firewood. Drew and I will take the horses and go fetch in a good supply for tomorrow."

"I hadn't given it a thought. As forthright as you've been in everything else, I surmised you would be equitable about that too." Then she offered a sincere smile of her own. "And now I would take this opportunity to be just as forthright with you."

The space between his straight, sun-bleached brows crimped in a frown. He obviously thought she was on the verge of some devious confession.

"Please," she said, placing a hand on his berry-died wool sleeve. "It's nothing that should cause distress. At least I hope it doesn't. I merely wish to make a trade with you. I shall give you the use of my pots each day after I've filled my quota if you will allow me to remain at your side as you work. I have so many queries I beg to put to you."

His sudden grin caught her by surprise. It reached all the way to his silver gray eyes. "I thought you were already doing that."

She felt her face burn with embarrassment, but she forced

herself to ignore it. This was much too important for her to turn fawn shy. "Every answer you gave me this morning only made me want to know more."

His grin softened to a tender smile that made her heart do another strange flip-flop. "Well, then, Miss Jessica Jane, I gladly accept your offer."

"You do?" She couldn't keep her exuberance from bursting forth. "Then I'll return directly. I have something to show you."

Jessica spun away and raced up to her cabin. Banging past the door into the dim interior, she tossed the sack of salt in the corner where cured beaver pelts were stacked along with a good portion of the dry goods—enough supplies to see her and her father through the winter. Dodging her eating table, she ran to a crate shoved against the wall opposite the hearth. In it she kept her keepsakes along with the prized newspapers and broadsheets she'd been collecting since she'd learned to read her first word. Squinting in the dimness, she rummaged through until she found the paper she was after. Tucking it inside her fur robe, she dashed out again, eager to show Mr. Reardon.

By the time her moccasin-clad feet padded to a stop in front of Noah, she was out of breath, but she didn't waste a second. Retrieving the Philadelphia newspaper, she carefully unfolded it and pointed to the picture printed on the paper. "See all those windows. Rows of them. Father says they all have what he calls 'plate glass' in them. Lots of squares of it at every window."

"That's right."

"And they're like thin sheets of ice. But so clear you can see through them as if nothing's there."

"You've never seen a glass window?" He dropped the load of wood close to the nearest fire. "No. Of course you haven't. Unlike shutters, they're wonderful for letting in light when it's too cold outside to leave the window open."

"I saw a small glass bottle once, but I couldn't see through it much better than through one of my clear stones. Tell me, how would a person go about making such wonderments?"

A smile lifted one corner of his mouth. "Actually, glass is made of—shall we say—a mixture of substances that come from the ground. A sand, if you will. Then it's heated until it becomes liquid and can be poured. You know, similar to when we heat lead and pour it into our bullet molds."

That still didn't make sense to her. "But lead is still lead before it's melted and afterward."

"You do have such a delightfully inquisitive mind. Especially for a female. Believe me, what I say is true. Cross my heart."

Her happiness expanded at the thought that he enjoyed her curiosity. Not once had he grown impatient with her questions as Father usually did. But what did he mean by "cross my heart"? She placed her hand over the hidden bejeweled cross just above her own heart. He must be wearing one too. And he swore to the truth by it. Perhaps it had some special meaning, like the Muskogee women wearing turtle-shell rattles around their ankles. "What does your cross look like?"

"My cross?" He stared at her oddly.

Perhaps he didn't want to expose his pendant anymore than she did hers.

Then Noah's wonderful smile returned. "You misunderstood me. I said, 'Cross my heart.' Like this." He ran a finger down his chest, then across it.

"I see. That's your sign for saying you're telling the truth?"

"Aye. With God as my witness."

"And which god is that?"

Mr. Reardon's mouth went slack. He stepped back and stared at her as urgently as he sometimes did Drew.

Had she said something to anger him?

Then he spoke in a rather severe tone. "The God of our fathers, of course."

Amazing. "You have a god just for your family?"

"For my family?" He stared oddly at her again, before he quickly collected himself. "No, the one true God who lives inside anyone who asks him in."

Jessica stepped back herself. She wasn't certain if she wanted to stand so close to him. "You have a god dwelling inside you? For truth? The Indians stay away from me because they think I have one. But I don't."

Mr. Reardon caught his breath. Then, expelling it, he called to his brother. "Drew, watch the fires for me. I need some time to speak to Miss Jessica."

"Alone?" Drew returned suspiciously.

"Just do what I say." He took Jessica's hand. "Come along, please."

Despite the fact that something she'd said had upset him, Jessica realized her hand did feel cozy in his much larger one. But he certainly was a hard man to figure.

Mr. Reardon led her up the barren rise to a cutaway in the rock surface that formed a natural seat. Pulling her down beside him, he continued to hold her hand as he looked intently into her eyes. He must have thought she'd lied to him. Did he think she really did have some spirit living in her, as the Indians feared?

Finally his expression gentled, and he spoke. "Have you never heard of Jesus, the Son of God, who came to earth from heaven above to die for our sins?"

"Jesus. Is that the name of your god?"

"My dear, sweet Jessica. You have something far more important to learn about this day than what lies east of the mountains. It's long past time you were introduced to your Savior."

As long as he looked at her so sincerely and called her *my dear, sweet Jessica,* she couldn't help but listen to anything he had to say.

7

Noah couldn't help enjoying the lively banter that had kept him entertained all morning on this, their fourth day of boiling down salt. As he watched Jessica Whitman stir pine coals beneath a pot, he especially relished the happy enthusiasm in her voice.

"*You're joking,*" she cried incredulously. "How could a young lady walk around wearing that many petticoats?"

Drew, pouring brine into a cauldron, laughed. "They don't, not that good, anyway. That's why we men have to keep helpin' 'em in an' outta carriages or anything else they want to climb up to. Remember Nancy, Noah? When she first started sportin' all that nonsense, she couldn't pass a table but what she didn't knock somethin' off."

Noah chuckled at the recollection of his younger sister. Even more cheering was the fact that he hadn't had to reprove Drew a single time in the past two days. Once the lad realized that Noah had meant what he said about the work and treating the lass with respect, he'd become an enlivened participant, especially in answering the multitude of questions Miss Jessica had come up with.

"Noah!" The summons issued from the top of the rise. Ethan Yarnell stood outside the cabin, motioning for him to come, then abruptly returned inside.

Yarnell's bearded face had not looked happy. Pizar Whitman must be driving him up a tree again. With a groan, Noah set down the bucket and started up the slanted slab surface. He, too, had come to dread the time he spent with the trader. The words that spewed from the man's mouth were as unsavory as the rest of him.

Before Noah reached the cabin, Yarnell strode out with his rifle, his powder horn slung across his lean chest. "Can't stomach any more. I'm goin' huntin'." Without waiting for Noah's response, the leather-clad frontiersman headed for the nearest line of trees.

Noah looked back with longing at the two he'd just left. He had no choice. Drew had guarded Pizar Whitman just before Yarnell, and now it was his turn to spend time in the gloomy hole of a place.

"Ah, a changing of the guard, I see," Whitman remarked in a sarcastic tone when Noah strode in. He sat slumped at the table, his unkempt head at a tilt and his bony thumb hooked in the ring handle of a jug. The only rope securing the puny man to the chair was wrapped around his waist and secured at the back with several intricate knots.

Since their captive was never left alone for more than a minute or two, they'd given him as much freedom of movement as possible.

"Aye," Noah replied tartly, "you've managed to run Yarnell off again."

"And in that traitor's stead I must endure the asinine posturing of the elder Reardon cur."

Noah chose to ignore the insult. "Have you eaten anything yet?"

"Absolutely not!" he answered in horror as if Noah had asked him to take poison. "It's much too early in the day to impose such traffic on my poor constitution."

"It's almost noon." Noah charged, then caught himself from saying anything further. He'd had too pleasant a morning to allow the argumentative drunkard to draw him into a debate. "Think I'll fix lunch and save Miss Jessica the effort." He started for the stash of food piled in the corner.

"Miss Jessica, is it now?" her pa sneered. "Cooking for *Miss Jessica*. And will you be using some of your own stores for a change? It's not bad enough that you keep me prisoner here whilst you rob me of my salt, but, like the blackest of ravens, you're devouring all the food I have stocked for winter." He pulled the jug close to his body as if it were a child he was trying to protect and pointed toward the shelves lining the wall to his left. "And you've been drinking up my rum."

"You'll not be able to blame your dwindling supply of rum on me. I'm a Baptist. It's against the ordinances of my faith to partake of such debilitating swill."

"My, but aren't you the hoity-toity one. Well, it's against the ordinances of my faith *not* to imbibe. And as for my food—it's a pity *that* isn't against your religion." He pointed to the far wall. "Look at that shelf. It's half empty. You gluttons are emptying out this cabin."

Sighing, Noah turned back to him. "I've told you this before. We are merely merging our supplies with yours to give all of us more of a variety. And as you and I both know, most of your food stores are kept in your daughter's cabin."

Whitman took a swig, then wiped the excess moisture from the stubbled beard that was growing in again. "Spend a lot of time up at her cabin, do you?" he insinuated accusingly. "You think you're so clever, hiding behind your religion and all. But I know your kind." He leaned forward, snarling through his nose. "I know what you've been doing with my girl whilst you've kept me tied up here for weeks on end. And since you won't let her come in here to me, I suspect she hasn't been a willing participant."

Outrage infused Noah—as much for Miss Whitman as for himself. But he refused to dignify her father's latest accusation with an answer. Unclenching fists that itched to rearrange the blackguard's swarthy features, he took a calming breath. "You seem to have lost track of time, my friend. We've been here only four days. And as for your daughter, I find Miss Jessica to be an honorable young lady with a lovely spirit and a bright inquisitive mind."

Whitman sputtered into laughter. "Inquisitive?" he hooted. "That's my Jaybird. I've entertained many a true friend for hours on end, encouraging her to ask the most outlandish questions. That fool of a girl's more fun than a barrel of monkeys."

The thought of Jessica's own father deliberately making her a laughingstock sickened Noah. He swung away toward the door. He had to get out of here before he did something dastardly to this miserable sot.

"Where do you think you're going?" Whitman railed, his voice rising in volume. "You haven't answered my question. I want to see my daughter. Now!" he screamed. "She could be dead for all I know. You've killed her, haven't you?"

Noah couldn't open the door while the man screeched like he'd been caught in a bear trap. He wheeled back to Whitman. "You want to see your daughter. Fine." He strode to the back of the man's chair and untied the rope. Then, ripping the loose-jointed man from his seat, Noah half carried him to the door and swung it open. "See? There she is. Down there, making her daily quota of salt just as you ordered."

The bleary-eyed man squinted in the brightness. "Then why is the lazy girl just standing there?" Abruptly, he straightened. "What's she looking at?"

Noah followed the direction of Jessica's gaze to the wide river below. A canoe of Indians came paddling toward shore.

70

Whitman gave a violent jerk, trying to wrench free. "Help!" the man shouted.

Noah yanked Whitman back inside before he could yell again. Noah's most pressing fear was being realized. Muskogee braves were arriving. Men who would gladly come to Whitman's aid . . . warriors trained since childhood to kill their sworn enemies.

Even as debilitated as Whitman was, he struggled with more strength than Noah thought the man possessed. It took close to a minute to secure the squirming, kicking man to his chair again and get a gag across his mouth—time Noah could ill afford.

Noah snatched the strap of his powder horn from around his rifle, uncorked it, and sprinkled gunpowder into the weapon's flashpan, all the while thanking the Lord that he'd had the fore-sight to load the barrel ahead of time— a habit he'd learned while serving in the army. He prayed that his younger brother wouldn't do anything foolhardy before he . . . *what?* Should he show himself or stay hidden and keep the Indians within his sights? And he had yet to discover how many there were.

Having only one shot before he'd have to reload, he could've kicked himself for removing all of Whitman's weapons from the cabin. But the Indians would have no way of knowing that, he realized while carefully cracking open the door.

The trader made some strangled sounds, but not loud enough to carry very far—Noah hoped.

Since the door opened toward the land, not the river, the first person he saw was Drew. The lad was moving away from the fires toward where he'd laid his own rifle. But he stopped short of it.

Noah poked his head farther out to see why.

Jessica. She was saying something to him, her expression very intent.

Without retrieving his weapon, Drew turned back to her and picked up the bucket of brine.

Leaving Drew to pour the salt water into the pots, the young woman walked unafraid toward the river—toward the Indians. Noah's first instinct was to fear for her, to stop her, to protect her. Then he remembered she'd lived among the Indians her entire life.

Another thought, far more disturbing, surfaced. If Miss Jessica ever planned to betray Noah and Drew, this would be the perfect time.

He squelched that discrediting thought. She'd proven herself to be unquestionably worthy of his trust. Everything he'd hoped Lorna would be. And more.

Noah leaned out the door a bit more until he saw the riverbank . . . and the approach of the canoe. The only one, he noted with relief.

An Indian, in attire similar to that worn by those who had been at the salt lick the day they arrived, jumped into the water a few feet from shore and pulled the sleek birch-bark vessel up onto the sand.

Noah saw only two other passengers in the slender craft. His confidence returned somewhat. But he still thought it best to remain hidden for the moment. Wait. See what transpired between them and Miss Jessica.

The other two Muskogee hopped out onto dry ground. The first carried two rifles, one of which he handed the brave who'd debarked earlier. Then Noah was encouraged to see that one of them was a young squaw. The braves would be much less apt to start trouble with a woman along.

As Miss Jessica approached them, the three stopped abruptly and backed toward their canoe as if to keep a wary distance from her. It would seem she had not exaggerated when she said that Indians feared her eyes.

She spent a short time conversing with them, though Noah couldn't hear more than an occasional wind-carried word of the Indian tongue.

One pointed up to Drew, who now added wood to the fires as if he had no interest in the Indians whatsoever.

Fearing again for his brother, Noah edged the door a little wider and grasped his weapon with both hands.

Behind him, Whitman started making gag-muted noises and tried to scoot his chair forward. It fell over with a clattering crash.

Noah's heart banged like a drum as he checked to see if the Indians had heard. None turned toward the cabin. Thank God for the steady noise of the river. Noah inhaled a fortifying breath.

Then he froze. The Indian who had pointed at Drew now started in Drew's direction.

Miss Jessica caught up with the Muskogee brave, smiling and talking in his language as if nothing were amiss. He thrust a hand out to ward her off. Keeping her distance, she continued on with him.

Noah swung up his long rifle and aimed. If the Indian raised his own, it would be for the last time.

Behind Noah, Whitman squirmed on the packed-dirt floor, trying to dislodge himself from the chair, but Noah could not divert his attention from the scene outside.

Drew, acting more coolheaded than Noah thought the lad could ever be, appeared almost relaxed. He smiled as the brave walked within a few feet, paused a second, then strutted right up to stand face-to-face with him. Staring back, Drew didn't give an inch.

Noah wasn't so confident. He eased back the flintlock hammer. One false move . . .

The Indian rocked his feather-decorated head from side to side, scowling at Drew, then peered behind the lad as if Drew might be hiding something.

Noah, becoming more unnerved by the second, hastily swiped away a bead of sweat stinging his eye and renewed his aim.

Miss Jessica moved into Noah's line of fire just then, blocking not only his aim but his view of the Indian. What was the matter with the woman? Surely she must know he'd be at the door. But she seemed oblivious as she chatted on in that strange language. She stepped closer to the Indian.

As before when she came near, the brave backed away, giving Noah a clear aim again. Though the dark-skinned man avoided Miss Jessica's gaze, he wore a broad smile, exposing a row of white teeth.

Noah watched as she held out half a bag of salt.

The Indian took it, switching the sack to the hand that held his rifle, then reached inside his deerskin robe and drew out a beaver pelt. He handed it to her, undoubtedly in payment for the salt—a very profitable exchange for her, considering the value of the pelt. Still grinning, the Muskogee flicked a last glance at Drew, nodded, then trotted down the rise to the two waiting by the canoe.

They were leaving. Just like that?

Noah couldn't believe they'd come upriver in this cold weather without wanting to check out the stores in the trading post. Still, not until the trio were back in their craft and moving swiftly downstream did Noah relax and lift the fallen Whitman and his chair up from the ground. He couldn't imagine what Miss Jessica had told the Indians, but somehow she'd prevented bloodshed . . . again. If he were the superstitious sort, he might put more stock in her remarkable eyes himself.

With Whitman resettled on what was now a lopsided chair, Noah grabbed his weapon and headed out the door for some answers.

Drew was already coming up the rise and met him halfway. "Did you see that?" he asked excitedly. "You did have a bead on them redsticks, didn't you? I was sure countin' on it."

"Aye, I did." In a sudden rush of unexpected emotion, Noah grabbed his baby brother into a fierce hug. "I did."

Drew returned the embrace with equal fervor, then just as quickly shoved himself away, embarrassed.

Noah, his own eyes a bit moister than he cared to admit, glanced beyond Drew to Miss Jessica.

A load of wood in her arms, she watched them with the first unguarded full smile he'd seen.

Noah's heart, which had only just begun to beat more slowly in the aftermath of the crisis, halted, then rebounded with a hard beat. The wide smile had transformed her elfin face into one of remarkable beauty. What a belle she would be, given half a chance.

Realizing that he was just standing there staring at her, he pulled himself together and walked to her. "You are a wonder, my lady." He took her bundle of sticks and carried them next to the nearest fire ring.

"I am?" She looked at him as if he'd just given her a diamond ring.

"Aye, that you are," he said as Drew came up beside them. "How did you get the Indians to leave so soon?"

"Oh, I just told them that Father was down with a fever."

"And Drew—how did you explain his being here? They surely didn't think he'd merely walked in alone from out of nowhere."

She glanced at Drew. "No, they most certainly would have questioned that. I fabricated that Father brought him here for me."

"For you? Me?" Drew sounded as surprised as Noah was.

"Aye," she said with a teasing lilt to her voice. Then all humor fled her expression. "So Red Bird wanted to take a gander at anyone courageous enough to live with me and my perilous eyes. The Indians call me Eyes-That-Have-No-Bottom."

Noah placed a comforting hand on her shoulder. "There's nothing perilous about your eyes," he said. "They're wonderfully unique."

If anything, she looked even more dismayed. She caught her upper lip in her teeth and shifted her gaze to the side. "What you really mean is, they're queer to behold."

Drew jumped in. "They ain't *that* queer, leastways not once a body gets used to 'em. For truth, I like 'em a lot."

She didn't look the least encouraged by Drew's words.

"Truly, Miss Jessica, they're not strange in the least," Noah said, giving her shoulder a reassuring squeeze. "Fact is, they're strikingly beautiful. Any belle in Baltimore would consider them quite the advantage. Besides, any man would count himself lucky to have a lass as true and loyal as you." *Unlike the jilting Lorna Graham,* he remembered.

The sparkle in her expression had returned as she gazed up at him. Suddenly she looked away and gave a nervous laugh. "I don't think Father would concur that I'm true and loyal."

Drew laughed along with her. "No, I don't reckon he would."

But Noah scarcely heard them. He couldn't rid himself of that split second of adoration he'd seen in her ice clear eyes. No one in his life had ever looked at him with such honest emotion. Especially not the flirtatious Lorna of the coy smile and the practiced charm.

Leaves crunched. A twig snapped.

Noah swung toward the sound with upraised rifle. In an instant, both Drew and Miss Jessica were at his side, their own weapons cocked and ready.

"It's just me," came a shout. Yarnell emerged from the deep shadows at a dead run. Not until he was a few feet from them did he slow to a walk. "I come back to warn you," he said, panting for breath. "I saw some redsticks out on the river."

"'Twern't no need to bother yourself," Drew said. "Me and Jaybird, here, we took care of it."

"You and *Miss Jessica,*" Noah corrected.

That earned him another flash of appreciation from the young woman at his side. One he couldn't help but enjoy.

What harm could there be in her becoming a little taken with him? He wouldn't be here much longer. Sometime tomorrow afternoon they should have their last sack filled with salt. By nightfall they'd be long gone.

He refused to allow himself to think beyond that . . . to how the enchanting lass would be left here alone to face her father's wrath.

8

It had come . . . the moment Jessica had been dreading. The men were packing their horses to leave. And here she was, hiding out in her cabin, too embarrassed to show her face until she could stop the tears from spilling down her cheeks.

Her last moments with them were being wasted. *Wasted.* Yet no matter how hard she tried, she couldn't stop the tears any more than she could stop the awful ache in her lungs . . . the burning in her throat. This was even worse than the day Spencer left. He at least had promised to come back for her.

But he never did.

She ran her hands down the sides of her deerskin day gown, fingering the coins she'd sewn into the seams —coins she'd managed to scrounge since the day Spencer left for Baltimore four long summers ago. He'd said she might need them to buy her and Little Bob clothes and other necessities when he returned for them. Even if she lost track of the years, the number of secreted coins attested to the length of time Spencer had been gone.

And now she'd lost Little Bob too.

Logic told her that Spencer was either dead or he hadn't thought her worth coming back for. Jessica took a deep breath. Both possibilities were too unthinkable. But another spring would not pass, she vowed, without her going across the mountains to learn the truth for herself. To wait till then with only Father for company would be unbearable. Yet bear it she must.

A happier thought surfaced. On her way to Baltimore, she'd drop by Henry's Station and find out where Noah Reardon lived. Mayhap she'd pay him a friendly visit first.

Aye, that's what she'd do.

The notion greatly improved her mood. Wiping her eyes, she went to her basin sitting on top of a covered barrel. Pouring water into it from a pewter pitcher, she splashed the cold liquid over her ravaged face. After repeating the process several times, she dried away what she hoped was the last of the evidence. Without a mirror, she couldn't be sure.

In a hurry now, she wrapped her bearskin around her shoulders, belted it, snatched up a ten-pound sack of salt as added payment for all her questions the Reardons had answered, and headed for the door . . . then she hesitated. Salt seemed like such a paltry recompense for all the kindnesses these men had shown her—especially Noah Reardon. She should give him something more special . . . perhaps something that would always remind him of her.

But what?

Her hand flew to the cross she wore hidden beneath her clothes. No, not even for him would she part with this lone link to her Baltimore family.

Instead, she went to her "treasure chest," as Spencer had always called the lidded crate. Surely she'd find something in there. Stooping beside it, she rummaged through the newspapers and prime pelts, pausing when her hand smoothed across the silky mink a trapper from the North gave her last spring . . . just because

she had a pretty smile, he'd said. She could give Mr. Reardon that
. . . if she didn't find something better.

Digging deeper, her fingers fell upon some strung shells. Pulling
them up to the top, she saw they were part of a necklace with a
medicine pouch attached—the one Little Bob had brought home
when they still lived out in Chickasaw country. Jessica smiled at
the remembrance. She'd just had her first monthly flow and feared
she was dying, so her baby brother had stolen one of Father's jugs
of rum to trade to the village shaman for it. Little Bob had taken a
bad beating from Father for his efforts, too.

Jessica clutched the necklace to her heart. She could never part
with something that had cost Little Bob so dearly. She tucked it
safely within the mink pelt, then reached down to the bottom of the
crate to other bits and pieces she'd collected through the years.

Coming up with a handful of stones and shells, she rose to her
feet and took them to the firelight. There, she discovered the
perfect token to give Mr. Reardon—a colorless stone she'd had for
many years. Though it was not nearly so clear as the window glass
they had talked about, when it was held up to the light, the softest
shades of blue could be seen within. All of her brothers had agreed
it was just like her eyes . . . the perfect token for Noah Reardon.

With a sudden urge to get back to him, Jessica dropped the
other stones back into the crate and hastened to the door. When
she stepped outside, though, and saw how rapidly the men were
working—even Mr. Yarnell—her grief threatened to overwhelm
her again. Fighting it off, she took long purposeful strides toward
the men. Remembering to be polite, she removed her hat when she
reached the first one, the bearded long hunter. "Fare thee well, Mr.
Yarnell. Keep your powder dry."

"You, too, little Jaybird. Take care now," he added, nodding in
the direction of her father's cabin.

"I will." And suddenly she was loath to take her eyes from
him—this man who had come and gone a number of times through

the years. Although his prior departures had scarcely bothered her, knowing that upon this leave-taking, she'd probably never see him again, she felt the sharp pain of loss, almost as much as she felt for Noah Reardon.

She turned next to Drew, who was tying off the pack of a patient horse. "It's been a supreme pleasure making your acquaintance, Drew Reardon. I do sympathize with you, though, because you never had the opportunity to go hunting. There is such an abundance of game moving down-mountain this time of year."

Drew's ready grin—a lopsided one this time—added a twinkle to his eyes. "Aw, plenty of time for huntin' once we get home."

Mr. Reardon stepped out from behind a horse, and Jessica turned to face him. The moment she dreaded had come. She forced herself to smile. "I particularly want to thank you, Mr. Reardon, for the many hours you patiently answered my multitude of queries. You've imparted upon me a veritable wealth of knowledge—knowledge I shall put to good use. Once the weather turns warm again and Father can get by without a constant fire, I'll depart for Greeneville up in the Watauga settlements. My brother Spencer said he'd leave word for me there if I left before his return. Then, hopefully, I'll be on my way to Baltimore," she added in as bright a tone as she could muster.

"You don't have to wait that long."

Was he asking her again to come with them, as he had already done twice this morning? Her heart leapt at the mere thought.

"I'm going to Greeneville to file some deeds," he continued, "as soon as we take these horses back to Henry's Station. I could make inquiries, ask if there's any word from—Spencer, isn't it?"

"Aye. Spencer Whitman."

"I'll send word to you on the first raft coming south."

She tried not to show her disappointment, though she'd already refused him twice.

"Better still," he continued, "change your mind. Come with us now. I don't like leaving you here with your pa so angry."

"I thank you, but I can't. Like I said, I'll have to wait till spring, or Father would most likely freeze to death during one of his drunken stupors. But I'd be much obliged if you'd check for a letter in Greeneville. I have a deep yearning to hear anything at all from my brother." She took his hand. "And to help you remember me, I'd like to give you this token." She pressed the stone into his palm. "If you hold it up to the light on a sunny day, you'll know why I gave it to you."

He glanced down at it, then kept her in a tender gaze for a long moment. "Thank you, Miss Jessica. I'm sorry I don't have anything to offer you in return." He paused. "Except I do hope you will think on those truths I told you about our heavenly Father. If you decide to take my words into your heart, that's the greatest gift I—and the Lord—could ever give you."

"I will think on it, I promise." The thought of taking his words into her heart, of actually sharing the same god with him, was most appealing, though she'd had a problem since he told her this invisible god was like having a second father. The one she had was more than she could handle. Yet Mr. Reardon had spoken of his heavenly Father in such glowing terms, explaining that his god, the creator of not only this forest she'd lived in her whole life but of the whole earth, the moon, and the stars. And that this god loved her, Jessica Jane, very much.

But then her father had told her he loved her too. More times than she could count. Usually after he woke up from one of his violent spells. Over and over he'd beg her to forgive him and tell her how much he loved her. However, it wouldn't be long before the drink had its hold on him again.

"Well, I reckon we better get a move on," Mr. Yarnell said, mounting his horse.

For one last time, Jessica looked up into Mr. Reardon's stalwart face, memorizing every pleasing line, every angle, his lips . . . his eyes that beheld her even now with such tenderness. "Godspeed," she whispered for his ears only. She'd heard that parting spoken by the occasional hunter and used it now herself, knowing it would please him.

"Are you certain you won't come?" he asked once more.

It took all her willpower to answer. "Aye. We all have our duties . . . me to Father and you to that valley you talk about so fondly."

He expelled a defeated sigh. "Well then, God be with you too, Miss Jessica."

Before she knew what was happening, he took her hand into his work-roughened one and brushed his lips across it.

At the feel of his warm breath against her skin, her own breath caught. Quickly she stepped back. She didn't want him to notice that she had begun to tremble. "I won't free Father until nightfall," she said, trying to collect herself. "That way he won't be able to go fetch the Indians until tomorrow. You do know he *will* hire them to reap vengeance on you."

Mr. Reardon's expression turned grim. "Aye, I expect he will. But don't you put yourself at risk over us. He knows we never allowed you to see him. Don't tell him any different."

Watching Noah Reardon mount and ride out with the others, Jessica hoped that his god was as real and loving as he said the invisible spirit was. And as powerful.

Mr. Reardon and his party reached the trees. Soon he would disappear from sight. Jessica could hardly keep herself from running after him.

Just before he was swallowed up by the dark shadows of the forest, he swung around in his saddle and took one last look at her—a serious, unreadable stare. Was Mr. Reardon truly as reluctant to leave her as she was to see him go?

With all her heart, she hoped so.

Jessica had stalled as long as she could; dark would soon descend. With a trencher loaded with food in one hand and her musket in the other, she left her cabin for her father's. She knew without a doubt that she was in for a severe tongue-lashing, if not worse. She could predict the exact accusations Father would fling at her. And she'd likely have to dodge a fist or two as well.

Crossing the upper half of the rock slab, she couldn't stop herself from gazing down at the salt works. In the last gloaming of twilight, no fires burned, no one moved about. There would be no more laughter as there'd been when the Reardon brothers joked with her. No more kind acts. No more conversations with the one man who lived every virtue she could hope for. He'd made her heart leap every time he smiled at her . . . but he'd left her to a vast emptiness—a vast, hollow void.

Even the birds in the trees seemed to understand. They had ceased their singing. No sounds could be heard except the low unending rumble of the Tennessee River and the padding of her moccasins across stone. Springtime . . . it seemed as far away as the moon and the stars. The sting of sorrow returned to camp behind her eyes.

Reaching her father's cabin, she balanced the food and her musket in one hand and reached for the wooden door handle. She hesitated, dreading the next moment. With a resigned huff, she flung it open and stepped into a blast of warm, stale air. Leaving the musket propped by the door, she noted the glowing embers in the fireplace. Almost out. She shifted her attention to the table where the oil lamp glowed with the lowest of flames. Beside the lamp, her father's head lay pillowed on one arm, while the other cradled a brown jug.

He appeared no different than when she'd walked in a thousand other times—he looked just as free to come and go as he ever had. So why hadn't he?

Moving past the table, she saw what held him. A length of rope secured his waist and both ankles to the chair, then wrapped several times around the chair's back legs and tied between them. Father would have had difficulty reaching the knots with more than one or two fingers. And in his usual state of drunkenness, he would never have managed to loosen them.

She set the trencher on the table with silent care, deciding to release the ties before waking him . . . a few more peaceful moments before facing his ire.

Stooping, she saw that the knots were tighter and more intricate than she had first thought. Even using both hands, she had quite a struggle loosing them, but she kept at it. "Finally," she whispered beneath her breath as she tugged apart the last of the knots.

"Finally?" Father's head sprang up, and he swung around, kicking free of the encircling binds, his fingers clamping around one of her wrists. His nails dug in painfully.

The old codger had been merely pretending to sleep.

"Is that all you have to say for yourself?" His foul breath blasted her face.

Still in a crouch, she would have fallen backward if he hadn't had such a tight grip on her. "The men are gone now, so I've come to set you free."

He rose to his feet, hauling her up with him. His bloodshot eyes narrowed. "How dare you allow those scoundrels to treat me like I'm some hog to be trussed up for days on end? And don't you try to tell me there wasn't a single time when you could've spirited past them to set me free."

"But, Father, there were three of them," she said, sidestepping his accusation.

Shoving her away, he started for the door in a stiff-legged stagger.

That was the end of his tirade? It wasn't nearly as bad as she'd feared. For the first time, she took stock of what a skinny little man he really was—especially when compared to Mr. Reardon. Not such a fearsome creature after all.

"How long have they been gone?" Still, the rasped-out words sounded plenty vicious.

"Not too long," she hedged.

He grabbed her musket by the door. "Which way did they go?"

No sense lying—any fool would be able to find prints left by five horses. "Up the river trace. But it's growing dark. Why don't you sit down and eat whilst the food's still hot?"

He turned around and came back.

Jessica could scarcely believe he was actually going to settle down so easily.

However, he didn't move past her. Stopping in front of her, he snatched the powder horn from around her neck. "Where are the other guns—my trade rifles?"

Did he actually plan to start out after them now by himself?

"Answer me, girl. Where are the rifles?"

"In my cabin. But, Father, the men have been gone—"

"*Your cabin?*" The skin above his stubbled beard went ashen, and his eyes seemed to turn to flame. "You had a whole arsenal in your cabin, and you left me here to rot?" With a hair-raising roar, he flipped the musket, and wielded it like a bat.

She dodged to the side. Not far enough.

The edge of the wooden stock clipped her cheek. Everything went to a starry haze. She grasped at air, trying to find something to latch onto.

"I'll kill you, you useless piece of trash!"

Finding herself down on the ground, she scrambled out the open door.

"Ye'll not get away so quick!"

Hearing the lethal click of the flintlock, Jessica launched herself to one side as the weapon exploded.

9

Noah hated the idea of putting out the fire. Gloves on, coat collar up, he huddled as close to the flames as he could while warming his insides with a cup of coffee. The night had been bitterly cold, especially when one was sleeping on the damp ground with fog dripping off the bare branches of a nearby beech. By morning his bedroll was sodden, and the molding leaves around him had turned to mush. Daybreak hadn't proved any warmer. Low drizzling clouds still grazed the treetops, and a mist blanketed the river.

Wrapped in a buffalo robe, Yarnell stood beside him, looking equally miserable despite the long scraggly beard covering most of his face.

In moments like these Noah was doubly glad he'd chosen the life of a landholder, living snug in a warm tight house instead of sleeping in the woods "free of responsibilities," no matter how romantic being a long hunter might seem. When he looked back at the end of his life, he'd have more than memories; he'd be surrounded by his accomplishments—his own place, the mill he owned with his older brother, an entire valley of God-fearing settlers who wouldn't be there if the Reardons hadn't brought them. A worthy legacy to pass on to his sons one day.

And perhaps someday, when Tennessee became a state, his neighbors would choose him to represent them in Philadelphia, the same way they'd chosen him now to file their deeds in Greeneville—a commission he was very late in completing. But as fast as he and his party would have to travel to stay ahead of Whitman's Indians, he was certain he'd be back to Henry's Station then on to Greeneville in record time.

Drew, who'd been the last to rise this morning, worked nearby, tying off the load on the second of the two packhorses. The boxed supplies and bags of salt were no problem to secure, but those large kettles had proven awkward.

Stepping away from the animal, Drew glanced down the back trail to the south. "I'd say we put a good eight to ten miles 'tween us and the salt lick yester's eve, wouldn't you, Yarnell?"

"I reckon." The hunter tossed the dregs of his coffee into the fire. "And if Pizar's gal kept her word 'bout not loosin' him till dark, that old sot won't ride out after his redsticks till after he wakes up today."

Drew's mouth tilted into that one-sided grin of his. "That'd be nigh onto noon, I'd say."

"Aye. I figure we got us a good two-day start afore he can fire them Injuns up enough to come out in this cold. But that don't mean we couldn't run into some of our feathered friends up yonder. Keep your eyes peeled and your ears flapped open."

But the Indians were the least of Noah's worries. The mere reference to Miss Jessica sent him into another spate of guilt. "I still say we shouldn't have left her to take her pa's wrath for our deeds. No telling what that old reprobate did to her when she untied him."

"You're wastin' your time frettin' over her," Yarnell said as he walked to his waiting horse. "That one can take care of herself. She's been dealin' with him on her own since her older brothers took off."

"I don't know," Noah said, shaking his head.

"What would you have us do? Add kidnappin' to the list of grievances Pizar's got agin' us? He depends on her for just about ever'thing." Yarnell raised a foot to his stirrup. "Mount up."

Noah knew Yarnell was right. Miss Jessica belonged to the old pirate, whether he liked it or not. Well, if nothing else, he'd do whatever he could in Greeneville to get a lead on that brother of hers. Spencer Whitman couldn't be much of a man, though, if he'd go off and leave his sister with nothing but empty promises.

Excuses aside, Noah had to admit he wasn't any better. He'd left her, too, with no intention of going back. And those eyes. How sad they'd looked when he bid her farewell. Pulling off a glove, he reached into his coat pocket and closed his fingers around the small, jagged stone she'd given him.

"Quit your dawdlin' and snuff that fire," his younger brother ordered. Then the lad picked up the spade and shoveled the fire over with dirt himself. "We've wasted too much time downriver as it is."

"Aye," Noah grumbled under his breath as he mounted the borrowed roan. All that kid could think of was getting back to the settlement and people of their own kind. Noah heeled his horse into a walk, pulling along the packhorse tethered to his saddle ring.

Drew did the same, the second pack animal secured behind him. Nudging his mount into a trot, he crowded past Noah, in an obvious ploy not to be last.

Let the lad have his way. Riding first, second, or third made no difference at all, but traveling away from the salt lick did. Noah's self-condemnation had grown with each mile yester's eve and had not lessened overnight. He swiveled in his saddle, looking down the back trail. He could send the other two on to Henry's Station with the salt—no sense risking their necks, too—and return alone.

Just then he caught a flash of movement where the brush-crowded path curved out of sight. It couldn't be Pizar Whitman's Indians this soon. Miss Jessica had said the closest village was a good ten miles away . . . unless he'd gotten to them and talked them into riding through the night.

Noah considered calling out to Yarnell and Drew, but since they'd already been swallowed by the dense woods up ahead, he decided not to draw undue attention to himself.

As quietly as possible, he maneuvered his mount and the other horse off the trail and into an overgrown ravine, pulling his long rifle from its scabbard as he went. He uncorked his powder horn and poured a smidgen into his flashpan, all the while watching for further movement along the river trace or in the surrounding forest. It was probably just an animal. Still, he had to be sure.

The way the leaves crunched and twigs snapped underfoot, he knew whatever was coming wasn't concerned about the noise.

More movement. Something dark, coming fast up the trace. Then it broke into full view.

A black bear.

No. Jessica!

Miss Jessica, on foot, running at a steady pace.

His first instinct was to ride up the embankment to her. But what was she running from?

He waited and watched. She didn't seem frightened. Not once did she look back as she neared, and he heard no other sounds but those she made. In mere seconds she would pass him.

He nudged his horse up from the gully.

Miss Jessica halted—an abrupt, shaky halt. Her eyes were large as moons, her breath spewed out in great racking bursts.

He guided his mount abreast of her, and she collapsed against his stirruped leg. She tried to speak, but nothing more than strangled sputters got past the heaving pants.

Noah swung down and caught her by the shoulders.

An ugly bruise marred her cheek. The sight of it was like a punch to his gut. He pulled her close against his chest. "I'm so sorry. Please forgive me for leaving you . . . to face your pa in our place."

More apologies poured out as he continued to ramble feeble amends until her breathing began to quiet. Then, remembering she'd been running, he held her at arm's length. "Are you being followed?"

"I don't think so," she finally managed. "It was almost pitch dark when Father took his first shot at me. By the time he reloaded, I'd made myself scarce."

Whitman had actually tried to shoot her? His own daughter? Noah's guilt drove deeper than ever. The man was even more of a wretch than any of them had suspected.

Her breathing still labored, she continued. "I don't think Father knew which direction I took, but if he'd saddled up and come up the trace after me, he would've caught up long before this."

Unhooking his water flask from his saddle, Noah removed the cork and offered Jessica a drink. As she reached for it, he noticed that she was empty-handed. "You've been out on the trace all night without your musket?"

Because she held the flask to her mouth, she could only nod.

"And without a horse," he added, stating the obvious. "You must have walked all night to reach us."

She swallowed the liquid and wiped her mouth with one of those delicate-boned hands. "And I still didn't catch up," she said, handing back the rawhide water container. "With the approach of dawn, I started running. I knew if I didn't catch you this morning, I never would."

"I thank God you did." He pulled her close again. If she hadn't reached them, she might not have survived.

Those great luminous eyes gazed up in profound relief that verily ripped at his heart. "I suppose I should thank your god too. I hope you don't mind, but I took the liberty of asking him to get me to you. You *did* say he hears everything we say, didn't you?"

"Aye, that I did," he whispered as emotion welled within. He diverted his attention to the ground, hoping she wouldn't notice . . . and his gaze landed on her moccasins and their ragged condition.

"Noah—I mean, Mr. Reardon . . ."

When she hesitated, he looked up again and saw that she'd caught her lower lip between her teeth. "Yes?" he urged.

"I was wondering . . . I'd be unequivocally obliged if you'd permit me to accompany you to Greeneville. I would do my utmost not to burden you unnecessarily."

Even if refusing her request weren't the furthest thing from his mind, how could anyone possibly deny such a valiant lass.

Swooping her up into his arms, he tossed her onto the saddle. "Scoot forward, I'm coming up behind you."

Two days later, her time spent entirely on horseback, Jessica really felt the effects. At the moment, she rode double with Mr. Yarnell, sitting behind his saddle directly over his animal's bony rump. But she dared not emit the smallest groan. He'd been adamant that they all remain absolutely silent, ever watchful, never knowing when they might have to make a run for it. She hadn't been able to ask a single question to further her education since she first joined them. Hand signals were used whenever the foursome stopped to rest their mounts or to transfer her from one rider to another.

Jessica didn't hold on to Mr. Yarnell's waist anymore than she had to. She knew he'd been the least happy to see her and especially to hear what she had to say. The usually easygoing long hunter had visibly blanched when she told him that her father had been so enraged when she freed him that he might have gone straight through the dark to the nearest Muskogee town in search of braves willing to come after them.

Mr. Yarnell informed the small group that, unlike himself, the Indians would know the lay of this southern country. They'd know the best river fork crossings, all the shortcuts, while their small party was obliged to follow this winding river trace.

And Jessica didn't have to be told that her extra weight added to the burden of the horses—an addition that could cost them all their lives.

For no apparent reason, Mr. Yarnell reined in his long-legged bay.

Jessica tensed. Leaning to the side of the frontiersman, she checked the trail ahead. Nothing. With the overcast daylight fading, deep shadows made it impossible to see more than a few feet into the forest on either side.

She shortly realized, though, that Mr. Yarnell merely planned to off-load her onto another horse. It was Mr. Reardon's turn to take her again. Finally. At the thought, her heart beat a little faster.

Bringing his mount alongside Mr. Yarnell's, Mr. Reardon smiled an honestly warm greeting and held out his gloved hands.

She gladly went into them. Not only did the decidedly handsome man always act pleased to have her with him, but his saddle was large enough for both of them to fit into. And there was the undeniable fact that she simply enjoyed being within his arms.

Settling herself beneath his chin, an unbidden sigh of pleasure escaped her lips. It soared out on a vapor cloud of warm air.

Mr. Reardon stiffened for a second.

He'd heard the telltale sound. Wholly embarrassed, she wished she could voice a plausible excuse, pretend she'd sighed for any other reason. From exhaustion, perhaps. But to break the silence was forbidden.

A lone snowflake floated on the breeze past Jessica's eyes, landing on Mr. Reardon's sleeve—a tiny fluff of white that melted almost instantly into the berry-dyed wool.

Snow? They would need a better shelter for this night.

More fat flakes made their way down through the branches, as the remaining light faded to near darkness. One floated featherlike beneath her hat to land on her nose. Several clung to the roan's mane.

Ahead of them, Mr. Yarnell veered his mount off the trail, motioning for them to follow him toward the base of a high stone wall.

A good choice for a camp, Jessica concluded, since the sheered rock blocked most of the breeze. A scattering of boulders at the bottom would provide more protection. A couple of the outer ones could be used as walls for a lean-to. Scanning the area, she also saw plenty of deadfall to build a shelter. Aye, a good spot.

Mr. Reardon lowered her to the ground.

Aware at once of the loss of his nearness, she ventured a last glance back at him as he secured the roan to a low branch. She moved to the closest packhorse, where she started untying the ropes. She wanted to do her fair share. More, if possible. Since she'd arrived with her dire report, the men hadn't chanced the noise of shooting their supper or risked the glow or smell of a cookfire, so they were forced to ration out their dwindling supply of dried meat and hard bread. She was certain they didn't appreciate one more mouth to feed.

Mr. Reardon stepped up behind her and helped her bring down the load, then smiled apologetically as he reached past her to retrieve a hatchet.

A deafening roar shattered the silence. A bullet whizzed past her ear.

Mr. Reardon's body slammed into her.

10

Jessica hit the ground hard.

Mr. Reardon came down on top of her, covering her with his body as more shots exploded around them. The front hooves of the frightened packhorse struck the earth dangerously close to their heads.

"I'm going for my rifle," Mr. Reardon whispered. "You crawl behind yon rock." Rolling away, he scrambled toward his own mount.

Frantically, she wished she had her own musket to go for. She dove for the nearest boulder, then noticed the firing had ceased.

How many shots had there been? Three? Four? She fervently hoped there were no more shooters out there. If they were all reloading, it would be at least twenty seconds before they could fired again.

Raising her head slightly above the waist-high rock, she scanned the woods but saw none of the marauders, just her companions. All three were at their mounts, snagging their weapons and ammunition.

Mr. Yarnell, she saw, bled from the shoulder, but it didn't slow him one whit. He pulled the cork from his powder horn and started sprinkling gunpowder into his flashpan with the same grim speed as the Reardons were doing.

A blood-chilling cry ripped from the shadows, and four painted, feathered Muskogee braves burst into the open. Hatchets raised, they charged. They must have given up reloading in favor of reaching the men before they could fire.

Two headed straight for Mr. Reardon.

Clicking back his hammer, he yanked up his weapon. Too late. The closest warrior swung his hatchet against the long barrel. The firearm flashed and roared. The lone bullet went astray, Mr. Reardon's rifle flying.

Jessica watched terrified as Mr. Reardon reclaimed his weapon and wielded it like a club. The Indian's hatchet blocked the blow. With his other hand, the assailant brought up a hefty knife.

Before Jessica could shout a warning, Mr. Reardon caught the Indian's wrist. Then, to her horror, she saw the other brave circling to Mr. Reardon's rear.

She vaulted up. A scream wilder than any Indian's tore from her as she ran toward them.

The braves halted like stunned deer, their eyes wide and fixed on her.

She lunged for the closest attacker. He leapt back as if he were being struck by a snake.

Mr. Reardon's attacker shouted something she couldn't translate. Then both Muskogee stepped away from him. Slowly . . . cautiously.

The two braves who had set upon Drew and Mr. Yarnell fell away as well. All of them backed away, their weapons held out in a sign of peace.

Mr. Reardon grabbed Jessica and pulled her behind him. "Get back. Behind the rocks." Swiftly he began the lengthy process of reloading. Fetch a paper-wrapped ball and powder from his bullet pouch. Rip it, pour a bit of powder in the flashpan. Feed the rest of the wad down the barrel. Unhook the ramrod from beneath. Jam it deep. . . .

"Ain't no sense workin' up a sweat," Mr. Yarnell drawled. "Them redsticks has turned tail."

That didn't slow Mr. Reardon one whit till he had the hammer cocked and the barrel leveled on the trees where the Indians had disappeared.

Jessica then noticed that Drew also held his rifle at the ready, though the deepening dusk along with the steadily falling snow made seeing farther than a few yards impossible.

"Are you certain they're gone for good?" Mr. Reardon scanned the forest. Taking a step back, he bumped into Jessica. "I told you to get back to the rocks."

"Ain't no need," Mr. Yarnell said, wincing as he pressed a cloth to the bloody hole in his buckskin shirt. "They done been scared off."

"It isn't like we were winning." Mr. Reardon took another uneasy look around, then centered his attention on the long hunter. "How bad's that wound?"

Mr. Yarnell moved his shoulder back and forth gingerly. "'Pears to've gone clean through without hittin' bone. Just need to get the bleedin' stanched."

Drew stepped closer, his youthful features marred with worry as he pulled a rag from his pocket. "That's an awful lot of blood, Yarnell."

"Aw," the frontiersman scoffed, "I've had worse cuts on my lip and kept right on whistlin'."

Maybe so, Jessica thought. But above the beard, his long narrow face was losing color and his hands were starting to tremble. "Since the Indians already know our location, we might as well have a fire. I'll see if I can find some dry wood," Jessica offered.

"Wait." Mr. Reardon wheeled around and caught her hand. "You can't go traipsing off into the woods."

"Ain't no harm gonna come to her," Mr. Yarnell grunted as he made his way to a flat rock and eased down. "Didn't you see the way them redsticks turned tail when they saw her? They're gone, for sure. Leastways, as long as we got the Jaybird with us." He croaked a wincing laugh. "They ain't takin' no chance on gettin' kilt and havin' that girl steal off with their souls."

Jessica was glad her eyes had saved these three she cared about, but there was something wretched about having people, red or white, take one look at her and run for their very lives. Doubts she'd been trying to lay aside resurfaced. Would she be just as unwanted in the white folks' towns as she'd been in the Shawnee, Chickasaw, and Muskogee villages?

Was this the true reason her brother had never come back for her?

Even knowing they had Miss Jessica and her exceptional eyes with them, Noah never ceased watching for another Indian attack during the next two days. The safety of all their lives weighed heavily on Noah, considering Yarnell's game shoulder and Drew's inexperience. And Jessica, for all her spunk, wasn't much bigger than a speckled fawn.

That's why he now insisted on her riding with him most of the time . . . at least, that's what he told himself. At this very moment, she sat in front of him on Storekeeper Keaton's roan. And though he didn't want to admit it, he enjoyed the fact that he could share his warmth with her on this bright but chilly day.

Like Noah, Miss Jessica continually watched the woods on either side as they rode up the trace. She seemed to take the dangers of this journey as seriously as he, especially since the sun had broken through the clouds this morning and the unusually early snow had started to melt. The sounds of dripping, the plopping of globs of snow falling from branches, had surrounded them in a cacophony of irregular noises that kept them all on edge.

At the front, Yarnell's bay suddenly whinnied, then broke into a trot. Noah's mount, though weary from carrying double for most of the afternoon, did the same. Rounding a bend on the trail, Noah was almost blinded by a splash of bright daylight ahead. They must be close to Henry's Station . . . home to the string of horses.

In mere seconds his eager mount carried them to the edge of the woods, and there before them lay an expansive clearing and in the middle, the fort. Its rows of standing pikes rose up from yellowed grass dotted with diminishing patches of glistening white. What a welcome sight in this vast wilderness . . . like a safe harbor must seem to sailors after a stormy crossing.

Drew let out a loud whoop. Leaning low over his animal's neck and hanging on to his hat, the lad gave his mount its head and galloped past Noah and Miss Jessica. Two of the cauldrons on the trailing packhorse clanged together as loud as a discordant church bell.

Yarnell reined in his impatiently prancing mount until Noah and Jessica drew alongside. "Nothin' like sneakin' up on 'em," he said with a wry smile.

Noah barked a chuckle, glad to see his friend's sense of humor returning. Yesterday, just staying in the saddle had been a chore for the injured man.

Then Noah realized his passenger had shrunk back against him. Was she frightened? This wisp of a woman who didn't hesitate when it came to charging into the midst of a war party was afraid to venture into what was supposed to be their safe harbor?

She'd saved him, saved them all. He could do no less than return the favor. He leaned as close to her ear as her floppy hat would allow. "Don't fret, Miss Jessica. I'll see you through."

Mr. Reardon's whispered words, though well intentioned, only confirmed to Jessica that she truly did have something to worry about. But she refused to show her apprehension. Straightening, she took another, closer look at the fort. It stretched up far taller than even the largest Indian lodges. It was huge. Ominous. Every pole that comprised the walls was taller than the combined height of two men, and the end of each pike had been hewn to a deadly sharp point. High up at each corner of the wall, log houses with small windows overlooked the fort and the surrounding country-side.

Only in her earliest memories did she remember such a struc-ture—at Fort Pitt, in the mountains to the north. The place where her mother had died.

She didn't see anyone watching from any of the lookout houses, but with the racket Drew's iron pots were making, not only the people in the fort but everyone for a mile around had to know they were approaching.

Without slowing, Drew charged through the wide-open gates, shouting his arrival.

Although she was determined to bravely face the people, Jessica pulled her hat down more tightly and tilted it forward. Merely to shade her eyes from the glare, she told herself.

Too soon, she and Mr. Reardon passed through the entrance also. To her surprise, she didn't see the many cabins she'd expected. Aside from the tall ones at each corner, only four other log structures sat within the great enclosure along with a few corrals and a stable. Over the nearest cabin's door was a board painted with the words *Keaton's General Store*. Over another's gaping opening was a sign that said *Blacksmith*. From that building came a fiery glow and the strong smell of brimstone and melting metal.

Drew had dismounted and now his riderless mount and his packhorse trotted past the ironworks, with the cauldrons clanging all the way to the stable.

Two men, one holding a red-hot horseshoe, stepped out for a look-see.

Jessica turned her head away.

Yarnell brought his tall bay alongside Mr. Reardon's sturdier roan as they reined their reluctant animals to the left toward the store. It was obvious the horses would have preferred going, instead, to the stable.

On a porch that ran the length of the store's cabin, Drew stood talking to three people. The one wearing a pure white shirt beneath an autumn-colored coat and vest left the others and came down the steps to greet the new arrivals with a friendly smile.

Jessica recognized him as Storekeeper Keaton, one of those who'd come to the salt lick several weeks ago. To her father he'd complained loudly, but unlike Mr. Reardon, had paid the price her father charged for the small amount of salt he purchased.

"Your brother says you boys came back with plenty of—" Mr. Keaton's attention shifted from Mr. Reardon to her—"and more."

Resisting the temptation to duck down into the coarse fur of her robe, Jessica lifted her chin.

"I'll tell you all about it," Mr. Reardon said as he swung down from the horse. "But right now we could use something hot to warm us up." Raising his hands, he beckoned for Jessica to come down into them.

She froze. The thought of leaving the safety of the horse sent her heart pounding.

For her only, Mr. Reardon mouthed, "Don't be afraid."

Swallowing hard over her closing throat, she made herself reach for him and slid down into his arms.

As Mr. Reardon set her feet on the ground and wrapped an arm around her shoulder, she kept her gaze fixed on the safe sight of

Keaton as he ushered them up the steps toward the two strang-ers—a man and a woman. Even so, she caught a glimpse of a long, dark green cloak and a gray skirt peeking out the slit. Except for a few sorely abused captives, she hadn't seen a white woman since she was four years old. She couldn't resist looking at the face as she approached.

The hooded woman stared back. Pasty white skin puckered the mouth, and a frown pinched her brows above a pair of light brown eyes. The woman looked as if she'd just eaten something sour.

Jessica quickly returned her attention to the storekeeper.

"Afternoon, Hagerty, Mistress Hagerty." Mr. Reardon touched the brim of his tricorn. Then tightening his hold on Jessica, he whisked her past the married couple and into the stuffy heat of the store.

Completely surrounded by such an array of goods, Jessica could only gaze in awe. The store was piled high with all manner of sacks and crates, kegs and barrels. Never had Father brought back such a variety of goods when he went over the mountain for supplies. Shelves on all the walls were lined with smaller boxes and sacks and devices made of metal and wood. She recognized hammers and hatchets and the pots of varying sizes but not much else.

Curious about the uses of the items she couldn't identify, she wanted to take a closer look but was distracted by the sound of footsteps and voices as the others came inside. She felt all their eyes on her.

"Heard you took a bullet, Yarnell," Storekeeper Keaton said.

Relieved that everyone's attention would now shift to the long hunter, she gladly let Mr. Reardon usher her toward the blazing hearth at one end of the store.

"Ball went clean through," Mr. Yarnell replied. "Reckon my shoulder will be stove up for a spell, but that's about it."

"Aye," Drew chimed in, his voice bright with the zest of his youth. "We run 'em off good and proper."

Mr. Reardon didn't correct Drew as Jessica expected he would. He only grunted his disapproval before turning to the storekeeper. "We brought back all the salt we'll need in our valley and enough to pay you for the use of your horses and equipment, plus a little extra. And I'd like to use that to trade for some presentable attire for Miss Jessica here."

Everyone started gawking at her again.

Mr. Keaton shook his head. "I don't think I have anything her size in the barrel of used clothes at the moment. But you could probably take something up."

"Mayhap Mistress Hagerty will." Mr. Reardon turned to the woman. "You have two or three daughters still at home, don't you? Could one of them spare a day gown that would fit the young lady? And perhaps she needs a good serviceable cloak."

"For how much salt?" the woman asked in a bargaining tone.

"I'd have to see the clothing first. If it's of good quality and not too worn, I'll be generous. Miss Whitman could do with a sturdy bonnet as well."

"A town dress, a cloak, and now you want a bonnet too?" Mistress Hagerty exchanged glances with her husband. "That's askin' a lot. Just how much salt did you plan on givin' in return?"

The woman spoke like a born trader. "If the clothes have plenty of wear left in them," Mr. Reardon said, "I'll not quibble. Say, twenty pounds."

"That's a mite stingy for all three." Mistress Hagerty plucked a twig off her cloak as if she'd lost interest. "Thirty pounds sounds more like it."

Mr. Reardon removed his tricorn and ran fingers through his sun-streaked thatch. "That's mighty steep." He brushed at debris caught in the folds of his hat. "I really couldn't spare more than twenty-five and still have enough salt to take back to my valley."

"I don't know," she said, shaking her head. "My gal's not gonna be too happy with me tradin' off her clothes as it is. . . ."

Jessica tugged on Mr. Reardon's sleeve. This really wasn't necessary. Rising up onto her toes, she whispered in his ear, "Please, may we converse privately?"

"Why, yes. Certainly."

He turned back to the Hagertys. "Would you excuse us for a moment?" Stepping past Mr. Yarnell and Drew, Mr. Reardon escorted her between rows of stacked barrels to reach the other side of the store, then—polite as always—waited for her to speak.

Clutching her bear robe, Jessica moved close and spoke in a low voice. "I do apologize for interrupting your transaction, but I don't want you trading your salt to buy me those clothes. You worked too hard for it."

"It doesn't matter," he insisted. "I'll not have you ever again be subject to people's stares because you're not dressed as they are."

Ever again, he'd said. How she wished he'd stay with her that long. But that was not to be. "I thank you for your kindnesses on my behalf, but I think I have more than enough coins to pay for the white woman's clothes and, hopefully, enough left over to cover my expenses until I find my brother."

"You do?" He sounded surprised.

"Aye." Glancing back at the others who stood watching, she rose up on her toes again. "I've been collecting coins from here and there for the past four years. I have them sewn to the inside of my day gown. They weight it down a mite, but I kept them close because of my father."

"If you don't mind my asking, how much do you have?"

She hesitated. "At our store we usually dealt in pelts. The only coins Father received were from leftover profit when he went overmountain to bargain for provisions. So I'm not certain what they can be traded for. Some are English, and some Spanish. And I think two are French."

He patted her hand. "We'll discuss the money later. I'll pay for the clothes today. It's the least I can do, after all you've done for us."

Heading back toward the others, he again addressed the older woman who, Jessica noticed, no longer looked so confident. "Mistress Hagerty, I'll give you twenty-eight pounds of salt *if* you'll deliver the goods back here by this evening. I've already lost so much time by going to boil down the salt myself—it's imperative that I start for Greeneville first thing in the morning. Do we have a deal?"

"I don't know. There's only a couple more hours of daylight," Mr. Hagerty observed.

"I'll ride along with you," Drew offered, "and fetch the clothes back." He grabbed the woman's bundles and ushered the couple toward the door, being more helpful and respectful of his elders than Jessica had ever seen. Jessica suspected that the fact they had daughters his age had something to do with Drew's eagerness.

Drew was already crossing the threshold when Mr. Reardon called out the last detail of the transaction. "Drew, have Keaton weigh out the Hagertys' salt before you go."

11

Jessica ran ahead of Mr. Reardon to the storekeeper's private cabin—lodging the kind man had offered her for the night. It stood next to the store where the men would sleep. Mr. Reardon followed with a tote chock full of things he and the storekeeper had decided a young lady needed, and she could hardly wait to examine them in private. She flung open the door, then stood back, ushering her tall, broad-shouldered champion across the threshold before her.

He graced her with a smile that matched the sparkle of his dove gray eyes. "Thank you. This time. But in the future, you're to let the gentleman open the door for you."

"Even when you have your hands full? That's silly."

"Well," he hedged, his expression still light, almost teasing, "if they aren't *too* full."

She swelled with happiness. This was turning out to be a really fine day. Stepping in behind him, she halted, and her jaw fell open. Never had she seen anything to match the sights that lay before her.

The plank floor beneath her moccasins shined like still water in the morning light. And so did several big crates that stood on end with knobs down the front. All the edges were curved and carved with the same care as the intricate cross she wore, and built so tight they showed no cracks on the tops and were as slick as the glass in the windows. Glass! She moved to touch the transparent panes with her fingertips. Draped around each window was thick green-and-gold cloth gathered and pulled back at the sides. And so much more! A big shiny table and chairs . . . that stood on a rug of many colors! At the other end, a bed was suspended high off the floor by more shiny wood—carved poles this time. And pretty clay dolls. Just as slick and elegant as everything else, they decorated a mantel board above the glowing fireplace.

The clatter of Mr. Reardon's emptying the contents of the tote onto one of the gleaming crates interrupted Jessica's exploration. The ribbons he'd selected to decorate her hair came spilling out last like so many streams of color . . . as many as were in the rug. With a joyful sigh, she gazed about her again. She had no idea there could be so much beauty inside a building. Then she realized that this must be what the homes in Baltimore looked like. Such grand places they must be.

"Why don't you freshen up and get some rest before supper?" Mr. Reardon suggested, then headed for the door.

A sudden panic gripped her. "You're leaving me?" Where was he going? For how long?

"I'm just going out to unload the packhorses, brush them down," he explained.

"Oh, then I should accompany you and assist in the labors."

"No." Thrusting out a hand, he stayed her. "For the next couple of hours I want you to think of yourself as a lady of leisure. Sit by the fire and warm up, tend only to your own needs for a change."

His rejection of her offer sounded sincerely kind, but as soon as he closed the door behind him, she felt out of place in another's dwelling, no matter how beautiful. It stood in the midst of a village hidden behind a fence so high she couldn't see the forest beyond . . . this settlement where everyone had stared at her.

She watched Mr. Reardon walk toward the stables. How handily he had taken charge of getting her outfitted. He had such confidence, always knowing the right thing to say and do. And, more amazing, he hadn't seemed to even notice the beautiful things in the room—they were that commonplace to him. This was a man who'd traveled everywhere, who seemed to know everything. And she had only a very short time to learn what she could from him. She desperately needed some of that confidence, because in three short days they'd reach Greeneville, where he would tend his business and be on his way back to his own valley. Three days, in which he'd said she could ask as many questions as she wished.

Once Mr. Reardon had disappeared from sight, Jessica's attention shifted to the glass pane only inches from her. Again, she ran her hand over the cold hard surface, one that truly was as clear as Mr. Reardon had said. Turning back to the beautiful room, she walked to the shiny crate where Mr. Reardon had left the wondrous things he bought her. The rainbow of ribbons felt smoother than the mink pelt she'd left behind. Beneath them were brushes; one was for her teeth, and the one for her hair had more bristles in it than she'd ever seen. And there were oddly shaped combs that were supposed to stay in the hair, as well as a dozen or so bent wires.

And perfumed soap. She picked up the hard block and brought it to her nose. It smelled like the sweetest flower. Lilacs, Mr. Keaton had said. Putting it down, she gasped and jumped back. Something directly in front of her had moved.

A person stared at her through a small window.

No, not a window . . . a looking glass that hung on the wall. She touched her own reflection—infinitely clearer than any she'd caught in any still pond. She stared in awe as she tipped her head this way and that, trying a frown, a smile. Her chin and jaw were more fragile looking, her cheekbones wider and more pronounced than she'd realized. Finally, she focused on the eyes that met hers.

The tribes had been known to call people with blue or gray eyes "white eyes," but hers gave far more meaning to the name. She leaned close to the framed mirror to be sure they were truly as they appeared. Except for a light aqua at the edges, the irises had almost no color—a startling contrast to the black pupils in the center and the lashes surrounding them. Small wonder, with all the superstitions the Indians had, that they thought their souls might be swallowed whole if she looked at them the wrong way.

But Mr. Reardon had not been frightened away. Fact was, he'd even said her eyes were beautiful.

Stepping back, she took an appraising assessment of her face as a whole. There was a thinness to it, like the rest of her, yet her eyes were larger and wider apart than Mistress Hagerty's . . . her lashes thicker and darker below the almost straight slash of her brows. Her mouth, too, was fuller. Touching its softness, she wondered if white folk thought thin lips were prettier. Another question in a long list that grew with her every new sight.

Then her gaze gravitated to her hair. She saw it was a terrible mess! The part was not straight down the middle as she'd thought but looked as if some frantic squirrel had run through it. And the rest was as haphazard as any robin's nest. Another reason the strangers had stared at her.

Not wasting another second, she ripped loose the thongs tying the ends of her braids.

Coming awake at a rumbling sound, Jessica took a second to recognize her surroundings. Then she saw she'd fallen asleep by the banked fire in a wonderful chair. The bottoms of its legs were glued to wood curved like a smile, and she'd rocked back and forth in it for the longest time.

The noise grew ever louder. Horses were galloping toward the fort. More people were coming. The fleeting thought that they might come to her door set her heart to pounding.

Rising, she hurried to the nearest window that flanked one side of the door. Three riders charged through the gates. When they were almost on top of the store next door, they reined in hard, skidding their mounts to a stop.

Jessica moved to another set of the glass panes to get a better view.

Three men. She couldn't hear much, but they appeared to be talking and laughing all at once as they swung down to the ground. She recognized one as a fellow who'd accompanied Storekeeper Keaton to the salt lick several weeks ago. Mr. Mackey, she remembered. There'd been something disrespectful in the way he'd talked to her, and she'd made a point of staying well out of his reach.

Mr. Reardon and Mr. Yarnell came out of the store and walked to the edge of the split-wood porch, where they stopped. Mr. Yarnell seemed more relaxed than Mr. Reardon as he returned the newcomers' friendly greetings.

She knew it wasn't polite to listen in on people's conversations, but her curiosity won out. She unlatched the window and swung it out until she could clearly hear their words.

Mr. Mackey lifted a large tote from over the pommel of his saddle and tossed it up to Mr. Reardon. "Mistress Hagerty told me to give this to you."

Catching it, Mr. Reardon's gaze narrowed. "Where's Drew? My brother was supposed to bring this." He didn't sound pleased.

The freckle-faced man laughed again as if what Mr. Reardon had said was highly amusing. "Got hisself invited to supper at the Hagertys'. So me and the boys, here, volunteered to bring the sack to you." He started up the steps.

Mr. Reardon still didn't look satisfied. "You three were all visiting at the Hagertys' when they rode up?"

"Nay. I seen Drew ride by our place with 'em, so I went out to see how you boys fared down at the salt lick. And I have to say, I was plumb surprised when Drew said you brung that queer gal back with you. We had to come see for ourselves. Didn't we, boys?" The rawboned Mackey turned to his friends. "The high and mighty Noah Reardon givin' up the gorgeous Miss Lorna to take up with a daft woodsy? You must be as touched in the head as she is."

A round of laughter followed . . . merriment at her and Mr. Reardon's expense. Jessica was used to trappers and hunters poking fun at her, but how could anyone treat Mr. Reardon so disrespectfully?

She was tempted to tell that Mackey fellow just what she thought of him. He was just as boorish as she'd remembered.

Jessica swung open the door. But before she could step out, another young man stopped laughing long enough to sputter, "We come to see for ourselves what she looks like."

She stopped in her tracks.

Fists balled, Mr. Reardon stalked off the store's porch and halted directly in front of the smirking Mackey. He glared down at the shorter but sturdy-built man.

Mackey shrank back, but only slightly, before he puffed out his barrel of a chest.

Was he challenging Mr. Reardon? Were they going to come to blows?

"Whatever the lady may or may not be," Mr. Reardon said tightly, "I would never subject her to such uncouth behavior. So take those bad manners back to where you got them."

Smirking, Mackey rocked his head in what looked like a taunt. Still, he did retreat backward. "It is true then," he crowed. Catching up the reins to his old horse, he hooked his boot toe into

114

the stirrup and mounted. "Be sure and send me an invite. I wouldn't miss this wedding for all the beaver pelts in Tennessee. Come on, boys. This news is too good to keep."

As fast as the three had come, they rode out, whooping and hooting like a bunch of celebrating Muskogee.

Mr. Reardon watched them go, his face rigid as slate and equally dark.

But was he enraged because they'd made sport of her—or him?

And just who was the gorgeous Miss Lorna? Hadn't Drew mentioned that name before? That first day when she overheard them talking? Hadn't he said something about Mr. Reardon's wanting to marry her? Could she be the *betrothed* he couldn't keep hold of? Whatever that had meant. Another of those questions she'd never quite worked up the nerve to ask.

Had Mr. Reardon really given up the gorgeous Miss Lorna? Or could she, at this very second, be waiting in his valley for his return?

Suddenly the outside chill seemed to go right through Jessica. She quietly shut the door and closed the window, then returned to the comfort of the chair that seesawed.

As kind as Mr. Reardon had been since he'd appeared at the salt lick, she really knew very little about him. The multitude of questions he'd answered for her had mostly been about life in the East. He had mentioned his valley on a number of occasions, but mostly to expound on its beauty, its rich black soil, and the future he envisioned for it. But he'd said nothing in particular about the other folks who'd come to live there beside him and his brothers. All she really knew was that he was dedicated to his settlement, and that he was not married.

He'd made her two promises, though. He'd vowed to see her dressed like everyone else so she wouldn't draw undue attention, and he said he'd take her to Greeneville—the settlement that was

115

to have been her brother's first stop after he left Chickasaw country for Baltimore.

And it was past time she stopped thinking about anything else. Quit her foolish dreaming. From now on she would concentrate on only one thing—finding Spencer and her mother's people. It was time to put the fact that she'd be traveling with Mr. Reardon for several more days completely out of her mind . . . days when she'd have Mr. Reardon all to herself. Aye, put it completely out of her mind.

Completely.

12

Smelling the tempting aroma of frying bacon, Noah stretched a kink out of his neck while stirring a pot of cornmeal mush. He certainly would be glad to get back to the comfort of a bed again.

Yarnell, beside him, flipped slices of the side pork he cooked over a few hot coals scooped onto the hearth. Though Noah's body ached from sleeping on the floor in the back room of Keaton's store, it didn't seem to bother the long hunter anymore than bedding down in the woods. Any stiffness Yarnell complained of was from his healing shoulder wound.

Keaton came stumbling out of the back room, rubbing the sleep from his eyes. Having slept in his clothes, he looked rumpled for the first time since Noah had started trading at the normally tidy man's store. "Smelled the bacon," Keaton said, combing fingers through his thinning hair. Walking stiff-legged past a row of barrels to reach them, Keaton wasn't faring so well either, Noah noticed with amusement. The thoughtful man had given up his bed and cabin for Miss Jessica.

117

"Is Drew still asleep?" Noah asked the storekeeper. The lad had not ridden in until long after they'd retired for the night.

"Aye," Keaton chortled. "I toyed with the idea of giving him a swift kick in the behind just now, for nearly beating the door down in the middle of the night. But then I remembered what it was like to be young and in love with every young miss in the neighborhood."

"Then you really should'a booted him," Yarnell drawled. "Keep him thinkin' we're watchin' all the time."

Keaton chuckled again.

Noah didn't. He'd be off to Greeneville this morning, leaving his brother behind. He might get into mischief, if last night was a precursor. He turned to his friend. "Yarnell, I've been thinking . . . would you mind hanging around here whilst I'm away? Keep an eye on Drew. He looks up to you."

"Me?" The man's narrow features stretched even longer. "I was thinkin' of headin' up to Boonesborough for a spell."

"Just for a week. I'll bring you back one of those good hunting knives the smithy there makes," Noah bribed. "It's like that one of mine you admire."

Yarnell expelled a breath. "Make sure it's extra sharp."

Noah handed the long-handled wooden spoon to Keaton. "Would you two finish up here? I'd better go see if Miss Jessica is up and dressed in her new clothes. Oh, and one more thing." Keaton had been a pretty good sport about giving up his bed for Jessica—Noah hoped he wouldn't balk at his next request. "Would you mind if the three of us ate breakfast in your cabin with her? You have all that fine china and silverware over there we could work with, and you probably have a better knack for which fork to use, and all that nonsense."

"Are you asking me to give lessons on table manners?" Keaton didn't sound amused.

Doing his best to look helpless, Noah pleaded with a shrug.

"I usually save my good table and service for special occasions. As you see, I don't even cook in the cabin where I keep my costly furniture."

"Think of it as your good deed for the year."

"You forget, I slept on the floor for her last night? But, all right," Keaton conceded. "I reckon it'd be the Christian thing to help the misfortunate lass get a new start in life. When the food's ready, Yarnell and I will bring it on over."

"*Not me,*" Yarnell vehemently declined, wagging his shaggy head. "Any manners she'd pick up from me wouldn't do her no good. None a'tall."

Laughing at Yarnell's aversion to anything remotely akin to the social graces, Noah started for the door.

"Let's just hope she's willing to eat with us at all," Keaton said as Noah strode out. "After what she heard Donald Mackey spouting yesterday, she's been real standoffish."

As aggravating as Mackey's remarks had been for Noah, he knew how much worse they must have sounded to Jessica. He really hated that her first day in civilization had been so recklessly and stupidly marred. Most assuredly, her next entrance into a township would not be as an object of ridicule. He'd see to that.

Within seconds after Noah knocked on Jessica's door, he saw the drape at the nearest window flutter; then he heard her lift off the bar before she opened the door . . . and he got a good look at her. She was gloriously colorful. She'd taken *every* ribbon he'd purchased for her and woven them into her braids. And her eyes seemed to pick up every hue. Simply breath-stealing. Even those delicately sculpted cheekbones bore a rosy glow. All a striking contrast to her ebony hair—hair she must have washed last night and brushed until it glistened.

No doubt, she was gorgeous . . . hilariously gorgeous. Yet he didn't dare crack a smile even if the plaits hanging down either side of her face did resemble maypoles.

119

Her expectant expression turned to angst. "La, I thought you admired my hair, but you don't."

Noah realized she'd read his every reaction. He took her hands into his. "Oh, I do. You're absolutely beautiful."

He obviously hadn't been all that convincing—her features relaxed only a little.

Then he noticed more. Though she'd had the presence of mind to discreetly cover her upper bosom by wrapping and tying the shawl collar over the wide scoop-neck bodice, she'd put the petticoats on *over* the faded yellow homespun dress. How could he tactfully inform her that if she walked out in public as she was, she would most assuredly be a laughingstock? His insides knotted at the thought. *Father in heaven, please give me the right words.*

He'd been silent too long—he knew he had to say something. "You've done a beautiful job with your hair. Truly you have." Removing a hand from hers, he picked up one of the many-colored weaves. "You would doubtlessly be the prettiest girl in any Cherokee town."

She still didn't look convinced. "We never lived near the Cherokee."

He took a breath—she wasn't making it easy. "Muskogee, then, or the Chickasaw. But in Eastern towns it's different. Only little girls wear braids that hang down like this."

"Oh?" Withdrawing her other hand from his, she shielded each plait as if to hide her shame.

He caught her hands again. "Please don't think they aren't wonderful—they are. But for your sake, I don't want anyone to stare because something about you is different from what they're used to."

Hurt filled her eyes as she pulled away and glanced toward the cherry-wood bureau where he'd left the items he'd bought her. "But I don't know what else to do." She started toward the chest of drawers. "These bent wires and strange-shaped combs . . ." Her airy voice cracked.

It tore at his heart. Quickly he stepped up behind her. "I don't know if I'll be much good at it, but I *have* watched my mother and sister do their hair. Let me see if I can help." He took one of her braids—heavier than he'd expected—and began undoing it, feeling clumsy from the start.

She gazed up at his reflection in the mirror, giving him a hopeful smile.

As the braid unraveled, he became aware of just how much hair Jessica had. With every unleashed inch, it seemed to grow thicker, swallowing the flashy ribbon strands within its sleek luster.

Loosing the last plait, he tossed away the ribbons and fluffed out his half as well as the hair Miss Jessica had just finished unraveling. Even wavy from the braids, her tresses fell in a shining mass well below her waist . . . the kind of silken glory any man would want to wade through.

Then, out of the blue, he recalled Lorna's hair. It had been even blacker than Jessica's. And instead of mere waves, it had been a riot of curls. And Lorna's eyes . . . they had no need to reflect the colors around them; they had so much color of their own—deep violet blue. Eyes that had looked at him with open admiration, much the way Jessica's now did.

No. Lorna's eyes had deceived him into believing she loved him. Only then she had abandoned him when she decided the comforts he offered weren't to her liking. But he really hadn't known her—the real everyday Lorna—at all. He'd met her and courted her during that brief summer month when he'd gone back to North Carolina for his sister's wedding. Marriage had been in the air, and Lorna, only fifteen at the time, had said yes. What had either of them known about each other? The two years of exchanged corre-spondence—fanciful love letters back and forth—had only added to their misconceptions of one another. Not once had he questioned her Christian faith . . . not until she ran off to the carnal pleasures of New Orleans.

Yet here he was, only a few short months later, starting to have serious feelings for another young woman he'd just met . . . and this time, one who freely admitted she didn't know the Lord. Not to mention, he thought with an inward smile, this one was so woodsy she couldn't even dress herself. But he couldn't let himself get caught up in her vulnerability. For all he knew, when she had learned all he could teach her, she might turn out to be just as fickle-hearted as Lorna. Especially since all Jessica talked about was going to Baltimore.

And that would be for the best, he tried to convince himself . . . since she didn't share his faith in Christ. He could never knowingly take an unbeliever to be his wife.

"Is something wrong with my hair? I brushed it until my arms ached."

"No, no," he assured her with a forced smile. "I was just admiring it. God has truly blessed you." He caught up the entire mass and lifted it high as if he knew what he was doing. "My mother always held her hair up like this, then twisted it round and round," he explained while he twirled the thousands of strands as well as his calloused hands could manage.

He sensed her attention on his every fumbling move. And worse. What if Keaton or Yarnell popped in about now and caught him at it? Glancing out the window, he suddenly had the truest understanding of just what it meant to feel out of place.

Noah thought he'd never get all her hair trapped, but once he did, he started coiling it at the top of her head as one might a long rope. More than ever he wished he had a third hand—the coil kept trying to slide downward—just as his gaze also found itself doing . . . to the creamy whiteness of her exposed neck . . . and her ears. They were ever so perfectly shaped and delicate . . . as if they were made of porcelain.

Suddenly Noah developed a need for more air. He took a deep breath and tried to return his concentration to her hair. "Miss Jessica, would you please hand me some pins?"

She stiffened. "You aren't going to poke them in my head, are you?"

He broke into laughter, much too loud. Then he regained control. "No, of course not. I'll use them to hook the coils together. And I reckon the combs will help to hold up the whole blamed thing. You certainly have a lot of hair."

"I thought you said that was good."

"Oh, it is. It's just me. I'm not used to fooling with a female's hair, and all my fingers have turned to thumbs."

"Not even Miss Lorna's hair?"

Where had that come from? Donald Mackey, of course. "No, you're my very first victim."

After several attempts to get all her hair to stay put, he stepped back to assess his efforts. And lo and behold, Jessica looked like any other young lady. Except maybe prettier. Much prettier. "Very nice, if I do say so myself."

Jessica jiggled her head back and forth, as she stared dubiously at herself. "But when I take off my hat, I don't think it's going to stay put."

"That reminds me," he said, "when ladies are being introduced, it's not customary for them to remove their hats—or in the case of what Mistress Hagerty brought you—your mobcap. Only men do that. Women curtsy."

She tilted her lovely head to the side. "Curtsy? What's that?"

"Nothing to fret about. I'll show you once you've put your petti-coats under your day gown."

She caught up a handful of the plain white layers. "Underneath? I think you're wrong about that. Mistress Hagerty wore hers on the outside."

Now it was Noah's turn to be confused, but only for a second.

"No, what you saw was her apron. She didn't send one of those for you." *Along with not including a bonnet,* he groused to himself.

When Drew came in late last night, he'd explained that Mistress Hagerty had said one wouldn't be necessary because the cloak had a hood. So she'd sent a mobcap, nothing but a flimsy circle of gathered cotton with only one ruffle decorating it. And though the dress and the dull blue gray cloak of homespun wool still had plenty of wear in them, there wasn't an extra adornment on either. Mistress Hagerty had certainly made a good trade for herself.

Jessica fingered the petticoats. "All these layers. Are they supposed to keep one warm?"

"I reckon that's how it started out, but now they're used mostly to make the skirt bulge out." He demonstrated by holding his hands out from his thighs.

"Aye! I know what you mean. I saw that in one of my pictures. I thought the woman was merely very fat from the waist down."

Noah couldn't help smiling. "Well, now you can be too. It's an Eastern ladies' fashion. Just like with the hair."

She opened her mouth as if to speak. Instead, she glanced down to the bureau and picked up the ribbons. "What about these? I thought you procured them for my hair."

"And I did," he said with more enthusiasm than he felt . . . now that he had to figure out where one would actually go and how to keep it there. He felt his fingers turning to stubby thumbs again. "Pick one."

"Only one?" Now, *she* wasn't happy.

"I'm afraid that's also the fashion. One in a color that goes with your dress." He scanned the ribbons, then shrugged. "I'd probably choose the yellow one because of your dress, since I'm not all that certain what colors go with what." He pulled the sunny strand from her fingers and held it up against her dark hair. "Yes, very nice."

In the mirror he watched her raise the thick lashes shading her eyes and look up at him. His mouth went dry. She suddenly seemed much older than eighteen.

Then a frown creased her brow. "There's so much to learn. So very much."

"And you shall. We'll talk all the way to Greeneville. Now that I'm beginning to see things through your eyes, I also see there's much that will seem foolish to you. But you'll need to learn even our foolish customs for when you locate your brother and he takes you to meet your family in Baltimore. In fact, Mr. Keaton is coming over with our breakfast any minute now. He and I will teach you what we know about table manners. You know, like which fork goes where."

Her mouth fell open. "You mean there's even a special place for a fork?"

"I'm afraid so. But first things first."

Somehow he managed to get the slippery satin strand wrapped around her coil of hair and a nice neat bow placed to one side of her middle part. Then, still standing behind her, he put his hands on her shoulders and positioned her directly before the looking glass. "How's that? Does it please you?"

"Aye. I suppose."

That wasn't the reaction he'd expected.

"You did a wonderful job," she amended. "It's just this white cloth I tucked down my front. It makes my eyes appear all the lighter."

Hmm, still worried about her eyes, was she? He turned her to face him. "I will never lie to you, so believe me when I say that in this new world you're about to enter, those eyes of yours will be considered your most advantageous feature." He gazed down at their ethereal loveliness. "And your hair. And when you smile, it's so warm . . . and your lips, they're . . ."

Not soon enough, he caught himself and wheeled away. "I'd better go see what's taking Keaton so long." Then remembering, he turned back. "Whilst I'm gone, don't forget to put the petti-coats under the dress." An instant picture of her performing that task—a flash of ankle—sent a rush of heat to the back of his neck.

What was he getting himself into? Even if he treasured her every word, her every glance his way, she wasn't a Christian. He had to keep that foremost in his mind.

13

"It's important to always bow your head and close your eyes whenever someone is saying a prayer," Mr. Reardon informed Jessica.
"Like I did this morning before we ate."

As he'd promised, he'd spent most of their first day alone on the
trail instructing her. While Jessica enjoyed the stories he told her,
such as one about a man named Moses who delivered his people
out of slavery, she was starting to get annoyed. Mr. Reardon had
spent most of his time conveying the teachings of his god, rather
than helping her know how to conduct herself in society. To make
matters more perturbing, he had insisted she ride sideways on her
saddle as was proper for women, causing her to get a stitch just
below her ribs. These supposedly civilized white people had some
of the silliest customs—especially concerning women. But at least
it was a valuable part of her education. And she had only two more
days to learn how to act like one of them before reaching
Greeneville.

Her patience was growing thin as she nudged her lagging mount closer to Mr. Reardon's. "Just how many more commandments and rules does this god of yours have?"

But it didn't bother Mr. Reardon in the least. He just laughed and reached behind him. Lifting the flap of a saddlebag, he pulled out the biggest book she'd ever seen. Hundreds and hundreds of pages. So much bigger than her father's thin volume of Shakespeare's sonnets, which he'd rarely allowed her to read.

Mr. Reardon leafed through it, then stretched closer, handing the open book to Jessica. "This is the Bible, the book about *our* God, mine and yours, if you will have him."

It was so heavy. And so many words! She pulled her rented chestnut gelding to a halt. "Someone wrote this much about just one god?"

"Not just one author. Down through the centuries, many have been inspired by our Lord to put down the things he wanted us to know. On that page, look just below where it says Chapter Five. There's something specific I want to show you."

At the top was the title Deuteronomy, not *Holy Bible,* but she wouldn't quibble. "Aye, I found it." She held the spot with her finger.

"Now move down from there to the line that starts with the number 6, and read that passage for yourself. Those are the Ten Commandments of God. Whether or not you choose to believe in him, these are what all our laws *and* a great many of our customs are based on."

Feeling a bit daunted by such an impressive book, she began to read and immediately learned that Mr. Reardon's God—spelled with a capital *G* as if it were his name—was a jealous god. Folks weren't supposed to worship any other god but him. Mr. Reardon had mentioned that before, and now here it was, written down plain as day. Not only that, but this god expected people to love him.

The next one wasn't quite so understandable, something about not using the Lord thy God's name in vain. She read on, hoping further words would explain, like with the first command, but they didn't.

Not wanting to take the time away from the book to ask Mr. Reardon, she read on. The next one she liked very much. It didn't just say it was permitted not to work one day each week; the words *commanded* it. One whole day every week!

Hmmm. She glanced over at Mr. Reardon. She'd been with him for more than seven days now and hadn't seen *him* stop working for even half of one of those days. Maybe he wasn't as perfect as his good looks and manner would make one think—which reminded her of the fact that he hadn't answered her when she'd asked him about his Miss Lorna.

But then the next commandment was like a slap in her own face: "Honour thy father and thy mother, as the Lord thy God hath commanded thee." She certainly hadn't honored Father when she'd allowed Mr. Reardon to keep him tied up.

Shaking off the niggling thought, she read on. "Thou shalt not kill." *That* she totally agreed with and wished everyone else did too.

The next command spoke of adultery being a sin, and she had a pretty fair idea what that was about, which brought her back to wondering about Mr. Reardon and his Lorna.

But before she could bring that elusive subject up, the next command stabbed right into her. "Neither shalt thou steal." Though anyone might think it a good law, she'd broken this one each time she'd taken one of Father's coins.

After that one, the commands just got harder. The next one said she wasn't supposed to bear false witness against her neighbor. Even harder to keep was the final one. It said she wasn't supposed to even want what someone else had. And first on the list of forbidden wants was that a man wasn't to desire another man's wife. And here she was, this very second, wishing there was no Miss Lorna.

She lowered the big black book to her lap. "I'm sorry, Mr.

Reardon, but these rules of your god are much too hard to follow. I'm breaking some at this very moment."

"Really?" Mr. Reardon glanced from her to scan the stripped November woods surrounding them. He was obviously confused.

In a small way it pleased her, his being the one off balance for a change. "For one thing," she said, starting with what she thought was the least offensive one, "I covet this book. I've never seen anything like it. I could read for days, *weeks,* before I came to the end."

Pushing back his tricorn, Mr. Reardon seemed to relax. "It's all right to want a Bible, just not a particular one that belongs to someone else. Wanting to take away what belongs to another is the sin. It leads to bad feelings and maybe even stealing."

"What if a young miss has feelings for a man, but he hasn't told her he belongs to someone else? Then later she finds out he does. Is she guilty of coveting? Or is he the sinner for bearing false witness?"

Instead of betraying his guilt, Mr. Reardon grinned, a sly grin she couldn't quite interpret. "Maybe I'd better show you another passage. It might help." He took the Bible from her lap and began searching.

She watched, amazed that in a book so huge, he would know which exact page held certain words. He must be much smarter than she could ever hope to be to have memorized so much.

"Here it is," he said as if it were no feat at all. "Matthew seven, verse twelve: 'Therefore all things whatsoever ye would that men should do to you, do ye even so to them; for this is the law and the prophets.' If you treat others as you want to be treated, you'll do all right."

"That's all very nice, but it doesn't change that I've broken several of those commandments, because I *have* done things I wouldn't want to have done to me."

With a sigh, he nodded. "So have I." And it was high time he started admitting his own imperfections.

"But God knew all of us would sin on occasion," he continued, without naming his own sin. "And the price of sin, even just one, is death. Yet because God loves us so much, he did something very special for us. He sent his only begotten Son to earth. Jesus walked among us for thirty-three years, and he is the only human being who never succumbed to temptation. He never sinned. Not once. Yet Jesus allowed himself to be taken and nailed to a cross and killed for false crimes in order to pay for our sins."

"That makes no sense at all."

"I just told you sin had a price, and Jesus paid it for all of us."

Jessica shook her head. This was a very complicated god.

Mr. Reardon looked up and closed his eyes for a second, then said more. "If we believe in Jesus and confess our sins, our sins are washed away by the blood Jesus shed for us. Then when we die in the flesh, we go cleaned of sin to live with God in heaven. That's the only way we can go there. You see, sin is not allowed in heaven. Heaven is the most marvelous place of eternal love and perfection. Something that is just as wonderful, I think, is that we'll be able to rejoin our redeemed loved ones who have gone on ahead of us. My pa died whilst I was away fighting the war. I felt really bad about not getting to say good-bye. I miss him, and I want very much to see him again."

Could it possibly be true? "Do you mean I could see my mother again?"

Mr. Reardon's expression instantly brightened, as if she'd just offered him some wonderful treasure. "Absolutely! If you believe what is written here, that Jesus died on the cross for our sins and—"

She cut him off. "A cross? I have a cross!" Reaching past her hooded cloak, she dipped in between the shawl collar ties and pulled it out.

At seeing her item of jewelry, his expression transformed into utter astonishment. "Where did you get that?" Reining his horse closer, he took hold of the chain-held pendant.

His hand was so close, she could feel the heat of his fingers near her throat. "It was Mother's. My brothers kept it hidden from Father until I was old enough to comprehend its value and keep it secret from him."

Mr. Reardon nodded his understanding without her having to say more. "May I study it up close?" he asked, letting it fall to the length of its thick chain.

She supposed, since it was him asking, it would be all right. Flipping back her hood, she carefully lifted the necklace over the mobcap from Mistress Hagerty and gave it to Mr. Reardon . . . this cross that was more intricate than the carving on Mr. Keaton's shiny crates.

After turning it over this way and that, Mr. Reardon looked up at her. "A large ruby set in gold—even the chain. This is worth a great deal of money."

"How much would you say in the way of trade goods?"

He stared at it again and turned it over in his palm before speaking. "Fifteen, maybe twenty, horses."

"So much? No wonder Spencer insisted I keep it hidden. But even if it was worth a hundred horses, I wouldn't let it go. It's all I have from my mother. And she inherited it from hers, who got it from hers." Jessica held out her hand, not wanting the keepsake to be away from her any longer. "May I have it back now?"

After she'd dropped the chain over her neck, she watched as it came to rest upon the shawl gathers. It did look pretty there.

"You'll still need to keep it out of sight," Mr. Reardon cautioned. "'Twould be a real temptation for folks to steal."

"I thought the people where we're going are all followers of the laws in your Bible book."

"I wish that were true. But I'm afraid not everyone is, though

132

they might pretend to be. And with us out here on a lonely trace
. . ." He shrugged.

She picked up the pendant, not quite ready to conceal it again.
"I showed you this because I thought that mayhap my mother and
those who came before her wore it as a reminder that your Jesus
died for them. They might all be in that heaven place right now,
waiting for me."

Mr. Reardon settled back in his saddle and closed the big book.
"Only God knows if they truly repented of their sins and believed
in him. But I'd say 'tis a very real possibility that they are all up
there at this very moment, enjoying each other's company, living
in perfect harmony. No strife, no sickness, no growing old." Then
he pointed to the cross. "The red gem in the middle probably
signifies the blood of Jesus, shed to wash away our sins."

Jessica caught her lower lip between her teeth and glanced away.
"It surely would take a lot of washing to get rid of all mine. With
every coin I took from my father, I have sinned."

Mr. Reardon started to say something, then hesitated. Finally he
spoke. "It's not right to steal, that's so. When you reach your
family in Baltimore, mayhap they'll reimburse your pa for what
you spent of his on your journey to reach them. Since he doesn't
even know you took the coins, I'm certain 'twill be a nice surprise
for him—as well as the fact that he'll learn you've safely reached
your destination. Because I'm sure once he gets over being angry,
he'll start worrying about you."

"He never worried about my brothers—just kept on cursing
every one of them for being traitors."

"Well, then," he said with a kindly smile, "we should start praying to our all-powerful Lord to soften your pa's heart."

"Father's heart? 'Twould take a very powerful god to do that."

"You'd be surprised what the Creator of all the heavens and the
earth can do. In fact, I wouldn't be surprised that God meant for
me to meet you."

She liked the idea. "You mean the way God sent that Moses character you told me about to deliver the Israelites out of slavery?"

Her words had pleased Mr. Reardon; she could see it in his expression as he said, "Something like that. God heard the pleas of the Israelites and sent Moses to them. I wouldn't be surprised if someone has been praying for you all along."

"For me?"

"It could very well be. Mayhap, those same people in Baltimore that you want to go to."

Jessica's thoughts were sent spinning. The very notion that Mr. Reardon's god would hear prayers from people all the way across the mountains—people who were actually worried about her—then find just the right person to send to her. Her very own Moses—even if he did have a woman waiting for him in his valley.

She clutched her cross. How very much more it meant to her now. "If this is all so, then I'm certain to find my brother. Very soon. After all, this Lord thy God knows you need to get back to your Miss Lorna."

Mr. Reardon's mouth tightened. No more being subtle. He wouldn't be able to dance out of it this time.

He cleared his throat. "Ah, yes, the lovely Lorna Graham. We were to be wed until a few months ago when the young lady changed her mind. By now, I reckon she's hundreds of miles away, seeking her happiness—and her fortune—downriver in New Orleans."

She stared at him, incredulous. "Moses parting the waters of the Red Sea would be easier to believe than that. How could anyone rebuff such a handsome, intelligent, kind-spirited gentleman such as yourself?"

She noticed a redness creeping up from his collar. Had she upset him?

Looking away, he started rubbing that telltale area above his coat. "Well," he said in a voice that sounded more apologetic than angry, "I reckon not everyone holds me in such high esteem."

Suddenly Jessica realized how rude she'd been, prying into his private, painful affairs. "I'm truly sorry anyone would feel they couldn't find happiness with you," she said, hoping to make amends . . . though in her heart she wasn't the least sorry Lorna Graham had gone elsewhere. She just hoped she could keep her smiling heart from showing on her face.

But would hiding her true feelings be bearing false witness? She expelled the breath from her lungs. La, but this sinning business was hard to keep straight.

"Thank you for your kind words," Noah said to this young woman so lacking in guile, then nudged his horse into a faster pace. It would be better for both their sakes if he put a little distance between them before any more was said.

But Miss Jessica was a caution, a pure caution. Despite having to delve into the painful subject of his being so callously jilted, Noah couldn't help but share some of the joy that had splashed over her face when she learned he wasn't bespoken. He knew he should tell her that it was unwise for young women to express their feelings about men so freely, yet it was very healing to be the recipient of such open admiration. He had to keep reminding himself that anyone as hungry for a little kindness as Jessica would be appreciative of whoever sincerely offered it.

She was quick witted, though. Noah had no doubt her knowledge of worldly matters would increase as rapidly as she'd been learning the social graces. In no time young men would be vying for her attentions, hoping she'd look at them with that same devotion she now gave to him.

Even in her simple clothes and lacking the more obvious womanly curves, she was a beauty. Added to her goodness and spirit, her lively curiosity would surely make her irresistible. And, oh, that big, wide, honest smile. Nothing coy there, nothing false.

In that instant he felt a great sense of loss . . . a loss at their imminent parting. Turning in his saddle, he looked back at her.

She waved and smiled that spectacular unabashed grin that she'd begun to display so often, now that she'd grown to trust him . . . and it caused unexpected stirrings in his heart.

Lord, you do know I'm going to miss this young woman. I pray those people back East truly have been praying for her, body and soul, and that they will see what a wonder she is. That some helpful Baltimore matron doesn't ruin her by teaching her how to tease with that smile, or to use it as a means of getting what she wants. Please don't let them turn Jessica into another Lorna.

14

Jessica huddled deeper into the dull blue cloak Mistress Hagerty
had sent to her, wishing it was a bit more substantial. Since the sun
had dipped below the western ridges, what little warmth that had
hovered on the floor of this river valley left with it. Every breath
she took turned to icy puffs just as the vapor spewed from the
nostrils of the scruffy blaze-faced chestnut she rode. Ahead of her
on a trail crowded by the spines of leafless bushes, Mr. Reardon
didn't look much warmer. He'd turned up the collar of his maroon
coat and hunkered into it against the frigid wind.

She did, however, have her bearskin robe tied to her gelding's
rump. More interested at the moment in staving off the cold than
whether she would look woodsy, she reached back to retrieve
it—and caught a sudden flash of movement.

A deer crashed out of the brush and onto the trace, dodging past
as if it were being chased. A doe. Her white tail flagged high. She
ran into a clearing, veered across a field, and leapt back into the
woods again, disappearing within seconds of her appearance.

Jessica scanned the trees but neither saw nor heard what had frightened the deer. When she turned forward again, she saw that Mr. Reardon had reined in his mount. He sat relaxed yet stared straight ahead.

Curious, she rode up beside him. A settler's clearing lay ahead. At the far end stood three small buildings. This was one of only a few farmsteads she'd seen since leaving Henry's Station. More often she'd merely smelled the smoke from their fires or spied tracks cutting into the woods, the way marked by a crudely carved wooden sign nailed to a tree next to this age-worn path.

"It'll be dark soon," Mr. Reardon said, stating the obvious. "I'd hoped to get to the settlement at the big bend on the Nolachucky before stopping, but I think we should see if these folks can put us up for the night."

"Put us up?" Instant panic grabbed Jessica, and her gaze shot to the closest cabin, where smoke billowed from its cross-logged chimney.

"Aye, see if they'll let us spend the night with them."

"Stay with strangers? All of us crowded into one small cabin? What'll I do if they ask me questions I can't answer?" She paused. "They'll stare."

"No, they won't," he assured her. "You'll do just fine." Reaching across to her, he put his gloved hand on her shoulder. "And even if you don't always say or do what they expect, that's all right too. Keep in mind you'll probably never see these folks again. Think of them as merely being here for you to practice on, just like when you were first learning to shoot."

She clutched the hand at her shoulder. "Don't leave me alone with them."

"I won't." His own grip strengthened. "I promise."

As they rode across plowed-under fields of last summer's corn and squash, Jessica was forced to guide her horse around a number of tree stumps. Then, closer to the cabin, she saw where someone had been trying to dig one up. White men certainly cleared a plot the hard way. Indians merely set a fire. And, unlike the white man, each brave didn't mark off a few acres with rod and chain just for his very own—they farmed together. An Indian didn't think he had to have a piece of paper to prove the land was his—like those papers Mr. Reardon was taking to Greeneville for the people in his valley to have recorded.

She'd noticed another thing different about white settlers. They were scattered out far from one another. Small wonder they'd been so vulnerable to Indian attack during the rebellion. Until now, she'd thought only people with something to hide—like her father—lived off to themselves. From what Mr. Reardon said, though, hundreds and hundreds of them did live in towns. Some towns, like Baltimore, had more than a thousand people in them.

A thousand folks all in one place!

As they neared the main cabin, Jessica saw it was not built nearly so nice as Mr. Keaton's. Whereas his was perched high off the ground and was fronted by a porch, this one sat squat in the dirt as hers did at the salt lick.

"Halloo the house!" Mr. Reardon shouted as they reached the front of the shuttered dwelling.

They didn't have long to wait. Almost immediately, a man came out of the split-wood door, huddled into a heavy coat and carrying a rifle. Outlined in the light from the slightly ajar door, he called back, "How do."

Jessica took only a cursory glance down at the sheathed musket Mr. Reardon had borrowed for her—the man didn't seem much of a threat. Even with his closely trimmed beard, he couldn't have been much older than her own eighteen years. He didn't look to have much meat on his bones either, certainly not enough to be wrestling with big stubborn tree stumps.

"How do you do. The name's Reardon, Noah Reardon." Mr.

Reardon pulled off a glove and extended a hand down to the younger man. "I have a place three days' ride west of Henry's Station."

The man offered his own hand in a greeting, the same as Jessica had seen her father and the trappers use countless times. "Duncan Finch here. Just passin' through?"

"Aye. We're on our way to Greeneville to file some deeds, and we were wondering if you'd be kind enough to put us up for the night. We'll pay, of course. Do you have need for some salt?"

"We could do with some." He stepped up beside Jessica's horse. "And we'd be mighty pleasured for the company. Don't have many folks comin' through now that it's turned off cold."

Not wanting to dismount until she was certain he wouldn't be put off by her eyes, she stared straight at him.

The young man didn't seem to even notice as he reached up for her with frayed sleeves. "Let me help you down, Mistress Reardon. My Winnie's gonna be plumb tickled to have another woman to talk to."

Not only had he mistaken her for Mr. Reardon's wife, but she would be expected to converse! Jessica shot a panicked glance to Mr. Reardon.

His attention was on the man. "I do apologize," he said. "I should have been more explicit. I'm merely escorting the young lady to Greeneville. Her name is Miss Jessica—"

"Jessica *Jane*," she quickly inserted, not wanting to be called by her last name in case her father's notoriety had stretched this far. "I was named after my mother, Jessica Jane Hargrave of the Baltimore Hargraves."

Sliding off her horse into Mr. Finch's arms, she suddenly realized her brother would've ridden on this trail, passed this very cabin, and that was of far more importance. "Sir," she asked as her feet touched the ground. "Perchance did a Spencer Whitman ever pass this way? Dark haired like me, but, of course, with much bluer eyes."

The square-jawed young fellow glanced off as if in thought, then shook his head. "Nay, that name don't have a ring to it. How long ago was it? Last month? During the summer?"

"Dear me, no. Four summers past would be more accurate."

"I'm sorry, miss, but we've only been here three." Stomping his feet against the cold, he turned toward the door. "You best go on in 'fore you freeze to death."

Just as she was steeling herself to do so, the door swung wide, and a reedlike girl stood in the opening, holding a babe while two small children clung to her skimpy day gown. To Jessica's surprise, the young woman's clothing had no more shape or fullness than that of the deerskin she'd worn until today . . . no tightness at the waist, no gathered skirt, no petticoats underneath. The undyed cloth of rough homespun had several stains spotting it. And her hair . . . it wasn't up in a neat knot, but pulled back in a single plait with loose strands of dull brown hanging down the sides of a heart-shaped face.

"How do, ma'am," the young mother said, her voice uncertain as she shifted the babe to one bony hip and began tucking the flyaway strands back into her braid. "'Tis a pure joy to have you."

"How do you do," Jessica returned, remembering to curtsy as Mr. Reardon had taught her. And that's when she saw them—the woman's eyes. They were almost as pale as hers. Feeling an immediate kinship with the woman, Jessica smiled. "My name is Jessica. It would be a supreme kindness if you'd bestow yours upon me?"

Mistress Finch seemed surprised by Jessica's words, but for only a second. She smiled as if she truly was pleased to meet her. "Winifred. But folks just call me Winnie. Come on in out of the cold." She stepped back, making way for Jessica to enter.

The two little round faces peeking from behind their mother's legs moved back with her.

"We are most obliged for your hospitality, Mistress Finch," Mr. Reardon said, coming alongside Jessica. Then he bent to her ear.

"Will you be all right whilst Mr. Finch and I put away the animals?"

Jessica glanced back at the woman—the first her own age she ever remembered seeing—and knew she had absolutely nothing to fear. "Aye, we'll be just fine."

As they all crowded onto benches lining both sides of the trestle table, Noah couldn't have been more proud of Jessica. From the moment she'd walked into the crudely furnished dwelling, she'd pitched right in as if she lived there. She'd finished the meal Mistress Finch had been preparing, while the young mother tended a baby who, from the odor it had emitted, sorely needed it. The little tyke now slept peacefully in a crate on the far side of the room.

Sitting across from Jessica, Noah was tempted to reach over and squeeze her hand but knew that would prompt more questions all around. He pulled his gaze away to the little fuzzy-headed girl perched on her knees between the two women. The sexes had naturally separated, with the boy child wedged between him and Duncan Finch. "What's your name?" he asked in his friendliest voice of the tiny girl.

Nonetheless he frightened her. She buried her cherubic face in her mother's side.

Then Noah felt his sleeve being tugged. The boy. No more than four, he had the same serious blue eyes and blond hair as his sister. "Her name is Susie. She's a-skeert of big men. I'm not."

"That's real good to know. And what might your name be?"

The boy sat a bit straighter. "Timothy Thomas. Just like my grampa," he said with a slight lisp. "He's comin' to see us next summer. Gramma, too."

Trying not to grin at the child's exuberance, Noah replied, "You must really be looking forward to that." Then Noah peered over

142

him to his father. "I'm certain your folks will be proud and pleased with all you've accomplished here."

"Hope so," Finch replied, pouring a cup of milk from a dented pitcher. But his words didn't hold much confidence.

Noah began to wonder if Duncan and his Winnie had recklessly run off together. That would explain why this was one of the most poorly equipped farmsteads he'd ever seen. And the young man didn't look much older than Drew, not nearly old enough to have three children and the sole responsibility of this farm. At the thought, Noah came to a sudden decision. He'd leave them all the salt he could spare. The preservative might very well be vital to their survival this winter.

"Mr. Reardon," the young husband said, drawing him out of his reverie, "we'd be plumb honored if a educated man like yourself would give the blessing."

Noah glanced around and saw that no one had begun filling the wooden trenchers with the simple meal of fried venison, boiled carrots, and corn bread. Everyone had been waiting expectantly. While he'd been sitting here judging this struggling little family, they had been intent on following the true order of things. "I thank you for the honor," he said, humbled. "Shall we bow our heads?"

Knowing his last words had been unnecessary where the Finches were concerned, he'd said it to remind Jessica. Then, while blessing the food and this household, he stole a peek at her, just to make sure she'd followed his instructions. But he didn't have to worry on her account either. Fact was, with those thick dark lashes fanning her cheeks and that ruffled mobcap framing her face, she could have been one of God's own angels herself.

He stumbled over his final words as if he were a dunce of a schoolboy. When he'd said "Amen" and they all started filling their trenchers using hand-carved spoons, Noah had to discipline his gaze from wandering across the table to her. Even in this smoke-blackened cabin and surrounded by the crudest of furnishings, even in the jaundiced yellow light of the tallow candles, Jessica glowed with beauty.

Yet she had no idea.

Winnie Finch leaned past her daughter to whisper something to Jessica. A small smile instantly appeared, and a blush added color to Jessica's cheeks.

The young mistress had undoubtedly read his thoughts and informed her . . . thoughts that he never should have given place. Shortly the two of them would be saying farewell, and most likely he'd never see her again. He knew, though, he'd be wondering about her and her quest for a very long time to come. And the Lord. Would she one day turn to the Lord?

Noah made a point of turning to Duncan Finch. It was past time to strike up a conversation with the farmer centered on safer subjects, such as crop yields and animal husbandry.

But within mere minutes the topic was redirected again when Noah asked young Finch if he'd tried dogwood bark for his animals' skin ailments.

The lad turned to his wife. "Did you hear that, Winnie? Next time ol' Caesar gets a rash, we'll just cook us up a good thick poultice."

Again Noah was humbled by the young man. At the Finch table everyone was included in the conversations.

Winnie shrugged. "It certainly couldn't hurt."

Jessica jumped in as if she'd known the Finches all her life. "The Indians have always applied dogwood to their dogs. That's why the tree is named that."

"My, my, Miss Jessica," Winnie said, slanting a sly glance at Noah, "that's real clever of you, knowin' things such as that." Noah had read Mistress Finch's motives correctly early on. Their young hostess had matchmaking on her mind.

But at the moment, Noah was more concerned that Jessica didn't say anything further about the Indians. Although there hadn't been any trouble with the tribes in the proximity of the Watauga settlements for several years, the fact that Jessica's pa had traded with them during peacetime and war might not set well with frontier folk. Most families west of the seaboard had suffered the loss of at least one of their own due to Indian attack.

He quickly changed the topic. "Miss Jessica has many fine qualities. One is her exceptional reading voice. Perhaps after supper she can read to us out of the Bible I brought."

Jessica's lips parted in astonishment by his mention of what he'd discovered this afternoon.

"You can read?" Winnie cried. "Oh, my yes, please read to us. I ain't heard no Bible readin' since we come here. Psalm one hundred. Read that. It always makes me happy to hear about folks all singin' and happy together."

From the wary tilt of Jessica's head, Noah knew she was again caught off guard, but he wasn't certain if it was because Winnie couldn't read, or if Jessica was wondering where Psalms was located in the big book.

Finch echoed his wife's sentiments. "Aye, that would be pure pleasure. But, Winnie, would you mind if Miss Jessica reads Psalm one twenty-one first? I'm not certain if I still remember all the words." He turned to Noah. "They been a real help to me."

Touched by the man's sincerity, Noah rose from the table. "I'll go get the Bible now. No sense letting half the evening go to waste." As he did, he caught Jessica gazing up at him with a searching look. As if by lightning, he was struck with the knowledge that they'd been meant to spend the night here . . . for Jessica's sake as much as for these good people's. Not only would she be exposed to God's love through this family's faith and hope, she'd also receive some much-needed confidence.

As he crossed the room to fetch his saddlebag, he also knew he needn't worry about Jessica ever again—the Lord would continue to look after her, even after they parted. If he had doubted before, he didn't any longer. Someone besides him was petitioning God on her behalf . . . someone she was on her way to.

But, oh, how he would miss seeing this butterfly, so newly out of her cocoon, stretch her wings to fly. Toward heaven, he entreated, *Lord, I do pray that she truly sees your eternal love in her deliverance and flies to you.*

15

"'Twas an unprecedented pleasure," Jessica said the next afternoon when the old deer trail widened enough for her to come alongside Noah. "Undeniably a halcyon experience, sojourning with the Finches," she added, raising her voice above the roar coming up from the Nolachucky River.

"Aye, quite pleasurable." Noah glanced over at her sitting sideways on her saddle with one knee hooked above the scant pommel. He couldn't help smiling . . . not merely for the happy mood she'd been in since they departed the young family early this morning, but because of her choice of words. Still, he knew he'd have to speak to her about it. When they'd passed through the Bend River settlement, there'd been merely the usual friendly exchanges until she used one of her rarely spoken words. The man she addressed gaped when such a high-flown word came from the mouth of such a plainly dressed miss.

Though he'd been putting it off, he couldn't wait any longer. In a few minutes they'd be riding into Greeneville, the closest thing to a town this side of the mountains.

"Jessica, I don't want to upset you, but there's something I've been meaning to speak to you about."

Despite his plea, the happiness fled her face. She raised a hand above her eyes to block the slanting sunlight and stared warily. "What's amiss?"

"Like I said, it's not anything that can't be effortlessly altered. It's about your using long words, such as *unprecedented*. Except for college professors and orators, most folks here in America don't talk like that. Long words like *sojourning*, for instance, are used in newspaper articles and essays, not in everyday conversation."

She stared at him, a crease deepening above her pert nose. "I don't understand. You incorporate them. You just used two long ones—*effortlessly* and *conversation*. Those have considerably more letters than *sojourn*."

She had him there. Since childhood, he'd had his own fascination with the English language. Plus, he'd always had rather grand dreams of someday hobnobbing with men the likes of Benjamin Franklin and Thomas Jefferson. He reined his horse closer to hers. "You're right, I do. My pa knew I had a penchant for learning. He planned to send me to a college. But that very year, classes were suspended because all the young lads wanted to join Washington's army. Besides, at the age of fifteen I thought fighting for freedom and justice sounded absolutely honorable and righteous *and*—" he grinned—"romantically adventurous. My brother Ike and I, we took off for Boston to join up."

"Then it must not be that unusual for lads to run away from home. All my brothers left to gain their freedom too."

"Aye, but there's a sad difference. Your brothers were running away from your pa's tyranny. We were running toward the ideal of ending British oppression. And we had the assurance of our family's prayers, and a home and hearth awaiting us when we returned."

"Spencer was going home . . . to Baltimore." The light was suddenly back in her eyes. She reached out and squeezed his arm. "We're almost to Greeneville. There'll be a letter from him. He promised he'd leave word. I know it's a long way from the Mississippi, but he grew up in the forest. I'm certain he found his way this far."

"I think so too," he assured her, though he only half believed it himself . . . too many miles through too many tribes' sacred hunting grounds. He put a gloved hand over her bare one, raw and chapped from the cold. "Do remind me to get you some gloves or mittens or something."

Her smile was just for him when she withdrew her hand. "Do you think the trading post will have some that are already made?"

"It's a big enough settlement. But if the store doesn't, we'll do what we did before—find a woman willing to part with a pair. But speaking of Greeneville, try not to use big words. You might not be understood anyway. Few girls are ever schooled in the language arts. Fact is, a good many don't even know how to read."

"Even in Baltimore?"

"Mayhap a few more there would read. But mostly it would be young misses of the wealthier families who have the leisure to pursue all the arts and sciences."

Surprisingly, her eyes narrowed and her generous lips stiffened into a hard angry line. "Father taught me all those words to make me an outcast in the white world, didn't he? Just as he used my eyes with the Indians. He never loved me as he said. He was nothing but a mean, spiteful villain." Then just as abruptly, her features smoothed out again. Taking a deep breath, she returned to the prior topic. "Tell me more about Baltimore ladies."

He knew this new revelation about her pa had cut deep. Yet he knew if she were ever to become a Christian, she'd have to forgive the man. There was so much Noah wished he had time to tell her about that, but she needed time for her anger to cool. He answered her question instead. "A young miss in the city learns what is known as the gentle arts. Fancy stitchery, how to set a table properly—like Keaton and I showed you. The young misses are usually taught some form of music to perform for friends and family. The proper way to dress and walk, the art of conversation. Some of the more affluent are taught to read enough to create invitations in a lovely, practiced script and so they might correspond with acquaintances." Lorna and her letters to him came to mind . . . letters, he now realized, that had no substance whatsoever, only girlish references to the adventure of coming west to be with him.

"My mother could read and write," Jessica reminded him, bringing him out of his morbid reverie. "So she must have been from an affluent family. Wouldn't you say?"

"Possibly. Or she could have been someone as eager to learn as you." He couldn't help smiling again. She always brought him out of the dreariest moments.

"But you haven't said what a young miss does during the rest of her day. Getting dressed and singing and talking simply cannot take up all that much time. You said most of them don't cook or clean. Do they just sit around and sew or write letters for the remainder of the day? I can't imagine anyone wanting to do that. They'd have nothing but sore fingers and tired eyes."

Noah pressed his lips together, trying to contain his growing amusement. "Young ladies do seem to find a plethora of things to talk about—what with parties to plan, the latest fashions from Paris, gentleman callers. . . ." Another remembrance of Lorna and her capricious flirting and chatter came to mind. He couldn't imagine why he'd thought she'd ever settle for being a frontier wife. He returned his attention to Jessica. "I really don't know what takes up all their time. For the most part Southern ladies have slaves to cook and keep house. But what I do know is that they *aren't* spending time learning big words," he added with a chuckle.

"Slaves? Indian slaves or the dark-skinned folk from Africa?" She didn't sound all that pleased.

"From Africa mostly," he said, wishing he hadn't mentioned the controversial subject. Colonists had always condemned the Indians for taking white people captive and making slaves of them, yet many of his people were doing the same to the Africans.

"I saw an African once," she mused. "His skin was deeper brown than any Indian I ever saw. Almost black. He was with a trader who stopped off at a post we had out West on the Cumberland. They were on their way to trade along the Mississippi. But what I remember most was how exceptionally distressed the slave was. He'd been taken from his wife and children, forced to come overmountain with his master. He didn't know if he'd ever see them again. And the Chickasaw were uncommonly interested in his hair. It was thicker and curlier than a buffalo's. But his master wouldn't let him have so much as a hunting knife to protect himself."

Noah understood her meaning. "I was hoping when we fought for America's freedom, it would be for everyone. Some of the lawmakers in the Philadelphia Congress have been arguing to free the Africans, but the opposition is fierce. It seems a Southern gentleman gauges his worth by the quality of his horseflesh and the number of his slaves."

"But doesn't your Bible say we're to treat our neighbors as we would ourselves?"

"Aye, but I'm afraid some folks get mighty picky when it comes to deciding who is or isn't their neighbor."

"Does Baltimore have any of these Southern gentlemen?"

"Yes. Quite a number of them."

Jessica's gaze slid away. "I had always dreamed that everything would be perfect there. I suppose that was childish of me."

"A lovely dream nonetheless. But, I'm sad to say, there's

precious little perfection this side of heaven." *You do come close though,* he wanted to add, *with your bright mind and your pixielike face framing those miraculous eyes.*

As the shadows lengthened in the weak sun, farmsteads became more frequent, until there was almost as much cleared land as forest. A man burning a pile of weeds waved as they passed. Any time now, buildings that were lined up on the town-sized lots of Greeneville would come into view. And at any minute now, he'd probably never be alone with Jessica again. The thought stabbed at his heart.

Another farmer waved, and Jessica waved cheerily back. She did love feeling accepted . . . which reminded Noah he'd never finished talking to her about her pretentious vocabulary. He guided his horse close again. "Getting back to what we were talking about— your use of unusual words. I don't want to mention it in front of others, so I'll merely rub my hand over my jaw any time you use one that's not common. Like so," he said, demonstrating. "At least until we bid each other farewell."

Her eyes instantly filled with emotion.

The sight only made him feel worse.

"Until we bid farewell," she barely whispered. Then suddenly she blinked away the moment and returned to the subject. "I always pestered Father for the meaning of every word I read . . . the one thing he was always patient about. And he always reveled in debating the latest political theories with me."

"I, too, have enjoyed all of our discussions." And he'd miss them too, wretchedly, when they came to an end. "Particularly our ones about the Bible."

He'd hoped for a response from her, but instead she cried, "Look! We're coming into Greeneville."

Jessica's excitement had been building all day. Even in the chill weather, people had been out on the trail. They'd passed no less than twenty, young and old, and not just on horseback. She'd ridden by several driving two-wheeled carts, and even one up on the seat of a very rumbly four-wheeled wagon. And there was so much cleared land—at every spot that was even remotely level. And cabins. All day, she hadn't had a breath of air that wasn't laced with woodsmoke from their hearth fires.

And now they were riding into a place where cabins were lined up right next to each other on both sides of the trail, with other lanes crossing the main trail with more cabins on them. And all with glass windows . . . that had people staring out of them as she and Mr. Reardon passed. And cooking smells coming from every direction, dogs barking. Other sounds that replaced those of the forest, a hammer pounding, an axe chopping wood. A door slammed. Children laughing.

It brought back memories of her early years among the Indians when her family lived near the big Shawnee town of Chillicothe on the Little Miami. Before Father insisted they pack up and leave in the middle of the night.

Two men stood arguing on the porch of a many-windowed cabin, steam puffing from their mouths as if they were chimneys. Passing by them, she heard one insist there was no need for a federal constitution. Any other time she would have wanted to stop and hear more about the happenings in Philadelphia, but not today. Today was the day she would learn about her brother.

She reined closer to Mr. Reardon. "Which direction to the place where they keep the letters?"

He pointed up the mud-churned road to a cabin on the right. A pole jutted out from one of the porch posts and a colorful cloth hung from it, fluttering on the afternoon breeze . . . red and white stripes, and in one corner, a circle of stars in a blue square . . . much different from the British Union Jack her father used to fly.

On a sign hanging from the porch roof were the words, *Pottinger's Dry Goods Store.* "That's where the postrider brings the letters—at least it was the last time I was here," Mr. Reardon said, pointing toward the log structure.

Her heart, already beating fast, began pounding like a Muskogee drum. Kicking her mount in the flank, she sent the gelding trotting toward the front steps—and almost lost her hold, riding in this ridiculous sideways fashion Mr. Reardon insisted upon.

But it made dismounting all the quicker. Not waiting to be helped down as Mr. Reardon had told her was proper, she slid to the ground and raced up three graduating wood rounds to the porch. Remembering she hadn't secured her rough-coated mount, she turned back and saw Mr. Reardon was taking care of that chore for her.

"That was thoughtless of me," she said. "I do apologize."

With a grin, this kindest of men waved her on. "I'll meet you inside."

Once through the door, it took a moment for her eyes to adjust to the darkness. They gravitated past shadowy stacks and piles to the firelight of a giant hearth. A few feet this side of it, two men sat in chairs.

Both had turned toward her.

One rose and came in her direction. Almost as short as she, he waddled like a walking barrel. "Can I help you, miss?" he asked, the folds of fat jiggling from his chin.

Jessica had no idea anyone could get that round. She caught herself staring. "Aye. I came to fetch a letter from my brother. A letter from Spencer Whitman. Do you still keep letters here?"

"Aye, that we do. But I need to know who the letter is to, not from."

"It's to me. Jessica Whitman. Or he might have written Jessica Jones—I don't know which."

"Ah, you've married," he said, then turned away toward one of the shelf-lined walls before she could correct him. "Well, I have been holding some for a Jessica Whitman. Fact is, I was thinkin' about throwin' 'em away; they been gatherin' dust so long."

"*Them?* There are more than one?"

"Aye. Two, in fact."

The door opened, and Mr. Reardon entered on a blast of cold air.

Jessica dashed to him and dragged him back with her. "There are two letters!"

"That's wonderful," he said, but in a subdued voice . . . and she thought he'd be as thrilled as she.

She turned back to the storekeeper.

And the man held them out to her!

She snatched them away and ran to the nearest squares of window glass. Her hands shook as she stared at first one, then the other. There it was—her name on each one of them. One, a smudged, water-stained square, also had written on it: *Greeneville, Watauga settlements, North Carolina Territory,* and in the upper corner, strange symbols. But there was nothing else. She flipped both of them over. Still nothing written anywhere, only big globbed-on spots of wax. Tears popped into her eyes. Hands shaking, she held them out to Mr. Reardon and choked out, "He didn't write anything but my name."

In two swift strides Mr. Reardon was at her side. "You have to open them, Miss Jessica." Pulling a sheathed knife from his belt, he sliced away the wax and unfolded the heavy paper, spreading it flat.

Wiping away her tears, she tried to laugh at her ignorance. "At least the letters prove he did get this far—from the Mississippi."

"Aye. He was a brave lad to come all this way alone." Mr. Reardon smoothed out the paper and handed it to her. "I pray this says everything you want to hear."

Her gaze flew to Spencer's words.

*If you are reading this letter, I know you and Little Bob got away
from Father and reached this place before I could come back for you.
I am on my way over the mountain to Baltimore. I will post another
letter to this town when I get there.*

Jessica turned it over on the other side, but there was nothing else.
A bit disappointed, she looked up at Mr. Reardon's waiting eyes.
"Spencer only said he was on his way to Baltimore. That's all."

"This one is from Virginia." Mr. Reardon handed her the
second missive.

With eager hands, she unfolded it. It had so many more words.

Dear Jaybird and Little Bob,
*I am in a town called Fredericksburg. It's in the colony of Vir-
ginia, or state, as they call themselves now. I met a postrider, and he
said he would make certain this letter gets all the way to Greeneville.
I have been traveling for 21 days since I left there. I had to trade
horses in a settlement at Lynches Ferry. Meshewa's hoof split.*

"Oh, that's too bad." Jessica looked up from the letter. "Spencer
had to trade off his black stallion at a place called Lynches Ferry.
He loved that horse."

"That is a shame," Mr. Reardon commiserated. "But crossing
the mountains can be hard on animals. Read on. What else does
your brother say?"

"I'll read it aloud," she said, remembering that Mr. Reardon
thought she had a lovely reading voice. "He said he was writing
from Fredericksburg," she recapped. "Oh, and here he says, 'The
postrider just came from Baltimore. He says it is an easy three
days' ride north of here. I will write you again as soon as I find
Mother's family. I can hardly wait for you and Little Bob to come
and see all the wonders I have seen. People here are all rich. I miss
you very much. Spencer.'"

"Spencer mentioned Little Bob," Mr. Reardon mused. "But then he wouldn't have known your little brother ran away with the Muskogee."

"He doesn't even know we left Chickasaw country." Then a dreaded thought resurfaced. "Do you think he went back there looking for us, and the Indians killed him over Father's cheating?"

Mr. Reardon wrapped an arm around her. "Don't make hasty assumptions." He turned toward the storekeeper, who'd gone back to sit by the fire. "Sir, are you certain these are the only two letters?"

"Aye," the portly man said. "Only the two."

"What about one for Robert Whitman?" Jessica asked in desperation. "Is there one with my little brother's name on it?"

"'Fraid not, ma'am."

"But there has to be another. He said he'd write from Balti-more." She swung back to Mr. Reardon and waved the letters at him. "Something terrible must have happened to him. A land pirate must've waylaid him before he reached Baltimore." Great waves of trembling shook her body.

Mr. Reardon caught hold of her. "Don't think the worst. Any number of things could have happened. Other letters from him might have been lost. The mail wasn't all that dependable in eighty-two. The peace treaty with the British had yet to be signed, and so many of us were still away with Washington's army."

"But Spencer never came for us. He would've come. He always took care of us. Protected us from Father. Spencer wouldn't just get so caught up in the wonders of Baltimore that he would forget us. Would he?" That thought was even more painful. She had to learn the truth.

Resolved to do just that, she pushed away from Mr. Reardon. "I've got to find my brother. I'm going after him. Now."

16

"Be reasonable," Noah said, drawing Jessica away from the store-keeper. "It may be only a week or so into November, but it already looks like we're in for an early winter. To start overmountain now would be foolhardy. We could send an inquiry by postrider to Fredericksburg and Baltimore."

"If a postrider can make it overmountain, so can I. I'll go with him." She swung back to the round little storekeeper. "Sir, where might I find the postrider?"

Mr. Pottinger, trudging back to his chair by the fire, stopped and showed his impatience with a shake of his jowls. "Postrider Clayborne is gone. He stops only long enough to drop off the latest pouch of letters, then heads straight back to Virginy. 'Specially now with winter comin' on."

"How soon before he returns?"

One of the storekeeper's paunchy cheeks bunched. "He ain't comin' again. Not till next spring."

Jessica turned back to Noah. "So it's too late to send an inquiry.

159

I'm going. Snow or no snow. Draw me a map of the quickest route to Baltimore."

"You can't take off by yourself." But the determination in her eyes told him something different. "I understand your need to go investigate. Perhaps . . ." He lifted his voice loud enough to reach the storekeeper, who'd just returned to the chair beside his grizzle-haired friend. "Mr. Pottinger, do either of you know of anyone trekking overmountain anytime soon?"

The two older men looked at each other and shook their heads.

"Nay." The storekeeper shrugged. "This time of year all the traffic is comin' our way. Mostly beaver trappers headin' on down the Tennessee, hopin' to catch themselves some prime winter pelts."

Noah turned back to Jessica.

Her lips had tightened into a thin line. "I don't really need anyone else. Merely an accurate map." She clutched her brother's letters to her stubbornly. "You said yourself there aren't any Indians east of here. And I'm exceedingly capable of taking care of myself. I know how to construct a shelter against any storm that might blast my way. And if a bear happens by, I'll simply have him for breakfast. And lunch and dinner," she added with a tight smile.

"Hear me, Miss Jessica. That would be the least of the dangers. Once you reach the other side of the mountains, a young woman simply cannot travel the roads unescorted. You would find yourself prey to some much craftier stalkers than bears or wolves. Men, shall we say, of unsavory character."

Her frozen expression told him she wasn't being swayed one whit.

Maybe she'd be more reasonable in the morning. He wheeled around and again addressed Mr. Pottinger. "Is there a place where we can get something to eat and lodging for the night?"

"Aye, Mr. Jones. Over to Maloney's Ordinary. Just head on out like you was on your way to Jonesborough. Last place on the left."

"Thank you. The name's not Jones, though. It's Reardon. My brothers and I have a valley about a week's ride west of here. Off Avery's Trace."

"I see," the man said, but by his expression, he was obviously still confused.

Taking Jessica by the arm, Noah strode out the door and was halfway to the horses before he realized why the man had called him Jones. The storekeeper had thought Jessica was married to him. That would need to be clarified, especially if Jessica were to stay in Greeneville until he could be assured she had a proper escort to Baltimore.

Noah was almost upon the ordinary before he spotted it between two white oaks. Set aways off the road, the two-story log house stood in front of several outbuildings and horse corrals, with fields of withering crops stretching to the rear. Like most folks in the new settlements, the Maloneys had more than one source of income.

A lad of about twelve came out the main entrance just as he and Jessica rode up to the front,

"How do," the boy called, an eager expression on his freckled face. "From whence do ye hail?"

"From out past Henry's Station," Noah said as he dismounted. He dug into an inside pocket and came out with a few pence for the lad. "Would you mind putting up our horses and feeding them? We'll be staying the night. And bring our totes in to us, if you'd be so kind."

"Aye, aye," the skinny kid agreed enthusiastically, his gaze locked onto the coppers in his hand.

Noah then reached up for Jessica.

She'd pulled her deerskin dress out of her bedroll and had it clutched to her—the one with her stolen coins sewn in it. "Nothing you can say will change my mind," she said, coming down into his arms. "I'm leaving tomorrow."

"I don't know about you, but I'm powerful hungry." He'd evade

the issue for the time being. At least she wasn't balking about waiting until morning. "Let's go inside and get settled. Then we'll
talk."

Without acknowledging his words, Jessica marched ahead of
him through the entrance with her woodsy garment tucked under
an arm.

The room was well lit with several candles set on each of four
trestle tables. Without even a second's hesitation, Jessica turned
toward the fireplace and hastened past the tables, the second of
which succored the only other customers, a trio of men who took
up one end. She then walked straight to a dust-capped and aproned
woman stooped at the hearth.

The generously fleshed-out mistress of middle years stopped
stirring a pot, which, as the hearty aroma indicated, held a stew of
beef or buffalo and vegetables.

Noah's stomach growled in anticipation. He felt as if he could
eat half a cow himself.

The woman glanced back at Jessica. "Welcome, strangers. I'm
Mistress Maloney, at your service. Are ye here just for supper, or
would you like a room for the night?"

"Do you have a room for just me?" Jessica asked.

The proprietress straightened up. "Aye, I reckon, lessen we get
more womenfolk comin' in." Mistress Maloney shifted her gaze
to Noah. Her brows were set deep beneath a thin line of brows
seemed all the more inquisitive. "Does it suit you, sir, sleepin' by
the fire? I only got the one room."

"That's fine." Noah glanced back at the hearth. Another night
on a hard floor.

"Could you direct me to my room now?" Jessica asked. Obviously, she couldn't wait to get away from him.

"Back yonder." The woman pointed to the opposite end of the
room where two doors flanked a long serving counter. "The door

to the right. You go freshen up, and I'll have supper on the table in a few minutes."

Without a word to Noah, Jessica left him . . . as if they were total strangers.

He stared after her. Was this how it would end? Her walking away without so much as a thank you? Literally shunning him or any further advice or assistance he might wish to offer?

Abruptly, Jessica turned back. "Mr. Reardon? Aren't you coming? I need you."

A deaf man couldn't have missed the scuffs and rustling sounds of every head in the room turning to stare.

Noah felt compelled to explain . . . until he realized a recounting of how they came to be together might sound more damaging than his silence. Schooling his features, he strode after Jessica.

"Close the door, and give me your knife," she ordered as soon as he entered the room.

"It's best if we leave it ajar," he said, surveying the sparse quarters that held nothing but a big sagging bed and a long bench that served as both seat and stand for a blackened lamp. The landlady had contributed a bit of color, though, with a quilt and curtains that were both made from patches of many hues.

"Your knife," she repeated, holding out her hand impatiently.

He handed it to her. "What are you up to?"

"I need to rip the coins out of my day gown." Turning the garment inside out, she sank onto the bed and held the newly exposed deerskin within a shaft of late afternoon light. "I need you to figure out how much I have and what it can be traded for on my journey to Baltimore."

Noah couldn't believe his eyes. Coins were sewn along both inner seams of the simple two-piece shift in an unbroken line and attached by what looked like the tail hairs of a horse. He sat down beside her, and she handed him the first, a gold coin with Spanish writing, but the number *20* was plain enough. And from its size, he judged it to be worth at least ten English pounds!

"Spencer told me to take care when I tried for the gold ones. He said Father would be more apt to notice them missing, so I have a lot more silver and copper."

True enough, she did, but by the time Noah estimated the value of the mostly English coinage—from those as nonconsequential as a copper penny to a twenty-pound gold piece—he estimated she had close to one hundred fifteen pounds sterling . . . more money than he'd ever had at one time in all his twenty-six years. And they were laid out on bedding made from nothing but poor folks' scraps.

"Will this be enough to get me to Baltimore, Mr. Reardon? I can hunt my supper along the way. And I don't have to stay in fancy places like Mr. Keaton's, or even one not quite so shiny—like this room." She grabbed his arm and shook it. "Mr. Reardon, say something. Is it enough to buy another horse if I need to?"

Fact was, with that much money, she didn't need him at all. Half the men in Greeneville would jump at the chance to escort her to Baltimore for a quarter of what lay there—even in winter. But with the temptation of that much money, not to mention the beauty of the lass herself, who could be trusted? Especially since he didn't know the true character of a single soul in this valley.

"*Mr. Reardon!*" Jessica was losing patience.

He held her in his gaze. "This is a great deal of money. It will easily take you to Baltimore, but—"

She leapt to her feet. "I know what you're going to say. It's not my money—it's Father's. Well, I've been deliberating on that, and I say he owes it to me. Between his cheating the Indians and intentionally making me the object of their fear and mistrust, not to mention his causing me to be the brunt of the trappers' ridicule. Truth is, I'm glad I stole from him. And if your god is the loving god you say he is, he'll side with me."

Noah shook his head. "Dearest Jessica, I know this is hard to understand sometimes, but merely because a person sins against you does not give you the right to sin against him. Since our Lord is willing to wash away every single wrong we ever committed or ever will, he expects us to forgive those who hurt us . . . to pray for those who spitefully use us."

Unyielding ice glowered back at him.

"I know this is a hard thing to hear, let alone do. But we can start by praying that you will have the desire to forgive him, then maybe pray for your pa to repent his ways."

The ice shattered into astonishment. "Pray for him?"

"Wouldn't it be a wonderful miracle to see him change into a loving parent?" Even as Noah said the words, he himself found them difficult to conceive. Pizar Whitman repentant? And if his memories of the foul-mouthed, rank-smelling man he'd known for less than a fortnight were still so raw, how could he expect one who had lived with him her whole life to believe it could happen? She'd probably never explored the possibility that loving fathers even existed. Yet he was asking her to embrace that idea as well as to believe in an *invisible* heavenly Father, one with what surely sounded like an unbelievable array of attributes—all-knowing, all-powerful, eternal . . . this God who doesn't merely love us, but is love.

All this while he told her that using the money she stole to find her lost brother would be wrong. In these, their last moments together, would he drive her from the very truth he'd been trying so diligently to help her see?

In that instant, Noah knew he couldn't leave Jessica just yet. He would take her overmountain, at least as far as Salem, North Carolina. To no one else would he entrust this precious young woman. He stood up and clasped her shoulders. "How about if I pray for your father until you're ready to join me? Until then, we can both pray that we have fair weather crossing the mountains."

She reared back from him. *"We?* You're going with me?"

"Aye."

Her expression was so ecstatic, tears stung his eyes.

"Someone has to be there to let you know when you're using one of those high-flown words," he explained with a smile.

Letting out a squeal, she threw her arms around his neck. "We'll most assuredly find Spencer now!" And she kissed him square on the mouth.

Caught off guard by her innocent expression of gratitude, Noah reeled at the sensation of her guileless kiss. Before he knew what he was doing, he found himself responding. His hand caught the back of her head, and he pulled her close, deepening the embrace, his lips exploring the sweet generosity of hers.

As the kiss suddenly, wondrously changed, a thrilling surge spiraled through Jessica with dizzying speed . . . all the way to the tips of her fingers and toes and back again, back to Mr. Reardon's mouth melding with hers . . . urgently . . . fervently . . . boldly . . .

A loud clanging crashed into Jessica's senses. Metal on metal. Intruding.

Mr. Reardon ripped himself away from her. "The supper bell! It's time to go in for supper." His words came out in a rush.

Jessica's head whirled, and she had a hard time concentrating on anything but the mouth that had so enthralled her. He'd taken over her kiss of gratitude and made it his own, and sent her soaring into an exhilaration she'd never known existed.

"Jessica, look at me."

It took a moment to make sense of those words. When she did and gazed up at him, he averted his own eyes.

But he kept talking as if his very life depended on it. "Pick up your money and keep it out of sight. That sum would be too tempting to anyone inclined toward thievery. The trip over the mountain will have enough difficulties without us being waylaid out on some lonely trail."

Jessica glanced down to the many-colored quilt. The coins did make a sizable pile. She started loading them into the pocket of her faded yellow skirt.

"No." He caught her wrist. Then just as abruptly, he let go. "They'll jangle." Reaching inside his coat, he withdrew a kerchief and spread it beside the coins. After placing all the money on it, he cross-tied the ends tightly, then handed it to her. "Just until you get them sewn inside your shift again. No one would ever expect that worn-out deerskin to be concealing so much value."

As she stuffed the bulging kerchief into her pocket, her gaze gravitated up to his mouth. She wondered if it tingled as won-drously as hers still did. No, it couldn't. The man looked as if he'd been slapped instead of kissed, and he was bent on getting out of the room . . . away from being alone with her.

He strode to the partially open door. "They're waiting supper on us."

Her disappointment gnawed worse than her hunger. And embarrassment. Had she shamed herself by throwing herself at him? Waiting until he was several feet ahead of her, she followed him into the main room.

The proprietress was busy ladling stew into wooden bowls that lined both sides of the long table where the customers sat. Instead of three men, there were now four seated at the end closest to the fire. All of them, along with the woman, stared unabashedly as Jessica and Mr. Reardon came toward them. Had they witnessed her shame?

She slowed to a stop. How could she face them or Mr. Reardon?

Mr. Reardon didn't give her a chance to escape. He returned for her. With his hand at the small of her back, he hurried her to the table where four extra bowls were set out—two, she assumed, were for them.

He helped her out of her cloak, then seated her beside one of the men on the long bench. Then just as he was about to take his own place beside her, the front door banged open.

In came the freckle-nosed lad who'd been tending their horses. He was burdened down with most of their gear.

"Just leave it by the door," Mr. Reardon said, striding toward the boy. "I'll separate my necessaries from Miss Whitman's after supper," he added with a backward glance to the woman with the ladle.

Letting everything fall in a heap, the lad ran for the table and hopped over the bench to sit beside Jessica—the last vacancy on that side. Mr. Reardon's place.

Jessica didn't know which would be worse—to have Mr. Reardon beside her or across the table at close staring distance. She tried to keep her humiliation from showing as he sat down, especially since the older woman had moved beside her to fill her bowl, not to mention all the others who were still staring.

Lowering her gaze, she tried to concentrate on her stew, as the proprietress filled the lad's bowl then moved around to the other side to spoon the beef and vegetables into Mr. Reardon's.

At the far end of the table, slurping of broth commenced as some of the men began to eat.

"Thank you," Mr. Reardon said to Mistress Maloney when she'd finished. He then turned toward the others. "I'm going to give thanks to the Lord now for our food. If any of you would care to share in the blessing . . ."

He left the sentence unfinished, but no more needed to be said. Those with spoons in their hands instantly put them in their bowls and bowed their heads.

The proprietress, too, perched on the bench beside Mr. Reardon—one more reminder that this god Mr. Reardon prized so much was not merely known but revered by the white people wherever she'd gone. She remembered the cross next to her skin.

Even as far away as Baltimore they worshiped him. Yet no one else seemed to mind how very demanding this god was. He expected far too much.

"Father in heaven," Mr. Reardon began, "we thank you for this bounty we are about to partake. I ask your blessing on this household and those who prepared the food. And I ask your merciful protection for Miss Jessica and myself as we embark on our trek over the mountain. We make this plea in the precious name of Jesus. Amen."

As the others picked up their spoons to eat, all Jessica could think about was the fact that she would be trekking over the mountain with Mr. Reardon tomorrow. The two of them alone. How would she be able to look him in the eye, speak to him after she'd made such a fool of herself?

But at the time, she really did think he had enjoyed the kiss as much as she.

Mr. Reardon plucked the coffeepot from the center of the table. First he poured some into a pewter cup sitting before Jessica, then filled his own. He was waiting on her, just as if they were a married couple. At the mere thought, a whole new flurry of emotions careened inside her. She almost forgot to say the all-important thank-you. Managing a whisper, she lifted her gaze only as far as his chin.

Mr. Reardon turned to the proprietress who'd slipped into the place beside him. "Ma'am? Might you know of a woman who would be willing to go overmountain with us? Act as chaperone for Miss Whitman here? She would be more than fairly compensated. I know this is asking a lot, but we'd like to leave tomorrow or, at the latest, the next day."

Chaperone? What was a chaperone?

But that didn't matter nearly as much as the fact that Mr. Reardon now wanted some stranger to go with them. So he wouldn't have to be alone with her? Face what had happened? Had the kiss been so impermissible? Or had it simply repelled him? Did he see her as merely some soul he was trying to save for that jealous god of his?

"Mighty late in the year," a plainly dressed fellow said. His long face was exaggerated by a receding hairline. "I doubt if you've got enough money to lure any woman up into the mountains this time of year. Cold as it's been, you could find yourself hip deep in snow."

Mr. Reardon turned back to the proprietress. "It's vital for Miss Jessica to have a female companion. Without one, her good name would be at risk." He sounded almost desperate in his plea.

"To be sure," the older, well-fed woman agreed, her penetrating green gaze detouring to Jessica. "And I think I have just the person you're looking for—a widow woman by the name of Izzy Stowe. She lives down the road aways with her oldest son. When the post-rider come through the other day, he brung word that one of her daughters is gravely ill. Izzy wants to go to her in the worst way— her daughter has a bunch of young'uns. But Izzy's son can't leave his place to take her till he has his own family set for the winter. At meeting on the Sabbath, Widow Stowe asked us to keep them all in our prayers."

"I'd say the Lord does work in miraculous ways, doesn't he?" Mr. Reardon rendered that warm smile Jessica always loved to see. Until now.

"Could you direct me to where the Stowe family lives?" Mr. Reardon continued. "I'll go speak to the widow right after supper."

It was as if he couldn't wait to fetch the woman. Surely he must have felt something when they kissed. Or was it possible that Jessica had merely conjured the lightning bolt that struck when her lips met his?

No. They still vibrated. . . . Or was even that sensation only a foolish figment of her imagination?

Questions . . . questions that might prove incredibly embarrassing, but she needed answers. "Mr. Reardon, I'll ride along with you. Keep you company."

"*No!*" burst from him much too quickly. His gaze then chased off, skittering from person to person at the table before returning to her. "Remember, Miss Jessica? You have that sewing to do tonight."

17

The following afternoon Noah sat on his horse, holding the reins of his horse and of the three extras on the north side of a swift stream. The weather was cooperating with only a few scattered clouds to mar the frigid blue sky. He took this opportunity to rest himself as well as the animals while waiting for his two companions to cross the water and rejoin him.

He watched as the long-faced, long-boned, *long-on-advice* Widow Stowe plowed headlong into the stream. The graying woman, who looked to be on the downhill side of fifty, whipped her black-and-white pony into the current with the same relentless determination she'd displayed since she arrived at Maloney's before dawn this morning and rousted them out. With her daughter gravely ill, the widow was bent on making forty to fifty miles a day, every day, even crossing the mountains, to reach Salem.

To expedite their departure, Mistress Stowe had helped Noah secure the extra mounts and had even convinced her son to file Noah's deeds, then take messages back to Henry's Station for him.

The first was to Mr. Keaton, extending Noah's rental of the store-keeper's horses. The second ordered Drew to go directly home with the coal and salt and whatever supplies Keaton would let him have on credit, since Noah and the cash money would be going the opposite direction. The third went to Yarnell, asking him to accompany the lad back to Reardon Valley.

But what would his older brother, Ike, think? There was still so much to do to prepare their place for winter, yet here he was, chasing overmountain with a lass he had just met. Ike would think he'd lost not only his good sense but his mind . . . especially the way Drew would tell it.

The widow was halfway across the stream now, seated astride her horse as she'd insisted Jessica, too, ride for greater speed and balance. The long-legged woman held her feet above the splashing water while shouting to her beleaguered animal, urging it across even as she added a few stinging lashes with her riding crop.

She'd scarcely clambered up the bank before her shouts shifted to Noah. "Let's get a move on. Time's a-wastin'." She snagged the reins of her extra horse from his hand. "Come on."

Noah did his best not to show his exasperation as he remained where he was, waiting to see if Jessica's crossing would be equally safe . . . though he was hesitant to actually fix his gaze on her. On her face, anyway. Each time he had looked at her today, her expression had grown rigid and distant.

He was still mortified when he remembered his response to her spontaneous, innocent kiss. Under normal circumstances, it would have been sufficient cause for a speedy betrothal or, worse, corporal punishment at the hands of the young lady's father or brothers. Knowing how Miss Jessica had been raised, Noah held her blameless in what had transpired between them. No, the fault was all his. And, coward that he was finding himself to be, he'd made every effort to avoid her, which the Widow Stowe had helped him do by her insistence on riding between them. The rather gaunt older woman took her duties as chaperone every bit as seriously as she did this journey. She'd even insisted there would be no stopping except to change horses and saddles. Considering the mess he'd already made of things, he didn't oppose her.

Now, using the widow's urgent quest as his excuse, he swung his own bay gelding around and nudged him forward, hauling the remaining horses behind at the very second the front hooves of Jessica's gray mare dug into the pebbly bank.

Transferring the reins of Jessica's second mount to her would have felt too awkward. Yet as he heeled his horse into a trot, he couldn't shake his guilt for refusing to discuss what had transpired between them yester's eve. He was pretending nothing had happened. Worse, he was letting her think she was a fool for assuming something had.

But what could he say until he'd sorted out his own feelings— his true feelings? A person couldn't be in love with one person, thinking of only her day and night for over two years, then forget her in an instant and start loving someone else.

He couldn't imagine himself being that cavalier, that fickle. As young as he'd been when he joined the army, he'd stayed throughout, despite the scores of soldiers in his own battalion who had deserted, not to mention that entire New Jersey regiment that had gotten bored waiting for some action and had simply gone home. He'd not deserted Ike or the hard labor of building a new life on the frontier. Until now.

Yet none of that mattered, since Jessica had not repented of her sins and given her life to the Lord.

Still he should not have ignored the sweet lass all day. In no way was he practicing what he'd preached about neighborly love just the afternoon before. Such a poor witness he was. A veritable stumbling block. He was going to have to apologize, to explain. But how? Everything he'd thought to say sounded like an ultimatum—either him *and* God or nothing. And she'd already balked at forgiving her father. The wrong words could very well cement her resolve against all the precepts of the Bible.

Noah looked heavenward, hoping the right words would come. None did. He noticed his horse had slowed to a walk. Without looking back, he cowardly heeled the gelding to greater speed.

The remainder of the afternoon, they never slowed the hard pace, whether climbing up a rocky ridge or slogging down into a muddy, brush-strewn ravine. Their goal was to reach Carter's settlement before they stopped for the night . . . a fifty-mile stretch if it was ten.

Noah, more saddle-weary than he could ever remember being before, was beginning to think they wouldn't make it, when in the last fading light of dusk, he spotted light twinkling through the trees and heard the distant roar of the Watauga River. The idea of spending the night in the woods after this wrenching day did not appeal to him in the least, nor did the thought of spending it camped with the two women—with nothing to say.

At the first substantial-looking farmstead they neared, he called back to Widow Stowe, "We'll turn off here. See if they can put us up for the night."

Looking as tired and beat as Noah felt, Widow Stowe only nodded.

Shifting his reluctant gaze to Jessica a few yards behind the widow, he forced a smile—a pitiful travesty of a smile, he was sure.

As they rode into the clearing, a bearded man came out the front door of his two-story cabin, carrying a lantern. "How do," he called, his gravelly voice sounding more surprised than welcoming.

"We're on our way out to Salem. We'd be obliged if you could put us up for the night. I'm paying cash money." Thank Providence for that one thing—he did have over twenty dollars on him . . . money that had been intended for his valley's supplies. But that couldn't be helped. He refused to spend Jessica's stolen coins.

The farmer came forward, lifting up his light. "Where'd you come from, Jonesborough?"

"Much farther. Greeneville," Widow Stowe answered for Noah. "It's been a long day. Are you willin'?"

The man was noticeably taken aback by the widow's bluntness. "We'd be pleased to have you." Then, remembering his manners, he moved forward to help her down. "You must be in a mighty big hurry to ride such a long stretch in one day."

"That I am," she huffed. "We'll be off again at first light." Lifting her leg over the saddle, she winced.

Noah squelched a smile. In her big rush, she'd undoubtedly forgotten to take into account that she'd be so saddle sore, she'd be hard-pressed to walk tomorrow, let alone ride. And the horses, after being ridden this hard, even taking turns, would be just as stiff legged. However, the horse problem could be dealt with.

"Name's Noah Reardon," he said, introducing himself, "from west of Henry's Station. We'll be needing some fresh mounts for tomorrow. Can you or any of your neighbors help us out?"

The man lowered the widow to the ground, then held out his lantern, but this time to study the lathered horses. He rubbed his bearded jaw. "I don't know. All the way from Greeneville in one day. They won't be fit for nothin' for a good three, four days."

"I'm willing to pay ten pence a horse for the inconvenience. I'll see your own horses are returned to you on my way back through."

"You two work this out," the widow said. "Come on, girl. Let's get in out of the cold."

Noah glanced back at Jessica and saw that she'd dismounted on her own. But she didn't return his look. Her hooded head was turned away as she followed the older woman inside.

Now she was ignoring him. But what could he expect?

"Might be I could trade you two horses," the settler said with more enthusiasm now that cash money was involved.

"Good. I'll give you an extra five pence if you'll help me get the other mounts I need."

The man didn't need any more incentive. Lantern still in hand, he hopped up on the horse Jessica had vacated and reined the sagging animal alongside Noah. "Name's Fulton. Howard Fulton from Prince Edward County up in Virginia." He extended a hand. "And I'd be plumb pleased to help you folks out."

Fulton had to take Noah to three different neighbors before they'd secured four more fresh horses for the next day. Riding with them back to his host's farm, Noah vowed not to let Mistress Stowe talk him into overtaxing this string as they had the others. Not only was it harmful to the animals, but he couldn't afford to spend money so freely.

But he knew he shouldn't blame the widow for the mistreatment of the horses. Ultimately, it had been his responsibility—one he'd shirked along with responsibility for his actions the night before. Heaving a tired sigh, he sloughed off the discomforting memory. He'd deal with the Jessica matter tomorrow. Somehow.

After Noah and the thin but wiry farmer put the stock up for the night, they headed for the cabin, which was lighted by a lone candle in an upper window. The rest of the house was dark—a good sign.

"Looks like the wife's got your ladies bedded down for the night," Fulton observed, carrying the lantern between them. "So, I'll say good night to you out here. Help yourself to what's in the pot." Fulton held out a gloved hand.

Noah took it. "Thank you, for everything."

"'Twas a pleasure doin' business with you." Blowing out the flame, the farmer led the way inside to a rush of comforting warmth.

In the soft glow of the hearth, Noah saw that the lower level was one big room, with a steep staircase rising to the second floor. Fulton headed up without looking back.

But Noah had only one thing on his mind. Where was Jessica?

He spotted her bedded down on the floor at the dark end of the room, close to the wall, with Widow Stowe on the outside. The women had rolled out his own blankets a respectable distance away. As quietly as his boots would allow, he stepped toward the fire and the smell of food that blended headily with woodsmoke. His stomach knotted with hunger. Still, he checked once more, making certain his two charges really were asleep. Satisfied, he breathed a sigh of relief.

Removing his tricorn and gloves, he dropped them on a long dining table that took up the middle of the room, then plucked a bowl and spoon from the mantel above the hearth.

In the stew pot Noah discovered mostly carrots and turnips—

Fulton's wife must have thrown in extra when she heard them ride up. Too tired to look for anything more, he poured himself some stale-smelling coffee and returned to the table.

He started to take a seat but realized he'd be placing himself in direct view of Jessica . . . a mere shadowy figure in her dark corner. Suddenly he wished he'd stirred up the fireplace coals, the better to see her.

Instead of sitting, he picked up his bowl and moved closer to where she lay—not so close that she might feel his presence and awaken—but near enough to see her face and the extraordinarily long night braid spilling across the feather pillow . . . hair he'd held in his hands, woven through his fingers only two nights ago. A few more steps . . . and he was filling his eyes with her delicate pixielike features. The fragile chin, the wide cheekbones that framed those gorgeous eyes, closed now, but still showoffs, displaying a thick fringe of dark lashes.

Tired as he was, he couldn't take his eyes off her. He ate his meal standing . . . knowing all the while this otherworldly innocent was fast becoming his forbidden fruit.

Either her or God? There was only one choice he could make.

Besides, she was on her way to family in Baltimore, and he had his own to get back to.

But for a little while, here in the still of night, he could dream.

A particularly sharp pain in the side brought Noah awake, but only enough to roll his achy body over on the hard plank floor.

Another jab of pain. Sharper. *Someone was poking him.*

"Wake up!" came an urgent whisper from behind. The widow.

Opening his eyes to pitch darkness, he quickly surveyed the deep shadows for an intruder. Spying nothing, he rolled back toward her voice.

"Help me," she ordered in a hoarse undertone. "I can't get up by myself."

Confused, but for only a second, Noah took perverse pleasure in her distress. She'd brought the soreness on herself, on all of them.

"*Hurry.* Time's a-wastin'. The sun'll be up soon."

He glanced past a crack in the window curtains and saw no hint of dawn. But he knew the stubborn woman wouldn't leave him in peace. With a huff, he tossed back the covers, exposing the rumpled linen shirt and breeches he'd slept in . . . then, gaining his own feet, he winced against a gripping stiffness. Even his bare feet rebelled at touching the icy cold floor.

He tried to improve on his stumbly gait as he hobbled to where the woman sat, then wondered how she'd managed to jab him from several feet away. He figured it out quick enough. With one hand stretched up to him, her other held what looked like a fire poker.

Probably had to use it for a cane last night, he mused. He glanced over at Jessica, still fast asleep. At least this sergeant of a woman had the decency to leave the lass to her rest.

He hoisted the tall woman to her feet.

She groaned in several octaves on her way up, then heaved a sigh and shoved down the dress she'd slept in before straightening the tuck of her shawl collar. "Better."

Not that Noah would ever discount her efforts, but she still smelled as much like horse as he did—and would until they got to a regular inn where they might purchase a bath.

"Just need to move around some," she hissed between her teeth. "You go on out. Feed and saddle the horses whilst I stir up the coals and fix us somethin' for breakfast. And be quiet about it. No need to wake the Fultons iffen we don't have to."

Noah remembered that his stockings and boots were all the way down on the floor. Gritting his teeth, he bent to fetch them, then eased onto a nearby bench to put them on before donning his outer clothes.

Supporting herself with the poker, the old woman limped past him in the dark, heading toward the hearth where only the faintest of embers still glowed from the back log.

By the time he had his warm outer clothing on, the widow had stirred up the coals and added enough wood to have a roaring fire going. Stepping beside her, he plucked a piece of kindling from the wood box. Flaming the end, he took it to light the lamp on the table.

"I could'a done that." Her voice, though barely above a whisper, sounded annoyed. "Get yourself out yonder to them horses."

He chose the better part of valor and didn't reply as he took his firestick to a lantern sitting on the mantel and flamed its wick. He had no intention of working blind in a strange barn.

By the time he had the lantern in hand, the woman had made her way on rodlike legs back to where they'd been sleeping. "Up, girl. Stop playin' possum, and get a move on."

Jessica awake? That sent Noah out the door quick enough.

By the time he'd taken care of his own morning needs, as well as

181

those of the fresh string of horses—plus bridling them and saddling three—the overcast sky began to show light in the East. Going over the high mountains today would be hard enough without snow, he reminded God, just before he blew out the lantern and led the animals out of the barn. Today he'd keep the extra mounts on a string behind him. Even if it didn't rain or snow, the women would have enough trouble keeping their seats . . . which reminded him of that bony woman's lack of natural padding. He smiled.

Sure that the pushy widow would have his breakfast ready by now, he started for the door, grousing to himself that he hadn't been ordered here and there so rudely since his army days. Well, at least *Widow Sarge* kept his mind off the mess he'd made of things with Jessica. Some of the time.

Stopping to regroup those wayward thoughts, he almost got hit when the door swung open. Out came Widow Stowe, wearing a sour expression.

Jessica followed close behind, her dull blue hood pulled so far forward, he couldn't see her face.

"Took you long enough," the woman accused on steam clouds of vapor. Handing him an unbleached cotton kerchief filled with something warm and lumpy, she walked away, carrying her bedroll and tote.

The smell of biscuits wafted up. Noah looked down at the knot-tied kerchief. She didn't expect him to eat out here, did she? He swung toward her.

She'd already selected her mount, the shortest one, and was busy securing her belongings.

"Mistress Stowe—," he said in a no-nonsense tone, but he got no further before she interrupted.

"Gimme a boost." Using both hands, she lifted her reluctant leg until her foot reached the stirrup. "Come on, lad, hoist me up. Time's a-wastin'."

He was sorely tempted to hoist her a whole lot farther than she expected. But he managed to maintain himself—though he did deposit her in the saddle a bit swiftly.

"That reminds me," she groaned, her hazel eyes narrowing beneath a bony shelf of salt-and-pepper brows, "You *did* leave my son's horses with folks who'll feed 'em good and not overwork 'em, didn't you? I don't want to come back here and find 'em all broke down and wheezin'."

This from the woman who nearly rode them to death yesterday? But it was understandable for her to be in a hurry, he conceded while entertaining a vision of his hands at her throat. Many more days of her mouth, and he'd be seriously contemplating murder.

God, give me patience.

Then he remembered his other problem. "If you'll excuse me," he said with a courtesy he didn't feel, "I'd better go help Miss Jessica."

The audacious woman grabbed his sleeve. "I'll be watchin' where you put your hands on her. And don't think you can dilly-dally whilst helpin' her up, either."

Speechless at her rude insinuations, Noah's mouth dropped open. And Jessica. What must she be thinking? He didn't want to know.

"Don't think that innocent look fools me," the woman spewed. "I didn't miss none of them calf eyes you two was passin' back and forth yesterday. It's plain to see you didn't get a chaperone for that li'l gal none too soon. A mite slack in your duty there, I'd say."

The woman had crossed the line. He jerked his sleeve from her claws. "I'll have you know—"

"*No,*" she overrode him. "I'll have you know I take my responsibilities seriously. When you came in last night, I wasn't really asleep—I raised my share of daughters, so I know better. And I had my eye on you the whole livelong time you was moonin' over that gal. Like some lovesick pup, you was. And just so you know, I had that fire poke ready just in case."

She'd spied on him! And was blabbing it out for the whole world to hear! Mortified, he swung around—and almost slammed into Jessica.

She stood not three feet away, offering him a steaming cup of coffee . . . and wearing the smuggest expression he'd ever seen.

18

Spying on her, was he? Mooning over her *"like some lovesick pup."*
My, but those words had sent Jessica's heart soaring this morning.
What a grand feeling it had been! Exhilarating! So much so, she'd
scarcely noticed the hard climb into the mountains or how much
darker the forest had become as the nearly leafless beeches and
maples gave way to dense evergreens . . . towering trees that
seemed to virtually grab hold of the clouds above and keep them
drizzling straight down on her.

But as the miserably damp day wore on, her high spirits began to
sag. If anything, Noah had been even more distant since Mistress
Stowe's outburst.

Had the widow been mistaken about his affections? Before the kiss,
Jessica and Noah had talked every chance they got. And laughed
together. He'd been her most agreeable and instructive teacher, told
her so many things—like about a strange contraption of bowlike
hoops that women wore under their better gowns. It supposedly
stuck out wider than a stag's horns and held out any number of skirts.

185

She remembered, too, how they'd both laughed when he told her about the big curly wigs Eastern ladies and gentlemen wore, powdered whiter than salt-lick dust. And big hats decorated with all manner of feathers and ribbons, gathers and ruffles sat atop the ladies' wigs. He'd even told her about a device called a goffer made for no other purpose than to iron those bows and frills.

Oh, what a grand time they'd had . . . before the kiss. Before she'd stepped beyond the bounds of this strange new world and he placed that cantankerous woman between them. What was odd, though, was that Mistress Stowe thought it was Jessica's good name she was to protect. Little did the widow know she'd been hired to keep Noah and his good name safe from ruin.

If he felt that way, why was he still escorting her across the mountains? Of course, she knew the answer to that one. Noah would not make a promise, then renege. That would go against everything he and his god stood for.

So, here he was where he didn't want to be.

And if he didn't want to be with her, she certainly didn't want him here. Jessica ground her teeth against the hurt and anger . . . and frustration, because she couldn't send him packing. Without having any idea which trails to take, she couldn't tell him to go back to his valley, where she knew he wished he was right now.

Not a single shred of pride could she keep. Of course, she mused, if she kept in an easterly direction, she'd eventually reach the other side of the mountains. "Civilization," as everyone was fond of calling it.

Jessica glanced at Widow Stowe riding ahead and knew she couldn't get rid of Noah or in any way slow their progress. The time-worn woman had an even more urgent quest than she did— a daughter who was dying. Grimly, Jessica smiled. The Widow Stowe had been particularly surly all day because she'd not gotten her way about the horses. Noah had refused to allow them to be pushed as hard as they had pushed their previous mounts.

However, despite the woman's mistreatment of the animals, Jessica admired her immensely for loving her daughter so much that she'd risk killing the horses to get to her. Just as Jessica had thought Spencer would have done to get back to her and Little Bob.

What happened to him? What if she never found him? What if she got to Baltimore and her mother's family rejected her as resoundingly as Noah had . . . after all his flattery and fine speeches?

Shaking off that alarming possibility, she glanced past the widow to Noah at the front leading the extra horses. He sat so tall and straight as if nothing whatsoever was amiss, as if he hadn't treated her so grievously—worse even than her father had. At least with Pizar Whitman, she usually sensed when the blow was coming. She knew when to duck and run. But Noah Reardon was more devious than Father ever thought of being.

Well, at least she wouldn't be stuck with the insincere man much longer. Just till they reached the other side of the mountains. That lifted her spirits. How much longer it would be, though, she wasn't quite sure, and she had absolutely no intention of asking their high and mighty leader.

Mistress Stowe would probably know. Jessica nudged her blaze-faced gelding into a trot, bent on catching up with the widow.

Crowding close to the widow's horse on the narrow trace, Jessica snagged her skirt on a thorny bush. Ignoring the rip, she swept back the damp hood of her cloak and hoped to gain the woman's favor with a friendly smile. "Pardon my intrusion, ma'am. But I was wondering if you'd journeyed to North Carolina on this trail before."

"Nay," the long-limbed sturdy woman answered. "I come on it a-travelin' *to* Tennessee country, not from it."

"I see. But mayhap you could still calculate how much longer before we reach your Salem-town."

Any good humor the older woman possessed vanished as she glanced at Noah. "I had thought only three more days. But as slow as that man of yours is going, it'll probably take four now."

Jessica started to assure the woman that she had no claim on Noah, except his promise to see her safely into North Carolina. But considering the widow's mutinous expression, she thought it best to remain quiet. Her question answered, she reined in her gelding.

But before she could fall back into line, the woman caught her horse's bridle, keeping her alongside. "I never should've left my Evaline," Mistress Stowe bemoaned. "The poor child's always been given to coughs and rattles in the chest, you know."

Of course Jessica didn't know that, but she fully understood what it was like to be on an angst-ridden quest to reach a loved one. "That is grievous," she commiserated. "Being so helpless to do anything to help her."

Widow Stowe released the animal's bridle but still held Jessica with her oversized eyes—eyes that lifted one's attention from her big teeth and long jaw. "I've got to get to her before that useless doctor back home has her too weak to save. All he ever wants to do is leech his patients, no matter what ails 'em. Leech 'em and leech 'em again."

"I don't understand this word *leech*."

"Not knowin' is your gain, child. To leech a person is to put the most disgusting, fat, bloodsucking worms all over some poor soul's body. The fools think they can suck out what's ailin' a person."

Jessica shuddered at the vile thought.

"And I gotta get to her, make her my special poultice." The older woman's large eyes sparked with moisture. "She just can't die—she's got four babies dependin' on her."

"Oh, la, I do understand your profound distress. So many days have already transpired since the letter was sent advising you. If ever there was a time for extra help, it's now." She swung her glance to Noah. He'd been dishonorable in flattering her into believing she was desirable when he didn't mean it. But mayhap what he said about the white folks' god was true. At least the almighty part. "Noah Reardon is quite an accomplished man of prayer. I'm confident he would pray for your daughter if you request it."

Some of the strain left the worried mother's face. "I'd like that. I'll go ask him straightaway. The more folks prayin', the better. And I'd appreciate your prayers too," she tossed over her gray-cloaked shoulder as she whipped her white-stockinged chestnut's rump.

"Mine?" Jessica started to call out that she didn't pray, then decided it might not be a good idea to divulge that. Besides, she had prayed that night she was running from her father and his musket. And hadn't everyone she'd met in the past few days put a very high value on their god? Even if this deity did ask some very hard things of his people. "I'd be supremely honored," she called after the older woman.

Watching Mistress Stowe maneuver her mount past the string of riderless horses, Jessica decided she actually would do it. If Noah's god was as loving as Noah said he was, praying couldn't hurt. He'd have to listen, especially when it was for a young mother. Small children needed their mother . . . as well she knew.

Perhaps her own mother would have lived if someone had been praying for her. The thought brought a new deep sadness to Jessica. Her hand went unbidden to cover the cross beneath her clothes.

Up ahead, Noah must have heard Mistress Stowe coming. He turned toward her with a stony expression.

Jessica chuckled at his distress. That woman had been a real thorn in his side since they left yesterday.

After Widow Stowe spoke, his expression softened . . . as Jessica knew it would. He really was a kindhearted man—no matter how he'd been treating her lately.

The word *leeches* rose above the others Mistress Stowe was saying.

Shuddering, Jessica wished she could see Noah's expression. What would he think about bleeding a woman to save her? Hadn't he said that God's Son, Jesus, already shed his blood to save everyone for all time? So what did this doctor need with the blood of this young mother? Just the thought of sucking worms stuck all over a body made Jessica cringe again.

Well, Noah had said God could do anything, even heal someone four days away. "Before the physician gets to her," she said out loud as she gazed up through the pines.

But could Noah's god really hear her prayer past the dark hovering clouds? She shrugged. Folks didn't seem to have any problem praying right through the shingles of cabin roofs. Besides, at worst, praying wouldn't cost her any more than a few extra breaths.

She remembered about closing her eyes. Better do it right, she thought, lowering her lashes. "Almighty Father in heaven? What I'm requesting isn't merely just because I want to be rid of Noah Reardon more quickly. But please keep those clouds from turning into a storm that would delay us. Help us to get to this Salem place as expeditiously as possible. And in the interim, don't permit that doctor to put his worms on Evaline, daughter to Mistress Stowe. She's in Salem, North Carolina. Noah says you know everything, but just in case, she's the sick one with four babies. Oh, and don't forget, babies do need their mothers more than anything."

Jessica opened her eyes and looked up, wondering if she would see or hear anything different.

But she didn't. Only the dripping of collected moisture from tree branches to the forest floor. Not a single creature rustled, not even a lone birdcall. With damp cold weather like this, the wildlife knew it was time to hole up.

Yet somehow the silence gave her comfort.

Then she remembered something else and squeezed her eyes shut again. "I have another request—if another one is permissible. My brother is missing. Spencer Whitman. He would be twenty-two now. If you have any idea at all where he is, could you keep an eye on him for me? I have some other requests too. In reference to Baltimore and a very uncomfortable situation here with Noah Reardon, but I don't wish to put too much on you at once. I know you must already be tremendously occupied with so many people praying to you all the time. But, this one about Evaline and the sucking worms is one I think you'll want to look into right away. . . . Oh yes, and, amen."

As the afternoon progressed, the peace Jessica had felt when she prayed lingered, and she was able to see the situation between her and Noah with more calm. Eventually, she'd settled on the fact that Noah was not without flaws, as he himself had implied when he said Jesus, the Son of God, was the only one who'd lived a perfect life without sin. Fact was, Noah was quite the hypocrite when it came to certain things, like keeping the Sabbath holy and, most assuredly, his misleading flattery.

After today, only four more days remained, and she'd be rid of the reminder of her shame.

Then Noah did something to ruin everything. Especially the peace she'd been savoring. He turned in his saddle and looked past Mistress Stowe to her with a pitiful hangdog expression and the saddest smile.

Her willful heart started that silly pounding again. She quickly glanced at the widow and saw that the older lady was busy read-justing her skirts and hadn't noticed.

Jessica looked back at Noah and saw he was still beholding her. Then, if she wasn't mistaken, he actually mouthed, "Forgive me."

At long last the widow was asleep. Jessica had never been so glad to hear the discordant sound of snoring as she lay beside Mistress Stowe in a rented room above a local ordinary. In another moment or two, she'd slip off this sagging bed and be out the door.

She couldn't believe she'd reverted again to sneaking around as she'd done so often when she lived with her father. But the widow was as unreasonable in this chaperoning business as her father had ever been about most everything, especially when he had a rum jug in his hand. Earlier this evening, she'd even caught the woman nosing through her things as if Jessica was trying to keep something from her other than that one epochal kiss . . . a kiss, she'd come to realize this afternoon, that had been equally significant to Noah.

And now all she wanted was the chance to speak to him, find out what his "forgive me" encompassed. But upon reaching the inn earlier, Mistress Stowe had insisted that the two of them be taken immediately to their room, away from Noah. She'd even ordered the tavern keeper to deliver supper to them upstairs, along with buckets of bathwater.

The bath had been a wonderful luxury. Especially since a tub had been delivered that was so deep, the water came all the way up to her neck. She'd been able to get the smell of horse off and warm up all her aching bones at once.

But being shut away up here she didn't like. Plus, the widow's reason had been exceedingly frivolous; she claimed that "Miss Jessica darest not be exposed to a place where there was the drinking of strong spirits and crude language." As if she hadn't been exposed to that almost every day of her life.

Well, being kept up here simply wouldn't do. No matter how tired she was, she'd never get any sleep until she spoke with Noah.

Lifting the heavy covers ever so slightly, Jessica slipped to the floor. She wore only the inner layer of her white woman's clothes—the shift—but that would have to be enough. Struggling into all the rest would make too much noise. Besides, the shift covered almost as much as her deerskin day gown had, and no one ever said that was indecent. Not taking the time to don her moccasins either, she tiptoed out the door in her stocking feet.

The hall was dimly lit by a single candle in a wall sconce and a shaft of light coming up from the stairwell. Reaching the landing, she heard the rumbling sounds of men's voices down in the main room. Thank goodness the inn had not as yet shut down for the night. That had been a real concern with Mistress Stowe taking so long to fall asleep.

It was also vital that Noah be among the patrons below. If he'd already gone to his own quarters, her plan would be thwarted. According to her chaperone, nothing was as scandalous as an unmarried miss venturing into a man's room.

Near the bottom of the steps, Jessica spotted men sitting at the far end on stools and a bench that they'd dragged close to the fire. She paused a moment, just staring at them—seven in all. Seeing that many white men together, all in one eyeful, still took a bit of getting used to, though she knew it was going to start happening on a regular basis now that they'd reached the North Carolina side of the mountains.

No one noticed her. The men were gathered around Noah, asking him questions about Tennessee country, and their respect for him was just as evident here as it had been at the inn in Greeneville.

"You'd have to travel farther west," she heard Noah answering. "As you go the land smooths out more. It's not all hills and narrow valleys like this mountain country. And richer. Like my valley."

He was talking about his land again. White men were sure partial to owning their own places.

"I can't imagine ever wanting to live anywhere else," he continued.

"Why's that?" one of the coarsely dressed men asked.

"Everything. Aside from those of us in the valley, there isn't anyone for fifty miles around. It's as if God gave it all to us. The trees, the animals. Everything grows bigger and in more abundance."

"How far did you say it is?" a man with his back to her asked. The interest was evident in his tone. Like so many, this one wanted to go where he'd never been, see what he'd never seen.

Suddenly Jessica realized these men weren't so different from her. She too was curious about places she had yet to see—and most particularly, Baltimore. Relaxing a bit, she started toward them.

A fellow holding a tankard spotted her first. He elbowed the man beside him and whispered something.

The other man swiveled toward her. It was the innkeeper, wearing an apron like most of the white women she'd seen. He scowled, then turned back to Noah. "Mr. Reardon, I do believe you have business to tend."

Noah followed the direction of the man's sharp nod. Seeing Jessica, he was on his feet in an instant, rushing to her as if something was terribly wrong . . . like the chimney had caught on fire, or worse. Still, he detoured long enough to snatch his maroon frock coat off a wall peg. The second he reached her, he tossed it over her shoulders. A body would've thought she was freezing to death. He turned her about and, by her elbows, practically carried her up the stairs.

As she tried to speak, to ask what the big hurry was, he shushed her. Not until they'd reached the dimly lit upper floor did he stop to speak.

But now it was her turn to silence him—which she did with a finger to his lips . . . those lips that had caused her so much distress—joy first—then distress. She placed a finger to her own lips and pointed toward the room where Mistress Stowe slept.

Nodding his understanding, Noah drew her to the other end of the hall. "Jessica," he whispered urgently, "you simply cannot come downstairs without your clothes on."

"I *have* clothes on. Not my moccasins, maybe, but plenty for in here where it's so warm."

He stared at her, his gray eyes much darker now as he loomed tall over her. Then, quite suddenly, he grinned. "I reckon I should've said, not without your outer clothes on. It's another of those white people's customs that I suppose won't make much sense to you."

"Well, I needed to speak to you, and—" she glanced past him to the widow's door—"and that chaperone you hired said I couldn't come down. You'd think she owns me."

"Until we reach Salem, she pretty much does," he added firmly. "You need to get back to bed before she finds you missing, or we'll never hear the last of it." Then he straightened slightly. "But first, what was so important it couldn't wait until morning?"

She stepped closer. "I needed to ask you about something."

He stiffened and stepped back. That hunted-animal look took over his eyes. A body would think this big strong man was afraid she'd try to kiss him again.

Suddenly she too lost her nerve. But she didn't want him knowing it. Brazenly, she smiled up at him. "There's nothing to fear. I merely want to borrow your Bible—to read so I won't keep making all these mistakes," she added for good measure. "I promise, I'll be ever so careful with it."

That seemed to relax him. "It's a very big book. Lots of books and letters, really. You should have someone reading it with you, someone who can answer your questions as you go along."

"Aye, that had been more instructive. But," she reveled in

reminding him, "you hired that woman to keep my instructor safe from me."

"Nay," he protested. "She's here for your protection, not mine."

"You could've fooled me." She took a step closer.

He backed up, banging his boot heel against his door; then quickly he regained his dignity. "Let me get that Bible for you."

He started inside, but he put out a hand to ward her off when she forgot the rule about not going into a gentleman's room and tried to follow. Then he shut the door in her face.

Staring at it, she shook her head at all this "civilized" nonsense she was having to abide.

Coughing sounds came from the adjoining room. Mistress Stowe! Had the widow awakened? Jessica spent the next moments anxiously listening for further sounds, but none came until Noah clicked open the door again.

He stood on the threshold, blocking the entrance with one hand on the jamb while holding out the big black book with the other. "Start with the book of John."

Taking it from him, she opened it and was reminded of just how many pages there were. She turned from Noah and slanted the printed words to catch the light from the wall sconce. Leafing through what had to be a thousand pages, she looked for one that would say John at the top.

Noah came up behind her. "Here, let me help." He reached around her, one arm on either side. Since it had to do with his God, he'd forgotten to shrink from her. Taking the book, he flipped the pages purposefully.

Her own concentration was lost. All she could think about was the fact that she was enfolded in his arms. Her breath died away, and she could hear her own heartbeat.

Or was it his? No longer could she feel the rise and fall of his chest either. But she did feel an added tension in the arms surrounding her, the beginnings of a tremble . . . the same as she'd experienced when he'd kissed her the other night.

Too soon he almost shouted, "Here it is!" His breath tickled her ear. Then he lowered his voice to a husky whisper. "If you have trouble finding it from now on, look for the numbers at the bottom. John starts on eight hundred and twenty-four."

Before she thought to take the volume from him, he shoved it into her hands and moved away.

She turned around, closing the gap he'd just created. "And I have something for you, too."

He blanched. The man really did fear being close to her.

She couldn't fathom why; nonetheless, it gave her a rousing sense of power. Her smile couldn't be stopped. "Your coat, kind sir," she said, shrugging it from her shoulders. "Merely your coat."

19

"I declare," Jessica cried, "another red door. And, look, that house over there. A blue one."

Riding beside her as they approached the outskirts of Salem, the first real town she'd ever seen, Noah took as much pleasure in watching her absorb the sights as she did in seeing them. After their encounter in the inn's hallway four nights ago, he realized that keeping such a distance from her had not been in her best interest. He'd been a very poor example of a Christian "neighbor." Her need for his spiritual as well as social guidance far outweighed any pangs of longing he felt.

He would never forget the moment she sent Mistress Stowe to ask him to pray for her ill daughter. Such hope that had given him—real promise that Jessica would convert eventually—something he must keep foremost in his mind every second.

Naturally he wanted Jessica to accept Christ first and foremost for the sake of her own soul. But Noah would be less than honest with himself if he failed to admit that he had a personal interest in the matter as well. If she never came to faith in Christ, the desire he had for her could be given no more place than if she belonged to another; in essence she did, since she wasn't part of the bride of Christ.

And time was running out.

Tomorrow or the next day, after he'd arranged for another escort and chaperone for Jessica, he'd be leaving her . . . unless she made that all-important decision. Thus far, though, she didn't seem ready. Not in the least. Her pa, who'd already caused so much suffering, stood in the way again . . . in the form of her hatred of him and his money she felt justified in stealing.

Still his heart ached. He tried not to think about how very much he'd miss her—and her every smile, every question, every look she gave him with her soulful eyes.

"Oh, look, a green door." She'd already grown accustomed to seeing painted houses sided with milled boards the past couple of days. But coming into Salem and beholding this scattering of more affluent homes with fancy shutters, colorful doors, and handsome brass knockers had her cheeks as flush as the roses he wished were blooming for her right now.

An enclosed carriage rolled past, drawn by two stylishly prancing hackneys. A red-coated Negro perched atop the jockey seat.

Jessica's delicate jaw went slack. Even Noah was surprised to see such evidence of wealth this far west. Salem must really be coming into its own.

Craning her neck around, Jessica followed the conveyance's progress for a long moment before turning back, her mirrorlike eyes glittering. "One of my newspapers has a drawing of a carriage like that, but I never dreamed they were so shiny . . . like a black-and-gold jewel."

"Hmm, I never thought about them quite that way," he mused, knowing all the while he must be beaming himself just because he was still with her.

Since he'd traded for fresh horses again in Yadkinville, they'd made good time today. There were still a couple hours of daylight left. And for a change, the sun shone with some warmth. He hoped the much-improved weather portended good tidings for Mistress Stowe.

She rode ahead of them, keeping the pace at a swift trot. Yet both she and Jessica were now obliged to ride in that awkward and not-so-safe side position on gear not made for it. Something he hoped to remedy for Jessica before he left for home. Surely the local livery would have a sidesaddle for hire.

Hopefully, the proprietor could direct him to a trustworthy escort—one of better character than he had proven to be—one who would see Jessica the rest of the way to Baltimore and, more importantly, continue helping her toward salvation.

Unexpectedly, Jessica reined her mount so close to his, their legs brushed as she leaned close. "Look! See the woman over there in the doorway. She has one of those hoops under her skirts. She'd have to turn sideways just to walk outside. La, but I do long to see under those skirts."

He laughed, as Jessica so often made him do. Too often. She was such a delight. He envisioned her in her own hooped gown of satin and lace. How much fun it would be to watch her trying to get around in one.

But in his mind's eye, she never appeared the least comical anymore. No, she was always more gracefully beautiful than any china doll on Keaton's mantel. And so much more . . . with her animated exuberance and quick wit. Point of fact, he couldn't think of anyone he'd rather have standing at his own painted front door, waiting for him to come home.

Noah gave an involuntary jerk on his reins at the forbidden idea he'd let slip in again. But it was hard not to. Accustomed as she was to the wilderness with all its hardships, she'd make a crack frontier wife. And such a lively conversant she would be evenings across the dinner table or sitting by the hearth. She'd willingly discuss every available subject as well as whatever they read in the Bible. No doubt, if he'd been an apt teacher, she would've long since learned all that etiquette business too.

Perhaps a requirement for the next chaperone he hired should be that she be proficient enough in the various graces to instruct Jessica along the way, prepare her to meet her family who must be fairly well situated, considering the expensive cross and the fact that her mother could read.

He glanced at Jessica's delicate profile. Such a lovely lady she would make if her mother's people did, indeed, have the extra money to dress her in those useless wide skirts that fascinated her so much.

For just a second, he allowed his gaze to linger unchecked on those wondrously full lips of hers. Lips that constantly reminded him of that brief star-shooting moment they'd touched his.

Jessica turned and caught him looking.

He glanced away but knew the damage was already done.

"Noah?"

"Yes?" he asked, afraid of what would come next. Thus far, she hadn't brought up his brash lack of restraint in Greeneville . . . that moment he would remember forever.

"I'm having a problem comprehending something." She spoke in an utterly serious tone.

He braced himself for the dreaded topic.

"You tell me that the Continental Congress's system of government is based on biblical morality, yet you say I cannot practice their legal statutes without sinning."

Now it was his turn not to understand. "What do you mean exactly?"

"Do you remember that courthouse we passed yesterday—the one with the barred windows?"

"Aye."

"That was proof that the new states are permitted to punish wrongdoers. The government even sanctions executions when it thinks a crime warrants it. The states also fine offenders—confiscate their money or property. Yet you say I must forgive my father of his wrongs and return his money. Money, I might add, that he earned by cheating, lying, and stealing." One of her brows spiked indignantly. "Tell me, how do you justify that?"

Though her heart was evidently still hardened against her father, Noah did appreciate the fact that she was now willing to debate her stand . . . open herself to be proven wrong. Sending a petition heavenward, he asked God for the right words—words that would not merely sway her mind but touch her heart.

But, just as he was about to speak, Mistress Stowe whipped her mount into a gallop. She turned back and shouted, "It's this way. My son-in-law's farm." Practically flying off her saddle, the lanky woman reined her horse off the main road and onto a set of wagon tracks that led through a muddy stubbled field of harvested grain.

Noah knew he should go straight to the center of town and inquire about a new escort for Jessica. He needed to get started back home while the weather still held. Yet he felt compelled to leave the main road and follow Mistress Stowe. He'd been praying for her ill daughter since he'd first heard about her tenuous condition. Thus far, he'd felt God had answered his prayers favorably, since the ominously black clouds had not burst over them while they crossed the mountains. He nudged his dun into a canter.

Remembering Jessica, he swiveled in his saddle to motion for Jessica to keep pace. But, of course, she already was.

Then an unsettling thought took hold in Noah's mind. At mealtimes during the journey, Jessica had witnessed a number of his petitions for Evaline Boyette, Mistress Stowe's daughter—petitions made to the God he'd professed as all-powerful. What if their providentially swift crossing had been intended to bring the widow here merely to comfort her son-in-law in his loss and to help with her grandchildren? If this young woman was dead, would Jessica's tenuous forays toward the Lord come to an abrupt end?

About half a mile down the track, the widow veered onto a path that ended at a simple, white two-and-a-half-story house with moss green shutters and stone chimneys jutting up at each end. Grabbing a handful of mane, the agile older woman vaulted off the black mare before it came to a complete stop. Her long legs stretched into a run; she reached the door almost instantly. Flinging it wide, she rushed in, yelling at the top of her voice. "I'm here! I'm here!"

Noah and Jessica reined in and waited. He wasn't willing to dismount. Not till he knew more.

He didn't have long to wait. No more than twenty seconds passed before Mistress Stowe charged outside again, a babe on her hip. "She's alive! My Evie's alive! And almost well! Praise the Lord!"

And emerging from the house behind the widow was a woman with the same identical features! Big-boned, long-toothed, and all. Mistress Stowe had a twin!

Noah's joy over Evaline's recovery was instantly tempered. One cantankerous Mistress Stowe had been more than enough.

After a round of introductions and explanations, Jessica felt a bit out of place when the relatives began fawning over each other with more hugs and kisses and a constant outpouring of joyous familial greetings in this room Noah had called a "parlor." With everyone talking at once, the chatter seemed all a-tumble, like a mountain stream spilling through clogs of boulders. Jessica stepped back and observed from a more comfortable distance.

The two older women were indeed twins. Introduced as Isabella and Elizabeth, they called each other Izzy and Lizzy.

The widow's daughter, Evaline, sat in one of those rocking

chairs like Storekeeper Keaton's. Though wrapped in blankets, she had ample color in her cheeks. She resembled the older women, except her hair was a light brown instead of gray and her chin smaller, giving her a prettiness her aunt and mother lacked.

The baby now sat in Evaline's lap, laughing and bouncing up and down in the excitement, while a pair of dark-headed boys of about three chased each other around their mother's chair. More twins!

Must run in their family, Jessica thought, then wondered if twins ran in her own. A new happiness surfaced, knowing she would soon find out when she reached her people in Baltimore. This happiness was soon followed by a sharp sense of loss, remembering that Noah would be gone from her by the next day.

Jessica reined in her thoughts and concentrated on the riches about her. Though only Evaline sat, the room held so many pieces of furniture, Jessica believed they all could have been seated.

Another boy, with light hair like his mother's and a couple of years older than the twins, was almost hidden in a corner near a spinning wheel. He had a tight hold on his father's hand. Like Jessica, the child seemed a bit overwhelmed by all the activity.

Evaline's husband, Samuel Boyette, though sturdy enough, wasn't any taller than Izzy and Lizzy. With a quirky smile, he turned to Noah beside him. "How about you and me gettin' out of here whilst the gettin's good? To the quiet of the barn. I'll help you put your horses up for the night."

Noah didn't hesitate. He headed for the door with Mr. Boyette. Jessica cut toward them.

"No," Noah said, stopping her. "You don't need to help us. Stay here and enjoy yourself." Then he was gone.

Enjoy herself? Why would these people want to visit with her when they hadn't seen each other in so long? Still, once in a while they would shoot a glance her way.

Then she sensed she was being watched steadily.

Standing next to a fireplace that wasn't used for cooking, just heating, the widow's grown nephew, Ben Coor, stared at her—not as if she were strange but more as if he were assessing her. Their eyes met and he smiled, a friendly smile that created deep creases on either side of his mouth. Then the large, loose-jointed man crossed the room to her in an easy lumbering gait. "I'll bet you could use something warm to drink. There's coffee in the kitchen."

His voice was coarser than Noah's, not nearly so pleasant to the ear. But his invitation made up for it. She'd hoped someone would offer her a cup from the moment she first walked in and smelled it. Nodding, she let the man with the largest hands and wrists she'd ever seen escort her through an inner door—a door painted a creamy peach color as was the rest of the parlor.

Once inside the big kitchen, Ben Coor pulled out a chair for her at the eating table and went to a cooking hearth from which also came other tantalizing aromas.

Her stomach knotted with hunger. She hoped the Boyettes had enough for everyone.

Mr. Coor collected a blackened pot from off some side coals and two crockery cups from a shelf above. This stranger was waiting on her just as Noah sometimes did. Perhaps she'd been mistaken that Noah was more special than other men. There could be a dozen men right here in Salem just as solicitous and just as handsome . . . well, maybe not so handsome. She couldn't imagine anyone who'd be as pleasing to the eye.

Realizing her thoughts were straying again toward sadness, she looked about her and saw that the Boyettes must be very wealthy. This home of many rooms didn't have just one fireplace in the kitchen, but two, the smaller one niched into the wall. Between them hung all manner of big utensils. Jugs and crocks and sacks of all sizes were stored beneath several worktables that lined the walls. Displayed on a shelf above them were pure white dishes edged with dainty flowers, while drinking vessels as clear as the glass in the windows lined another. Yet another held a collection of odd-sized bowls along with wooden spoons and paddles. And pots—they too came in all sizes, some with legs and some without. Strange inventions seemed to be everywhere she looked. Not wanting to seem ignorant by questioning the stranger about their uses, she wished Noah would come back inside to explain.

She glanced longingly toward the back door. It would still be awhile before Noah returned.

In the rafters above she noticed a great abundance of herbs and dried fruit hanging in bunches, along with a huge store of tallow candles. Light from other candles was everywhere—melting away on the mantel and on every table. This family seemed not to care at all about such extravagance.

"Cousin Evie stocks a good house, don't she?" Mr. Coor remarked. "My Sally did too, before . . . before the pox took her and our baby boy."

"Oh, I am sorry." She couldn't think of anything else to say, not having expected such a personal confidence from him.

"No, I'm sorry. I shouldn't have mentioned it. It's been four years, so the tellin' comes easier now," he said, pouring them both a cup. "Me and my folks live two days' drive west of here. Near Hillsborough. We come to help out till Aunt Izzy could get here. From what my aunt said, you are unattached and with independent means."

"Unattached?" She knew what that meant but was puzzled about the other. His embarking upon her unmarried state without any preamble, though, made her uneasy.

"Not betrothed," he clarified with a smile. Setting the sooty pot and the plain everyday cups on the table, he pulled a chair close to her and sat down. "I find that hard to believe. You bein' such a pretty little thing and all."

"I—uh—" Jessica wasn't certain why Widow Stowe had told him all this or what the proper response should be. She smoothed the lay of her wilted shawl collar, stalling for time. "We—uh—resided in a rather remote location."

"Aye. From what Aunt Izzy said, your pa was in the fur trade." That seemed to please him. He settled back in his chair, his impressive size causing the slender frame to creak. "From your smile, it looks like you got a mouthful of strong white teeth too. They say that's a sign of good health."

Would he be wanting to check them next? "I'm certain yours are just fine too," she countered.

"Aye." He opened wide, displaying the slightly crooked lot. "Nary a cavity. Yessir," he said, taking a sip of coffee. "And I've got my own home over to Hillsborough. Bigger than this one. I decided from the start I wasn't bringin' a wife into my ma's house. She's so bossy, she'd scare any little gal off, 'specially someone so tiny and dainty as yourself."

Jessica took a sip of her own brew, then another. This was obviously more than the usual pleasant conversation Noah said neighbors bandied back and forth.

"Built my own house before I even settled on a bride," he said, showing off his teeth again. "I got me four bedrooms just like Evie has here. But I got me a summer cookhouse too. I think it's important to keep the main house cool in summer, don't you?"

"I reckon."

He cocked his burly head and continued to behold her. It was obvious he expected her to contribute more to the conversation. But what? He surely wouldn't be pleased if she shared what her pa's cabins had looked like.

Mistress Stowe rescued her by bursting through the door, followed by the rest of her family. And again Jessica was surrounded by the clamor of voices, the only relief rendered by the twin boys when they ran, laughing, out the back door.

"Set yourself down there," the widow said, addressing her daughter, who was, as Jessica expected, just as tall as her mother.

Jessica was beginning to feel very insignificant among these giant women. But from the way Mr. Coor continued to study her, he didn't seem to mind.

"Need to get back to fixin' supper," his mother said. "Izzy, you slice the bread. Ben, see if you can round up enough plates and forks for everyone. And, little gal," she said, turning to Jessica, "you go stir that pot of beans. I'll see how the pork roast is comin' along. Should be about done."

Pork! That's what smelled so good. Jessica had tasted it so seldom in her lifetime that she'd almost forgotten.

While the others commenced with their assigned chores, she went to the hearth. Noticing the bean pot hung on one of those swinging poles Noah had told her about, she grabbed a long-handled iron fork and swung the bar along with the pot toward her.

Feeling Mr. Coor's eyes burrowing into her back, she took an extra long time stirring the beans as well as a pot of stewing apples. She was in no hurry to face the presuming man again.

"Aunt Izzy," she heard Ben Coor say, glad his attention had shifted, "I was just tellin' your Miss Jessica about our farm."

Jessica knew then that he had not stopped watching her.

"Did you know," he continued in his gravelly voice, "I cleared five acres of my own last year. Carted the wood into town and sold it off, then I bought seed with the cash and planted it all in cotton. Picked the cotton *by myself*," he boasted. "Then I floated it downriver all the way to New Bern. Sold it straight to a ship's captain myself. No middleman for me," he boasted again. "So you can see, I ain't just sittin' around waitin' for Pa to pass on so's I can inherit the family farm. Not that it ain't makin' a fine profit too. But I plan to have a tidy sum put away long before that. I'm thinkin' on buyin' more land in the next year or two—maybe sooner—" he added with emphasis—"and doin' the same as I did this year. Who can say? Mayhap I'll be able to buy myself a slave or two in a couple of years. No, sir, I don't plan on just sittin' around twiddlin' my thumbs. Before I'm through, them bigwig plantation lords along the river won't have nothin' on me."

"Glad to hear you're finally takin' hold," Widow Stowe answered, seemingly unimpressed by his account. But at least she did fill the silence that had followed his boastful speech.

Unable to dally at the hearth any longer, Jessica turned to face the room . . . and quite suddenly Mr. Coor became vexingly loud at setting the table. His attention was most definitely *not* on his chore or on the baby in Evaline's arms. The infant jumped as another of those lovely plates clunked onto the painted wood surface.

From the moment she'd walked into the house, Jessica had very much wanted to ask Evaline about the leeches, but she instinctively knew that if she said anything on any subject, Mr. Coor would manage to redirect the conversation back to his accomplishments. She'd known trappers like him. Father called them "ear-benders."

Noticing that the wood box was only half full, she started for the exit the twin boys had taken. "I'd better fetch in some more wood splits." And out she went, closing the door on the bold fellow.

The sun had yet to set on this crystal-clear day, painting the western sky subtle shades of pink. She quickly identified the wood-shed from the array of other outbuildings that yesterday Noah had explained were usually toolsheds and houses for things like smoking meat, storing roots, and even one that sat over a spring to keep things cool. The cultivated fields behind seemed to stretch forever.

Small wonder these people had so much.

The woodshed, attached to the chicken coop, faced the main house. Just as she reached it, a light flickered to life in the barn where she knew Noah was working. She was sorely tempted to skip doing her own chore and go join him. So little time was left before he would leave her. But she knew she should return inside, or Mr. Coor would rightly guess she'd gone out to avoid him.

To her dismay, she heard the back door open and close before she'd managed to gather two splits. She didn't bother to check on who it was. She knew.

"You forgot your cloak," Ben Coor called as his great legs ate up the space between them. "Don't want you comin' down sick like Evie. Almost lost her, we did. If I hadn't brung my ma here to tend her, she'd a'been a goner." Reaching Jessica, he draped the cloak over her shoulders, taking his time adjusting its fall.

"Thank you, sir," she said as graciously as possible, considering her annoyance.

He then wrested the wood from her arms. "I'll do that. You don't want to get splinters in those tiny little hands of yours."

Her first thought was to leave him to do it and go back to the house. But she knew instinctively that would be considered rude. After all, he was only trying to help.

"Aunt Izzy says you're headed for Baltimore to find a brother you ain't heard from in almost five years. And that you got plenty cash money of your own to pay your way."

Aunt Izzy talks too much—just like him. And just how did she find out about the coins? Since Noah had not allowed her to spend a single one of her "stolen" coins, they were all still sewn inside her deerskin day gown.

"My farm's right on your way. I'd be mighty proud to have you see it. Show a girl from overmountain, such as yourself, what a congenial life we lead there. Hillsborough has much better stocked shops than Salem. Our womenfolk don't ever have to spend their time spinnin' and weavin'. A young miss there can have her pick of all manner of finely woven goods from London and Paris. Printed cloth too, with as many colors and flowers as a woman could ever wish for. I'm not the stingy sort—I'd be proud to see my wife had all the pretty gowns she needed."

Jessica had already become aware that her coarsely woven day gown was not the least fashionable on this side of the mountain. And now Ben Coor was confirming it. She would need to buy another one. "How much would one of those pretty gowns cost?" she asked as pleasantly as she could manage. She had absolutely no intention of handing herself or her money over to some fast-talking stranger.

"That's not anything you need to bother yourself with. Me and Ma'll be headin' back to Hillsborough in a couple of days. You just come along with us in our wagon. Like I said, it's on the way to Baltimore. I promise, you won't regret it."

Had Noah told Mistress Stowe about her money or had the woman ferreted the coins out on her own? Considering what was taking place now, the latter was more likely. "But, sir, I don't even know—"

"Miss Jessica." A voice from behind startled her. To her vast relief, it was Noah . . . and none too soon. "You're needed in the kitchen."

How would he know that, coming from the barn?

Mr. Coor's gaze narrowed, but for only a fraction of a second. "Too many cooks in there already."

Noah stepped to Jessica's side. "And I'd say there's too many hands out here fetching wood." His voice had that same edge he'd used with Mr. Mackey last week outside Mr. Keaton's store. He'd obviously overheard Mr. Coor's remarks. But this time neither she nor Noah had been insulted.

Then a sudden realization struck. They were acting like two stags in a standoff—ready to lock horns . . . *over her.*

That exciting thought quickly died away. Noah hadn't given her any reason to think he wasn't heading back to that blamed valley of his the first chance he got.

"If you gentlemen will excuse me . . ." Whirling away from them both, she marched toward the house.

20

Jessica noticed every eye glance her way as she returned inside the Boyette house, and not simply as someone new coming into a room. The twin sisters passed suspiciously covert looks between them. For once, though, she didn't feel anything but anger. A plot to take over her life *and* her money was brewing.

"Is my Benny fetchin' in the wood for you?" Mr. Coor's mother asked with a sly smile. She set a large bowl on the dining table that was already loaded with food. Then in two long-legged strides, she reached Jessica and started pulling her toward the table. "He's such a kind and thoughtful man. A real catch. Firstborn, you know. The farm will go to him when his pa dies."

"Aye," Mistress Stowe agreed, moving to the other side, sandwiching in the much smaller Jessica until she didn't have room to pull out her chair. "And Ben's wife was plumb silly about him, she was. Said he was the best husband any girl could have."

"That's a pure fact," Lizzy Coor agreed, leaning down to look Jessica square in the face. "I know at least three of our local gals who shine up to him every time we go to church. And speakin' of church, he'd raise his family by the Good Book, he would."

Jessica had spent her life listening to the opening forays of trading, and this was how it always started—flourishing and flattering what they had to offer. And Lizzy Coor's son was being touted as if he were a bundle of prime beaver pelts.

Confirmation of Jessica's suspicions came from the recovering Evaline's flyaway glance when Jessica looked straight at her. Still seated, the young mother suddenly seemed engrossed with the gurgling giggles of her gap-toothed babe.

In the fever of the sell, Mistress Stowe picked up where her sister left off, praising the acreage *strong* and *capable* Mr. Coor could plow in a day.

But Jessica knew that in any trade, both parties had to bring something of value to the barrelhead. The twin sisters were quite readily offering him and his farm . . . to some lass who had no idea even how to be a farmer's wife.

Noah had said the coins in her day gown were worth a goodly amount, and no doubt Mistress Stowe coveted every one. The very second the widow knew her daughter was safely on the mend, she'd gone straight to her sister and nephew with the information. The painful thought fed Jessica's ire. To think she'd actually thought all this family's hugs and whispered greetings had been over Evaline's recovery.

Again Jessica wondered whether the widow had discovered the coins on her own. Or had Noah told her about them? Had he used the money as bait in the hope of getting these people to take Jessica off his hands? He'd certainly left with Mr. Boyette quickly enough, leaving her to them.

No. If that were so, he would have left her and Ben Coor uninterrupted out at the woodshed.

Mistress Stowe pulled out a chair across from Evaline and pushed Jessica into it, then sat down beside her, still bragging on

Ben. "'Course, him bein' so handsome and all, the gals just naturally swarm all around him. But, wonder of wonders, that boy's set his sights on you. I told him you been livin' in the backwoods your whole life, but he's willin' to overlook your lackin's."

At that comment, Jessica began to seethe.

"Aye." Widow Stowe's twin scooted into the chair on the other side, wedging Jessica between them. "My son was a mite put off at first by you bein' so tiny and all. But I told him that don't just out an' out make you sickly. And it would be a treat to have young'uns with them pretty eyes of yourn."

Even trapped as she was between the two giant women, the fact that Ben's mother would want grandchildren with the same eyes as Jessica's was not lost on her. One pearl to be found in all the tripe they were heaping on her.

"Since the onliest folks you got," the widow chimed in, "is a brother you haven't seen in almost five years, any young woman would be a fool not to latch onto such a fine offer. There ain't much call for woodsy brides this side of the mountain."

"Would you care to freshen up before supper?" Evaline abruptly asked. "You can use my room. First door at the top of the stairs."

Before either twin could stop her, Jessica shot to her feet. "I thank you for your most gracious offer," she said to the benevolent young woman. "And I fervently appreciate your hospitality."

As Jessica rounded the table toward the doorway that led to the staircase, Evaline plucked a lit candle in a ringed holder from the table. "Here, take this to light your way." Her voice was warm with empathy.

Upstairs and alone at last, Jessica felt as if she could breathe freely again. On a side wall of her hostess's bedroom, she spotted a small table with a large pitcher and bowl both painted with flowers similar to the dishes in the kitchen. Above them hung the largest mirror she'd ever seen.

In it she could see most of her reflection—which wasn't all that pleasant a sight. She cringed. The knot of hair beneath her mobcap sagged it down pitifully, and several long dark strands streamed over her shawl collar. Plus, both the white fabric and her face were smudged with travel dust.

There was no way anyone could've thought her comely in such a sad state. Clearly, Ben Coor and the sisters had only one thing on their minds—the money in her day gown.

Muslin cloths edged with artfully colored stitching hung on either side of the looking glass—even Evaline's washrags were fancy. After pouring herself some water, Jessica took a small square, wet it, and started scrubbing her face.

As she did, she wandered around the room, surveying pieces of polished furnishings similar to those Storekeeper Keaton owned. Four deep chests lined one wall. It was hard to believe that the young wife had that many treasures to store. Another stood tall with drawers. On the wall at the foot of the big bed, Evaline had three gowns hanging on wooden pegs.

Jessica moved to them and fingered one of plain indigo. It was of finer weave than her own unadorned and faded yellow gown. The next was pink striped with vining flowers. Very pretty. The last, though, was stunning . . . a shiny pale blue with row upon row of white lace marching down the center of the skirt and more dripping from the sleeves. It was easily as gorgeous as the woman's gown she'd seen earlier . . . which meant Evaline would have that hoop thing Noah had told her about!

She looked up. There it was. The curious-looking contraption hung above the fancy gown. It resembled a harness made only of bent strips of wood. Noah had called it a "pocket hoop."

She glanced behind her to make certain no one had come to the doorway, then reached up on tiptoe and unhooked it. Turning it horizontally, she held it out before her and let the pieces fall into place. Sure enough, a center hoop fitted around the waist while bowed strips fanned out on either side, arranged as neatly as any rib cage. Placing it against her, she saw the exaggerated width. She was tempted to put it on under her skirts to see how it would look on her, but didn't dare. Any second someone could come into the room and catch her nosing around . . . as Mistress Stowe must have done in her things.

Carefully Jessica replaced the pocket hoop, then returned to the small table to see if she could put her hair in some semblance of order before she was called to supper . . . supper with the pack of circling wolves.

Noah watched Ben Coor, piled with an armload of wood, stalk toward the house. He was relieved that the fellow hadn't tried to knock him cold. Instead, Coor had spent quite a spell at the well getting a drink of water—cooling off, no doubt. It was hard on a fellow, trying to court and fight at the same time.

But the big farmer's sudden interest in Jessica was a puzzlement. When they were introduced, he hadn't seemed to take extra notice of her in her tired bedraggled condition. So what could have prompted him to get so fired up in the short time Noah had been in the barn? And why such forward behavior from what seemed to be a rather plodding sort?

Had Jessica inadvertently said or done something to make Coor think she was a wanton? Or had she unwisely told them about her money?

Noah glanced back at the barn where he'd left Sam Boyette with the horses when he'd spied Ben Coor following Jessica out to the woodshed. Rightly, the chore of feeding and brushing down the animals was his own to finish. But from her distressed expression, she'd seemed in far greater need of him and still might be. Wasting no more time, he, too, headed for the kitchen door.

Reaching for the knob, he heard the low murmurs of a hurried conversation. Only out of politeness did he knock before entering the kitchen. As he expected, the instant he strode in the talk ceased. No one except Evaline Boyette smiled at him, yet they all stared.

Jessica was missing. But Ben sat there. Noah relaxed slightly.

Widow Stowe stepped toward him purposefully. "Mr. Reardon, my nephew says you got the wrong idea about him. You know I wouldn't allow no carnal goings-on in my daughter's house. Ben, here, has the most honorable of intentions."

Her words sounded far more convincing than her gaze, which started to drift. Then her last words took hold. Noah glanced at Coor—who scowled back at him—then swung back to Mistress Stowe. "Honorable intentions? Surely your nephew doesn't plan to ask a total stranger to marry him—to trust the rest of her life to him—between now and tomorrow, does he?"

"Well, I—"

Noah didn't wait for the widow to come up with the right words. He turned to the lady of the house, who sat rocking her babe back and forth. "Mistress Boyette, I thank you and your husband for your generous offer to accommodate Miss Jessica and myself this eve, but you're overrun with guests already. I think it's best if we ride on into Salem and find an inn for the night."

"I wouldn't hear of it," Evaline said with what seemed to be genuine dismay. "I owe you a good night's sleep, at the very least. You brought my mama here. It'll be the first Christmastime that we'll have her with us since before the twins was born. Blessin's upon blessin's," she sighed, smiling at her mother. "And besides, I'm certain you must be famished." She rose laboriously to her feet and handed the baby, scrunched blankets and all, to her mother. "Ben, you go out to the barn and fetch in all my men, whilst I go check on Miss Jessica."

Noah didn't have the heart to refuse the quiet-spoken woman's invitation—at least not until he'd had some of her tasty-smelling food. "Well, thank you, Mistress Boyette. We'll stay for supper, anyway."

While unbuttoning his frock coat and hanging it on a peg by the back door, Noah recalled a bit of the conversation he'd had with Evaline's husband out in the barn. Sam had said his wife was like "still water." When she'd been near death, he'd feared he would lose more than his life's mate . . . he'd lose his safe harbor. And now Noah understood Sam's meaning. Even in her weakened condition, the gentle young mother had almost effortlessly taken back her kitchen from two very formidable older women, not to mention the hulking Ben.

Noah relaxed. Maybe supper at the Boyettes' wouldn't be so bad after all.

"That coat of yours could use a good brushing, Mr. Reardon," Ben's mother noted. "I'll do it for you after supper."

"Thank you, ma'am," he said before realizing he'd just committed himself to staying on past the meal.

"You sit here," Mistress Stowe ordered. She pointed to a chair next to the head of the table, then turned toward the back door as Ben Coor came lumbering back in from his mission. "Benny, you better sit down at this end."

Noah came close to smiling as he took his place. The widow was separating them as if they were two squabbling schoolboys.

Before Coor was settled, their host, Sam Boyette, along with his three young sons, came stomping through the back door, the children talking all at once.

Scant seconds later, Evaline brought Jessica in through the parlor entrance.

Jessica looked much more appealing now than when they'd first arrived. Hair combed, her enchanting face shining, and, he noted, with most of the smudges removed from her ruffled cap and shawl collar. If Ben Coor had merely pretended interest before, now he really would be enticed. She was a hundred—no, a thousand—

times prettier than the other women in the room. And the candle-light only accentuated the startling contrasts of her coloring. Her dark hair peeking from beneath her white cap now seemed as sleek and lustrous as the black coach they'd passed on the road today. For some reason, Jessica kept her gaze lowered, not looking at anyone in particular. Had that clumsy farmer made her uncomfortable?

"Shall we all be seated?" Evaline suggested. "I think all the food's on the table now."

"Here, dear." Mistress Stowe caught Jessica's hand and led her to the other end of the table, seating her directly across from the bounder, Ben Coor. The widow was being deliberately duplicitous. Of that Noah had no doubt. And after he'd been kind enough to deliver her here posthaste.

As everyone else took a seat, the three-year-old Boyette twins crowded onto the same chair opposite Noah, both kneeling and trying to grab for a bowl of spicy stewed apples.

Their pa, at the head of the table, swatted their hands away from the treat. *"After* prayer, boys."

Noah was almost certain Sam Boyette was oblivious to the prevailing undercurrent in the room. There was no hint of it as he gave thanks for the food and the arrival of his mother-in-law, as well as for the help he'd received from the Coors, particularly for a special concoction Lizzy had plastered on Evaline's chest to break up her cough.

After a slight pause, Boyette said in a voice thick with emotion, "And, dear Lord, I thank you, not just for your kind indulgences this week but for your indulgence in giving my Evie to me in the first place. I promise never to forget your great mercies. In the name of our Lord Jesus, amen."

Noah glanced up just in time to see Sam and Evaline exchange tender glances. Their love for each other was obvious. Noah leaned forward with a sudden desire to see Jessica seated on the other side of the much larger Lizzy Coor.

Jessica had leaned forward as well and was looking at him. Quickly she sat back out of sight. And after she'd been such a chatterbox all day.

"La, Mr. Reardon," Mistress Coor said as she passed him a platter of sliced pork roast. "From what Izzy says, you've traveled very far afield. She says your place is almost to the Mississippi."

"No, not really," he corrected politely. "I live inside the great Tennessee River bend."

"I thought," Sam remarked from the right, "the territory betwixt the Watauga settlements and Nashville was nothin' but Injun country." Their host seemed to have a good grasp of the geography.

"The Indians have moved farther west for the most part, now. Of course, the various Creek tribes are still to the south of the Tennessee." Just the mention reminded Noah of his own bloody encounter with the Muskogee not much more than a fortnight ago.

"Nonetheless, Mr. Reardon," Ben's mother pressed on, "Izzy said you been gone from your home quite a spell longer than you expected. Had to send your kid brother home with some lazy hunter. Sounds to me like you need to be gettin' on back. A farm don't run itself."

"We all know what it's like to be away from our kin," the widow chimed from across the table. "And since you did me such a good turn, we'd like to return the favor."

"Aye," the other sister picked up seamlessly, "we've talked it over. You don't have to waste any more time looking for a suitable escort for Miss Jessica. Me and my Ben, here, will take Miss Jessica off your hands. We'll be goin' home to Hillsborough in a few days, and later they can catch a coastal packet for Baltimore—if she still has it in her head to go find her brother."

Aha! The plan unfolds. Ben wouldn't have to ask Jessica to marry him this very night. He'd have hours and days to work on her. "It's kind of you folks to offer, but Miss Jessica needs to get to Baltimore as soon as possible, and despite my need to get back to my valley, I made a solemn vow to see she gets there as quickly and safely as possible. And as you yourself said, you won't be leaving here for several days."

Noah glanced at Ben Coor at the far corner. The muscles in the man's jaw were bunched like so many hazelnuts—Noah's rejection had not been to his liking.

Coor started to speak, but his aunt beat him to it.

"What difference could a few days make?" the widow argued. "Jessica's brother has been gone without a word for almost five years. Either he'll be there or he won't. Besides, the dear girl could use the rest."

"I'm sorry, but Spencer Whitman's been missing much too long for the matter to be delayed an unnecessary minute. I'll be securing an escort for her, hopefully tomorrow morning, and she'll be on her way again. That is her wish. And, of course, I'll hire a suitable chaperone. One," he added as he turned his attention to Ben Coor, "who'll see she's not bothered by unwanted attentions along the way."

The big farmer's shoulders flexed, almost doubling their size.

And it came to Noah that he really might have to fight his way out of this place.

A chair screeched back. Not Ben Coor's.

Jessica was on her feet and heading for the back entrance, without saying a word. Without even a glance back, she grabbed her cloak from a wall peg and slammed out the door.

Ben Coor did thrust himself out of his chair now—right along with Noah. "I better go see what ails her."

"No!" Noah commanded. "I will. She's in my charge."

The cold rage in his voice must have impressed Coor. After only a second's hesitation, the man slumped down to his seat.

Not bothering with his heavy frock coat, Noah strode after Jessica in his vest and shirtsleeves, undaunted by the temperature's drop since sunset. He caught a flash of white in the beam of a three-quarter moon and saw her running for the dimly lit opening to the barn.

Noah hastened after her. Pausing at the cracked door of the yawning building, he spotted her in the glow of a lone lantern that was hooked on a post. Amid the pungent smell of animals and old straw, he started unhurriedly toward her. Had he overstepped his bounds? Did she really want to go with these people? Who was he to stop her when he couldn't offer for her himself?

Jessica was several yards inside, her back to him, rummaging through the saddle blankets draped over the top rails of the animal stalls. She already had a bridle in hand. She found the blanket she'd apparently been searching for and pulled it off—the one that went under her saddle.

For lack of a more courageous comment, he questioned the obvious. "What are you doing?"

She scarcely glanced over her shoulder as she started down the aisle separating the stalls. Stopping at one near the end, she flapped the blanket over the gate.

Before she could unlatch it, he caught up to her.

Glancing first at the hand that stopped her, she scowled up at him.

He felt obliged to let go.

Ire sparking in her eyes, she took a step closer. "I ran away from one tyrant only to allow you and that Mistress Stowe to order me about. A tremendous error on my part. Now you and that greedy threesome in there are treating me like I'm nothing but a sack of meal to be tossed back and forth as if I have no mind of my own." Her fists dug into her hips, setting the bridle in her hand to jangling. "Did you tell that woman about my money? I swear, she's got the Coors salivating worse than some old hounds."

223

"I didn't tell her. I thought maybe you did." He found himself on the defensive again.

Jessica's eyes narrowed. "That old witch! Going through my things." She whisked past him, heading straight for where their totes and saddlebags had been dumped. She ripped through them until she came up with her deerskin dress. In a flash, she had it turned inside out, her fingers counting the coins down one seam, then the other.

She looked up at him. "Well, they're all here. It would seem Mistress Stowe's not an out-and-out thief. She merely plans to get her hands on the coins by handing me over to her nephew." Her words were ripe with disdain. She started rerolling the dress. "I now truly understand the value of these coins. That man in there is willing—no, eager—to take a total stranger to wife *for life* just to get his paws on them."

"Yes, it is a sizable amount. And Coor hasn't even seen your pendant yet. Or has he?"

Her hand flew to her throat; then she eyed him again.

If he didn't know better, he'd think her ire included him.

"I thank you for your invaluable assistance thus far, but I'll be traveling on my own henceforth. The roads are wide, and folks are most helpful with directions. I obviously have a plentiful supply of money, tainted or not. And, as you've mentioned before, there's no shortage of inns between here and Baltimore."

"That's ridiculous. You can't—"

"No, *you're* ridiculous if you think I'm putting up with any more of this. I came across this mountain seeking my freedom, not more tyranny."

Then, quite suddenly her whole demeanor softened. "Forgive me for being so horribly ungrateful. Of all people, you don't deserve my wrath. I know you've gone weeks out of your way to help me, letting your obligations to home and family suffer at my expense." She thrust the leather gown at him. "And you've been the truest friend I ever had. I want you to quit being so stubborn about my money and take whatever you've spent on me thus far and enough to pay for your time and trouble."

"I don't want your money." He tossed away the fringed dress. "I doubt I'd take it even if it was honestly yours." Taking hold of both her hands, he turned her toward the light—he needed to look into her face. "Jessica, I truly believe that I was meant to meet you and take you to that freedom you cherish so much. But not necessarily as you've imagined it. Only through giving yourself up to a new life in Christ, only if you follow his teachings will you find any lasting freedom."

"What you really mean is you want me to give the coins back to my father and forgive him his trespasses—along with that greedy den of thieves in there." She shot a glance over her shoulder to the Boyette house.

Cupping Jessica's chin, he turned her face back to him. "And me. Especially me. Forgive me for being thoughtless and clumsy. And worse. You have not been able to see the healing love of Christ through me. I let my own inner struggle get in the way. I'm sorry, but I haven't been thinking clearly since I kissed you."

"The kiss . . ." Her expression became a potpourri of emotions: fear, confusion, hesitant anticipation.

He tried not to display his own emotion—misgivings about bringing up something that he still couldn't think about with any objectivity. He quickly moved on. "I accused Ben Coor of being presumptuous when I'd done much more. The activity of kissing, in the manner I kissed you, is to be reserved until one is properly betrothed to wed."

"I see," she said softly. "And that, of course, we are not."

Before she looked away, he glimpsed the hurt in her eyes. Rejection. One more in a lifetime of rejection.

Without thinking he took her arms and pulled her close. "Please don't think you aren't someone to be wanted, cherished. You are.

You will be." A harsh laugh escaped him. "Probably by more young men than I ever want to think about."

More aware than he should be of her nearness, he took a step back. Lifting her chin, he forced her to look up at him and continued, "And that's why we need to find that brother of yours as quick as we can. With all those young swains asking for your hand in marriage, he'll be the one they'll be going to—the one they'll have to convince that they're good enough for you."

His words hadn't cheered her. She stepped out of his hold. *"If I find him."*

"We will. If you'll still have me, I'd be honored to continue on with you to Baltimore."

"What about your other responsibilities?"

"They can wait. You're more important."

Then what he'd been longing to see happened. Her lips, those lips that tempted him so, spilled into spectacular glory.

Just before his desire to kiss her one more time got the better of him, she whirled away. "We'd better get back inside. As Mistress Stowe puts it, I'll need my beauty sleep if we're to get an early start in the morning." On an airy laugh, she swept up her skirts and took off for the house.

Noah watched her run, so light of foot, so graceful. She had the aura of a woman who had her man exactly where she wanted him.

And he reveled in the sight. How hard it was becoming to remain true to his avowed beliefs.

21

In Salem it had been as easy to hire a chaperone for Jessica as it had been in Greeneville. It seemed that older women were often looking for an opportunity to be escorted to some distant town to visit a son or daughter. All Noah had done was seek out the local clergy, and he'd been directed to a Mistress McKinney, a round little woman with a congenial nature, who would be stopping off in a town less than a day's ride short of Baltimore. Unlike the Widow Stowe, this chaperone was a much better instructress in female pursuits than she was a horsewoman. To accommodate her inexperience, Noah had slowed the pace by half, which was made easier by the fair weather they enjoyed the first several days of the trip north.

Then the rain started.

It had been raining steadily since they crossed the border into Virginia before noon, and now, to make the journey more miserable, a cutting wind began to blow, straight into their faces. Noah was already damp to the skin and chilled to the bone, despite the

227

oiled sailcloth cloak he'd purchased a few days ago—one for him
and one for Mistress McKinney. Though she had refrained from
complaining, he knew she fared no better than he did.

Jessica, on the other hand, had assured him on several occasions
that she was relatively comfortable. Despite the chaperone's
entreaty, "Surely, you're aren't going to wear that, are you?"
Jessica had donned her bearskin robe and floppy felt hat, which she
pulled low. It protected the back of her neck from the icy down-
pour much better than the chocolate brown, front-billed bonnet
he'd helped her select in Salem to match the set of traveling clothes
she wore beneath the robe—those that polite society and Mistress
McKinney had deemed proper for travel.

He had to smile as he looked over at Jessica seated on her proper
yet not so comfortable sidesaddle.

This main artery north was a wide one, allowing both women to
ride beside him. While Mistress McKinney huddled cold over her
horse's neck, Jessica sat as straight and tall as her diminutive height
would allow.

Among the six horses quite a lot of mud was being churned up.
He watched it splash up the hooves of Jessica's latest mount,
covering its two white stockings. A fine-boned black mare, its
rain-slicked coat was virtually covered by the coarser black of the
bear fur.

Aye, here they were in the civilized East, where folks naturally
stopped to stare at the girl in the animal skin, yet he couldn't have
bought anything that would protect her better.

Fact was, she looked no different from the first time he saw her
stirring her pots at the salt lick. Yet he knew she was. She truly was
becoming what he'd insisted on calling her from the start—Miss
Jessica Jane Whitman. But it was "Jaybird" who'd first touched
him so deeply . . . Jaybird Jones, with her insatiable curiosity and
the grandest of smiles.

Suddenly the rain came down so blindingly, they were riding

directly between two roadside buildings before Noah noticed they'd reached what looked like the beginnings of a village. A hinged sign jutted out from the closest structure, squeaking as it swung in the wind. Shaped like a basket, it read *Brooms & Baskets, R. Fulton.* The purpose of the building across the road was painted across the front in big red letters: *Leatherworks.* Beside the word was a drawing of a boot. About a fifty yards farther, he spotted another advertisement board hanging from a pole near the road, and through the haze, the sign stated exactly what Noah had hoped it would: *The Wayside Inn.* A painting of a coach and horses stretched out above the words.

How sad they couldn't be riding in something like that right now, he thought, something warm and comfortable. But alas, all the passenger stages were nothing more than canvas-covered wagons with rows of bone jarring backless benches for sitting.

"Ladies!" he shouted against the torrent and pointed toward the haven, then reined his mount onto the sweeping gravel driveway. He brought his gelding to a crunching stop before one of several ringed poles that had been grounded in front of the large fieldstone building that was framed and shuttered in green. Even in midafternoon, light shone brightly from all the windows on the lower floor—a welcoming sight.

After dismounting and tethering his animals, Noah lifted the two women down.

"Why are we stopping so soon?" Jessica asked, water dripping from around her hat.

"I'm soaked clean through. I need to dry off."

"Me too," the chaperone said through chattering teeth. Her full rosy cheeks were showing signs of chapping.

Jessica's eyes filled with sympathy. "We need to get you in and dried out." She protruded a velvet jacket-sleeved arm from out of the fur and wrapped it around the soggy cloaked shoulders of the equally short woman.

Noah enjoyed seeing this mothering side of Jessica. She'd even been the one to suggest the slower pace, not wanting to overtax the chaperone. "Take Mistress McKinney inside, sweet girl. I'll be right behind you."

Grasping their horses' reins, he quickly looped them through the waiting rings, then reached the big entrance door in time to follow Jessica inside.

They had entered a wide hallway that ended with a stairwell.

Archways led into rooms at each side. Above the one on the left was printed *Taproom,* and over the opposite one, *Food & Lodging.* "To the right," he said, removing his tricorn and dumping the rainwater trapped in the folds.

As he stepped inside, Noah noticed the amazed expression on the only person in the barnlike room—an elderly man with receding white hair. Noah was certain the old fellow hadn't seen anything quite like Jessica's woodsy getup for quite some time—if ever.

"Afternoon," the man said, rising from one of several rocking chairs near the fireplace.

Returning the greeting, Noah spotted some nearby pegs and helped Jessica off with her bearskin. He shook out what must have been five pounds of water from it as she helped her chaperone off with her cloak, then removed her own black cloak he'd purchased for her in Salem.

"Don't wait for me," he said to the woman. "Go on over to the fire and warm up." Removing his own outer clothing, the pungent smell of his maroon frock coat slapped him in the face. Its mixture of woodsmoke, wet wool, and horse was as ripe as any he'd smelled since his winters on the road with General Washington. He really hadn't been prepared to be gone from home this long. He'd had no choice but to purchase a used suit of clothes for when he took Jessica to a church service—which he planned to do the very next Sabbath now that they were down in the more populated areas.

Food, lodging, two outfits of clothes for Jessica and the one for him. This was costing him more than he'd thought. Thank goodness, he'd had money for the salt he never purchased and the other supplies the settlers had ordered. He'd asked Drew to buy the supplies on credit. Whatever he was short when he returned overmountain, he'd have to fetch from home back to Keaton's store. A loss of yet another week. He grimaced.

Taking some of Jessica's proffered coins was becoming more of a temptation all the time—but one he absolutely would resist.

Smoothing down his maroon waistcoat, he followed the women past a dozen cloth-covered tables to reach the warmth of the hearth.

"You look like a drowned rat," the slightly stooped proprietor said to Mistress McKinney as he circled a spindle-backed rocker. The poor woman's silver-threaded chestnut hair was straggling down from beneath her soggy mobcap. The old innkeeper then smiled his approval that Jessica was down to her quite dry, quite civilized brown velvet travel costume. "What can I do for you?"

"We're riding north to Baltimore," Jessica said enthusiastically, her spirits not dampened one whit by the foul weather. "Have you ever been there?"

His sagging face brightened—she had a way about her that just naturally lightened a person's mood. "Can't say as I have." As Noah came up behind them, the proprietor turned to him. "Riding, are you? Folks in these parts are more apt to go by sea."

"We didn't want to take the extra time." Noah felt compelled to explain since Jessica had made the man privy to their plans. "Ride down to some port only to find no coastal packet ready to sail for a week or two. And once you board, you're at the mercy of the capricious winds." He caught scent of a tempting aroma. "Something certainly smells good. Do you have a good hearty soup or stew ready and hot? And a pot of tea? We need some quick warming up." Noah smiled his empathy to Mistress McKinney, who stood so close to the fire, her generous behind was practically in it.

"Sure do. Set yourselves down by the fire, and I'll go roust out the wife. She's upstairs mending her good dress for tomorrow. Last Sunday an ember popped out of the fire and burnt a hole clean through it."

As the old man shuffled past the red-checked tables and out to the hall, Noah realized he'd lost track of the days. He called after the innkeeper. "Is tomorrow Sunday?"

The balding fellow turned back with a friendly smile. "Losin' your memory awful early, ain'tcha?" For an old codger, he had a sense of humor. "Aye, lad, 'tis the Sabbath."

"The Sabbath," Noah repeated and stuck his hands toward the fire.

Sighing pleasantly, Jessica pulled the rocker closer to the hearth and sat down in it. Hiking up her dark velvet skirt, she thrust her small moccasined feet toward the flames. Though she had cobbled shoes now, with shiny buckles, she refused to chance ruining them in bad weather.

Mistress McKinney cleared her throat.

Grinning sheepishly, Jessica lowered her skirt. Her decorum rarely slipped anymore.

Jessica's expression abruptly turned to dismay. She leapt to her feet. "Mistress McKinney, do take this chair. It's a wondrous thing. It'll make you feel so much better."

"Why, thank you, my dear." The older lady's voice sounded hoarse as she eased herself into the proffered seat.

Noah hoped the chaperone wasn't coming down sick. That could slow them up for days. Just to be on the safe side, he decided not to take her back out in this icy rain again today. He knelt beside her. "As soon as the proprietor returns, we're getting you into bed with some heated bricks to warm your feet."

"But there's still a couple hours of daylight left," she argued, her voice a husky whisper.

"I'm doing it as much for me as for you," he returned. "I don't want to go back out there today either."

Relief eased her plump features.

As soon as the proprietor returned with his wife, Noah sent him back up with Mistress McKinney, with Jessica helping. By the time Jessica returned, bowls of steaming thick potato chowder were on the table for the two of them and another was being taken up to the older woman.

After Noah said grace, adding to it his concern about the chaperone's health, Jessica smiled, warming him even more. "You made a good decision, Noah. I'm certain she'll be better by morning."

"Speaking of that, I'd like to join the good people here for church tomorrow—it being the Sabbath. A day or two one way or the other won't make much difference as to when we arrive in Baltimore."

"I can't believe you're asking that, considering Mistress McKinney's condition." Spoon in hand, she cocked her head and peered at him as if he'd lost his mind. "You want us to go all the way back to that church? Just to hear a bell ring? That's almost a half-day's ride. Then we'd have to come all the way back. I don't need to hear it again. And I'm equally certain Mistress McKinney would gladly forgo the pleasure."

Now it was his turn to look askance. "Whatever do you mean?"

Setting the spoon down, she frowned again. "You really must be losing your memory. You just brought it up. The big white house with the point sticking up where the giant bell hangs. You're the one who told me what was making the noise."

"Oh yes, the church just before we crossed into Virginia. But we don't have to go back there. Almost every village has a church. Larger towns have several."

"I suppose the more bells, the better." She shrugged. "That way more folks out and about can hear when it's nine o'clock or noon, like you said. Or when there's a fire. But why would a person want to waste a whole day waiting for a bell to ring?"

It took the greatest effort not to laugh. "Dearest Jessica, remember the commandment about keeping the Sabbath holy?"

"Aye, the one about not having to work. That was really my favorite."

"Well, you see, on Sundays the bell calls the congregation to the church where we gather to worship God. We sing and pray and a learned man gets up and tells us about things in the Bible."

Her whole demeanor livened. "Oh, will they ask you to speak?"

Noah did grin now. "Not likely. It will be an ordained minister. One who's had years of special schooling," he added, knowing that for her, it would be an irresistible inducement.

"Oh, really? Perhaps staying here would be pleasurable. As you said, Mistress McKinney needs the rest. Besides," she added with authority, "that commandment also says we're supposed to let our animals rest on the Sabbath, which we've neglected to do." Then her expression softened to something almost wistful. "And I do enjoy hearing folks sing."

Maybe she hadn't said the exact words he wanted to hear, but she was willing to go. And soon, very soon, he prayed, she would come to think of the Lord as her own. Why else would God have placed her in his care?

"And mayhap your god will stop this infernal rain by Monday. Do you think the people at the church would help us pray for that . . . like when we all prayed for Evaline Boyette?"

He was tempted to say nothing and let God take credit if the rain did stop naturally. But he knew that would be a cheat. "The weather, like life, Jessica, can rarely be ordered up like a cup of tea. Mistress Boyette's recovery was a wonderful blessing. It may even have been a miracle. We can't say for sure, since we weren't there to witness her recovery. But it's more important for you to under-stand that God wants us to believe in him on faith, not because of the miracles we see. And to love him . . . because he first loved us. His Son, Jesus, said we are to be as his bride and he our bride-groom. And that's the most powerful kind of love."

Easing back in her seat, Jessica looked up at him, startled, then quickly lowered her lashes to half-mast. "I can see how that would be a very powerful kind of love, this bride and groom kind."

How quickly the conversation had taken on a much more per-sonal tone. Of all the biblical examples of God's love, why had he picked such an intimate one? But, then, it was hard to think beyond his very personal desire with Jessica so close . . . so tempt-ingly close.

With each passing hour, it had become harder to keep his feel-ings to himself. And here he was, beholding a face that showed nothing but her love and gratitude for being rescued from her father. But an unknown future lay ahead of them in Baltimore. Even if he were free to do so, how could he ask her to commit herself to him for the rest of her life when she didn't have the first inkling what awaited her?

"Oh, good," she said, looking behind them at the sound of approaching footsteps. "The tea."

Noah turned and saw the proprietor coming with a tray bearing a matching porcelain tea service. He rose and intercepted the man. "I don't believe we've properly introduced ourselves. I'm Noah Reardon, and my charge is Miss Jessica Whitman, and upstairs is Mistress McKinney. If you have another room available for me, we'd like to lodge here for two nights and perhaps on the morrow accompany you and your good wife to church."

"The name's Edmund Pratt, owner of the Wayside Inn." He set the pewter tray down and extended his hand. "With no stage-coach through here until Monday night, and what with the pea-soup weather outside, I don't expect much supper business from the locals, so you are more welcome than you know." He picked up the teapot to pour. "Will any of you be wanting a bath?"

"Aye, that we would." Noah said, taking the blue-and-white porcelain pot from the proprietor. "Let me take care of the tea, whilst you tend to that."

Mr. Pratt looked from the teapot to Noah and frowned as he turned to leave, but he didn't make the obvious remark. Custom dictated that the women serve tea to the menfolk, not the other way around.

Noah grunted a chuckle. To look at Jessica in her tailored jacket and skirt, no one would guess she'd probably never even seen a full tea service, let alone know how to perform the ritual. Too bad Mistress McKinney retired before she could instruct her. He poured the golden liquid into two fluted white cups, then glanced up. "Sugar? Cream?"

Again her face transformed into one of gentle, trusting love— a veritable Renaissance madonna she was. "However you prefer your tea shall be fine for me."

But to him, her simple innocent reply, her congenial expression seemed to say, *Whatever you want of me, whatever you wish . . .*

Whatever he wished . . . "I like plenty of both," he scarcely managed. "Plenty of both."

Jessica heard the distant ringing of a church bell as she descended the stairs. This morning she knew the pealing of the bells was to call people to worship. And she would be one of those people . . . all decked out in the more elegant of the two outfits Noah and Mistress McKinney had helped her select back in Salem.

She was sad that her chaperone had felt the need to spend the day abed to recoup her strength. But then she was also glad. Just for this one day, she could pretend Noah was all hers, pretend they were like any other Eastern couple spending the morning in church all dressed up in their finest.

And this gown truly was fine. It even sounded beautiful when she walked, making a whisking sound. Mistress Pratt, the proprietor's wife, who'd helped her into it, said the stiff and shiny russet material was called taffeta.

As Jessica's shiny new black and silver-buckled shoes carried her downstairs, the wide band of jet embroidery at the hem, lent extra motion to the skirt. Her only regret—it wasn't designed to go over a pocket hoop. Those wide gowns, Noah had said, were usually reserved for social gatherings in the evening. Along with the powdered wigs she had yet to see.

But she shouldn't complain. After Mistress Pratt finished tightening the back laces, the bodice fit as smooth as a pigskin glove . . . ever so much more neatly than the bulky traveling jacket. And her cross pendant suspended most elegantly just above the jet black ruffles and stitchery at the scooped neck. Both Mistress Pratt and her chaperone, who lay propped up in the bed they'd shared last night, had said so.

Jessica had a pang of guilt about displaying the cross when Noah had warned her not to. But, she argued, if she couldn't wear it to church, where could she wear it? And just this once she wanted to look as beautiful as possible for him—even if she was such a reed of a girl.

Reaching the bottom step, she heard male voices in the main room. Making certain her new frilly lace mobcap was exactly centered, she went to join the men.

Stepping through the archway, she saw Noah at the other end of the common room. He faced the fire while talking to Innkeeper Pratt. She saw he wore what he'd called a "not-too-worn" suit of clothes he'd found for himself in the general store at Salem.

She smiled. She'd had so many more articles of clothing to pick from than he—an advantage, he'd said, because of her smallness. Nonetheless, from where she stood, she thought the dusty blue velvet knee breeches and waistcoat were a fine fit.

Her "civilized" shoes made a tapping sound as she traversed the center aisle between tables, causing Noah to turn to meet her. . . . And all thought, save one, fled her brain.

She paused and stared at the most unimaginably handsome man she'd ever seen. At the top of a pristine white shirt, a matching cravat artfully wrapped his neck, setting off an evenly tanned face of the most appealing angles. His sun-streaked hair, tied at the back with a cobalt blue ribbon, flared at the temples to frame eyes that had taken on the color of his waistcoat—eyes that stared back at her with their own fair amount of admiration.

He strode toward her, not in his tall brown boots but in shiny black shoes with silver buckles, like hers, along with creamy white stockings that displayed his manly calves.

Her heart picked up pace. My, but he made the most dashing figure.

"I'll be the envy of every man at the service today," he said in an enticingly mellow voice. "For I shall have on my arm the most beautiful woman in all the American states."

"If that be so, kind sir, then we'll be the most beautiful couple in all those states." Belatedly she remembered to curtsy. "Because no one in the whole wide world could be as handsome as you are right now." And he smelled really nice too, but from what, she wasn't sure. She quirked a smile. "I just may have to take along a stick to beat the ladies off."

A happy laugh rumbled up from his chest.

Quite suddenly, Jessica no longer found what she'd said all that amusing. Fact was, any woman with eyes in her head could see that Noah was—as the cantankerous Mistress Stowe had said about her nephew—the catch of the county, or any other, for that matter.

"The gown is even more stylish on you than I imagined," he said, his gaze traversing it.

"Aye," Mister Pratt agreed. "A sight better than when you folks washed in here yesterday. Thank goodness, there's only a light sprinkle out there this morning."

"And the ruffled tucker," Noah continued as if the innkeeper were not even in the room, "displays your cross to perfection. I'm so pleased we're going to a place where you can safely show it off. I'm afraid, though, once we return from church, you'll need to keep it hidden again. I don't want any passing ne'er-do-wells getting a look at it."

Touching her cross, she nodded. "I know." And she did. He'd said it was worth more than all her coins combined. And she'd seen what they could've bought—a husband for life.

She did, however, wish Noah would accept some of her coins for the expenses of this trip—that had been their biggest bone of contention. He'd merely said he'd recoup from her family if they were able.

"I'm ready," came a woman's voice from behind. It was Mistress Pratt, who had been much nicer and more helpful to both Mistress McKinney and herself than Jessica would've expected from one with such severe features. "Shall we fetch our cloaks and be off?" The workaday apron no longer hid the simple elegance of her finely woven black wool with white lace trim.

Yes, Jessica thought, the four of them were all in nothing but their Sunday best, as Noah had put it, and on their way to where the bell rang!

Her heart leapt beneath her heavy cross. They were going to a house that had but one purpose: to bring folks together to learn more about God and the Bible. That big black book truly must have the most incredible writings in the world if every township went to such trouble to build a special place to hear about it and gather there every single Sunday.

Maybe Noah had been right about his unbelievable god all along. Mayhap it was all true.

Still, she'd have to wait and see.

22

As always, Noah demonstrated he was the most considerate of men. Upon their arrival at the white-trimmed brick church, he quickly secured both their mounts alongside the other horses and vehicles. Lifting Jessica from the sidesaddle, he carried her above the mud toward a slate walk. He hadn't wanted it to spot her taffeta gown.

Though she told herself not to enjoy the short journey in his arms so much, she couldn't help absorbing some of that enticingly spicy scent wafting from his cleanly shaven face.

When he set her feet on the dark gray stones, she allowed him to hasten her along behind the Pratts, up the steps, and through a set of tall carved doors.

Other folks in front of them and behind seemed just as eager to get out of the weather. She felt a kinship with the people as they laughed in their hurry. She saw some of the men carry their womenfolk just as Noah had carried her.

The room they entered was wide but only a few yards deep, and the people crowded in, chatting nonstop as they removed their outer wear. Most were taller than Jessica, and as much as she tried, she couldn't see what lay beyond the next doorway.

Noah bent close to her ear. "This room is called a vestibule where folks hang their coats. The sanctuary where we gather is straight ahead. Let me take your cloak."

As she handed the black wool garment to him, Mistress Pratt stepped close. "I do hope you two enjoy our new minister. He's fresh out of seminary with some new ways of doing things. But he does fill the church, even on a day like today."

"How's that?" Noah asked.

Jessica detected concern in his tone.

"Nothing to fret about, Mr. Reardon. Reverend Stevens is an appreciator of religious poetry and music. He fashions his sermons after a different composition each week. Most of his preaching has been quite inspirational. He doesn't use all those long-winded, drawn-out words so many of the clergy try to impress us common folk with."

"I see." He still didn't sound all that convinced.

Mr. Pratt, his own cloak disposed of, spoke to Noah. "I'd like you to meet a friend of mine. He's thinking of moving west."

As the innkeeper ushered Noah away to a cluster of men, he looked back at Jessica with an apologetic smile . . . a dear smile. . . .

When she remembered to turn back to Mistress Pratt, a young woman about her own age stood before them, carrying a tiny baby. Her forest green gown had leaves of a lighter shade and small pink flowers printed right on the material. Very pretty, Jessica observed, but the fabric didn't have the body or shine her own did—not quite as much to her liking.

"Has a new family moved to the neighborhood?" the young blonde asked in a leisurely lilt as her gaze gravitated to Jessica's necklace and stayed there a moment too long. "Or are they some of your kin come to visit?"

"Neither," Mistress Pratt answered. "Merely guests passing through on their way to family in Baltimore. Miss Whitman, I'd like you to meet Mistress Stanwix. Her father-in-law owns a tobacco plantation to the west."

Jessica curtsied.

The other woman bobbed into her own hasty one as if she'd forgotten her manners. This added to Jessica's confidence, knowing that others sometimes forgot one of the huge list of customs.

"We're so pleased to have a lady such as yourself," Mistress Stanwix gushed in that syrupy voice that didn't seem quite real, "to honor us with your presence here today . . . and in such foul weather. Thank goodness our carriage is watertight."

As the young mother smiled politely, Jessica sensed that Mistress Stanwix had meant to impress her by mentioning ownership of a carriage. But Jessica's attention was instantly plucked away by the sight of the tiny baby nuzzling against the young mother's bodice. Wisps of the finest hair looked so soft, she had the strongest desire to reach out and touch it.

After Mistress Stanwix moved away from them, Jessica couldn't stop thinking about the baby and what it would be like to hold such a cuddly little bundle. A yearning she'd never experienced before welled within her. Even while Mistress Pratt introduced her to other ruffled and plumed arrivals, she couldn't think of anything else.

What would it be like to have a babe of her own? she mused, then took this new desire a leap further. To have Noah's baby. Just the thought sent a thrill spiraling through her—a thrill abruptly cut short when she realized Noah's hesitation to mention marriage might very well be due to her lack of stature, the same as Ben Coor had questioned. A man as stalwart as Noah might not wish to take a chance on his sons inheriting their strength and build from one as spindly as she.

Noah came walking back to her, and she was doubly glad—he interrupted a very disturbing thought.

"Shall we go in now?" he asked, tucking her hand into the crook of his arm. "The Pratts have their own pew box. We'll sit with them."

"Pew box?"

He leaned down and whispered for her ears only. "Their own seats." Never would he dream of shaming her unnecessarily. How could she not love such a man?

"Come along," Mistress Pratt beckoned from where she and her rather stooped husband had taken their place behind people streaming into what Noah had called the sanctuary. She, too, held on to her man's arm.

Despite the dreary day, the sparkling white plaster of the high ceiling lent a brightness aided by sconces spaced between the side windows. Straight ahead, a huge double ring of candles hung down from a black chain. Walking toward it, Jessica passed rows of seats that were sectioned something like horse stalls, only with solid walls of polished wood that matched the frames of the arched windows. Each sectioned-off pew box had its own gate. Standing near the front, Mr. Pratt held one open for them to enter.

The aisleway before them had now emptied of people, and directly ahead of her . . . beyond a low fence made of slender spindles . . . past a table covered in a lace-edged white cloth . . . she saw the huge window. Four sections were set with diamond-shaped panes of every color imaginable. As stunningly beautiful as it was today, she could only imagine what it would look like on a sunny morning. But, impressive as it was, what separated the four sections of panes caught her breath. The panes set off a lustrous brass cross.

Emotion swelling her lungs, she touched her own cross.

Then, from where she couldn't be sure, came the loudest flute sounds she'd ever heard. Any number of them. Jessica scanned the long hall for the flute players but saw none.

"Over there." Noah nodded toward a man in a black robe seated before a strange boxlike contraption. "It's an organ."

Both the man's hands and feet were pressing down on bars, his feet on long ones and his fingers up higher on much smaller ones. And out came the most glorious music. It seemed to come from everywhere, rising in such rich tones it virtually filled the cavernous hall.

"Step into our pew," Noah urged, and Jessica realized she'd been standing there, openmouthed and blocking traffic.

Quickly she complied. She sat next to Mistress Pratt, and Noah slid in beside her. With a clear view of the organ only three rows straight ahead of her, she could watch the black-robed musician to her heart's content.

Noah took her hand in his, lacing his fingers through hers.

She glanced up at him and found him smiling warmly at her. But, strangely, his eyes sparked with unshed tears. Perhaps the music moved him even more than it did her.

Too soon, the player brought this glorious feast for the ears to an end. As he did, a loud voice resonated from high above. "O sing unto the Lord a new song!"

Did the invisible god actually speak to the people in this place? Fear gripped her. All her sins were still lurking inside her. And he would be able to see each and every one.

Then she saw that it was not a disembodied voice, but a human being speaking. High above her, a flame-haired man stood in a wide-sleeved black robe. He looked heavenward with his arms outstretched, reminding her of a great bird. He was on a platform in the far corner of the front wall. Like the pews, it, too, was enclosed by a half wall.

"Sing unto the Lord, all the earth!" came his next impassioned cry. "Sing unto the Lord, bless his name. Show forth his salvation

. . . from day to day. Declare his glory among the heathen! His wonders among all people. For the Lord is great! And greatly to be praised!"

As the last word echoed from the rafters, the man, whose florid face stood out against his draping white collar, lowered his gaze to the congregation. "Now let us do just that—sing his praises! Please, turn in your hymnal to page ten— 'Mighty God, While Angels Bless Thee.'"

Without a second's delay the organ player struck the bars again. Music came forth, this time much faster.

Those gathered rose to their feet. Noah brought Jessica up with him.

"Here, dear," Mistress Pratt said, handing Jessica a thin volume.

People all around her began to sing along with the organ. The entire room suddenly vibrated with the most marvelous blending of sounds and voices. "'Lord of men as well as angels, thou art every creature's theme.'"

Taking the book from her, Noah held it so they both could see as he began to blend his deep rich voice with the others.

Nothing had prepared her for such beauty of sound. She'd heard a few trappers singing after downing some of Father's rum, a lively tune on a reed pipe now and then, but they couldn't even remotely compare to this. Her pride in Noah multiplied with every one of his melodious notes.

Not knowing the tune and embarrassed that she might make a mistake, she didn't join in the singing, but she followed every word while taking in every wondrous nuance. Surely this must be what the shepherds heard when the angels came the night the Lord Jesus was born.

Not only did the exquisite rendering move her tremendously, but the last two lines touched her deeply: "'From the highest throne of glory, To the cross of deepest woe, All to ransom guilty captives; Flow my praise, forever flow!'"

As the music came to an end, Jessica couldn't contain her gratitude for being brought to such an unimaginably wonderful place. Squeezing Noah's hand, she smiled up at him.

The warmth of his returning expression, the squeeze from his hand, made her heart soar even higher, to the vaulted ceiling and beyond.

The congregation treated her to several more stirring hymns praising the Lord before the Reverend Stevens bade them all bow in prayer. His following utterances were similar to those Noah prayed at mealtime, except the minister spoke with so much more flair.

Afterward, he asked everyone to be seated again and began what she'd been told would be the preaching part.

"Dear friends, our sermon for today will be taken from the words of the most reverent Isaac Watts— a great man of God who brought us so many of the insightful hymns we sing today. I do hope you will be as inspired as I am by the words to 'Alas! And Did My Savior Bleed?'"

The minister picked up a small volume and held it aloft. "'. . . and did my Sovereign die? Would he devote that sacred head for sinners such as I? . . . Was it for sins that I have done, he suffered on the tree? Amazing pity! Grace unknown! And love beyond degree!'"

As Jessica listened, each word, each phrase spoken with such fervor only reiterated everything Noah had already told her about Jesus choosing to die for sinners such as she.

"'Well might the sun in darkness hide,'" the pastor shouted with passion, "'and shut his glories in, when Christ, the great Redeemer, died for man the creature's sin.'" The preacher's voice dropped into a hushed tone. "'Thus might I hide my blushing face while his dear cross appears. Dissolve my heart in thankfulness, and melt mine eyes to tears.'"

The mere suggestion of Jesus' great sacrifice, his suffering for her, brought moisture to Jessica's own eyes as the minister continued with more emotion.

"'But drops of grief can ne'er repay the debt of love I owe; Here, Lord, I give myself away—'Tis all that I can do.'"

As a profound silence fell upon the room, those last words continued to ring in her head. *"But drops of grief can ne'er repay the debt of love I owe; Here, Lord, I give myself away—'Tis all that I can do."*

The pastor began to speak again, in more moderate educated tones now, but the words were lost on Jessica as her thoughts, her very soul cried out.

What a fool she'd been! If the Lord loved her so much that he died to save her . . . she, who had lied and stolen and hated the father she was supposed to honor . . . she, who had refused to give back what was not hers—how dare she refuse to repent her sins? How dare she insist on keeping what belonged to another, no matter how gravely she'd been mistreated, no matter how much she thought the money was owed her. How dare she not pray for her father's health and safety until she could return to bring him this wondrous hope.

Unbelievably, she felt all her bitterness melting away, and in its place, a buoyant sense of joy and love . . . especially for her desperately miserable father, lost soul that he was.

"Here, Lord, I give myself away," she cried silently, repeating the words she'd just heard. *"'Tis all that I can do." Thank you for taking my sins and for loving me. And most of all,* she added to the verse, *I thank you for wanting my love in return.*

Looking up to the cross at the window, she placed her hand over the cross resting on her bosom and felt the bloodred stone. Such love Jesus had for her; he'd never reject her love. He wanted it for all eternity.

As if she were an empty vessel, she felt herself being filled with even more joy, indescribable joy and peace and love . . . so much, she thought she would burst.

Noah had been utterly right when he'd called Jesus the bridegroom and the church his bride. She was one with the Lord now, together forever.

Small wonder Noah had been so dedicated to sharing his God with her. He'd said all the words, but she'd been utterly blind to their true meaning. How easy it was to understand now. And there was so much more she wanted to know. So very much.

Reveling in this wondrous new knowledge and the sensations that filled her and wrapped around her all at once, she didn't realize the minister had stopped speaking until the organ began to play again.

Noah took her elbow and whispered, "Stand up." He had the hymnal in his hand and already opened to page seventy-six.

As the others began to sing, Jessica again found herself floating on a stream of glorious song.

"'May the grace of Christ, our Savior,'" the congregation harmonized, "'and the Father's boundless love, with the Holy Spirit's favor, rest upon us from above. Amen.'"

The young minister, arms raised high, dismissed the congregation with, "May the Lord be with you and keep you, till we meet again . . . whether it be here next Sunday or in our heavenly home."

At once, everyone started moving toward the aisles; with Mistress Pratt on her heels, Jessica had no choice but to follow Noah. But she couldn't bear to tear herself from this awe-inspiring place just yet. It was too soon—much too soon. As they started up the aisle, she tugged on Noah's coat sleeve. "Could we wait till the others leave?"

That dear gentle expression she'd grown to love reappeared. "Of course." He guided her to one side to make way for those behind them.

Within scant moments the house of worship emptied, and

Jessica let the stillness in the sanctuary fall over her . . . and through her. She gazed up at Noah. "Thank you so very much for bringing me here. I never knew music could sound so thrilling. And there's so much more. Now I understand . . . really understand all that you've been trying to tell me."

"You have yourself to thank, sweet girl, with your unquenchable desire to learn."

"But there's more, so much more." She rushed on. "You see, I know now what you meant when you wanted your God to be my God. It isn't merely so I might attain a glorious end. The end starts at the beginning with Jesus. And every day from this moment on. With so much love, there's no room for hate. Even for my father. I can never thank you enough."

The spark of tears that she'd suspected seeing in his eyes earlier now became a reality.

He hugged her to him and whispered fervently, "And I thank you . . . for bringing me back to the fullness of my own faith. I've had my own struggles these past few weeks."

After a long moment, he took a deep shuddering breath and held her at arm's length. His emotion-filled eyes beheld her for a long-spun moment. "Whatever tomorrow brings, sweet girl, you and I have the Lord's promise: 'Fear thou not; for I am with thee: be not dismayed; for I am thy God.' Together we can face anything . . . no matter what awaits us in Baltimore."

23

The next several days flew by, despite the numerous times Noah was obliged to stop. Jessica plied him with such a barrage of questions about God and Jesus and the Holy Spirit, more than he or Mistress McKinney could answer. Therefore, they scarcely passed an inn along the post road without pausing for another perusal of Scripture.

Still, he couldn't have been more pleased—not only for her sake but for his own. Until Jessica came along and forced him to take a closer look at his own walk with the Lord, he hadn't realized how far he'd strayed. How wrong he'd been never to have questioned Lorna about the depth of her spiritual commitment. He had just taken her faith for granted since she attended church with her family.

More crucial, he'd never asked the Lord if Lorna was the right wife for him. Instead, he'd let his lusting eyes make the decision for him.

Thank heavens, the Lord had saved him from his folly. And,

thank heavens, Pizar Whitman decided to stake out the salt lick for himself. Like Jessica, Noah could no longer have ill fillings about any man who'd been instrumental in bringing them together and, ultimately, her to Christ.

Now all he had to do was share his feelings about everything with her, especially his feelings about wanting her for his wife. And he would, but not until they found her family, and she knew more about who she was and what she wanted. He wouldn't have anyone accusing him of taking advantage of a vulnerable young woman.

"Look, Noah! The sea." Jessica reined in her mount along with her extra horse at the top of a knoll and pointed through a break in the trees. "Does that mean we'll be there soon? In Baltimore?"

The visible slice of Chesapeake Bay was a silver blue glitter, reflecting the clear afternoon. "Aye, anytime now, we'll start seeing town buildings." The angst he'd been suppressing all afternoon tried to surface once again. He inhaled deeply. *Trust in the Lord,* he told himself one more time.

"Oh, I do hope I look presentable." She fussed with her brown velvet bonnet.

"For a person who's been on the road for weeks, you look stupendous."

She didn't act convinced as she brushed lint from her black cloak—the better of the two she now owned. "You always say I look fine. I wish Mistress McKinney was still with us."

"Well, Bladensburg was as far as she was going. Of course," he said, attempting some humor, "if you don't trust my judgment, we could always go back and ask her."

She slanted him an annoyed glance. "It's been a good three hours since we dropped her off."

"Then I guess you're just stuck with my humble male opinion."

"It would seem so." Her own amusement started to show.

But for Jessica, one aspect of this last week had not been amusing and especially not spiritually uplifting. During the past days of traveling through the Virginia countryside, she had become increasingly aware of the multitude of African slaves. Just the idea of their suffering had ruined the beauty and grandeur of the many plantations they passed—plantations she knew were built and maintained by their forced labor. "Shameful," she'd told him time and again.

A couple of days ago, she'd been particularly appalled when they passed a slave gang laying cobblestones up to a fine planter's manse. An overseer on horseback was harassing them by snapping a long whip scant inches above their backs. When he struck one slave, Jessica actually unsheathed her musket. It had taken quite a bit of talking before Noah and Mistress McKinney calmed her down, especially since Noah couldn't give her any better reason for stopping the abuse than interfering was against the law. Other than that, there simply was no moral ground to stand on. Once she'd rather bitterly asked if any white people at all worked in Virginia.

Then there had been the disheartening inquiries about her brother in Fredericksburg, from where he had mailed his second letter.

Since yesterday, though, when they ferried across the Potomac into Maryland, all her questions and expectations had been running ahead of her on this last stretch of road to Baltimore. . . . Since yesterday, when his own concerns took solid form. Noah knew from studying the Bible that he should turn all his worries over to the Lord, but they continued to plague him.

"Tell me what you smell," he urged as they descended the hill with the four horses . . . anything to keep his mind from drifting.

She wrinkled her nose and frowned. "Smells faintly like the salt lick."

"Aye. The ocean is salty too. Not as briny as the lick, but too salty to drink."

"How much farther?" Her mind really wasn't on salt, just on getting to Baltimore. Too much so.

The traffic was becoming heavier and more roads intersected now. "We'll probably see it over the next rise."

Jessica's excitement showed in her expression as well as in her unusual silence as they maneuvered around wagons and carts, one after another, being driven down to the city on the muddy thoroughfare that kept growing wider.

Assorted creaks and grinds began to surround them as the crowd thickened, along with the shouted greetings of people on their way to and from the port or marketplace. If Noah's memory served him correctly, there were three market locations in the bustling metropolis that rose on gentle hills above an inner bay. This city of Jessica's dreams . . . this place Noah fervently prayed would not disappoint her. Or him.

What if, once she met her family, she no longer wanted him, if, indeed, she really did even now. No actual words of love or commitment had passed between them.

Several times this afternoon he'd wanted to grab her horse's bridle and turn her around, take her away from all the uncertainties. Convince her to forget all this and go back to Tennessee with him.

But she'd come so far to find her family. Even if she did confess her love for him, would she be willing to return with him? If not, would he be willing to stay here to be with her? Forego his dreams for her . . . the valley he and Ike had worked so hard to develop.

None of it mattered, though, if she really wasn't as enamored with him as he thought. Oh, he was pretty certain she cared about him now, but aside from her family, she'd be meeting any number of splendidly dressed, dashing city men who had comforts and diversions to offer her right now, rather than the hard work of a settler and the someday promises he could offer her. Baltimore even had quite an array of churches from which she could choose.

They passed a brickyard across from a large plowed-under garden. Then came a wheelwright shop and a cabinetmaker's shop.

Down the way stood a cooperage and ever more businesses along the roadsides. Cross streets began to appear, with shops and houses lining them as well. There'd been a tremendous building boom since the war and, from what he'd heard, Baltimore now boasted of some eight thousand residents.

Eventually the road changed from muddy ruts to cobbles, creating more traffic clatter and rumbles. Folks on the street scarcely noticed them, the coming and going of strangers being so common here.

Noah reined his mount closer to Jessica's. "Let's stop and ask one of the tradesmen where the nearest parish house is."

"A parish house?"

"Where a minister lives. Considering your cross, I would expect your mother's family to attend church regularly."

"Aye." Her mirrorlike eyes reflected her emotion. "The ones who've been praying for me."

"That's just a guess, Jessica. We don't know that for sure." That had sounded a bit mean spirited, but it was true, he told himself.

She gave him a patient smile. "I know, but it is such a lovely thought."

Seeing a pasty-faced man standing in the doorway of the silversmith shop, Noah stopped in front of it. "Sir," he called to the fellow, who was dressed impeccably down to every shining silver buckle and button—an obvious advertisement for his wares. Even his wire-rimmed spectacles were of the same metal. "Could you direct us to where the nearest minister lives?"

The man eyed them both, then the extra horses. "Thinking of getting married, are you?"

No doubt they looked like they were on the run from some irate father with two mounts each. "Not today," Noah replied. But it really wasn't a bad idea. He shot a quick glance to Jessica.

She grinned back at him.

Too bad there was such a thing as the posting of the banns—

a two-week delay. Marrying her before finding her family now seemed like the smart thing to do. Why had he decided to be so all-fired noble?

"I can direct you to St. Paul's rectory, if that would do."

Noah glanced at Jessica's eager face. "It's as good a place to start as any."

Not more than a few minutes after the silversmith directed them to the parish house, they stood within a neat wrought iron–fenced yard at a conservative-gray door.

Noah hesitated to lift the brass knocker.

But not Jessica. So excited, she was on her toes, banging it up and down on the plate.

Much sooner than he wished, a Negro maid, dressed in crisp white cap and apron, answered. "May I help you, sir?" she asked woodenly.

"We'd like a moment with the minister, if that's possible," Noah requested against his better judgment.

"It ain't," the dark-skinned woman said. "The master ain't here just now. But they's a slate on the hall table. If you put your mark on it, he'll come see you when he can."

"We don't live here. Could you tell us how long he'll be gone?"

"Don't know. I has to go ask."

"Thank you," Jessica called as the woman left them at the half-open door; then she turned to Noah. "What if he's gone a long time?"

"We'll simply find another minister," Noah reassured her. "I'd rather ask someone we can trust, not just anyone on the street. Port cities attract all sorts."

What looked to be the mistress of the house came in the servant's stead. Although she was dressed rather plainly in dark green wool, the expensive thick tatting on her cap and collar added a dignified elegance to the sagging-cheeked older woman. "My husband left for Philadelphia yesterday. Perhaps I may be able to assist you," she said, folding her hands benignly.

Noah removed his tricorn. "We're from overmountain, ma'am, and we're looking for the whereabouts of some of this young lady's relatives. By any chance would you happen to know of a family named—"

"Hargrave," the minister's wife supplied with certainty. She smiled then and stepped closer to Jessica, catching her by the chin. "It's the eyes, my dear. Just like Mistress Hargrave's—God rest her soul."

"She's passed on?" Noah asked.

"I'm afraid so. A good ten years ago. But I'm certain the rest of the family will be more than delighted to see you."

The city was a mass of trails going every which way, and there had to be hundreds of buildings. Street after street was lined with them. Yet, miraculously, the very first person they'd asked about her family didn't even have to be told their name. In the blink of an eye Jessica's prayer had been answered. And now they'd reached the very street her family lived on. Anticipation filled her to the point where she could scarcely breathe. If finding the Hargrave home was this easy, surely Spencer had found it too . . . if he had ever reached Baltimore. She desperately hoped he had, since no one had known anything about him when they'd questioned the residents of Fredericksburg.

"This way," Noah said as he reined his mount off the street and through an open set of wrought-iron gates that were taller than Noah as he sat upon his brown gelding.

"Here?" A sweeping driveway led past trees and gardens up a rise to a brick house larger than any of the coaching inns they'd visited.

Did amazing happenstances never cease?

Jessica nudged her black mare abreast with Noah's mount as they rode the considerable distance to the entrance. "It must be a very big family."

Noah only grunted—not a happy grunt.

She glanced at him and saw a sternness in his face he hadn't worn since Salem. "Noah, what troubles you?"

"Nothing."

But she knew that wasn't true as she watched him dismount. Then he lifted her down with more haste than usual. This was the moment of moments she'd waited for for so long, and he wasn't happy for her.

Brushing at a mud splatter on her black cloak, she led the way up several steps to a stately porch, its roof held up by two round pillars. And there before her was a door of her favorite color. Red! Delighted to see such a happy welcome, she refused to let Noah's dour mood dampen hers.

Everything about the entry was a feast for her eyes. The door was framed by a narrow window on either side that had flowering vines etched into the glass. Another window fanned out above the door. Hand trembling, she banged the knocker, then remembered to check the ties of her brown velvet bonnet.

Noah, approaching much slower, stopped just behind her so she couldn't see his face. *Please, God, let him be happy for me. Is he afraid this will change how I feel about him? It couldn't.*

A rattle at the handle. The door swung wide. In the opening stood an elderly Negro woman dressed as neatly as the servant at the rectory. Her coal eyes widened. She gasped. A hand went to her throat—the other hand slammed the door in Jessica's face.

"What? Why—" Jessica swung around to Noah.

He looked no less stunned.

The door opened again, and Jessica whirled back.

The same woman, just as wide-eyed as before, peeked around. Then she slammed the door shut again. But this time Jessica heard her shouting as she retreated, "Mastah William! Mastah William!"

How could they reject her so resoundingly? Without even giving her a chance to speak. Tears brimming, she turned to flee.

Noah caught her. Pulling her close, he reached out and banged the knocker again. Hard. "I will not let them treat you like this. We won't leave here without some answers."

Just as he raised the knocker again, the door swung swift and wide. This time a rather tall, old white man filled the space. Husky of build but worn-looking, he stood there in shirtsleeves, his feet slipped into a pair soft shoes. And like the elderly servant, he stared unabashedly at Jessica.

Perhaps she and Noah had been misdirected to a place where mad people were kept.

Then slowly the white-haired man reached out with a shaky hand to touch her.

Jessica backed into Noah, but she couldn't help noticing the cleft in the man's chin. Spencer had a very similar dent in his.

"How do you do?" Noah said. "We've traveled a long way. Could you tell us if this is the Hargrave residence?"

"Aye," the man answered absently, but his faded blue gaze never left Jessica. He cleared his throat. "May I touch you, lass? I won't hurt you."

She wasn't all that certain he wouldn't. But with Noah watching over her, she risked putting out her own unsteady fingers.

He took them in his aged but soft, uncalloused hand. "Pray tell," he asked very quietly, "what is your name?"

The moment of truth was upon her. Would he know of her? "Jessica Jane Whitman. Daughter of Pizar Whitman and Jessica Hargrave."

"Thank God," he sighed, one broad but rounded shoulder sagging against the doorjamb. But he didn't let go of her—he pulled her with him. Then he yelled back into the house, "It's all right, Famar! It's not a ghost! It's my granddaughter!" Returning his attention to Jessica, he straightened his stance. Though much taller than she, he was still a few inches shorter than Noah. With a belated welcoming smile, he patted her hand. "Please forgive our foolishness. Do come in. Both of you."

Upon entering, she saw the staircase and stopped, speechless. Ever since she'd left the salt lick and started traveling, the homes, the inns, and the towns had gotten progressively larger and grander, but nothing had prepared her for the wide-railed steps that swept upward in a graceful curve as if floating on nothing but air. Even her joy at finding her mother's father couldn't keep her eyes from it . . . until she saw the most exquisite chandelier made of nothing but streams of glass cut in myriad shapes and angles. It sparkled like a thousand diamonds. Mirrors on both side walls reflected its splendor. Under each looking glass rested a cushioned bench that looked too delicate for sitting. Each was flanked by side tables that were equally dainty, and . . .

". . . no, we're not married," Noah was saying to her grandfather.

She realized they'd been conversing without her, and she returned her attention to the two men.

"I've been her escort from overmountain in Tennessee country."

"I see," her grandfather said, with an accusatory tone to his gravelly voice. "Her *lone* escort?"

"No," Noah defended. "We departed from our traveling companion Mistress McKinney just before noon in Bladensburg."

Jessica couldn't help smiling. Noah had been right all along about the necessity of a chaperone.

Noah's explanation seemed to satisfy her grandfather. The old man's humor improved immediately. "Come along to the parlor where we can get acquainted in comfort. I'll have Famar bring us some refreshments."

"I's already on my way, Mastah William." The elderly servant had been watching from one of several doorways that led off the big hall they stood in. "Welcome home, Miss Jessica," she added with a dear round-faced smile.

This Famar sounded as if she really meant those words. "Thank you," Jessica said, already feeling affection for the woman.

"Come in, come in," her grandfather beckoned impatiently as he led them through a set of double doors at Jessica's left. "There's something I want to show you."

Noah's arm came around her as he went with her into another room easily as large as the one they'd exited—but with much more of the beautifully crafted furniture, as well as magnificent draperies, sheer curtains, and elegantly painted vases and urns! And figures of animals and willowy people on all the tables! And . . .

Jessica stopped in her tracks. Above the ornate mantel hung a very large portrait . . . *of her!*

She grabbed Noah's hand. "Look!"

Her grandfather was at her other side. "Aye, that's what I wanted to show you. That's my Janie, my wife. I had it commissioned soon after we were married. Almost forty-six years ago. Wasn't she beautiful?" he said in a wistful tone.

"Yes," Noah answered, his own voice hushed, and his eyes now on Jessica, "very beautiful."

24

"The cross!" Jessica cried. "Look, Noah, she's wearing my cross." Ripping the ties loose from her wool cloak, she drew the necklace from beneath the collar of the brown velvet riding jacket.

The elderly man's faded blue eyes fell upon it. Slowly, almost reverently, he slipped his trembling palm beneath it and ran pale fingers over the design. "The Berkshire Cross . . . it's been gone a very long time."

"What's all the commotion about?" came a female voice from the doorway.

Jessica turned from her grandfather to see a woman, perhaps in her forties, hasten into the room. She wore a full apron stained with every color imaginable, and she carried a tiny broomlike brush.

"Oh!" She halted, startled. "My . . ." After a moment, she composed features that were as comely as any figurine in the room. She came forward again, extending a smile and her empty hand. It, too, had several shades of paint on it. Noticing the smudges, the woman quickly withdrew the proffered fingers. "You must be

Charles's Caroline." With the back of her hand, the woman smoothed back a strand of her reddish blonde hair. "You should have informed us you were coming. We would have sent our driver down to the docks to fetch you."

"Melissa, this isn't Caroline from Halifax," Grandfather corrected. "This is Jessica Jane, Jessie's daughter."

"Jessie's daughter?" Forgetting the mess on her fingers, she pressed them to lips registering her surprise. "I knew Jessie had a pair of boys before she and Captain Whitman left for Fort Pitt. But I—" She stepped closer, her lovely autumn eyes taking on a sadness. "We were heartbroken to hear about your mother's passing, my dear, at such an early age. An officer returning from the frontier informed us. But, alas, it was two years after her death. We had no idea she had a daughter."

"And another son. Robert," Jessica supplied. "He's four years my junior."

"La, but we did lose touch. We received only the one letter from your mother after she left for the wilderness post . . . that I know of." Melissa shot an accusing, if fleeting, glance at the older man.

"I scarcely recall my mother," Jessica informed her. "It's been fourteen years now since her demise. But George and Spencer said she always spoke fondly of her Baltimore family."

"Where she should have stayed," the elder Hargrave muttered.

Jessica knew her mother had married against her family's wishes, but Spencer had assured her that all would have long since been forgiven.

"Your father, Captain Whitman—I'm surprised he even allowed you to come back here," her grandfather stated, his tone tinged with bitterness. "We didn't part on the best of terms. Or has he gone on to meet his *just* reward?"

"No, sir. I came of my own volition. This was the dying wish of my mother—that I, along with my cross, return to Baltimore some day. My brothers kept it hidden from Father until I was old enough to keep it safe."

"My hat's off to your brothers! And to you, too!" He wrapped an arm around her. "You have no idea what it means to me to know your mother regained her senses before she died." He turned to Noah. "And who might this handsome young buck be?"

Noah had been giving the threesome time to get acquainted. Now Jessica pulled him into the circle. "This is my friend, Mr. Noah Reardon. A veteran of the Revolution and a most learned man. He's a prospering land speculator with a beautiful valley of his very own."

Noah seemed nonplused by her introduction. "I'm not nearly so educated as I'd like to be. And as for the land, it's in virgin country west of the Tennessee."

"Tennessee country! My, that is a long way to come," Melissa observed. Then her brows raised slightly. "And did the two of you travel such a long distance *alone*?"

Jessica saw Noah tense—that chaperone business again. She jumped to his defense. "Absolutely not. Noah insisted on hiring a chaperone to accompany us. I've had two. The first one was a real tyrant."

Melissa's smudged lips eased into a dimpled grin. "I'm glad to hear that. William, why don't you take their coats and offer them a seat whilst I go clean this mess off my hands."

"You might take a swipe at your mouth too, dear," Grandfather William teased as he began helping Jessica remove her cloak. "Green doesn't become it."

"Oh, my." On a light laugh Melissa started for the door. "I'll be back soon, and we can have a nice long talk. I want to hear everything."

"And I just want to look at my Janie for the next year or two," Grandfather William said as if he really meant it.

An old Negro man, neatly dressed in black accented by a white cravat and stockings, stepped into the parlor entrance and waited, his glance sliding surreptitiously to Jessica.

"Yes, Solomon?" her grandfather asked.

"The horses out front, sir? Does you want 'em fed and put away?"

"Aye," he answered. "Tell Tonab to take good care of them. They've come a long way." Walking toward the ancient servant with Jessica's cloak over his arm, he collected Noah's heavy maroon coat. "Take these things and hang them in the armoire out in the hall." His attention then returned to Jessica. "Do come sit by the fire."

"I need to know something first." She caught Noah's hand for emotional support. "My brother Spencer . . . he hasn't been here, has he?"

The old man's brow furrowed, further extending a widow's peak that was already pronounced by thinning at the temples. "Why, no. Is he on his way too?"

"He was. Back in the summer of eighty-two. I possess a letter he posted to me. It came from Fredericksburg about a hundred miles south of here. He said he'd send word overmountain again as soon as he found you. But that's the last I heard from him."

"La, that is disturbing news, child." Her grandfather's sagging jowls lifted with an empathetic smile. "I'm truly sorry, but he never came."

Jessica sagged into Noah. The probability that Spencer was dead pierced her deeply. "Something must have happened to him on the road." She couldn't bring herself to suggest any further possibilities.

"Come, sit down." Noah ushered her to a plush cushioned couch with graceful hardwood arms. He came down beside her.

"Yes, do sit." Grandfather said, running his hands through the white hair fanning out from his temples. He sat in a chair next to Jessica. "Dear child, rest assured I shall hire men first thing tomorrow morning to scour every inch of the road between here and Fredericksburg. I vow, if your brother can be found, we will find him."

Noah untied her bonnet and carefully removed it, setting it on her lap. "Don't lose hope just yet, sweet girl. The war wasn't quite over in eighty-two. A lot of soldiers were on the road. Perhaps he was invited to go on an adventure with one of them. Or he could've met a pretty young lass, or . . . who knows?"

She knew he, too, was trying to comfort her. But he didn't know Spencer.

"At least wait until after the investigators' report," her grandfather cajoled.

Jessica attempted a smile. She didn't want to ruin this reunion with her family. "I will." She straightened. "Now, do tell me all about the Hargraves. The only information I have is that my mother's mother gave this cross to her when Mother was sixteen, as her mother had done before her."

"Ah yes, the Berkshire Cross. Janie's people, the Grants, came from Berkshire County in England. Goldsmiths, they were. Still are, actually. My oldest son, Grant—Melissa's husband—is named after them."

"Oh, then Melissa's not your daughter," Jessica concluded.

"I do apologize. She's my daughter-in-law. I was so flabbergasted at seeing you, I failed to properly introduce her. I also have another son besides Grant. He runs the Hargrave enterprises in Halifax. My three daughters are all wed to trading partners and live in other port cities as well. And as you do, my child, they all carry the middle name of Jane. But none quite compare to my Janie." He reached across the small table separating them and patted her hand with his own too-soft one. "Until now."

The intensity of his words and gaze made Jessica strangely uncomfortable. Still, she smiled politely.

"You seem to have another tradition," Noah interjected. "Each of your daughters is married to a merchant."

Without taking his eyes from Jessica, Grandfather William nodded affirmatively. "We've found that having family ties in other ports is most advantageous. I'm afraid, Jessica, your mother was a bit headstrong, though." He turned to Noah. "She eloped with the overly clever Captain Whitman. When the British command transferred him to Fort Pitt, rumor had it that he was sent under a cloud, if you know what I mean. But enough of that."

No doubt Father had been caught cheating or stealing.

"My son, Grant, has followed my lead. He's made excellent matches for all his daughters." Grandfather returned to Jessica with a wooing smile. "Our only regret is that his Sally succumbed to yellow fever on the Dutch island of—" He stopped midsentence, his attention darting to the doorway.

Melissa stood there with a stricken expression on her lovely oval face. She'd removed the mussed apron and now looked as elegant in a coral-and-beige striped gown as a matron of this grand house should. Schooling her expression, she moved toward them. "Yes, our home has been empty of all young voices for over a year now. Since Grant sent our last child, our son, to school in England. Marvelous contacts at Oxford, you know." Though subtle, there was a definite bitterness in her cultured voice.

Jessica had no idea how to respond.

Thank goodness, the servant Famar came in not far behind Melissa, bearing an exquisite silver tea set on its own tray, along with china cups and saucers so delicate, Jessica feared she might crush them if she held on too tightly. They were lavishly painted with pink-and-rose flowers and braided in gold. Beside the china, a silver platter held little tidbits that looked too pretty to eat.

Hoping she remembered what Mistress McKinney had taught her about the proper procedures of afternoon tea, Jessica glanced at Noah beside her. She would hate to embarrass him.

Seeing the uncertainty in Jessica's eyes, Noah smiled reassuringly. She'd do fine. With the chaperone's help, she'd been diligently practicing the niceties of afternoon tea since their fateful stay at the Pratts' inn outside of Hicksford.

But what did worry him was this family's penchant for marrying off their daughters for profit. And without Spencer here as her closest relative, they would naturally assume guardianship. He'd have to ask this very wealthy man for her hand.

And an affirmative answer seemed less likely by the second.

What a fool he'd been to chance waiting until they arrived here to ask Jessica to marry him! He should have convinced her to stop off in Richmond or Alexandria. Two weeks, that's all it would have taken to have the banns posted so they could wed. He should have walked in this door with her as his legal wife.

Mistress Hargrave, now seated directly across the serving table from Noah, prepared and poured the tea with the quiet elegance that Noah knew she would. "Cream? Sugar?" she asked each of them in her soothing melodious voice.

But then, a Hargrave wouldn't have a wife who wasn't the epitome of graciousness. However, she did seem genuinely pleased to see Jessica.

"Mistress Hargrave," Noah said after thanking her for the cup she handed him, "this is a truly delightful room." He felt it was past time to slather on some of his own charm. "The wall coverings and furnishings are exceedingly tasteful. And your choice of peaches and mauves complement your extraordinary coloring to perfection."

"Why, thank you, kind sir." She lowered her burnished lashes in an unexpected moment of shyness, then quickly regained her composure. "And we're exceedingly pleased to hear youthful voices in this big house again. I've missed that more than you can know." She handed Jessica her cup. "And, my dear, having you here is like having both your mother and grandmother back again. Although I didn't meet Mother Jane until she was forty, you really do favor her. Even in the timbre of your voice. If you continue on as you have thus far, you will age most gracefully."

"Aye," Mr. Hargrave agreed. "My Janie was beautiful till the day she died."

Noah caught a glimmer of hope and clung to it—the man had obviously loved his wife very much. Surely he would want the same happiness for his granddaughter.

The front door clicked opened, then shut, and was followed by the tapping echoes of a lone pair of shoes, as someone crossed the marble tiles of the voluminous entry hall.

Mistress Hargrave gave a last stir to her father-in-law's creamed and sugared tea, then quickly rose. "That must be Grant. I'll go fetch him."

A moment later, the matron returned with a man who looked like a younger version of William. Taller and straighter, he carried more solid bulk and had less of a pronounced widow's peak. He also sported the cleft chin that rode just above the white cravat of his dark blue suit. The frock coat was generously trimmed in gold and managed to maintain a businesslike neatness while conveying the man's exceptional prosperity.

Noah set down his cup and came to his feet, wishing he'd listened when Jessica had been concerned about her appearance and done something about his own. He should've rid himself of travel dust and put on his Sunday suit.

Jessica rose from the settee, forgetting that propriety didn't dictate that she should.

"Grant, darling," Mistress Hargrave said, "you're simply not going to believe who has virtually dropped out of the sky. The daughter of your long-deceased sister. Jessica Jane."

The younger Hargrave paused but a second before walking over to them with the assurance of a man in his middle years who was fully in control of his world. "Niece Jessica, what a pleasure it is to have you under our roof."

The fact that, of the entire household, Grant Hargrave was the only one who didn't seem the least amazed by Jessica's existence was not lost on Noah. The man didn't even seem fazed enough to mention her identical likeness to the portrait. Had Jessica's brother Spencer made it to Baltimore after all? Told this man about her, only to be sent packing?

Or worse.

These people were well enough connected for any kind of foul play. Had Grant Hargrave seen Spencer as a threat? After all, it was one thing to have a marriageable young woman come home after almost twenty years . . . a young beauty who could be parlayed into a lucrative asset. But to have an unexpected heir show up?

"And Grant," his wife was saying, "I would like you to meet the gentleman who spirited Jessica safely away from her father and brought her to us from the wilds of Tennessee."

Noah extended his hand. "How do you do. Captain Noah Reardon of the North Carolina Rifle Company." He rarely flouted his past rank. But with this man, he felt the need.

Grant Hargrave returned a firm but brief handshake as he looked Noah up and down . . . obviously noting the plain waistcoat Noah had worn all the way from Tennessee and the rumpled shirt. His perusal completed, the purposeful man turned to his wife. "Dear, why don't you take Jessica up and find her something pretty to wear for dinner. I trust the girls left any number of suitable gowns. And I'm certain she'd relish a nice soak in a hot bath too."

"Oh yes." Mistress Hargrave seemed a bit flustered as she took Jessica by the hand. "I have been woefully remiss. I was so thrilled to see you, I completely forgot my duties as mistress."

Jessica looked back at Noah with a hint of distress in those trusting eyes. He nodded reassuringly, but he himself felt anything but confident.

"Has my father shown you the fine horses he's breeding out in the stable?" Grant Hargrave asked as Noah watched the women exit.

"No, the subject hasn't come up." Nor did he see any reason for it to now.

"Well, then, come along. I think you'll be duly impressed."

"Yes," William encouraged. "Do come see my hackneys. I believe I have the finest in the colonies."

Noah was reluctant to be separated from Jessica. Her they'd whisked upstairs, while he was being relegated to the stables where, he had no doubt, Grant Hargrave intended to impress him with a whole lot more than his father's livestock. But with both men ushering him to the door, Noah had little choice.

25

"Don't forget your coat," Grant Hargrave reminded as he reached into the elegant mahogany closet standing near the entrance. He pulled out Noah's mud-splattered frock coat. "This is yours, I presume." His disdain was thinly veiled as he handed it to Noah.

Noah knew it smelled of horse, woodsmoke, and pitch, verifying a long ride the younger Hargrave evidently wished he hadn't made. A thank-you would have stuck in Noah's craw, but he was relieved of the necessity of saying it when Grant strode purposefully out the front door ahead of him and the older William.

The back flaps of Hargrave's blue-and-gold, knee-length coat bounced against his sure legs as he set a fast pace across neatly laid cobbles. Striding past an extended wing of the brick house that looked like a kitchen and servants' quarters, he led them toward a large outbuilding uniformly constructed of the same red brick.

Grant stopped abruptly. "Father, before going on to the stables, why don't you show our guest the carriage house. I think Mr. Reardon would enjoy seeing the new landau that arrived from

Bavaria last week. I need to speak to Caleb a moment. I'll rejoin you at the stables." Without waiting for an answer, he left them standing and walked toward a slave working by what looked like a garden shed.

"My son is so used to barking orders down at our warehouses, he sometimes forgets to stop when he's come home," William said in a roundabout apology. "But do come see our latest addition. It *is* a beauty. I think I'll take Jessica out in it on the next warm afternoon. Show her off. All my old chums will be so surprised to see her."

Aye, Noah thought, anyone who'd known her grandmother would be as amazed to see Jessica as this household had been.

Except Grant.

When they entered the large high-ceilinged building, Noah couldn't help but be impressed. This family didn't have just one elegant stretched-out open carriage that would hold at least six comfortably plus a driver and a footman, but they also had a four-passenger phaeton and a sporty two-wheeled gig.

"Quite a lot of transport for only three people," Noah remarked, wondering if the old man would acknowledge the excessive extravagance.

"There are four of us now," William corrected with a contented smile. "Besides, different-sized rigs are all the better for showing off my hackneys. Since my doctors won't let me go down to the docks anymore, raising horses has been my only pleasure. Until now," he added with obvious meaning, then returned to the prior subject again. "I intend to make a rousing success of my latest venture."

Noah ran a hand across the highly lacquered half door of the emerald green landau, more aware than ever that he should've checked these people out before bringing Jessica here. No matter what her wishes might be, they were not going to willingly let her leave here with him. William may have mellowed with age, but it was plain that he was as addicted to power and prestige as his son was. Added to that, he was obviously already obsessed with Jessica.

"Let me show you the upholstery," William offered, opening the door to velvet seats the same shade as the exterior. Undeniably enthralled with his carriage, he took his sweet time, showing Noah every golden accoutrement adorning the new arrival, then moved to the other two conveyances before finally suggesting they adjourn to the stables to see the magnificent steeds that would pull the luxury vehicles.

Stepping outside, Noah glanced back at the second-story windows of the main house, wondering which room Jessica had been taken to. As large as the manse was, there would be no less than a dozen rooms upstairs. At this very moment, with the male Hargraves doing their eloquent best to make Noah feel inadequate, was Jessica being dazzled with elegant gowns and wigs? Would she become so enthralled with all the riches that she'd forget everything that had passed between them these past weeks . . . every word . . . every touch of their hands . . . their souls? Why hadn't he declared himself before now? At the very least, he should have told her what was in his heart.

And this place looked like a fortress. *Lord, help me. Help us.*

In its own way, the stable was as impressive as the rest of the estate. Constructed of brick like the other buildings, its white double doors didn't appear to have a speck of dust marring them anymore than the pristine rails of the half-dozen paddocks flanking either side of the long structure. Noah had no doubt that the Hargrave stock would be equally well groomed.

A servant riding bareback on a surprisingly unstylish gray gelding came charging out the stable door and down the cobbled drive at a hoof-clattering trot. The slave's legs hugged tight to the horse's bulging sides as he urged it through the big iron gates, then galloped away.

For a family who spent every breath bragging on their wealth, it seemed almost cruel that they wouldn't suffer their poor slave the use of even an old saddle.

Noah was still musing about the inconsistency as he and William entered the shadowy confines of the stable. Inside was as he'd expected. A long straw-strewn center aisle stretched between stalls and connected the wide doorways at either end. He heard the sounds of animals rustling about, snorting, and smelled their distinctive odor.

Near the entrance, a slave was busy oiling a harness. Another raked straw at the opposite end.

Grant lounged at the gate of the first stall to Noah's left, patting the sleek neck of an intelligent-looking, large but compactly built bay. "Father's prize stallion," he said with a leisurely smile before starting toward Noah and William.

Everything seemed in order as they went to join Grant, but Noah sensed a tension in the air.

A trap?

He wheeled around.

The slave who had been oiling the leather now stood at the entrance, pointing a rifle straight at him. His own rifle!

Noah did an about-face and saw that the workman at the other end guarded that exit with what looked like Jessica's weapon.

"I didn't see any need to beat around the bush," Grant said, donning a complacent smile.

Noah couldn't believe he'd allowed himself to be ambushed like this. The signs had been there . . . as surely as the fact that Spencer was *not*. He should have trusted his instincts.

"Thought you'd found yourself a golden goose, didn't you?" Grant casually toed some feed sacks piled at the side of the first stall as if they were discussing the price of oats. "Well, my friend, we Hargraves didn't get to where we are today by playing the fool."

Before Noah had time to weigh his options, William contributed, "It's not to say we're not indebted to you for bringing home our darling girl." He at least seemed to be feeling a degree of guilt.

But not Grant. Noah aimed his reply at him. "If anyone thinks of her as a golden goose, it's you. I'd bet my valley you've already decided which of your business associates will be her husband."

"Absolutely not!" her grandfather retorted as he shot a worried glance to his son.

"If and when we do give her to someone," Grant clipped arrogantly, "it certainly won't be to a backwoods ruffian like you. You may have gained her trust and, if I'm not mistaken, weaseled your way into her affection as well, but—"

Fists clenched, Noah closed the space between him and the younger Hargrave. "You know nothing of where Jessica came from or what it's taken for her to appear as you see her today."

At Noah's advance, Grant tucked his chin like a stubborn bulldog. "And whether you thought so or not, your appearance here today does not deceive us." His bravado weakening, Grant shrank back slightly. "Nonetheless, I have no intention of cheating you out of just compensation for your trouble and expense on our Jessica's behalf." He reached inside his coat and pulled out several banknotes. "Thirty pounds is more than a man like you sees in a year. It should be ample recompense."

Money. Being paid off was the last straw. Noah reared back a fist.

All smugness fled Grant Hargrave's face. "Caleb! Fontaine!" Backstepping several yards, he glanced both ways to his armed men.

Noah halted in his tracks, but his anger raged unabated. "What are you going to do," he slung, "have them shoot me? Is this how you got rid of Jessica's brother? Did you ambush him too? Shoot him with his own gun?"

Noah heard William's sudden intake of breath and saw Grant's eyes flair wide, but for only the briefest second before the junior Hargrave pulled himself up in a display of indignation.

"I refuse to honor that accusation with a response."

The man protested a bit too vehemently. The fact that he immediately turned away didn't say much for his innocence either. Grant stalked to the next stall and flung open the gate. Grabbing the bridle of the horse inside, he led it out.

Noah saw that it was one of his own horses, saddled and with all his gear tied on—except for the rifle that was supposed to be in his scabbard. Following close behind came his extra mount.

Stepping to the side of the first horse, Grant stuffed the money into one of Noah's saddlebags. He was a very thorough man.

But Noah couldn't just ride out, leave. "Jessica has a right to know what you're trying to pull here." Taking his chances, he pivoted around and started for the entrance.

The slave blocking the exit stiffened. A look of fright took over the man's broad features as he jabbed the rifle in Noah's direction. "Stay back! Please, mistah!"

Noah took advantage of the man's hesitancy—knowing the slave feared the possible consequences of shooting a white man—and kept walking.

"Halt!" came from directly behind. Grant.

Something hard poked Noah in the back. He stopped, then slowly turned around.

Grant Hargrave was even more thorough than Noah had suspected. He had a dueling pistol aimed at the center of Noah's chest. His blue eyes were rock steady. "My boys might not shoot, but trust me, I will. Now, you can either go the easy way or the hard way. Makes no difference to me."

Noah had no choice . . . for now.

"Oh, and by the by," Granted added, "don't think you can sneak back here in the dead of night. The rider that passed you on your way in here—I sent him down to the wharf to fetch some of my bully boys. They'll be posted on the premises from now on, keeping guard over what's ours."

"You mean, your latest asset." Noah's rage began sliding into devastation at his loss. What would become of that sweet lively spirit who thought coming East was coming to the land of freedom and justice? Feeling utterly defeated, Noah gathered up the reins to his horse and mounted. Even if he asked the local law officers to help him get her out of here, they would side with the Hargraves.

"You needn't worry about her," the old man assured. "We'll take good care of her."

Noah turned to his last hope. Jessica's grandfather. He nudged his brown gelding toward the old man. "But she loves me as much as I love her . . . with the same depth that you loved your wife. How can you be a party to this? You don't have the vaguest idea where she came from or what she needs. And she's only just begun to trust in the Lord."

"I'm sorry, but please understand. She's a Hargrave. And once she's been with us awhile, a poor fellow like you would just become an embarrassment to her. A clean swift break now will be best for everyone in the long run."

"I'm losing patience," Grant clipped off. He waved his pistol toward the doorway.

There was nothing left to say. His heart ripping apart, Noah rode out.

26

Bathed, perfumed, dressed, and coiffed, Jessica stepped outside the suite of rooms she'd been given, thinking that for the first time she really did look like the "Miss Jessica" that Noah had so often called her. She could hardly wait for him to see the results of three hours of her being treated like royalty.

Aunt Melissa had proven to be as kind and generous as she was lovely when she'd insisted that Jessica don an unbelievable dinner gown her daughter had outgrown shortly after it had been finished. Pale lavender silk now draped and spilled all around her, its delicate overlays of transparent lace at the bodice and sleeves shimmering the same as a silvery mist through the trees. With her cross cosseted among the "mist," she felt like one of the English aristocracy her father had often spoken about. And not only did the fine fabric feel more pleasing to the touch than a baby's cheek, it whispered softly as she walked.

Crossing the many-colored carpet of the open seating area Aunt Melissa had called the upstairs sitting room, Jessica could hardly contain her excitement at the thought of actually descending the sweeping staircase in the hooped and swaying gown . . . with Noah waiting for her at the bottom. Already her smile was blooming at just the thought of him watching her coming on feet clad in matching orchid slippers. Imagine, shoes that were made to match just one gown!

Just before she reached the landing, Dicy, the servant who had helped Aunt Melissa with Jessica, came hurrying out of a nearby room.

Jessica turned her happy smile on the slave. "I want to thank you again for the magnificent dressing of my hair. I had no idea there were so many ways to whirl and curl it."

"Just doin' my job, Miss Jessica," said the young woman with a head sporting such tight curls, she would never have to endure the ministrations of a hot curling rod. "I gots to get on down now and fetch Miz Melissa her laudanum. Mastah Grant don' like her comin' down to supper without it."

Another thing Jessica had never heard of. "Is laudanum something I should wear too?"

Dicy exploded into throaty laughter. "Laudanum ain't for wearin', child. It's for spoonin' in. We calls it her happy juice. Otherwise she gets a mite weepy from time to time."

In such a wonderful house with all these riches around, Jessica found it hard to believe that anyone could be unhappy. Then she recalled that her aunt had expressed a sadness that she no longer had her children about her.

Together, Jessica and Dicy reached the top of the stairs, but Dicy didn't descend along with her. The servant continued toward the opposite wing's hallway. "I thought you were coming down," Jessica called after her retreating figure.

The wiry woman in her simple black-and-white apparel stopped, mob-capped head tilted, and swung an amazed look back to Jessica. "Honey, them's white folks stairs. We ain't allowed to traipse on them."

"I see," Jessica said absently as she watched the woman reach the far end of the passage and disappear down a dark narrow staircase. But she really didn't. It seemed that no more than a few minutes ever went by without her discovering something else she didn't understand. She had so much to ask Noah when she next got him alone.

Descending the grand stairway wasn't nearly as much fun now that she knew it was forbidden to the Africans. When she reached far enough down to view the expansive entry hall, she saw no one stood there, waiting for her, as she'd hoped. No Noah.

But what could she expect? Aunt Melissa had kept her busy until well after the sun dipped below the horizon.

Reaching the bottom, she heard male voices coming from the archway opposite the parlor. Her excitement building, she took the carefully measured steps her chaperone had taught her and fairly floated across the marble floor, beneath a crystal chandelier alive with flaming candles. She crossed the threshold into a room with two smaller chandeliers sparkling between wall mirrors and above the biggest table she'd ever seen! A score of people could easily be seated there.

Looking past the surrounding tall-backed chairs, she saw Grandfather William and Uncle Grant on the far side of the room, standing by another smaller serving table. They each held a sparkling glass bearing amber liquid. Both were as splendidly dressed as she in what also looked like silk, only shinier than her gown.

Grandfather's legs were encased in a subdued shade of green, and he wore a waistcoat of cream brocade that matched his stockings. And all was softened even more by ruffled lace at cuff and neck. He also wore one of those white wigs Noah had told her about. For a man his age, he struck a very impressive figure.

As did Uncle Grant in creams and golds from neck to knee. He sported his own wig as curly as the hair of the servant Dicy, only his was powdered a light gray.

They were talking business. Grandfather was demanding that Uncle Grant not make some sort of arrangement with a Parker Weston in the Bahamas.

She had thought Grant the forceful one in the family, but he warded off the older man with a raised hand. "Very well, Father. Whatever you say. Not for at least a year."

But where was Noah? Most likely still upstairs, getting the same treatment she'd received. She smiled as she rounded the long table and moved toward the other two—she could hardly wait until Noah joined them. He would be so handsome they couldn't possibly refuse him when he offered for her . . . *if he offered for her*.

She thought he'd been on the verge of confessing his feelings for her any number of times this past week after she'd found the Lord. They'd become so close, almost as though their souls touched. It was in his eyes every time he looked at her. When the tradesmen had mistaken their reason for asking for the minister, she'd been almost certain the next words out of Noah's mouth would be a marriage proposal.

But he'd waited as Mistress McKinney said any honorable gentleman should—until he could speak to the head of her family.

Had he already spoken to her grandfather? The expectation caused her bosom to swell against the stricture of the tight bodice. She quickly smoothed her hand over the silvery lavender. If he hasn't asked for her, he would, once he saw her in this gown. How could he not?

And even if she was smaller than most young misses, her grandmother had proved that a tiny woman could have strapping sons. Uncle Grant was certainly proof of that.

As if he'd known she was thinking about him, Grant looked up. Seeing her, he smiled a warm greeting. "Jessica. You look every bit as lovely as I knew you would."

Grandfather William didn't merely look up. He set his glass on the serving table and banged past his son to reach her. "Oh yes, yes." Collecting her hands, he looked her up and down, then drew her close, and his eyes filled with emotion. "My Janie . . . returned to me."

Jessica smiled uncomfortably within his grasp. He sounded as if she truly were his Janie.

Her grandfather leaned down, and without her expecting it, he kissed her first on one cheek, then the other.

Unaccustomed to such attention, she reared back.

He must have realized he'd alarmed her. "La, do forgive this old man his exuberance." He moved a few inches from her. "I promise not to overwhelm you so again."

"Here, my dear." Uncle Grant stepped forward, offering a lovely stemmed goblet like the one he held. Hers contained a sparkling rose-colored liquid.

Taking it, she raised it to her lips—then quickly turned her face away. Although it didn't look the same, the smell reminded her of Father's rum. "Do forgive me, but . . ." She left the cause for her rejection unsaid. For some reason she hadn't yet explored, she hesitated to tell them about her life with Pizar Whitman.

"Perhaps you'd prefer cider," her grandfather suggested as Uncle Grant turned back to the table that held a collection of pitchers and glass-stoppered bottles. But instead of choosing one, Grant plucked a silver bell from an equally shiny tray and rang it.

Within seconds, a servant appeared at a side door. Older than Dicy and of a more rounded figure, this new one bobbed into a curtsy.

Jessica was beginning to wonder how many people it took to tend this family's needs. How many had to lose their freedom so Uncle Grant wouldn't have to fetch her some apple juice.

"Cassa, bring a ewer of cider for Miss Jessica."

285

"I do apologize for making extra work for you," she said to the dark-skinned woman.

The servant bobbed another curtsy, this time in Jessica's direction. "That's what I's here for, miss."

Jessica stepped forward and returned the curtsy. "Perhaps I could go and assist you."

The woman shot Uncle Grant an uncertain look, then hastened away as if her very life depended on it.

Had she offended the servant? Jessica started after her.

Uncle Grant caught her by the arm. "Let Cassa tend her business." Maintaining his grasp, he turned to Grandfather William. "Father, Jessica is obviously unfamiliar with the correct treatment of slaves. Before you commence with any of your other plans for her, she'll need instruction in that area. We don't want her putting wrong ideas in their heads."

"I'd be glad to take on that task myself," Grandfather said, smiling down at her. "First thing in the morning."

"In the meantime, Niece," Grant instructed, "I would consider it a kindness if you would simply pretend the servants don't exist."

A specific manner of treating the slaves seemed crucial to her uncle. "Of course," Jessica agreed, though she felt that deliberately ignoring anyone was rude, and it particularly ran contrary to the "love thy neighbor" passage in the Bible.

"Good evening," came a woman's voice from the hall doorway. Aunt Melissa.

Jessica glanced past her, hoping to see Noah behind her. Hiding her disappointment, she returned her attention to her aunt. "My, but you do look beautiful."

And she did. From head to toe, Melissa was a vision in shades of sunset. In the candlelight, even her silken overgown seemed magical. As the lady walked toward Jessica, the folds and drapes of the split skirt seemed to change from amber to rose and back again. Layer upon layer of ruffled toffee lace down the front further set off her honey red hair and creamy complexion. And all was accented by crocheted roses in her coif and down her bodice.

Everything and everyone in the room was so beautiful Jessica could hardly believe that only a few weeks ago she lived in a hovel and wore animal skins. *Thank you, Lord, for bringing me here. This must be what heaven looks like.* All these years they had been here, waiting for her. All these years . . .

And it seemed that long since she'd last seen Noah. What was delaying him so? She wanted to share every happy moment with him.

Uncle Grant gave his wife the dark pink drink he'd offered Jessica a few moments before. "How was your day, dear?" he asked in an offhanded manner as if he didn't expect any more of an answer than is expected when one asks, How do you do?

"The portrait I'm painting isn't going as well as it might," Aunt Melissa answered nonetheless. There was a sadness in her eyes as well as in her cultivated voice. "Try as I might, I couldn't quite get Marcie's fingers the way I wanted them. You remember, Grant, the graceful way our daughter always held them when she spoke."

Jessica glanced down at her own hands. Was there even a way one was supposed to move the fingers?

"No sense fussing over it," Uncle Grant said and downed his drink. "No one notices a person's hands in a portrait."

"But Marcie *was* her hands." Though quietly said, there was a hint of desperation in Aunt Melissa's tone.

Then Jessica understood. "La, but I am sorry to hear of your sadness. The passing of a dear daughter must be unbearably heartbreaking."

Uncle Grant raked a scathing gaze across his wife, then softened his expression for Jessica. "Our Marcia is not dead. She's married into a very prosperous merchant family in Bristol, England."

"Oh, I see." Jessica did feel foolish. "But I do sympathize with Aunt Melissa's lament. I, too, have been deprived of all my brothers as they each left in search of their futures. I miss hearing their voices, their laughter, their touch, and, yes," she added with a nostalgic chuckle, "even their teasing. I had so hoped to be reunited here with Spencer, but . . ." Not wanting to burden them with the depth of her disappointment, she merely shrugged a shoulder.

Uncle Grant rang the bell again.

Before he had time to replace it on the table, the servant Cassa came through the side door, bearing a cut-glass pitcher with the cider he'd requested. She didn't look at him as she rushed forth to place it beside the other decanters. "I's sorry it done took so long. Had to tote up a new jug from the cellar."

Uncle Grant waved her away. "Tell Hannah we want dinner served now."

Now? But Noah had yet to join them. Not wanting to deliberately ignore the servant, Jessica didn't speak until after she left. "If you all don't mind, I'd rather wait until Noah joins us."

Her uncle and grandfather exchanged odd glances.

Grandfather William offered a smile, but it seemed forced. "Noah won't be spending the evening with us."

"He won't? Is he ill?" Why had she waited so long to ask?

"No, child." Grandfather pulled out a nearby chair. "Do be seated."

She ignored his request. "I don't understand. Noah should be as hungry as I am."

"He said something about wanting to go visit a relative."

"His mother?"

"I believe that's who he said."

"But she lives somewhere in North Carolina. When did he leave?" Pushing past her grandfather, she lifted the weight of her skirts and headed for the entry hall.

William trailed after her. "He's been gone for some time."

"No!" she railed back. "He wouldn't do that. He wouldn't leave

without telling me." She reached the front door. Flinging it wide, she ran out onto the lamp-lit porch. "Noah! Noah!" She searched the darkness beyond . . . the long wide path that led to the gates.

He wouldn't leave her. He wouldn't.

Descending the steps two at a time, she ran toward the street. Even if he hadn't said the words, she knew he loved her. He would never just ride away. She ran faster.

The pointed toe of her shoe caught in the skirt hem. She hit the driveway in a sprawl.

While trying to untangle herself from all the blasted layers of clothing, she heard footsteps fast approaching. Before she could regain her feet, strong hands lifted her up and did not let go.

She tried to jerk free.

"Stop this. You're making a fool of yourself."

She couldn't quite make out the features in the dark, but the voice was Uncle Grant's. "Unhand me."

His grip only tightened. "I want you to take control of yourself before we go back inside." He grabbed her other arm and turned her to face him. "I can see where a young girl might think the fellow was handsome—in a rustic sort of way. But he understood as well as we do that he is not an acceptable suitor for a Hargrave. Reardon took payment for bringing you to us and left."

"Not acceptable for me?" *Noah not good enough for her?* An ignorant backwoods girl? It was as if the world had just turned inside out. The very idea was utterly laughable. Besides, Noah would never let her family pay him off. *No. Uncle Grant is lying.*

Again she tried to wrench free.

"Please, don't do this." Grant's voice then turned unexpectedly gentle. "Father is so thrilled to have you here. He looks better than I've seen him look in months. He's not going to live much longer, so please don't break an old man's heart. Let him have his Janie back, even if it is just for a spell."

Suddenly Jessica felt as if she were being ripped in two. The

Hargraves pulling her one way; her heart, the other. *Oh, God, what is happening? This was supposed to be the happiest day of my life.* And now Spencer was most likely dead, and Noah had simply ridden away . . . simply abandoned her to an old man who looked at her as if she were his long-dead wife.

Tears spilled over her lashes and ran unchecked down her face. Convulsive sobs racked her from her very depths.

Now other hands were on her, pulling her from Grant.

Grandfather. He drew her within his circling arms. He pressed her head against his chest and held tight. "Everything will be fine, my darling. You'll see. Everything will be just fine."

27

Noah had dismounted some time ago, and now his legs were as shaky and faltering as those of both horses he'd ridden hard since leaving the Hargrave house . . . as if any amount of expended energy or distance could erase his rage, his anguish. Only the most draining kind of exhaustion could bring him down.

He looked into the starlit sky and saw by the position of Orion's Belt that it had to be two or three in the morning.

His arm ached from dragging the reluctant horses along the road behind him this last mile or so. He switched the reins to his other hand, astounded at the depth of anguish that had caused him to abuse those poor animals as he had.

Yet the anger and frustration and the grinding helplessness he'd felt when he'd been forced to capitulate had scarcely lessened. He still wanted to lash out, to smash, to destroy. Even in this debasing weariness, he still ached to shout out that same boast he'd once heard Drew use against the Mackey brothers: *"When it comes to shootin' or fistfightin', I'll match me and my brother against you two any day of the week."*

No matter how childish Drew's threat had been, overmountain those words would mean something. But here, the Hargraves were the kings of the hill—with just one reach into a coin purse they could make anything happen.

And he had no doubt, Grant Hargrave's threat to dispatch him the *hard way* had not been an idle one. Cold-blooded intent had been in the man's eyes. If Noah had resisted, Hargrave would have shot him and gotten away with it.

That thought only exacerbated the terrible gnawing knowledge that Jessica should never have been left with those people. Not just because he wanted her, but for herself. She'd gone to Baltimore to find love and freedom, not more tyranny, no matter how beautifully the Hargraves might package it.

Noah stopped trudging forward and took some strengthening breaths. To no avail. He was too far gone tonight to return and do anything even if an opportunity presented itself. Yet he refused to leave her there. No matter the danger to himself, no matter how long it took, he would find a way to rescue her.

He'd left her to her fate when he rode away from her at the salt lick, and he'd been given a second chance to do the right thing by her when she ran away from her pa and followed him. But he couldn't count on that happening again. The Hargraves were not the drunken fools Pizar Whitman was.

Oh, how easily Noah had played into the Hargraves' hands . . . just like a country bumpkin, a simpleton. And now that Jessica was in the midst of all that wealth, would they soon have her seeing him through their eyes, too?

He couldn't let himself think such thoughts. He had to find a way to get her out of there. Her fragile beginnings of faith in God may very well depend on it. "Lord in heaven," Noah cried into the night, "you promise that those who belong to you cannot be snatched out of your hand. I'm relying on that."

Still, he could not shake his doubts. As he remounted and

resumed at a slower pace, he reflected upon Jessica's reaction to her newfound family. When they'd walked into the Hargrave manse, she'd been so enthralled with everything—her Baltimore dream-come-true—that she'd been blinded to the underlying reality. Would she even believe him if he told her Grant intended to package her in the glamorous Hargrave fashion, only to sell her off to the highest bidder? The man had done no less with his own daughters.

But even if she didn't believe him, the two of them had come too far together—*she'd come too far*—to be thrown to the lions without a fight.

"God in heaven, you love her as much as I do. This can't be your will for her, to have me walk away and leave her to that fate. Tell me it's not."

Noah strained to see past the stars. He listened. Just once he wished the Lord would come right out and talk to him as he had with Moses on the mountain. But no bush burst into flames, no heavenly host began to sing, nothing broke the silence, only the plodding horses' hooves and their heavy breathing as they followed behind Noah.

Somewhere in the distance came the woofing of a dog. Another answered. Then from a different direction, another dog barked.

He'd been traveling through a stand of woods but now realized he must be near a village. He tugged on the reins. "Come on, you two. Just a little farther, and I'll find you a stable for the night."

Noah woke with a start.

Somewhere a door had slammed. Glancing around in the predawn light, he saw nothing but the man sleeping in the bed next to his.

Shaking the haze from his brain, he began to recognize where he was . . . in some inn near the ferry crossing of the Potomac, sharing a room with another traveler. He'd ridden forty miles from Baltimore before he'd regained his senses enough to stop—much to the innkeeper's exasperation when he'd rousted the poor man out of his warm bed.

Noah rolled over—he'd been in bed only a couple of hours. Then, before he felt it coming, the desperation of his loss got a stranglehold on him.

He couldn't breathe. He sat up.

"God!" he grated out in a hoarse whisper. Why was the Lord doing this to him again? So soon after Lorna. Why had the Lord given Jessica to him, even let Noah be the instrument of her salvation, only to have her ripped away so cruelly?

No! He threw back his covers and grabbed his boots. He'd gotten past that kind of hopeless thinking. Otherwise he wouldn't have managed to get any sleep at all. At the very least, he'd learn if she even wanted to be rescued.

His entire body ached and creaked like an old man's as he walked down the stairs to the main room, telling him that he hadn't given his body nearly enough time to restore itself. But it couldn't be helped.

He was driven to write Jessica and send the missive by the first willing person heading to Baltimore. And he'd be very clear about it. The man must reach the Hargrave house and deliver it to Jessica while Grant was still down at the wharf.

In the letter, Noah would propose marriage as he should have done a week ago. It wouldn't take more than a couple of days for her return answer. Whether her reply was favorable or not, at least she'd know he didn't merely go off and abandon her.

And if no word at all came back to him, he'd know Hargrave had intercepted her personal mail. In which case he'd be meeting her family again . . . on *his* terms this time. "Whatever that means," he mumbled sarcastically to himself as he glanced around the unlit common room.

Wondering where he might find some writing materials, he followed the smell of coffee into the kitchen.

Two aproned women turned from their chores at the twin hearths of a big cluttered room and frowned. "Breakfast ain't ready yet," the younger one said.

"Set yourself down out in the ordinary," the other plump woman said, pointing with a knife. "You're not allowed in here."

He grunted over a smile. "I've been hearing that a lot lately. Just wanted to know where I could get a quill and some paper."

"There's a writin' table in the main room, under the front window. Now, shoo," the plump cook said. "I'll send Ellie out with a cup of coffee soon as it's brewed."

Heading in the direction they'd ordered, he made one more plea. *God, I beg you, is this how I should handle it? Should I stay here and wait or go straight back? I can't go home until I know more. I pray you'll show me what to do. But I still don't understand. You say you love me. How can tearing her away from me be for my good?*

Shaking his head, he picked up the writing quill. *I just don't understand.*

Finally, morning.

Jessica rolled out of the tall, oppressively soft bed. At long last, the worst day of her life was behind her. What little sleep she'd managed had been troubled, since no amount of prayer had given her heart peace from the bitter disappointments of the day before. She'd thought God would always be there for her, but his fruit of the Spirit had vanished with her double loss—first Spencer, then Noah.

On bare feet she padded to the glass-paned door that led out to an icy balcony that faced the front grounds and the street beyond the wall. Unable to stop herself, she scanned both directions in the hope that Noah would ride forth . . . coming back to tell her he hadn't really let himself be paid off like some hired man who'd delivered the goods only to leave on his merry way.

But neither he nor anyone else, for that matter, was down on the street. The only men she saw were the two night guards posted at the gates. In Baltimore she'd thought there wouldn't be a need to fortify. Another of her misconceptions.

She turned back to a room whose lovely pink decor no longer held any fascination for her. A day gown of Scots plaid had been laid out for her. After taking care of her morning needs, she quickly donned the many layers of clothing as best she could, considering the bodice laces were in back. Her hair she scarcely bothered with at all. Coiling her night braid, she pinned it up and dropped a mobcap over the top, then left behind this room of her midnight mourning.

Hearing no other sounds of awakening on the second floor, she tiptoed downstairs and into the dining room.

Again, no one was there.

She heard muffled voices and the smell of coffee coming through the doorway from whence the servants had appeared last night. A cup of the vitalizing brew would be nice.

She eyed the silver bell Uncle Grant had rung the night before. But it seemed so rude . . . almost as rude as pretending the servants didn't exist. Most unchristian.

Choosing to do neither, she left the dining room through the servants' door and found herself following the sounds of happy chatter down a long hall with windows on both sides. From the windows she could see both the front and rear of the estate and realized that she was actually walking through a passageway that led to another building altogether.

The hallway opened onto the largest kitchen she'd ever seen. She stopped at the threshold . . . and yet another wonder lay before her.

Two giant blazing fireplaces held up facing walls along with adjoining bread ovens. In the cozy warmth, there were tables and shelves, containers and stores, the likes of which she'd never seen, even in the mercantiles she and Noah had frequented on their journey here. And devices galore. How could a single family of three need so much?

But then there weren't just three, she was reminded. Ten African slaves sat around a big table in the center of the room. Three men, four women, a lad of ten or twelve, and two little ones were gathered for their own leisurely repast before their masters awakened.

Dicy, fork in hand, burst out laughing. "I did not say that."

"I heared you, I surely did," chuckled one of the men, before he abruptly cut short his merriment and looked up at Jessica.

"Good morning," she said, hoping they wouldn't think she'd been eavesdropping.

The old man, Solomon, rose from the table, his expression turning somber, as did everyone's except the two tots'. "Beggin' your pardon, miss, but we never heared y'all ring."

"I didn't." She stepped farther onto the plain brick flooring. "I didn't want to be a bother." Seeing the coffeepot sitting on the hearth to the right, she veered toward it. "I'll just fetch my own coffee."

Famar, the older woman, was up in a shot. "No you won't!" She bustled toward Jessica. "I don't wants to be disrespectful, child, but you don't knows your place." The older woman opened a cupboard and filled a tray with fluted blue-and-white cups and saucers. "We knows you come from some faraway place that ain't got no slaves. But if you don't wants us to catch the very devil, you gots to stay over to the big house. Now go on. I'll be right along with your coffee and the fixin's."

"Please finish your breakfast first. I can wait."

Dicy's chair scraped loud across the brick as she sprang to her feet. "Now that's just what Famar's talkin' about. If Mastah Grant come into the dinin' room and sees y'all waitin' till we finish our breakfast—we'd likely lose a layer of skin."

At the end of Dicy's disturbing onslaught, Jessica replied as quietly and smoothly as she could muster, "Then I suppose I'll have my coffee now, please." Turning on her heels, she started for the doorway, feeling even more melancholy and lonely than before she'd found them.

Then like a warm wind, a rush of love suddenly filled her, and she knew she wasn't totally abandoned . . . God was with her. She turned to the slaves once more. "Just one more thing. Since I'll probably never have the chance to say it after this, it's very nice to meet you. May God bless and keep you all in his infinite joy and peace."

Solomon took a step toward her, a deep sadness in his great dark eyes. "And we wish the same for you, Miss Jessica. We surely do."

As she returned down the hall, she couldn't erase from her mind the passion he'd put into those last words. Something in his bearing made her sense he'd wanted to say more—to warn her perhaps? But about what exactly?

Scant moments later, Cassa came into the dining room and left the tray, which also contained an assortment of muffins and a silver coffee server.

After pouring herself a cup of coffee, Jessica felt foolish at the thought of sitting alone at such an enormous table. Instead, she wandered out to the entry hall that was as large as the dining room. Taking a sip of coffee from the delicate cup, she noticed that besides the arched double doors that led into the eating room and the parlor, another set stood at the back wall, to the left of the staircase.

She decided to explore.

If nothing else, it would keep her mind off the lonely questions that were trying to steal the flush of hope she'd felt just before leaving the kitchen.

The room she entered was immense, barnlike in size, yet had almost no furnishings. The entire center was empty. Only a scattering of chairs lined the edges, along with a few tables. Yet, in keeping with most of the house, the walls were papered in harmonious shades of peach, which were reflected in the many mirrors. Between them hung huge colored paintings set in gold frames— pictures of people frolicking.

Taking another sip of coffee, she recognized the purpose of the room. This was one of those ballrooms she'd heard her father talk about, where music played and beautiful people dressed in their finest and danced the night away. A place of gaiety.

Two rows of chandeliers marched to a bank of many-paned doors and windows that opened onto rear gardens that she had no doubt would be as beautiful in spring bloom as the interior of the manse now was.

Music, laughter. When Aunt Melissa's children were still here, this must have been a very gay household. Small wonder she missed them.

Jessica closed the doors of the ballroom behind her. There was still another exit off the entry hall to explore.

It stood at the right, hidden by the staircase. She found the doors opened onto nothing but a narrow hall that was soon intersected by yet another hallway. Amazing, a house so enormous it actually had trails in it—trails that crossed!

She turned down the new one and noticed that the first door she came to was ajar. Pushing it open, she couldn't believe this latest of wonders. On two walls, row upon row of books climbed to the high ceiling . . . surely enough books to hold all the written knowledge in the world. Everything she could ever hope to learn was at her fingertips.

Just the thought made her giddy.

She let her hands bump along the rich leather bindings, feeling them as she walked around the walls. Hundreds, maybe a thousand books. It would take months, *years,* to read them all.

If she was allowed to. Oh, they simply had to let her. As soon as Aunt Melissa rose for the day, she'd ask her.

With such a veritable feast for the mind tempting her, she had to force herself to leave the room before she actually picked one up. She and Noah would have so much more to talk about!

It wasn't until she was out of the room that she was hit again by the fact that Noah was gone. The now familiar ache returned. And the room of books lost its charm.

At the end of the hall Jessica noticed a glass door that led outside. Perhaps she should dash out into the morning chill and fetch in her things from the stable—the one thing the servants had been remiss about. Perhaps they'd been forbidden to bring an old bearskin into this fine house. But her father's coins were wrapped inside. She should fetch in the deerskin shift, at least, until she found a way to return the money.

The odd odors that had permeated Aunt Melissa's clothes yesterday came from the open door of the room near the end of the hall. Curious, she peeked in. Instead of books this time, two walls were almost entirely windows, making the interior as bright as the outdoors.

She wanted to cry when she thought of all the years she'd spent in dark dingy cabins. But then, she'd wanted to cry the livelong night.

Concentrating on something else, she looked for the source of the strange odors. As she did, she noted that the other two walls held quite a number of paintings. More were on stands, circling a chair and small table that held an assortment of brushes similar to the one Jessica had seen in her aunt's hand when they first met. Small cans and jars also cluttered the table, along with a thin slice of wood smeared with as many colors as had been splattered on

Melissa's apron. This must be where she was painting the portrait she had spoken of last night.

Jessica walked within the ring of easeled canvases and saw a number of young people staring back at her. Aunt Melissa's children, Jessica knew instinctively . . . a lonely woman keeping her children close the only way she could.

Would Jessica, too, find herself in here painting beside Melissa, trying to capture Noah from memory . . . the tilt of his head when he smiled . . . or those silvery gray eyes that could pull her close, hold her tight, with that one special look. . . .

"I won't let that happen to you."

With a start, Jessica whirled around to find her grandfather standing in the doorway. A splash of her coffee hit the floor. "Good morning, Grandfather William," she offered as she reached for a rag on the table to wipe her mess.

He came farther into the room. He was dressed in yet a different set of clothes than the two sets she'd seen him in the day before. "I've already told Grant you are not to be married off to one of his far-flung business contacts. He will have to find you a husband right here in Baltimore . . . right here where I can see you every day."

"Uncle Grant will pick my husband for me?" Surely she had heard him wrong.

"Of course, dear. A beauty like you will garner any number of offers. But I've told him to bide his time. I want you to stay here with us for a long, long time."

She had to ask again. "The man with whom I'm to spend the rest of my life is to be chosen by Uncle Grant? I'm to have no say? Is that the way it's always done?"

"Darling, I can't believe this surprises you. Of course it is. We would never leave such an important decision to an impressionable young girl. I'm sorry to say your dear mother was proof of that folly when she eloped with your father." He placed an arm around her shoulder. "Come along, sweet child. Let's see what there is for breakfast."

As Jessica allowed herself to be escorted away from Melissa's portraits, she felt the walls of this great house closing in. Everything Grandfather William had said, she'd heard before from Noah when he'd talked about a suitor going to a girl's family to ask for her hand in marriage. She simply had not been listening.

All the progress she thought she'd made, and yet she was still an ignorant backwoods girl if she imagined the freedom she sought could be found here in Baltimore . . . the freedom touted in all her treasured old newspapers. That same freedom so many had died to achieve. Life, liberty, and what she'd thought would be her own pursuit of happiness.

She had no more say-so over her person than those hapless folk in the kitchen.

28

The remainder of the day involved so much activity that Jessica had little time to think about Noah or her brother or anything else. As soon as Grant had risen for the day, he'd sent a servant into the city with messages to a variety of shopkeepers and tutors and, of most importance to Jessica, one to a man who would start the search for Spencer. Not long after breakfast, the tradesmen began arriving with samples of their wares and their expertise—all brought for the sole purpose of turning Jessica into a Baltimore lady.

Yet, with every rap on the door knocker, Jessica's heart had leapt with the hope that it heralded Noah's entrance . . . that he'd changed his mind and returned to her. And each disappointment sent her spirit plunging back to earth again.

It was late afternoon before the last townsman left—a Mister Standish Hanson, Esquire, Master of Elocution, who'd been hired to slow her speech into the genteel modulations of Aunt Melissa's.

What a busy, amazing day this first one had been.

In a simple afternoon gown of moss green, Melissa looked as exhausted as Jessica. She ordered tea sent upstairs to them in the family parlor, then dropped down on a lounge chair. Putting up her feet, she began chatting aimlessly about the day.

Jessica, restless despite endless hours of trying on wigs and shoes and being measured and draped with untold numbers of fabrics, wandered to the glass doors onto the balcony overlooking the street and the city, just as she'd done so often today. *Where was Noah?* The gray blue waters of the distant Chesapeake Bay drew her to them . . . they were the same shade that Noah's eyes had been the day he wore his new set of clothing to church. What an indescribably grand day that had been.

A shuddering sigh escaped.

Aunt Melissa must not have noticed. She didn't pause in her rambling discourse. ". . . and you have no idea what it means to me to have someone young in the house again."

Jessica squelched the temptation to remind her that there were other young people in the house—the three that had been in the kitchen this morning. But she knew slave children didn't count, except maybe to herself. And to God.

"We'll open up the ballroom and give you a big coming-out party as soon as the dance instructor deems you sufficiently accomplished. And you'll wear that one gown design we decided on, remember, the one we picked for the red-and-gold brocade? Yes," she drawled in her soft voice, "we'll have the grandest Christmas ball this old town has seen since the war."

Still gazing in the direction of the waters, Jessica noticed a church spire. "Which church will we attend on Sunday?"

Her aunt emitted an exhausted sigh and laid back her head. "Sunday . . . do you feel you'll be ready to start meeting a host of friends and all of Grant's business associates so soon? I was hoping to keep you to ourselves a little while longer."

"But what about keeping the Sabbath holy?"

"Oh yes. Well, I suppose you could do that right here at home until you're ready for your debut, so to speak. I'm certain Grant has a Bible in the study you could read—he seems to have books on everything. He ordered crate-loads from London."

Uncle Grant had merely written his request on a piece of paper, and two walls of books simply appeared! Jessica wagged her head at how easily the impossible happened if one was a wealthy Baltimore man.

Then it dawned on her. For all their riches, Melissa didn't even know whether or not they owned such a crucial volume as the Holy Bible.

Just as she started to address the matter, a tall man rode up to the gates.

Noah!

Her heart leapt in that brief exhilarating instant before she realized her error.

As the guards passed the rider through, she noted that this one wore rugged outdoor clothing, rather than the city attire of the tradesmen who had come and gone throughout the day.

Mayhap this man brought a message from Noah.

Just below her, he dismounted and drew out a missive from inside his heavy coat.

Her pulse began to race. A letter, please let it be from Noah, saying he'll come visit this evening. Surely Grandfather William had misunderstood Noah's intent when he left yester's eve. Noah had too much honor to simply dump her and ride away.

The knock at the front door echoed up the sweeping stairwell.

Jessica swung away from the glass panes. "If you'll excuse me, Aunt Melissa, I'll go see who's at the door."

"Don't be a ninny, dear," her aunt said, taking a sip of her tea. "That's what we have servants for. If the caller is for one of us, we'll be informed."

Determined to go anyway, Jessica halted at remembering the

warning the slaves had given her this morning about the consequences of her usurping their duties.

Unwillingly, she moved back to the windows just as the man reappeared from the front porch just under the window. He mounted and rode back down the driveway.

Jessica listened for the sound of footsteps coming up the stairs. There were none.

Still, her throbbing pulse would not slow. She had to know if the letter was for her. She turned back to Melissa. "May I have permission to go to the library to see if there's a Bible?"

"Oh yes, the Bible. Of course, dear." Melissa waved her away with an indulgent smile.

Jessica fairly flew down the stairs. Just before she reached the bottom, she saw her grandfather tucking the letter inside his yellow brocade waistcoat. Even though it didn't appear so, she couldn't help asking, "Is it for me?"

Grandfather William gazed up at her with his usual adoration. "My beautiful Janie—you don't mind if I call you that, do you?"

"No," she said but knew she lied. "The letter, was it for me?"

"No, my darling girl, it most definitely was not for you." He beckoned her with a lace-enshrouded hand. "Come with me into the parlor. I want to show you the jade figurine I gave your grandmother on our wedding day."

As she neared him, she had an odd thought. If his Janie truly had not been given her choice of husbands, had she loved him as much as he obviously loved her? Jessica hoped so for her grandmother's sake.

Then she remembered the Bible. "Could you wait a moment? I left Aunt Melissa upstairs whilst I came down to fetch a book."

He caught her hand as he did every time she came within reach. She quelled her instinct to pull free.

"You're just the tonic our Melissa needs too." He added as a second hand covered hers. "You've brought back the heart of this house." Slowly, reluctantly, he let go of her. "I'll be waiting in the parlor."

Hastening toward the library, Jessica was grateful for the opportunity to be free of both her doting relatives for a moment or two. From the way they talked and acted, they were becoming as dependent on her presence as Father had ever been. The Bible she sought was no longer an excuse. She had a very real need of her own . . . its strength and guidance.

In the library, the mantel clock ticked away several minutes—minutes she knew her grandfather awaited her—before she finally found a Bible. It was carelessly stashed so high not even Noah, as tall as he was, could have reached it without a ladder.

And of course, one was provided. A very clever one. With rollers and suspended from a ceiling track, it could be slid to the needed spot.

Climbing up, she retrieved the thick volume and clutched it to herself. Immediately, she found solace and strengthening. If she simply trusted, God would see her through this painful time. His Word promised faith sufficient for the day . . . today, tomorrow, each day, one at a time. He would see her through.

Starting down the ladder, another realization came to her. From the location of the Bible and from the comments Aunt Melissa had made, Jessica knew these people were not seekers of God's Word. To them, this had been just one more book in the many crates that had been purchased. They didn't ask the Lord's blessing at mealtime or seem to depend on him for anything. Only on themselves did they rely—and their vast fortune.

Yet with all they possessed, both Grandfather and Aunt Melissa seemed so lonely and strangely lost. From what Melissa said, they did attend church. But somehow they hadn't learned about the Holy Spirit. The Comforter.

She'd forgotten about the Holy Spirit for a while herself today. She must never let that happen again. And though she'd treasured another notion about these people, she now knew they had never prayed for her deliverance nor for her brothers'.

The door banger clanged again.

Noah. This time it had to be Noah. Her heavenly Father wouldn't take her from one godless house only to deliver her into another.

Tucking the Bible under her arm, she clambered down the remaining rungs. She would see who had arrived this time, whether or not the Hargraves approved.

Before reaching the entry hall, she heard the door open and heard Grandfather William's voice instead of a servant's. "Yes, may I help you?"

"I'm here to see Grant Hargrave," came from outside, and to Jessica's utter disappointment, the male voice was not Noah's. So many people had come today, but not Noah. Never Noah.

"I'm afraid my son hasn't returned from our warehouses as yet. You should check down there for him."

Coming through the doorway behind the staircase, she tried to see past her grandfather on the remote chance she was mistaken.

"He's not there either." A coarsely dressed young man with a trim beard and knit cap pulled low pushed rudely past Grandfather. "I'll wait here."

"You can't come barging in—" Grandfather's words were cut short, and he stepped back.

The man had pulled a pistol!

Jessica's first thought was to grab for her musket. Where was it? She'd forgotten to bring in her things from the stable this morning. Hoping the man hadn't noticed her, she deftly started backing toward the door she'd just entered. She needed to make a run for the stable.

"Stop!" the intruder commanded. "You stay put." Then the man's angry scowl slowly disappeared, and he relaxed his gun hand. His eyes grew wide. "Jaybird? Is that you?" He took a step toward her.

Who could be calling her that? She, too, moved forward. Then she recognized the eyes. Blue like— "Spencer? . . . *Spencer!*" Laughing and crying, she flung herself at him. Hugging him, kissing . . . her brother, full grown, who smelled as briny as the salt lick. "I thought you were dead. No, I didn't. I knew you were alive. No—I didn't." The words tumbled over themselves between kisses in a surge of elation Jessica couldn't even attempt to restrain.

Tears streamed down Spencer's weathered face. He laughed, a deep mature laugh, as he moved aside the front of his marine blue jacket and tucked the pistol into his belt, then held her at arm's length. The lad who went away four years ago had come back a tough, lean man. "That's my Jaybird, all right. Always chattering away even when you're all dressed up like a fine lady." He clutched her arms tighter. "How did you get here? When?" Not waiting for an answer, he hugged her again. "You don't know how glad I am to see you . . . out of Father's clutches and looking so well."

"You look even more wonderful," she said and squeezed him back.

"And Little Bob. He must be as tall as I am now." Spencer glanced past her.

"He is, he is. Almost. But he's—"

Spencer overrode her. "I've prayed day and night for you two." He leaned down for a closer look. "Day and night for the past three years since I found the Lord, I prayed you would get away safely. And my prayers were answered. I just didn't know it. You're here, both of you. Safe . . . and in this house, of all places."

Before she could explain about Little Bob or ask about the miracle of his own conversion, Grandfather pulled Spencer from her. The expression lifting his sagging face was almost as profound as when he had first seen Jessica. "You're the lost brother! I'm your grandfather, William Hargrave. Take off your cap. Let me get a better look at you." He didn't stop talking as Spencer complied, exposing a shaggy head of dark but sun-bronzed hair. "Where have you been for the past four years? Your sister was very worried about you."

Spencer's deep blue eyes turned almost black. That deadly cold temper she remembered was back. "Four years," he clipped off. "Four years, five months, and twenty-three days. I was impressed into service aboard one of your company's ships—I believe that's the polite word for being kidnapped, isn't it? And I've pretty much been sailing around the world ever since."

"But how? I don't understand."

"Oh, it's not hard to figure. That conniving, scheming, self-serving son of yours hired some thugs to carry me aboard and keep me in chains until the ship was well out of port. And to make certain I didn't return too soon, he gave orders to have me put under lock and key any time we sighted land." His rage was back, full force.

And he had a gun.

Disbelieving, Grandfather shook his head, rejecting Spencer's charge. "We don't do that sort of thing."

"Maybe you don't, but your son does. And I've come here expressly to tell him what I think—no—to *show him* what I think of him." He placed a hand over the lethal-looking weapon stuffed in his belt.

"This has to be some sort of misunderstanding." Grandfather darted a glance to Jessica. "I'm certain if Grant had known who you were—"

"He knew exactly who I was. And once he got over the shock of seeing his dead sister's son, he couldn't have been more welcoming . . . especially when he ordered his men to show me to my quarters. It's taken years to free myself from his captain's clutches and find another ship back here."

Grandfather sucked in a breath, then slowly expelled it, his rounded shoulders sagging. "Grant always did want to eliminate the competition. Even when it came to his brother Charles. He won't admit it, but I think he incited his brother into siding with the English. Charles ended up having to run for his life to Halifax."

"Well, I plan to cut short Grant Hargrave's days of inciting anyone to do anything ever again." Spencer stepped back from Grandfather and glanced out the door that still stood wide. But only a cold breeze streamed in . . . at the moment.

Jessica slammed it shut, then swung around and whisked the gun from Spencer's belt. "Oh no you don't. If you shoot Uncle Grant, the authorities will come and lock you up. And then they'll hang you. I won't let you leave me again, just when I've found you. I came all this way in search of you. I arrived only yesterday. And when I heard you'd never even been—"

"You arrived here just yesterday?" Spencer asked incredulously. "I did too. But our ship had to anchor out in the bay until there was a slip available at the wharf." With an exuberance that took her a moment to understand, he picked her up and whirled her around—long-barreled pistol, Bible, and all. "By George! Now, that *is* a miracle, that's what it is—a *miracle!*"

"Aye, 'tis that." Still held high in the air, she hugged the Bible to her. "And that's not the only miracle. Your prayers sent Noah to bring me out of Father's hell, just as the Israelites' prayers sent Moses to save them."

With a confused frown, Spencer put her down. "You mean Noah as in Noah and the ark?"

"I'll tell you about that later. But I'm sorry to say your prayers haven't all been answered. Little Bob didn't come with me. He ran off with a tribe of Muskogees three months ago."

"Muskogees? When I left, we'd just left the Shawnee and moved into Chickasaw country. Oh . . . ." Spencer gave a knowing lift of the brows. "Father got caught cheating the Chickasaw this time."

"Aye, watering down the rum again."

"What are you two talking about?" Grandfather William glanced from Spencer to Jessica.

"Everything's been in such a whirl since I arrived, Grandfather, I haven't had a chance to tell you about where I came from. You see, Father quit the army to go trading with the tribes. Then when Mother died at Fort Pitt, Father took us with him. Deep into Indian country. I hadn't seen a white town since I was four years old. Not until a few weeks ago." Looking at her brother again, she continued, "I need to fetch my things out in the stable. I think it's best we leave here before Uncle Grant returns, and that temper of yours gets the best of you."

"You've been living among savages for fourteen years?" Grandfather sounded appalled. "We learned that Whitman left Fort Pitt with his children, but I had no idea."

"You would have if that son of yours had a drop of decency in him." Spencer's eyes narrowed beneath a crimped line of dark brows. "I told him I'd come seeking refuge for Jay Jay and Little Bob. He knew they were out there in a dark and heathen land with a violent drunkard." Rage building in his voice, he reached for the pistol in Jessica's hand.

She stepped back, avoiding him. "No, Spencer. Killing Uncle Grant is not worth sacrificing you. Leave his judgment to God. Please, let's just go."

Grandfather clutched Jessica's shoulder painfully. "You can't leave. You just arrived."

"I'm sorry, Grandfather, but I don't see how Spencer and I can stay. And I don't think I could have stayed here even if Spencer hadn't come. I care for you and Aunt Melissa, but there are too many reasons I can't stay. For instance, the fact that you hold slaves in bondage. That, I could never accept."

"Sweetheart, we don't mistreat our slaves. They're treated like—"

Jessica silenced the old man with a finger to his lips. "I'm sorry, Grandfather, but there's nothing you could say that would make that loathsome practice acceptable to me. I know exactly how hopeless it feels to be at the complete mercy of someone, and I also know what it's like to be an outcast, to be barred from all the social gatherings. But I promise to write as soon as I know where we'll be. And, Grandfather, once Spencer and I are settled, we'd love to have you come visit us. You must, you really must."

Grandfather swung from her to Spencer. "Wait, please. If you'll stay, I'll—I'll make you captain of your own ship." His desperation was almost tangible as he sought his grandson's face.

Spencer's expression softened. "Thank you, sir. But if I never walk another ship's deck again, it'll be too soon. I have to go where I'm my own man. I'm going back overmountain. If that's acceptable to you, Jaybird."

"Aye." How could it not be? She had her brother back. She had Spencer, whom she trusted with her life. "One thing, though. Now that I, too, have found the Lord, I want to go find George and Little Bob and tell them all about him. Even Father, in time."

Spencer scowled, then eased into a grin. "All right, Jay Jay. Even the old goat."

"But the winter snows are coming," Grandfather argued, catching hold of both of them, still unwilling to concede. "At least stay here till spring."

"What do you mean?" came from the stairs above. It was Aunt Melissa. She descended the steps, her pleasant features marred with concern. "Who's leaving?"

Jessica went to her aunt, whom she'd left forgotten in the upstairs parlor. "My brother Spencer has finally arrived. Isn't it wonderful? An absolute miracle! Please come meet him."

Melissa stiffened—she'd caught sight of the pistol in Jessica's hand.

At that moment the door opened, and Grant strode in.

29

Grant Hargrave's authoritative scowl landed on Jessica's brother. "I suppose you're the one my men at the gate said was looking for me. It's after hours, so state your business, and be quick about it."

A vein bulged in Spencer's forehead. Fists balling, he returned Uncle Grant's glower. Wheeling to Jessica, he grabbed for the pistol.

Standing between the two, she dodged away from Spencer. The last thing he needed in his present state was a weapon.

To her utter dismay, Uncle Grant snatched it from her. He aimed it at her brother. "What in blazes is going on here?"

Spencer lunged for him.

The end of the barrel stopped him.

"Father, what's going on?" Grant shoved Spencer back with the pistol.

Spencer eased off, but only a step, his body rigid, his face dark with anger. "You don't remember me, do you? But, then, it's been quite awhile—four years, five months, and twenty-three days, to

be exact. I'm your nephew, Spencer Whitman, back from the seas
... where you sent me."

Grant blanched and reared back his head. "Oh. I see." The
voice had lost its roar. He retreated a pace.

"Spencer Whitman?" Melissa asked incredulously from the
stairs. "Spencer? Jessica, is this your lost brother?"

"Aye, ma'am," she said without daring to take her eyes off the
two adversaries. "Uncle Grant had him abducted and taken aboard
one of his ships."

Melissa gasped.

"And I'm here to make certain he doesn't play God with anyone
else's life." Spencer, on the advance again, filled the space Grant
had vacated. "Ever again."

Grant warily added a second hand to secure his hold on the
weighty pistol.

"Is this true, Grant?" Aunt Melissa demanded as she descended
the remaining steps.

He flicked a quick glance at his wife. "Stay out of this, dear. It
has nothing to do with you."

Undeterred, she crossed the space dividing them in that calm,
ladylike manner of hers, stopping to stare up at Grant for a long
moment. "You're right." Her voice, her tone, were oddly quiet.
"Kidnapping your dead sister's son and shipping him off to heaven
knows where has absolutely nothing to do with me. Nor should
your despicable actions surprise me. Since you've done no less to
your own children." She perused him a moment as if he were no
more appealing than a pot of beans gone sour. "You will do
anything and everything to maintain supreme power over your
little empire. Isn't that how it goes? Well, as you said, it has nothing to do with me." She whirled around, her sea green chiffon
skirts flying. *Not anymore.*

"This is not the time, Melissa," Grant growled, his gaze still
trained on Spencer.

Grandfather William, in a sudden move, grasped his son's wrist and shoved with surprising force for a man his age.

The barrel veered away as the pistol misfired, exploding thunderously in the grand hall. A mirror shattered. Glass sprayed across the marble floor.

"I'll not have family killing family," the old gentleman said, plucking the spent pistol from his son's hand.

The elder slaves, Solomon and Famar, burst onto the scene through different doors, their eyes wide and wary.

Melissa, however, picked up her skirts in an elaborate show of calmness and started for the stairs. "Famar, would you have Dicy come up to me? I have immediate need of her help. Oh, and Solomon, would you please have my trunks brought up from the basement?"

"Grant," Grandfather said, turning back to his son. "It seems to me you have a lot to answer for." He pointed the empty gun in Spencer's direction. "And you can start by apologizing to your nephew. Then you'd better get upstairs and try to reason with your wife if you want to keep her."

Like the sails of a big ship in a sudden calm, the wind was taken out of Grant . . . but for only a second. He straightened to his full height, hiking his proud cleft chin. "Everything I've done has been for the betterment of this family."

"Whose family is that?" Grandfather retorted. "Certainly not mine. Spencer is as much my grandson as your own son is. Maybe he's not in line to inherit the real estate as Grant Edward is, but he has every right to a portion of my worldly fruits. As do all my grandchildren, no matter how far away you've managed to disperse them."

Grant's face turned bloodred; veins bulged at his temples.

Almost certain Grant would attack the old man, Jessica braced to leap. Instead, he wheeled away, toward the front door.

"Not so fast." Spencer started after him.

Grandfather caught Spencer's arm. "Let him go. If you have a bone to pick with someone, it might as well be me. Whatever happened to you is as much my fault as your uncle's. After my Janie died, I buried myself in my own self-serving grief. I just walked away and let Grant take over the business and the family. I knew he was getting ahead of himself. I should have put a stop to his riding roughshod over everyone. But I didn't. If you want to shoot someone, start with me." He handed the spent weapon to Spencer, butt first.

A grand gesture—but was it genuine? Or would Grandfather's anger soon be reignited as easily as an empty gun can be reloaded?

Spencer must have had his own doubts. A veritable battle raged across her brother's face as he glanced from the useless weapon to the door Grant had exited. "You expect me to forget what he did to us?" Flipping the weapon, he caught it, barrel first, and started after Grant.

Jessica leapt up, wrapping her arms around his neck, the forgotten Bible banging against the back of his head. "Think what you're doing, Spencer—what it will do to us! You must let it go! You must! Vengeance belongs to the Lord."

He ripped one arm loose.

But she wouldn't give up. She thrust the Bible under his nose. "We have our miracle. Please don't throw it back in God's face."

They stared eye to eye for what seemed an eternity of warring wills.

Finally, she heard the air whoosh out of his lungs as he relaxed and pulled her closer. "All right, Jaybird, all right. Get your things. I want to be as far away from here as humanly possible before we stop again." He lowered her to the floor.

"Let me get my cloak." Straightening the fall of her plaid skirt, she hurried to the armoire.

"Wait, child," Grandfather William pleaded as he started after her. "Not so fast."

Collecting her hooded garment, she turned back to the kindly old man. "I'm sorry, Grandfather, but even you must see this is the only way to restore harmony. We must go—for now anyway," she added to soften the blow. Pulling his rumpled old face down to hers, she kissed his cheek, then ran for the door Spencer held open. "Follow me to the stables. I have my horses and my overmountain things out there."

Following close behind in the waning light, Spencer collected the horse he'd left near the entrance.

"No, wait!" Grandfather hurried down the porch steps after them. He still refused to give up.

One of the men who'd been stationed at the front gates came hurrying up the long drive. "What was that shot?" he called on vapor puffs of the chill air. "Mr. Hargrave rode outta here as if the very devil was after him."

Jessica heard her grandfather pause to explain as she and Spencer hastened on to the stables.

At the yawning doorway, Tonab stood watching their approach. "Was that a gunshot I heared?" he too asked, his concern as evident as the guard's.

"It was nothing," Jessica provided. "No one was hurt. I need what I came here with. Can you please tell me where my musket and bedroll are?"

"You mean that rolled up ol' fur?" the groom asked, screwing up one side of his face. "Y'all sure you wants to take that thing into the big house?"

"Please, where's my bearskin robe?"

He schooled his dark features into a placid expression and pointed to a corner next to the stalls. "Over there."

"You still have that old bear fur?" Spencer asked, a grin giving his own expression a much needed lift.

"Aye." She smiled.

319

"Let me." Spencer picked up the weighty bundle for her and carried it to his horse.

Jessica suddenly realized she still had the treasured Bible in her hands. It seemed as if an hour had passed since she'd found it in the library, yet she'd never had a chance to open it. Reverently, she set it on a stack of feed sacks. She hated leaving it behind, but it didn't belong to her. She started for the stalls to find her horses.

"Fine." The lone word preceded her grandfather into the darker confines of the stable as he rushed to catch up to her. His breathing was labored. "I understand the need for you to leave the Hargrave house at the moment. But that doesn't mean you have to leave Maryland too." Taking in some much needed air, he continued. "Let me buy you a little cottage nearby. Then—"

"Then what?" Spencer finished for him. "Live here beholden to you? I'm a man full grown. I have to make my own way."

"But where's the shame in taking your inheritance early?" he insisted desperately. "And if you want to earn your own way, I commend you for that." He caught Spencer's heavy wool sleeve. "I'll tell you what—instead of a cottage, let me buy you a little horse farm I've had my eye on. And . . . Tonab." He swung to the stableman. "Bring out Chelten and three of our best mares." He turned back, his eyes—the same shade of blue as Spencer's—full of hope. "Best coaching horses in the colonies. They'll make a fine start."

Shifting the bearskin roll to one arm, Spencer's demeanor gentled, and he clasped the old man's shoulder. "I thank you, I truly do, for restoring my belief in my mother's family. Perhaps someday we shall come back. But right now we have two brothers to find."

The disappointment in Grandfather's face was exaggerated by the deeply shadowed lantern light. He looked from one to the other and sighed. "Yes, you must find your brothers—my other lost grandchildren. I suppose I can't stand in your way any longer."

A gate clicked shut behind Tonab, and he brought forth a magnificent bay stallion. The animal's arched neck was elegantly exposed by the braidings of his black mane, adding to his regal bearing. "Mastah? You still wants me to bring out Chelten?"

"Aye. And the mares. Hitch two of them to the phaeton and tie the others to the back."

Tonab looked surprised but said nothing as he went to fulfill the order.

"But, sir—," Spencer began.

Grandfather swung back to Spencer and Jessica. "No grandchildren of mine are riding out of here empty-handed. The four hackneys are yours, son." He turned to Jessica, and his eyes melted into a glisten of tears. "And the carriage is for my Janie. To bring her back to me." He grabbed her hands and held tight. "You must come back. No matter how long it takes. Promise me."

"I'll do my utmost." She couldn't honestly say yea or nay. But her grandfather needed so much more than her presence. She pulled him with her to where she'd laid the Bible. "Your gifts to us, I know, are worth a fortune, and we will treasure them." Retrieving her hands from his, she picked up the heavy black book, then pressed it to him. "There is only one gift worthy enough to give you in return. Please, Grandfather, open it, read the book of John. There is someone very special in that book I'd like you to meet."

He looked down at it confused, turned it to the light. "But this is—it's a Bible."

Jessica took the precious emblem at her neck and held it out to him. "Because this cross came from Grandmother Janie, I'm almost certain she's in heaven. If you read what is written in St. John's words and believe, your loneliness for her shall be eased. Because then you will know for a certainty that you shall rejoin her someday. As surely as I will join you. Whether it's in this life or the next. I promise you—no, the Lord promises us both—we shall be together again."

"But you will come back." His eyes held such pleading.

"Yes, Grandfather, I promise." She could no longer deny him the words he so urgently needed to hear.

Tonab strode by, leading all four matched horses out of the stable.

"It's time to go," Spencer said as he came alongside Jessica. "Where are your horses?"

As Jessica pointed them out, her grandfather caught her arm. "I say, what's that huge furry thing you've got there?"

"Jay Jay's cloak." Spencer called from the black mare's stall. His bitterness still lay close to the surface. "And her deerskin shift. The clothes she was relegated to wearing these past four and a half years because I was prevented from going back to fetch her and Little Bob," he said, leading out the fine-boned black mare.

Jessica sent Spencer a reprimanding look, as Grandfather's mouth fell open.

The old man made no further remark about the bearskin as his sagging features lifted to their faces. "I'll walk with you to the carriage house. But, Spencer, you must promise that when you find your brothers, you'll bring them home to meet me."

Reluctantly, Spencer grunted, "I promise," then went ahead with the two mounts and their gear, while Jessica strolled at a slower pace with her grandfather.

He looked overly tired now. His arm lay heavy around her shoulder. "Write me, sweet girl. I want to hear from you every day."

Her throat tightened, and she could hardly speak. "Noah called me 'sweet girl' sometimes," she sighed wistfully. "It sorrows me deeply, knowing he didn't care enough to even say good-bye." She took a second to regroup her emotions. "Of course, I'll write to you, Grandfather, as often as I can. Now that I know where to post the letters."

"You'll need money for postage." He reached inside his waistcoat. "And traveling expenses, and—" He stopped in his tracks, obliging her to do the same.

"Is something amiss?"

His face was almost unreadable in the growing darkness, but the sorrow was still evident. "This has turned out to be a day of facing quite a number of hard truths. And I suppose I have one last truth to confess. I lied earlier when I said the letter that came was not for you." He pulled forth the missive. "It's from your young man, Noah Reardon."

30

Noah rolled to his other side. Again. Having slept away a good portion of the day before, sleeping through the night was becoming impossible.

But he knew he couldn't blame his restlessness on that. The real reason never left his thoughts. When he'd stopped a postrider at the ferry dock yesterday morning, the man had promised on his honor to deliver the letter to Baltimore before nightfall and wait for Jessica's reply . . . the letter that laid bare his feelings for her, that asked her to consider marriage to him.

He had little doubt she cared for him. But it was the last sentence he wrote that kept him tossing and turning. After she'd seen all that the Hargraves possessed—riches she couldn't even envision a month ago—would she turn her back on all that to go back with him to the hardships in Tennessee?

He knew he couldn't stay here, even for her. *Especially for her.* There was no future for him on this side of the mountains. The virgin land he and Ike had been awarded for their years of service in the Revolutionary War was all he had to offer her—that and his half interest in the gristmill they'd set up on their creek.

Then there was the matter of a grandfather who'd unabashedly worshiped her from the moment she walked in the door, who was ready to lavish all manner of attention and luxuries on her.

The bed squeaked loudly as he sat up and swung his legs over the side. Thank goodness he had the room to himself tonight, or any fellow travelers wouldn't be getting much rest either.

Again he played through his mind the postrider's trotting up to the mansion, knocking on the same grand door he and Jessica had stood before not thirty-six hours ago. Would she answer it herself, be just as anxious to hear from him as he was to hear from her? Would she readily, eagerly, send the return answer he so desperately wanted to receive?

Or would a servant answer the door? That was more likely, he knew. Had Grant Hargrave given orders that she not receive any correspondence from him? That was his worst fear—that they'd deceive her into thinking he had callously ridden off without giving her another thought.

He couldn't have that. *He wouldn't.*

He knew he couldn't just sit here and wait. He'd go mad. Grabbing his breeches from off the bedpost, he rammed a foot into each leg, then, in the faint light of his sole lamp's trimmed wick, found his stockings and boots.

But how would he get past the guards Hargrave had hired—guards who were probably ordered to shoot him on sight? Though he'd prayed more these past hours than ever before in his life, no insight, no plan had come to him.

If he remained here and if Jessica had received his letter, he had no hope of hearing from her until tomorrow evening at the earliest . . . unless she rode all through the night to reach him. He kept remembering she'd done that once before, and on foot, and neither the threat of bears nor wolves nor Indians had stopped her then.

Noah chuckled at the childish twist his musing had taken. She hadn't been running *to* him—she'd been seeking refuge *from* a crazy father who was trying to shoot her. And what was that old saying? Lightning doesn't strike twice in the same spot.

Shoving his feet into his boots, he sprang off the bed. The clock downstairs had chimed three times not long ago. If he hurried, he could be back to Baltimore before noon.

He heard a rumbling sound. Horses' hooves!

Feeling as silly as he had when he'd checked out the two previous travelers who'd passed by since midnight, he couldn't keep himself from going to the window.

It was too dark to see very far in the moonless night, but the sound grew louder . . . hooves, creaks, squeaks, wheels churning.

He groaned. "A wagon." She'd be on horseback.

Still, he waited a couple more seconds. Two spots of light emerged from the trees. A carriage.

Disappointed as before, he collected his belongings and started out the door of his room. Halfway down the stairs, he heard the coach roll to a stop outside. The poor proprietor was destined to be forced out of his bed again tonight. He himself had been the culprit who'd interrupted the man's rest in the wee hours last night.

And these people really meant business. Almost immediately, someone pounded on the door without ceasing.

"I'm coming! I'm coming!" came a very irritated cry from above. The innkeeper's stumbling about and cursing on the second floor only added to the uproar.

Reaching the main room lighted only by the embers of a couple of backlogs in the giant fireplace, Noah tossed his saddlebag on a table and hurried to unbar the door before the entire inn was rousted out. He swung it open to a small cloaked figure standing in the dark entrance.

"Noah? Is that you?" The woman flung back her hood.

Jessica? She'd come! She'd really come!

He pulled her into his arms. "My sweet, sweet girl." Unable to stop himself, he trailed kisses all over her face, her hair, her hands . . . her lips, pulling her close, ever closer. She was really here.

He leaned back slightly to make sure. Yes. He could smell lilacs in her hair, could taste her lips. He had felt her breath on his cheek and her arms around his neck. His heart was pounding with hers.

"Noah," she sighed.

"Jessica." Lifting her up in his arms, he captured her lips in a hungry, searing kiss.

"Now that you've established each other's identity," a male voice came from behind, "I'll thank you to disengage yourselves."

Dragging his mouth from hers, Noah was in no mood for intruders. "And who are you?" he growled impatiently at a young bearded man bearing a lantern.

"The name's Spencer Whitman. And I strongly suggest you put my sister down, and let's all get in out of the cold. I need some answers from you. The right ones."

"Spencer Whitman?" Noah set Jessica on her feet and looked at her as she flashed that big splashy grin of hers. "You found your brother? How? Where? *He's alive!*"

"Very much so," the young man answered for his sister as he ushered them inside and closed the door behind them. "And I'll thank you not to change the subject. My sister has kept me from my bed this whole miserable, damp night to come all this way just to tell you something." The irritation in his voice had a weary edge to it. "Do you have any idea what it's like having a frantic female driving you and your poor horses to exhaustion? Or having to stop every hour to change teams? In the dark?"

Noah's trip from Greeneville to Salem with the Widow Stowe quickly came to mind. He grinned. "Aye, I believe I do."

"Ah, then you know what a night I've had. So let the girl get on with it. Then maybe we can all get some sleep."

"Amen," came from the bottom of the stairs. The craggy-faced innkeeper had been standing there listening in his long nightshirt and cap. "When you're through palavering, put the lady in the room across the hall from yours. We can settle up in the morning." Without waiting for their response, he trudged barefoot back upstairs.

Noah tore himself from Jessica's side long enough to stoke up the fire. She came alongside and handed him some kindling from the wood box . . . ever his helpmate.

He glanced up and saw the firelight dance across her eyes, the same as it had the first time he ever saw her at the salt pots . . . his beautiful, fragile darling.

"Yes," she said in a low breathy voice, as if he'd asked her a question.

Had he? He didn't think so. "Yes?"

She pulled loose the bow tie of her cloak. "Your letter. I say yes to everything in it."

"Everything? Even Tennessee?" He had to ask—to be sure.

Her lips trembled ever so slightly as she said yes again.

She was actually choosing him over the Hargraves? Coming home with him to be his wife? Cupping her sweet face in his hands, he leaned down to her. "Truly, you will?"

She smiled and nodded.

His heart threatened to burst from his chest. "You'll marry me, be my wife?"

Tears swam among the flames reflecting in her eyes as she nodded again.

He kissed them away, each and every one, with all the love and promise and hope he'd been longing to give her.

She came up on her toes and returned his ardor with no less passion or promise. When at last she drew back, she took his face into her own hands and whispered, "I love you, Noah Reardon."

"And I love you," he roughed out through his own emotion-clogged throat. "My sweet, sweet girl."

329

"Say it again," she breathed past a warm smile.

"I love you, Jessica Jane Whitman."

"No, the 'sweet girl' part. Call me your sweet girl again."

A chair complained loudly as Spencer dropped down on it with an exaggerated groan. "I suppose you intend to keep this mush up for some time, don't you?"

"Aye," they both returned, laughing and pulling each other into another hug.

"And nothing I could say would convince you otherwise?"

Noah's mouth was mere inches from Jessica's now. "Wild horses couldn't drag her from me." He returned his rapt attention to her lips.

The chair gave another loud, irritating creak, stealing Noah's attention again.

Jessica's brother had folded his arms behind his head, and looking quite comfortable, watched them with a big, lazy grin. "Wild horses, you say. Well, you couldn't blow me out of here with a twelve-pound cannonball. But come to think of it, I reckon we've got plenty of time. Aye, all the time in the world."

Noah and Jessica burst out laughing. Tonight *she'd* had the good sense to bring a chaperone.

But that was all right.

Everything was better than all right.

Pulling Jessica close again, Noah sent a heartfelt thanks heavenward.

Tomorrow he'd find out what miracle of miracles had brought her and her brother here in a fine coach and in the middle of the night. Then he'd get those wedding banns posted. But for now, he was just going to enjoy the moment.

A lot.

Epilogue

Ten Months Later
Reardon Valley

At the sound of cooing, Jessica Reardon turned from the hearth where she'd been checking the tenderness of a pot of carrots.

The round-eyed baby girl sitting on her mother's lap gummed a toothless grin. It was the first one Jessica had received from her tiny niece. Her hand gravitated to her own swollen belly. In a few months her little "bundle of joy," as Annie, her sister-in-law, liked to call newborns, would make its appearance. Then she and Noah and the babe would be a family all their own. "When did Mary Lou commence smiling?"

Annie looked up from the rocker with a mother's tenderness still glowing in her green-and-gold eyes. "Last week. I 'spect she was savin' that one special just for you."

"A special smile for a special day." Jessica glanced out the open door of her cabin to see whether her husband, his brother Ike, and their very welcome guests were returning yet from their walk of the property. Yester's eve Grandfather William had arrived with Noah's most gracious mother, so this was a day of celebration for everyone.

Grandfather had rallied remarkably from his ill health last winter. So much so that he'd arranged to collect Louvenia Reardon in North Carolina and escort the tall, rather regal-looking woman to the valley—with the assistance of three hired men, of course. A trying journey, nonetheless.

Jessica had been nervous about meeting Noah and Ike's mother, until she'd actually arrived and given both of her daughters-in-law exuberant, rib-crushing hugs. What a wonderment to be surrounded by so much love. And Grandfather was so impressed with this bounteous new country that he no longer felt she'd made the wrong choice. That alone pleased Jessica no end.

"Everything's just about ready to set on the table," Jessica informed Annie, hooking her big spoon on a spike beside the fireplace. Untying her apron, she removed the covering from the lovely, lace-trimmed lavender gown Grandfather had brought for her. Then one last time she surveyed the table that took up the center of this main area of Noah's and her three-room cabin. Linen cloths and the last flowers of summer added to the lovely china Grandfather had also brought. They really dressed up her simple log home. "I'll go ring the dinner bell."

Shading her eyes against the late afternoon light, she stepped outside their cabin, one of three facing a meadow that gently sloped to the Carey River beyond. Seeing no one moving about, she paused to admire the view spread before her. She didn't think she would ever get tired of walking out across the meadows and fields her new kinfolk had cleared and plowed. Off to the left, the late corn stood tall, waiting to be harvested along with a patch of squash and pumpkins. In the tree-lined river, she knew fish were jumping. At her right, a large barn rose up with a loft big enough to store their bounty, and below there was plenty of room to protect the milk cows and horses and hogs from the winter's cold. Beside it stood a chicken coop with laying hens and fryers. All surrounded by family. Who could ask for anything more? This truly was God's country.

Jessica swung the rope of the bell attached to the side of the house and rang it hard. With no sign of her dinner guests, she surmised that Noah and Ike had taken them down to see the gristmill.

Guests. Jessica loved the sound of that word. She only wished more of the family had been here to greet them. Accompanied by Ethan Yarnell, Spencer and Drew were off searching for George and Little Bob. They'd been gone all summer, returning home for a short respite only once after scouting up North for George with no success. Too many years had passed since he had run away with the Susquehannock nursemaid—he could be anywhere from Canada to the Mississippi.

Spencer had reported that Father, too, was gone. He'd abandoned the salt lick and moved on with an Alabama squaw he'd bought. Sending a prayer heavenward for the poor woman, Jessica rang the bell again. She'd always expended too much concern over her father's earthly fate. One way or another, he'd always seen to his physical needs. Perhaps one day their paths would cross again and she could address his spiritual dearth.

Now Spencer and the others were deep in Muskogee country hunting for Little Bob. She was sure they'd succeed in finding him since Jessica knew which clan the lad was with—if they didn't lose their scalps first. Every night she prayed they would prevail against the dangers in the wilderness.

From the direction of the water mill Jessica spotted Noah approaching with Grandfather. Her breath caught, as it often did when she first sighted her husband. At the moment, a golden halo outlined his blond hair in the late afternoon light, giving his outward appearance the same glow she always felt was within him . . . especially when they spoke of the babe she now carried within her.

How foolish she'd been to think he wouldn't want her for the mother of his children. And what a wonderful father he would make. Such a gentle and patient man. And loving. He had proved to be more loving than she'd ever dreamed possible. In so many ways, she mused playfully, as a smile spread easily across her face.

Jessica noticed Ike and Mother Louvenia strolling up the rise behind the first two. She raised a hand and waved. But no one noticed. They all stopped and turned southward.

Stepping farther away from the cabins, Jessica saw four riders coming at a trot from down valley. An odd time for neighbors to come visiting. She doubted she had enough food prepared to feed four more.

Then she recognized the big bay stallion—the one Grandfather had given Spencer in Baltimore. "Spencer!" Picking up her lavender dimity skirts, she ran down the path separating the squash from the corn . . . toward men and horses who now broke into a full gallop. Spencer was back! With Yarnell and Drew and an Indian lad. No. It was Little Bob in buckskin!

Spencer and Yarnell reined in hard when they reached Noah and Grandpa. But not her little brother. He kept coming, straight for her. "Jaybird!" Reaching her, he vaulted off his mount before the roan had a chance to come to a complete stop. "Jaybird!"

They threw themselves into each other's arms, hugging and kissing.

"Little" Bob was as tall as Spencer now but more gangling. Eventually, he held Jessica away from him and stared at her. Happy disbelief filled his dark blue eyes. "Aren't you pretty as a picture book."

"Yes, she is," came from behind, and Noah clapped Little Bob on the shoulder. "Welcome home, Robert. Welcome home."

Not completely letting go of Jessica, Little Bob turned to Noah. "You're the husband Spence told me about." He extended his hand. "I want to thank you for rescuing Jay Jay. I've been feeling real guilty about leaving her at the salt lick with Father. But I couldn't stay any longer, and she wouldn't come with me."

"Well, there won't be any need for you to leave your family again, not unless you want to."

"That's right, Bob," Noah's older brother had sauntered up to join them. "I'm Ike. I just want to say that this is your valley now too. And we're all here set to love you, just like we've already come to love Spence and little Jess. Ain't that right, Noah." Ike grinned at his brother with that same disarming Reardon smile.

"Aye." Noah glanced beyond Little Bob. "And there's someone else I think you'll be pleased to meet." He motioned for Grandfather to step forward. "This is your mother's father. He's come all the way from Baltimore in the hope of meeting his youngest grandson."

Little Bob's eyes doubled in size in his deeply tanned face. His mouth dropped open. "Baltimore?"

"Come here, lad. Give me a hug."

Jessica watched as Grandfather in his stylish buff-and-cream waistcoat pulled the primitive-looking young man into his arms—feather-adorned braids, fringed-and-beaded leather and all. Grandfather had come a long way from Baltimore in more than miles. Jessica knew that he now could see past his own needs and into the hearts of others. William Hargrave had made friends with the One the apostle John had written about in his Gospel.

And now her youngest brother would have that opportunity as well.

Noah wrapped an arm around Jessica's shoulders and pulled her close. With his thumb he wiped a tear that she hadn't been aware of from her cheek.

Jessica looked up through a happy mist to the love she always saw in his silver gray eyes. Blessing upon blessings. "I suppose giving thanks to the Lord this evening is going to take you an extraordinarily long time. Supper's going to get exceedingly cold."

"Probably so." Chuckling, Noah leaned close and nuzzled her cheek. "Probably so."

A Note from the Author

Dear Reader,

It was a joy for me to meet and get to know the heroine, Jessica, with her insatiable curiosity and unquenchable hope for the future. And Noah . . . what a guy! He could be my hero in real life any day of the week.

But seriously, I do hope you've had as pleasurable and as spiritually uplifting a journey as I had. I pray that everyone who reads this novel will come away with the reminder from 2 Corinthians 6:14: "Don't team up with those who are unbelievers. How can goodness be a partner to wickedness? How can light live with darkness?"

Many of us Christians have thought that once we marry that wonderful nonbeliever who embodies every quality we ever wanted, he or she will see Christ in us and become a believer. I'm one of those people. I'm grateful to God and to my prayer partners that my husband eventually did become a Christian, but only after twenty-one difficult years of each of us pulling in opposite directions. For those contemplating marriage, take heed: It's a lifelong journey. I pray you'll be wiser and more trusting in the Lord's desire for you than I was, that you'll receive the many blessings of taking that journey with someone already traveling the same path.

If you missed the first of this series, *Freedom's Promise,* I think you'll have an entertaining and insightful trip with fiercely independent Annie McGregor as she learns to trust not only God but the man she grows to love, Ike Reardon.

The third novel of the series will hit the book stands in spring 2001. *Freedom's Bell* will feature Crystabelle Amherst, an overly educated young belle with some very radical ideas for 1794. She thinks she should have as many rights and choices as a man, including the right to become Reardon Valley's first schoolteacher. Thrust into the mix is Drew Reardon, who vows not to marry until he finds a woman who is willing to give up everything to explore the vast wilderness with him. Sounds like they're both in for a few lessons in humility.

I thank you for your lovely letters. They are my inspiration to keep writing.

Blessings to you and yours,

Dianna Crawford

About the Author

Dianna Crawford lives in southern California with her husband, Byron, and the youngest of their four daughters. Although she loves writing historical fiction, her most gratifying blessings are her husband of thirty-eight years, her daughters, and her grandchildren. Aside from writing, Dianna is active in her church's children's ministries and in a Christian organization that counsels mothers-to-be, offering alternatives to abortion.

Dianna's first novel was published in 1992 under the pen name Elaine Crawford. Written for the general market, the book became a best-seller and was nominated for Best First Book by the Romance Writers of America. Three more novels and several novellas followed under that pen name.

Dianna says that she much prefers writing Christian historical fiction, because our wonderful Christian heritage is commonly diluted or distorted—if not completely deleted—from most historical fiction, nonfiction, and textbooks. She felt very blessed when she and Sally Laity were given the opportunity to coauthor the Freedom's Holy Light series for Tyndale House. The books center on fictional characters who are woven into many of the real-life adventures and miracles that took place during the American Revolution. Her HeartQuest novels, the Reardon Brothers series, are set soon after the Revolution.

The Freedom's Holy Light series consists of *The Gathering Dawn, The Kindled Flame, The Tempering Blaze, The Fires of Freedom, The Embers of Hope,* and *The Torch of Triumph.* Dianna has also authored two HeartQuest novellas, which appear in the anthologies *A Victorian Christmas Tea* and *With This Ring.* She is the coauthor with Rachel Druten of the novel *Out of the Darkness* (Heartsong Presents).

Dianna welcomes letters from readers written to her at P.O. Box 80176, Bakersfield, CA 92240.

Current HeartQuest Releases

- *Awakening Mercy,* Angela Benson
- *A Bouquet of Love,* Ginny Aiken, Ranee McCollum, Jeri Odell, and Debra White Smith
- *Dream Vacation,* Ginny Aiken, Jeri Odell, and Elizabeth White
- *Faith,* Lori Copeland
- *Finders Keepers,* Catherine Palmer
- *Freedom's Hope,* Dianna Crawford
- *Freedom's Promise,* Dianna Crawford
- *Hope,* Lori Copeland
- *June,* Lori Copeland
- *Magnolia,* Ginny Aiken
- *Olivia's Touch,* Peggy Stoks
- *Prairie Fire,* Catherine Palmer
- *Prairie Rose,* Catherine Palmer
- *Prairie Storm,* Catherine Palmer
- *Reunited,* Judy Baer, Jeri Odell, Jan Duffy, and Peggy Stoks
- *A Victorian Christmas Cottage,* Catherine Palmer, Debra White Smith, Jeri Odell, and Peggy Stoks
- *A Victorian Christmas Quilt,* Catherine Palmer, Debra White Smith, Ginny Aiken, and Peggy Stoks
- *A Victorian Christmas Tea,* Catherine Palmer, Dianna Crawford, Peggy Stoks, and Katherine Chute
- *With This Ring,* Lori Copeland, Dianna Crawford, Ginny Aiken, and Catherine Palmer

Coming Soon (Fall 2000)

- *Lark,* Ginny Aiken
- *Prairie Christmas,* Catherine Palmer, Elizabeth White, and Peggy Stoks
- *Glory,* Lori Copeland
- *A Kiss of Adventure,* Catherine Palmer
- *A Whisper of Danger,* Catherine Palmer
- *A Touch of Betrayal,* Catherine Palmer

Other Great Tyndale House Fiction

- *As Sure As the Dawn*, Francine Rivers
- *Ashes and Lace*, B. J. Hoff
- *The Atonement Child*, Francine Rivers
- *The Captive Voice*, B. J. Hoff
- *Cloth of Heaven*, B. J. Hoff
- *Dark River Legacy*, B. J. Hoff
- *An Echo in the Darkness*, Francine Rivers
- *Embers of Hope*, Sally Laity & Dianna Crawford
- *The Fires of Freedom*, Sally Laity & Dianna Crawford
- *The Gathering Dawn*, Sally Laity & Dianna Crawford
- *Home Fires Burning*, Penelope J. Stokes
- *Jewels for a Crown*, Lawana Blackwell
- *The Last Sin Eater*, Francine Rivers
- *Leota's Garden*, Francine Rivers
- *Like a River Glorious*, Lawana Blackwell
- *Measures of Grace*, Lawana Blackwell
- *Remembering You*, Penelope J. Stokes
- *The Scarlet Thread*, Francine Rivers
- *Song of a Soul*, Lawana Blackwell
- *Storm at Daybreak*, B. J. Hoff
- *The Tangled Web*, B. J. Hoff
- *The Tempering Blaze*, Sally Laity & Dianna Crawford
- *Till We Meet Again*, Penelope J. Stokes
- *The Torch of Triumph*, Sally Laity & Dianna Crawford
- *Unveiled*, Francine Rivers
- *A Voice in the Wind*, Francine Rivers
- *Vow of Silence*, B. J. Hoff

HeartQuest Books by Dianna Crawford

Freedom's Promise—For the first time in Annie McGregor's life, she's free. *Free!* Her years of servitude drawing to a close, Annie hears there's a man in town looking for settlers to accompany him across the mountains into Tennessee country. Could this be the answer to her prayers?

Isaac Reardon is on a mission to claim his betrothed—along with a preacher and a small group of settlers—and return to the beautiful home he has carved from the rugged wilderness. He is devastated to learn of his intended wife's betrayal. And now to make matters worse, he's confronted with a hard-headed, irresistible young woman who is determined to accompany his wagon train—without a man of her own to protect her!

Together, Annie and Ike fight perilous mountain passages, menacing outlaws, and a rebellious companion. As they do, both are shocked to discover their growing attraction, which threatens to destroy the dream of freedom for which they have risked their very lives.

Book 1 in the Reardon Brothers series.

A Daddy for Christmas—One stormy Christmas Eve on the coast of Maine, the prayers of a young widow's child are answered in a most unusual manner. This novella by Dianna Crawford appears in the anthology *A Victorian Christmas Tea*.

Something New—An arranged marriage awaits Rachel in San Francisco. But her discovery on the voyage from the Old Country threatens to change everything. This novella by Dianna Crawford appears in the anthology *With This Ring*.

Other Great Tyndale House Fiction
by Dianna Crawford

Freedom's Holy Light series, Sally Laity and Dianna Crawford

The Gathering Dawn—This story portrays the fervor of the growing American Revolution—and the yearning for spiritual fulfillment—through the lives of an Englishwoman and an American patriot.

The Tempering Blaze—Hunted by the British Crown, Ted and Jane Harrington and Dan Haynes must run for their lives, leaving Susannah a prisoner in her own home.

The Fires of Freedom—Hostilities break out between the colonists and the English troops in 1774. Daniel Haynes is arrested and charged with aiding his brother-in-law Ted Harrington in deserting the British army.

The Embers of Hope—The exciting and gripping Revolutionary War saga of love, betrayal, and forgiveness continues when Emily suddenly finds her dreams in ashes and has to struggle for a new life and love.

The Torch of Triumph—In the captivating conclusion to this Revolutionary War saga, patriot spy Evelyn Thomas is taken captive by Indians and has only one hope for rescue—her true love.